Praise for Tim Parf
Adventures in Madrid.

M000197704

'*Parfitt is no ordinary Englishman ... his light touch and neat line in self-deprecating humour perfectly suits this entertaining urban spin on the old tale of Brits having fun under the Spanish sun.*'

— The Sunday Times

'*Hugely entertaining memoir ... frequently laugh-out-loud funny.*'

— The Daily Express

'*A love letter to Madrid ... brilliantly captures a truly eccentric and hedonistic place.*'

— The Daily Mirror

'*A Load of Bull chronicles his Spanish experiences in often hilarious detail.*'

— BBC

'*Magnificent ... brilliant and moving, hilarious and truthful.*'

— La Vanguardia

The Barcelona Connection

Tim Parfitt

MARAVILLA
PRESS

Published by Maravilla Press 2023

ISBN: 978-1-7393326-1-7

Ebook ISBN: 978-1-7393326-0-0

To Juliane

Paranoiac-Critical Method

'*A spontaneous method of irrational knowledge based on the critical and systematic objectivity of the associations and interpretations of delirious phenomena.*'

Salvador Dalí

'*Investigating a crime scene is an art, not a science.*'

Benjamin Blake

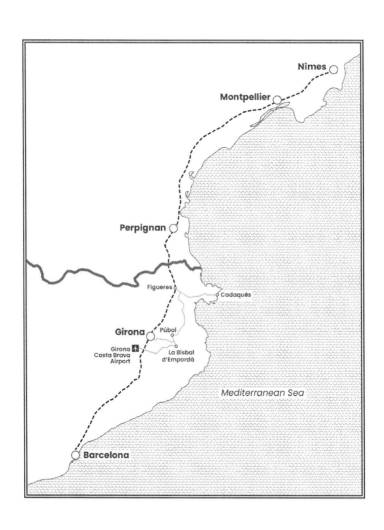

Nîmes

Montpellier

Perpignan

Figueres

Cadaqués

Girona

Púbol

Girona
Costa Brava
Airport

La Bisbal
d'Empordà

Mediterranean Sea

Barcelona

Part One - Location

1

Benjamin

Monday 4 June, 5am – somewhere in Catalonia.

Light gusts of wind, a distant police siren and a chorus of chirping crickets helped Benjamin to recover consciousness. Flat on his back and gazing upwards, his eyes slowly adjusted to a starlit sky that looked like remote pinpricks, but with a silver-white moon providing enough light to see by.

He hadn't a clue where he was at first; his head throbbed like hell, and he could feel a lump at the back of his skull. When he pulled his fingers away and saw the blood, he nearly passed out again, so he shut his eyes and rubbed his fingers against the side of his shoe and on the hem of his khaki pants, anything to wipe away the red stain. The pain was intense. He was spinning, but he could still make out the bloated figure on the ground, about fifteen metres away near a row of parked vehicles. Benjamin called out, but it was more of a groan.

'Hey, what happened?'

No reply.

'What happened?'

Very slowly, he managed to stand, then staggered nearer to the motionless figure. There was a wide gash across the man's bald scalp, which was glued to the ground in a sticky puddle of blood. A ball of cloth was wedged in his mouth. Benjamin immediately felt nauseated again. He crouched down, squinting to avoid sight of the bloody skull, then yanked the gag free from the man's lifeless jaws. He reached for his wrist, searching for a sign of a pulse to see if there was anything he could do. There was nothing. He'd been talking to a corpse.

Whatever frenzied attack had just taken place, he was thankful to have survived it himself. Glancing around, he finally realised he was at a service station, with the body lying away from the fuel pumps and shop – all closed. There was a van alongside, and a few other lorries and trucks parked nearby, but no one else was in sight.

Benjamin checked his watch. It was just after 5am. He could recall pulling in here late last night, before midnight, carefully reversing into the carport area, with the vehicle's boot tight against a barrier and impossible to break into. He'd grabbed his jacket and got out, locking the car behind him. He'd caught a faint glimpse of a van pulling away fast but had thought nothing more of it as he'd dashed across to the shop just before it closed, keeping his car in sight. He'd used the washroom and bought a sandwich, was opening it as he returned to his car, unlocking the door when the blow came, and then he was out cold.

He could vaguely remember someone yelling before he'd been bludgeoned. He'd seen a word on the side of the van that had sped off, and something else – a piece of fabric – as he'd slumped to the ground. He rubbed his eyes. Whatever he'd seen, it had gone; but then something else nearby caught his eye. He reached to pick it up. It was a small, white button, like a shirt button. He peered at the body again, dressed in track-suit bottoms and a bloodstained T-shirt. The button didn't come from there. He put it in his pocket.

Suddenly, he realised his car had gone – *with the painting.*

Fuck. They'd stolen the painting.

Benjamin didn't lose paintings. He'd never lost a painting. What he did was track down art thieves and forgers and retrieve paintings.

How many had there been – one, two thugs? They'd obviously waited for him to return to the vehicle, to get the keys out of his pocket to open the door. They'd taken the car, but it wasn't even his, it was a hire car. It was the painting they'd targeted. Had the bastards then also savaged the figure on the ground? Why? Because he'd witnessed something?

Benjamin looked around again. There'd be security, surely, possibly a CCTV camera, but then he saw that it was pointing towards the fuel pumps and not where he'd parked and been attacked, which was also too dark.

He still had his jacket on, with his wallet and passport. He tugged out the wallet, wincing as he did. They hadn't taken his money because they clearly just wanted the painting, but his phone? Shit, it was also in the car. Going through his pockets he found his airline boarding pass and a lecture leaflet from yesterday. Slowly, he started to recall the sequence of events, now fully aware of the critical situation he was in.

He'd only been in Spain a few hours, but he was already stranded without his phone at a service station alongside a dead body in the early hours of the morning, and with the painting and his car stolen. He was in trouble. Big trouble.

Whoever took the painting was also a killer. He had to find them and get the painting back, and the best way, in fact the *only* way to do that was to first find his car. He had to move, immediately. He looked down at his footprints in the blood alongside the disfigured corpse. He should not have touched it.

2

The Marqueses de Guíxols

Nineteen hours earlier.
Sunday 3 June, 10am – La Bisbal d'Empordà, Catalonia.

The painting had been discovered on Sunday morning in an old trunk in a cellar at the country home of the Marquès and Marquesa de Guíxols, in the Baix Empordà region of Catalonia. On the outskirts of the old town of La Bisbal d'Empordà, seawards from Girona and a hundred-and-twenty kilometres north-east of Barcelona, the rambling *masia* house had been in the family for several generations.

They found the trunk and then the painting while searching the cellar for some antique table linen for their daughter's forthcoming wedding reception. After the housekeeper had helped to bring the trunk up to the main hall, Jaume, the Marquès de Guíxols, a tall, distinguished, silver-haired gentleman with half-moon spectacles and a ruddy, flushed complexion, carefully propped up the painting on an oval oak table to study it. By contrast, his petite wife, Montse, her taut features highlighted by wide, almond eyes, was barely able to control her excitement.

'It's beautiful,' she said. 'It's exquisite. But is it genuine? And is it … is it ours? If we sell it quickly, we could clear the debt. We could give her the wedding she really wants.'

Jaume keyed in some numbers on his phone to make a call. Waiting for a reply, he turned to his wife.

'Montse,' he said. 'Look at the painting. What else do you see in it?'

3

Marcos Constantinos and Brigitte

Sunday 3 June, 3pm – Hampstead, London.

Marcos Constantinos sat waiting for a phone call, even though he didn't possess his own phone. He didn't own a car either. He cycled to and from his office each day on a foldable, eco-friendly bicycle, now propped up outside his self-sustaining, prefabricated pod. He liked to describe it as his 'intelligent home', and if homes had brains, then this one sure was a smart ass.

It looked like an ugly, minimalist, white luminous sculpture. But it could capture and reuse rainwater, sink and shower water, and then heat all that water under the floors to warm the house, all on solar power. It was a home that apparently *understood*. It was big enough, with glass walls and steel frames that had saved countless forests, especially as the building industry consumed over fifty percent of the world's natural resources – and how much space did one need to live in?

Go-getting, goatee-bearded Constantinos was the owner of a multi-million pound cosmetics empire founded on environmental, ethical and animal rights values. Always donating to green causes, he'd made his money from soaps and fragrances using vegetable ingredients, but had since launched 'Cell Conscience', a solar-powered cell phone. His kinky new squeeze, Brigitte, now appeared with the latest model, excited that it was ringing. It was her phone, not his. Marcos didn't own one; he just wanted everyone else to.

'Marcos,' said Brigitte, offering him the phone. 'They're calling.'

'I hardly know them,' he said, hesitating. 'Promise me it will be symbolic only.'

'I promise,' said Brigitte. Her eyes shone.

Marcos sighed and took the handset.

'Yes?' he said. There was a pause. 'When?'

Brigitte was watching and he couldn't resist her.

'Okay,' he said. 'Do it. But no violence, you understand? The collective will cover any legal repercussions. Do it.'

He switched the phone off and Brigitte undressed in front of him.

'Come here,' she said.

At first Marcos didn't obey.

'*Come. Here.*'

Marcos moved towards her.

But then her phone started ringing again.

4

Benjamin and Sir Anthony Hughes

Monday 4 June, 5am – somewhere in Catalonia.

Benjamin Blake, forty-one, art detective, currently dressed in a battered corduroy jacket with bloodstained back collar, frayed polo shirt and khaki cargo pants, was … English. He was also peculiarly handsome with a kind, inquisitive face, often distracted and reckless yet still intellectually brilliant, but above all, *English*.

With a passion for art, food and wine, he had a slight yet permanent frown that creased his forehead, making him look frequently baffled, and bushy hair that had a life of its own; currently also matted with blood at the back.

Benjamin could be blunt, awkward and unpredictable, but not in a bad way; regardless of his quirkiness and flaws, he was well-intentioned, considerate and selfless. He didn't want to hurt anyone's feelings, even though it meant battling a deep rebellious nature that was pushing to rise up against his innate sense of courtesy.

Despite his gentle looks, he possessed a gritty, inner toughness, hardened over the years by threats from the criminal underworld of stolen and forged art. Keen to appear calm and composed, even if he wasn't, his tenacious character and quick-witted intuition had helped him to survive several lethal encounters up to now ... but only just.

Benjamin's impressive art historian's résumé was complemented by a PhD in forensic science, with a specialism in counterfeit criminology in the arts. Since starting his own art loss detective agency, however, he'd moved on from purely analysing works of art using forensic science in the laboratory. He was now regularly called upon to investigate art crime – be it theft, forgery, looting, illicit trade or smuggling – and he'd become an expert in developing criminological and psychological profiles to better understand the art thief or master forger.

It went further, too, because Benjamin believed that by viewing *any* crime scene as a work of art, the forensic scientist could become the connoisseur, evaluating the entire scene to draw conclusions from often overlooked details, clues or traces. For Benjamin, investigating a crime scene was an *art*, not a science.

But there was an issue. Or rather, Benjamin had an issue. Several issues, in fact ... and not just because his wife had also recently filed for a divorce.

A man of few words, he faced the daily paradox of working in the art world while being unable to stomach the aloofness of the art Establishment itself.

Art had to be freely available for everyone, as far as Benjamin was concerned, and there had to be equal opportunities for anyone wanting to study or work in art.

He abhorred bullies, cronyism, snobbery, the self-serving elite and the super-rich (especially if uncharitable), and he had little time for the many pompous and patronising figures he encountered, even though some of them eventually became his clients.

With his unorthodox and maverick attitude towards bureaucracy, protocol and authority, he sometimes found himself in precarious situations through a combination of circumstance, haplessness and rash decisions. It meant that things didn't always go the right way for Benjamin; but when they didn't, he had a stubborn if also perilous determination to put them right.

Right now, stranded at a service station in Catalonia with the painting and his car stolen, he knew he'd also suffered concussion because every so often things appeared in slow-motion. He wasn't sure if he was confusing the real with the surreal, and if it was partly due to the double images of the painting that kept swirling in his brain, or if it was something he'd seen before he was attacked … *something on the ground*.

His head was still throbbing incessantly. He felt he had punch-drunk syndrome, and it dawned on him that whoever attacked him had really tried to kill him. Inflicting injury to the head was one of the most effective methods of homicide; maximum damage with minimum effort. Someone knew exactly what they were doing when they'd struck him, and he was lucky to have survived. Unlike the poor bastard lying nearby.

Just hours ago, he'd been sworn to secrecy about the painting, and he had no choice but to keep his word. He now had to retrieve it without fail, if it hadn't already been bartered for something else. He started to piece together his whereabouts prior to arriving in Spain last night, trying to fathom out who else knew that he'd put it in the boot of his hire car …

≈

Sixteen hours earlier.

Sunday 3 June, 12.30pm – Norfolk, England.

Benjamin had been participating in a brunch lecture in the Sainsbury Centre at the University of East Anglia in Norfolk, when he switched his phone back on and immediately received two calls.

The first was from Walter Postlethwaite, his divorce lawyer, or at least the chap he'd appointed to try and defend him against the far-fetched demands of his soon-to-be ex-wife's lawyers. The divorce hadn't been

Benjamin's idea or, he believed, his making, but the sooner Walter reached some sort of an agreement on his behalf, the happier he would be.

'Hello, Benjamin, it's Walter Postlethwaite.'

Benjamin knew only one Walter, and one was enough. Walter clearly didn't realise that his full name might be logged in Benjamin's phone contacts, either, as he still announced himself every time he called.

'Hello again, Walter,' said Benjamin, as Walter had been calling rather a lot. Before he could explain why he was calling this time, Benjamin was already making his excuses. 'It's not the best moment, to be honest, Walter,' he said. 'I've only just finished a −'

'You remember I have the meeting with your wife's team tomorrow at noon?'

Benjamin winced at the 'team' reference. It was his wife's Champions League team of unreasonable and exorbitant lawyers against non-league Walter, a one-man band. Benjamin wanted to help, but Walter's timing was appalling.

'Yes, but it's not a great time to talk right now,' said Benjamin. 'I'm in Norwich. I'm also hoping to see my daughter this evening, to discuss it all with her, so it would be better to chat first thing tomorrow morning, perhaps −'

'Okay, but −'

'Okay, thanks, Walter, that's great, speak tomorrow, bye.'

Benjamin cut him off, then immediately felt guilty about it.

Just seconds later, Anthony Hughes called.

He started the call abruptly with: 'I presume you have that passport with you.' Cold, business-like, not even a hello or an introduction. The opposite to dear old Walter.

When Benjamin didn't reply, he said, 'Is that Blake? It's Hughes. Anthony.'

Hughes was the chairman of Sotheby's worldwide and it was actually 'Sir' Anthony, but Benjamin avoided the term. He'd met him only once but spoken to him several times, having been sent on assignments for Sotheby's in the past. He was another one of those prominent yet condescending types, but also an important client.

'Anthony –' said Benjamin.

'I've been trying to speak to you for nearly an hour. Do you have that passport?' Hughes insisted.

Benjamin did. He always did. After arriving back in London late on Friday from Florida, where he'd been advising and finally dismissing as a forgery a painting at auction, initially believed to have been on the FBI's National Stolen Art File, he'd headed to the tiny flat he was renting short-term in Clapham and then slept most of Saturday.

He'd planned the day-trip event to the university in Norfolk on Sunday to also catch up with his daughter, Sophie, a promising young singer, and to take her for a drink or dinner if she wasn't rehearsing, before grabbing the last train back to London. Even though he hadn't brought an overnight bag or his laptop, he still had a small backpack stuffed with some notebooks and a passport. Assignments could crop up anywhere in the world and at any time.

'Of course,' he said, but then his phone bleeped.

'Can you hear me?'

'Yes, but I think my battery's running low −'

'Let's get straight to the point then,' Hughes said.

'Let's.'

'A painting, possibly a priceless Dalí, has been discovered just outside Barcelona by an old friend of mine. I want you over there immediately to see if it's genuine.'

Benjamin hesitated. It wasn't that he didn't provide an appraisal service, but he preferred the more lucrative and secret assignments working for Scotland Yard's Art and Antiques Unit, or for Interpol on international stolen or forged art cases, even though it often dragged him further into that vicious criminal underworld. Insurance companies that monitored the art theft databases run by the FBI or the International Foundation for Art Research paid him far more than private collectors, curators or auction houses.

He also felt inclined to remind Hughes that they'd been forging Salvador Dalí lithographs for years, and that he wouldn't need to go to Barcelona to authenticate anything. All they had to do was email him some good quality photos of the front and back, the signature, the dimensions and any other relevant documents, like the original invoice for the print −

'It's not a lithograph,' Hughes snapped. He went

on to say that his friend was the Marquès de Guíxols and that the painting was oil on canvas. 'I'm also calling you as I understand the work could be a study for a painting that you know very well, the hallucinating bullfighter or something –'

'Excuse me?' said Benjamin. '*The Hallucinogenic Toreador?* Yes, I did a thesis on it, and it's included in the current series of talks about deceptions and discoveries that I've been invited to take part in. He glanced down at an image of the painting on his lecture leaflet while Hughes was talking to him. 'But it's impossible that there's another study.'

Hughes wasn't listening. Instead, he told Benjamin that he needed a specialist in Barcelona before the Marquès approached anyone else, and that *he*, Benjamin, was going. Not only that, but he wanted him there 'incognito'.

'When?' Benjamin asked, hearing Hughes mumbling to someone else.

'Now,' came the reply. 'Since I've got hold of you, we've confirmed a flight for this afternoon. Don't let me down, there's little time. The Marquès has some financial and personal issues and he's not even sure the painting is his yet, so it's very delicate. He doesn't want anyone to know. If others get wind of the fact that you're meeting him then they'll all be sniffing around. He'll want to sell it quickly and privately, and I've offered to assist him. Total confidentiality is crucial, you understand? A flight's been booked from Stansted to Girona using your agency details. Best we could do.

Finding a hotel was tricky because of the summit but my PA has booked you in somewhere. Hang on, I'll pass you over –'

A minute later and Benjamin had scribbled down the flight reference and hotel details, as well as the Marquès de Guíxols' address and phone number on the back of the lecture leaflet, all from a text message that he received, just before his phone went dead. It was already 1.15pm, with the flight leaving at 5.15pm.

Due to roadworks and diversions, he eventually made it to Stansted just an hour before the flight was due to depart. Unable to recharge his phone in the taxi, he had to pay extra at the Ryanair desk for not checking in online, or having a digital or printed boarding pass, which wasn't a great start.

Many people assumed that his international art assignments involved private jets, helicopters, a yacht, a jet-ski, endless dry martinis, a luxury hotel and a chauffeur at each airport greeting him with something like, 'Welcome to Berlin, Mr. Blake' – but it wasn't like that at all. Nothing was glamorous in his job, and chaos usually followed wherever he went. Danger, too. There was always danger.

Once through security, he rushed to buy a European plug adapter for his phone charger, exchanged a wad of sterling into euros, and then sprinted towards the departure gate – conscious that Sotheby's had booked him a hotel but not a return flight. Sure, he had a passport, driving licence, credit cards and cash, but he had nothing else at all, no toiletries, no change of clothes, just his jacket over a polo shirt and the small backpack of notebooks.

He was certain the job wouldn't take long, anyway. It often took less than two minutes to dismiss a painting, as most discoveries turned out to be fakes. He used 'image, location, time' as his strategy for authentication; most art failed the image test, without having to worry about the location of its discovery, or the date and time period of its creation.

On the flight, he mulled over the call from Anthony Hughes. If his client had wanted a simple appraisal, he could have called the Salvador Dalí Foundation in Figueres, north of Barcelona, although it would have hindered any hope of a quick and discreet sale, *if* it was genuine. Benjamin had a good enough relationship with the Dalí Foundation, and he'd advised them on several fakes in circulation in the past. There was an elderly specialist he'd met in Figueres, too, years back when he'd been doing a thesis – Conso Puig was her name – and they'd kept in touch.

His flight touched down at Girona-Costa Brava Airport at precisely 8.15pm, local time. With no baggage to collect, he unwrapped his plug adapter and found somewhere near the car rental desks to start recharging his phone, then paid cash to hire a modest VW Polo for two days.

Once his phone was showing signs of life, he checked his scribbled notes on the lecture leaflet and then keyed in the address of the Marquès de Guíxols on Google maps. It was about a forty-minute drive from Girona airport, heading east towards La Bisbal d'Empordà. His hotel was in Barcelona, about an hour away, south. No time to lose, Hughes had insisted, so Benjamin decided to visit the Marquès immediately, to view the painting and then locate his hotel later. At least that was the plan.

~

Nine hours later.
Monday 4 June, 5.15am – somewhere in Catalonia.

Benjamin realised that he was now back near Girona airport. From the service station, he could see a radar and control tower in the distance across the fields, and even at this early hour planes were already taking off.

He'd pulled in here last night, after visiting the Marquès. Someone must have followed him, knowing he had the painting in the boot of the car, and that he was taking it to Barcelona for further examination. There were only four people who knew that – the Marquès, his wife, two staff members, and possibly Hughes. Did one of them really have him targeted? He would need to find out, but he had to move fast.

Suddenly, lights started to flicker across the fuel pumps, and a light went on in the shop. Moments later, Benjamin was banging on the window.

5

Elena

Sunday 3 June, 8pm – city of Girona, northeast of Barcelona.

Elena Carmona signalled to her father to turn down the volume on the TV in her cramped apartment on the east side of Girona. Despite the open window and a fan rotating slowly in the corner of the room, her T-shirt still felt glued to her skin. Neighbours could be heard shouting, dogs were barking outside, a baby was crying, and reggaeton was blaring from a car. It was a deprived neighbourhood, but not as bad as the one she and her brother had been brought up in and which her father, Diego, still refused to move from, even since her mother died.

Dressed in boxer shorts and a vest, Diego was only staying with her now, temporarily, because he was unable to look after himself. His right foot was in plaster after a bad fall, and it was currently propped up on a low table in front of Elena's TV, with his crutches lying on the floor beside him. A sixty-four-year-old taxi driver, the foot fracture meant he couldn't work, and he needed to, despite Elena and her brother taking it in turns to drive the taxi and keep some cash coming in.

Diego had spent forty years as a labourer, barman and farm worker, whenever he could find work, before finally saving enough to acquire his own taxi. Like hundreds of thousands of Spaniards who'd moved from the poor west and south to the industrialised northern cities in the late 1970s, Diego's own parents of Romany origin – persecuted and harassed under the Franco regime – had finally brought him from Andalusia to Girona when Spain was in transition from a dictatorship. With the cities unable to accommodate the influx of migrants, Diego had been brought up in a dilapidated district on the edge of Girona, an area of social exclusion but where his roots still firmly and proudly remained.

Elena, thirty-one and streetwise, had always juggled several jobs, too, whenever she could find the work. Fiery, olive-skinned, stunning, with sleek, jet-black wavy hair, cut short at the back in a French bob, her eyes literally sparkled, yet she was also often snappy and on edge, and even more so this evening.

She was working on her laptop in the corner of the room, with one eye on the Twitter newsfeed while calling someone on her cell phone. She needed her father to turn down the TV news about the G20 and UN Climate Change Conference starting in Barcelona, not only because she couldn't hear herself think but because she also hated the way they were reporting on it all.

For the last year, Elena had gone back to studying, to further improve her English and finally kickstart a proper career with a qualification in journalism, initially specialising in sports journalism – *periodismo deportivo* – her passion.

She'd made the decision to restart her life just before her thirtieth birthday, soon after losing her mother. She'd wanted to put the clubbing, failed relationships and other issues behind her. There were boyfriends she regretted, cute yet stupid guys, but then there'd also been an assault that had left her emotionally scarred, mainly because the police refused to believe her side of the story or take things further – and she knew why. It was one of the reasons she'd wanted to learn journalism: to eventually expose hypocrisy, cover-ups, corruption and the chauvinistic bastards in authority who'd treated her the way they'd treated her. But first she had to learn the ropes, and she'd chosen sports journalism.

A few years ago, she was fit, very fit, running half-marathons, playing volleyball and padel, even kickboxing. She was still in great shape, but instead of taking part in competitive sports, she planned to report on them instead.

She'd paid for the two-year course by registering with a temp agency specialising in bar, catering and hotel work, and she'd been regularly employed whenever it fitted in with her study hours. She was the oldest on the course, and her overall assessment would be based on all the essays and audiovisual assignments to date, as well as the final media dissertation due next month. She was anxious to finish it on time and there was still much to do. In the meantime, she'd been approaching online newspapers in Spain with some articles related to the climate conference, in the hope of getting some byline credits to add to her portfolio.

'Hi, it's Elena Carmona ...'

She was speaking on the phone now, seeing that Diego had finally worked out how to use the remote control to mute the volume on the TV.

'We spoke on Thursday, and you asked me to email the piece over, which I did. So, have you read it and are you going to use it?'

Silence filled the room. Diego gazed across at her as she listened to the reply from the other end of the line.

'Yes, I know it's Sunday evening,' she said, 'but the G20 starts in thirty-six hours.'

Silence.

'No, it was about climate emissions from the agricultural sector, reducing meat consumption to cut greenhouse gas emissions, and very relevant at the moment with Spain's track record on factory farming.'

Another silence.

'Well, I emailed it, can you check? No, I can wait. No ... I'll wait. *No.* I said I'll wait. You can check while talking to me, no? What? It was a thousand words.

Well, it's relevant now, today, but it might not be in a few days, so I need to know if you're going to use it, or I'll take it elsewhere. What? Why didn't you tell me that on Thursday? You could have –'

Elena was cut off. She stared at her phone.

'*Go to hell*,' she shouted. '*Dickhead.*'

Diego shook his head and turned up the TV again.

Elena jumped up, cursing, and then called another number as she went across to her kitchenette to prepare some food for her father, with the phone pinned to her ear by the shoulder.

'Yes, it's Elena Carmona,' she was soon saying. 'If you remember I sent an email with my article about factory farming in Spain in light of the key issues at the climate conference. No, it's not unsolicited. We spoke last week, and you said send it in. Have you had a chance to read it yet?'

There was a short silence, then: 'I've never seen anything on your site about factory farming.'

Silence.

'Well, if he's your climate change correspondent then he should have looked at the issue –'

Silence again.

'Qualified to know? What do you mean he's more qualified to know? What do you mean by that? Qualified in what sense? Qualified because he's a man?'

It wasn't long before Elena had banged a saucepan down hard on the counter and tossed her phone to one side.

'*Bastard.*'

She knew deep down that she wasn't as qualified as others to write about climate issues, but she couldn't stand being patronised, and always by male editors. Throughout the course, she'd had to put up with a macho lecturer who'd kept flirting with her, while repeatedly telling her that she had the looks to be a TV sports presenter. The jerk. She hated that. *Hated it.* Sure, she'd love to report at major sporting events, but she didn't want to be there for any looks. She didn't want to be anywhere for her looks. If anyone else ever tried that line on her, she'd probably kill them. Her looks had let her down badly in the past. They'd got her into situations she didn't feel comfortable with. Why was that?

She continued to prepare some food for her father and checked her phone for messages from her brother. There was nothing. He was as unreliable as ever.

'Hey, papi,' she called over to her father. 'Did Pablo confirm he's okay for the taxi shift from 6am?'

Diego didn't reply.

'Papi?'

6

Benjamin

Monday 4 June, 5.30am – near Girona-Costa Brava Airport, Catalonia.

'Internet?' Benjamin called through the glass.

He was banging on the window of the service station shop because the shop itself was still closed. There was a stocky, dark, middle-aged man inside, with a beard fading to white. He was mopping the floor. Had he driven here? Benjamin hadn't seen the head-lights of any vehicle arrive. Had he walked here? It wasn't yet dawn, but the air was already warm and balmy, with the symphony of chirping crickets still reverberating from the surrounding trees and hedgerow.

'Internet?' he called through the glass again.

The man inside shook his head and waved him away.

'No, listen, *please*,' Benjamin shouted, with more urgency. 'I need to get online. I need to use a phone or a computer.'

The man now waved aggressively and shouted back in Spanish through the glass.

'*Vete a la mierda, cabrón! Me cago en tu puta madre!*'

Benjamin could guess from the tone and twisted body language of the man with the mop and bucket that he wasn't shouting anything very pleasant or friendly back through the glass, but he had no idea that he was being told to run along and fuck himself, or that in a purely literal sense, his elderly mother was at risk of being shat upon.

What he *did* know was that he had to inform someone about the dead body, although he had no intention of calling the Spanish police and waiting for them to arrive. He'd be detained while he explained what he was doing here, and the last thing he should do was report a lost painting. It would affect his under-cover work, his clients would never take him seriously again, and anything the police might do, he could do himself.

Whoever stole the painting and attacked him must have also been responsible for splitting open the skull on that corpse. He'd find the painting by finding the hitman. It wouldn't be the first time he'd had to track down a killer.

He had no intention of calling Anthony Hughes or the Marquès de Guíxols, either. He simply couldn't tell them that he'd lost the painting. Also, if, just *if* he'd been targeted by either of them, then it would hardly help matters if he suddenly called to announce that he was still breathing.

He was certain, however, that the Marquès and his wife hadn't ordered someone to follow him. Why target their own painting? Last night, the old aristocrat had almost been threatening Benjamin to authenticate it urgently, which is why he'd insisted on him taking the painting to Barcelona for further examination. He'd go stark raving mad if he knew it had been stolen, whether it was genuine or not. And what if it *was* genuine?

Benjamin hadn't wanted to admit that there was a slight chance that it could be genuine, not with the aristocrat's threatening tone, but he now shuddered at the thought of losing a canvas that could be worth a fortune. As for the Marqueses' housekeeper and maid, they appeared to hold some sort of grudge against their employees, and they also knew he'd put the painting in the boot of the car. But who else? The corpse? Who was it? Had he followed him and then been attacked himself? If so, who had the painting now? Benjamin had to move, he had to immediately locate his car, and there was only one chance he had to do so …

'*I need Internet,*' he shouted through the glass, much louder now, but the man started waving aggressively again and yelling back in Spanish.

'*Vete a la mierda, cabrón!*'

It didn't sound good. Benjamin briefly considered

his options. Smash the glass, smash the whole shop window, and then demand access to the man's phone, if he had one, or the shop's computer, if there was one. Not the most sensible idea. The man would retaliate, it would set off an alarm, the police would surely arrive, and Benjamin would be taken away and possibly held as a suspect for the body in the carport area.

'Right,' said Benjamin, as if in response to his own thoughts. 'I'm going to leave, then, okay?'

The man glared at him through the glass.

'But you need to call someone,' said Benjamin. 'It's because over there – *look* – there's a body. It's way over there …' He pointed. It was all he could do.

The man continued to simply glare at him.

'Airport? Walking?' Benjamin tried. He stretched his arms out wide, and then swayed from side to side to make them look like the wings of a plane, but it made him feel dizzier. He then used his fingers to indicate someone walking.

This time the man pointed towards a gate across the forecourt, shouting back through the glass in Spanish again.

'*Joder, vete de una vez!*'

It was time to leave.

Benjamin could see the illuminated runway lights across the field as he pushed through the gate and staggered along the grass verge down towards the airport. He had no time to lose to get online.

7

Séverin and Jürgen

Monday 4 June, 5.45am – central Barcelona.

Séverin enjoyed hurting and killing people, if they deserved it. It was as simple as that. He was paid to do it, too, which made it even more enjoyable.

His propensity for violence and a lack of any remorse started when he was just nine years old. Teased at his French school for being ugly and monstrously oversized for his age, Séverin learnt how to defend himself by becoming a callous bully.

Because his mother had an allergy, Séverin's parents never allowed him to have a pet. Other kids taunted him, telling him it was because he was a future serial killer. All serial killers harm animals at an early age, they said, and that's why his parents wouldn't let him near animals. He retaliated by turning violent towards anyone who did hurt animals.

Witnessing a classmate throw a stone at a cat, he beat the kid so hard that he lost permanent sight in one eye, and no one ever questioned or teased Séverin again. He'd beaten him senseless because he believed he was doing the right thing; he was proud of it. From then on, he made temporary friends by agreeing to belt anyone who they said deserved it, and the pride in doing so stayed with him forever.

Progressing from school bully to a professional bruiser and savage debt-collector around Marseille in France, combined with part-time jobs as a labourer and gardener, his big break in finding his true vocation as a hitman came with his first paid-for killing.

He received a fat fee from a Saint-Tropez nightclub owner who claimed a rival had been harassing his four-teen-year-old daughter. Séverin used pruning shears to remove the scalp of the suspected paedophile, gouging out the man's eyes before strangling him with just one of his meaty hands. The police never found the killer. As far as Séverin was concerned, someone had behaved badly and had to be erased. He was simply putting the world right; he was the good guy.

After that first assignment and over the next fifteen years, Séverin's trademark contract killings carried out for French gangsters never involved any firearms – only his bare hands, or the tools of his building and gardening jobs. He often wore a leather tool belt around his waist when out on a mission, like a double holster. Instead of guns, he carried screw-drivers, pliers, a meat cleaver, a couple of claw hammers or his favourite pruning shears and secateurs.

As and when required, 'Sev' became an expert on severing arms, hands, fingers, feet, toes, even genitals … getting a kick out of keeping his victims alive during bit-by-bit mutilation, before putting them out of agony. All along, his victims had to have done something wrong, something very bad. They really had to deserve it. Otherwise, it wasn't fun, and it definitely wasn't 'right', in his twisted code of ethics.

Deep down, perhaps in the dark pit of his depraved mind, Séverin believed he had many likeable qualities … although he wasn't aware that his looks weren't one of them.

Physically immense, he appeared rather insane, with sinister, deep-set hooded eyes that portrayed a cold, dark stare, and a demented, pudding-bowl haircut with a fringe like Star Trek's Spock. He had brown, nicotine-decaying teeth, around which his twisted, menacing mouth spat out rancid saliva and vile breath to anyone within reach.

With no remaining family that he knew of, he was a loner and had never had any success with women, much to his on-going frustration. Many prostitutes refused to go with him, and would then receive a hard slap or a gob load of phlegm from him instead. He would not stand for being disrespected or made fun of.

Never a heavy drinker, he got off on various substances instead, plus a lot of creepy porn. Recently, he'd moved from crack cocaine to hallucinogenic angel dust, which only enhanced his penchant for savagery. PCP or phencyclidine could be snorted, taken as a tablet, a capsule, in liquid, or even injected, but he'd been soaking his marijuana in it ... a lot.

After years of well-paid butchery, Séverin had been considering semi-retirement. He'd saved enough money and was thinking of setting up a florist's shop as a front for his other horticultural interests; he knew enough about plants, especially hemp, from his part-time gardening.

But then while researching tulip bulbs as a pretext to finding cannabis suppliers in the Netherlands, he was approached by a Dutch gang looking for logistical support for a mission in Nîmes, his hometown, and with a connection to Barcelona. After a few clandestine meetings, he accepted the job, as it reminded him of the very first retribution that he'd carried out at school.

Right now, however, in the early hours of the morning and wearing a red hoodie emblazoned with the logo of Nîmes Olympique football club, he was in the centre of Barcelona, raging and seeking revenge. He'd driven here in pursuit of the Dutch bastards who'd left him stranded, and who still owed him eight thousand euros in cash. He'd been betrayed, and no one ever betrayed Séverin and got away with it ...

Jürgen was on edge. Dressed in black jeans and T-shirt, with a shaved head and long hipster beard, he was perched on a stool in the corner of a cafeteria within Barcelona's Sants railway station. He was relieved to be rid of the sadist, Séverin ... but for how long?

Violence had never been part of the original plan, let alone murder. Jürgen's world was green, dedicated to healthy living, saving the planet and the well-being of animals. It was about promoting veganism, non-violence, anti-capitalism, spirituality, peace, love, weed, and a lot of radical free-thinking. There was no space in his world for a contract killer.

Back in the Netherlands, Jürgen had lived in a squat in The Hague, and then in a commune of canal boats in Utrecht, where the idea for this stunt had first been conceived. He'd then moved to Barcelona, where they'd planned everything. But then along came Séverin, the so-called 'facilitator' from the South of France, recruited by someone from the organisation in Amsterdam. Had they even carried out any background checks on him?

Over the past month, Jürgen had visited Nîmes a couple of times to coordinate things with Séverin, and to pay him a first instalment. Séverin had also visited Barcelona, and they'd met at a hotel. Jürgen thought the Frenchman was sinister from the outset, and he was worried about his mental state, even more so once they'd received the final go-ahead for the mission. Now things had gone drastically wrong, and he was in a panic about his own safety.

Even at this early hour, Sants station was teeming with commuters, tourists and security guards. During the past ten days and before travelling to Nîmes for the last time, Jürgen had blended in with the crowds, using the toilets and left-luggage facilities as a virtual campsite.

He'd come to the station an hour ago to pick up a cell phone that had been deposited in the luggage locker. He'd left his Dutch colleague, Hendrik, guarding the hostage back at the safe house – but nor did he trust him. Hendrik had got on too well with Séverin when the Frenchman had come to Barcelona last month, and he'd seen them doing drugs together.

Checking the phone, Jürgen saw a text confirming that the pre-recorded voicemail had been delivered to fifteen media groups, in Spanish and English. It was, they said, a 'robocall', reciting the same message through auto-dialling software ... but it wasn't the exact message he'd recorded.

What the fuck had they done?

He quickly dismantled the phone, snapping it into tiny pieces, and then dropped the fragments and SIM card into two separate bins near the cafeteria.

He tried to remain calm. At least he still had all the cash. He would need it to get safely back to Amsterdam, once he'd removed all trace of himself at the safe house. When this mission was over, Jürgen had planned to leave the part-time job in Barcelona and return to his own utopia, a small houseboat near the artistic colony of Ruigoord, in the west harbour of Amsterdam.

But he now feared it might never happen ...

8

Benjamin and the Marqueses de Guíxols

Monday 4 June, 5.45am – near Girona-Costa Brava Airport.

'December, November, October, September …'

Benjamin was muttering to himself as he hurried down the lane that ran parallel to the AP-7 motorway towards the exit for Girona airport, with his shadow bobbing two steps ahead of him, cast by the moonlight.

'August, July, June, May …'

He was putting himself through the type of pitch-side concussion assessment that rugby players might receive, being tested to recite the months of the year backwards or being asked to stand for twenty seconds with one foot in front of the other, and so far, he'd passed, even though he knew he'd suffered concussion.

His head was spinning, and the déjà vu feeling was still there; double images of the painting flashed through his mind, or was it something that he'd seen on the ground, just as he was attacked?

He had no idea how bad his skull injury might be, but nor did he have any intention of letting it delay him. He was in severe pain, yet he had to overcome it.

There were links between repeated concussion and early-onset dementia and other neurological diseases, chronic traumatic encephalopathy, they called it, or dementia pugilistica, a pathology often seen in former boxers. With a possible fractured skull, he knew he had to avoid further brain trauma to limit neurological impairment; his own studies in biochemistry had taught him all that. But just the thought of a blood clot, aneurysm or brain haemorrhage was enough to make him feel dizzy.

In truth, he sometimes wondered if he was a bit of a hypochondriac, but he'd never shared that thought with anyone. Certainly not with Claire, his soon-to-be ex-wife. She'd always said he was neurotic.

'April, March, February, January.'

He probably could have gone on to do a full forensic pathologist course if it hadn't been for sporadic fainting at the sight of blood, or vasovagal syncope, as it was officially known. He'd quickly discovered that blood splatter analysis, decomposing human remains, postmortems and autopsies weren't for him.

Instead, following on from his master's in the restoration and conservation of works of art, he'd finally done a PhD in forensic science specialising in document examination, art forgery and counterfeiting.

And it meant that last night, at one point, the Marquès de Guíxols even insisted on calling him 'doctor' …

∽

Eight hours earlier.
Sunday 3 June, 9.30pm – La Bisbal d'Empordà.

It had taken about an hour to reach the aristocrat's home after hiring the car from Girona airport. On taking a toll ticket to join the motorway, he'd headed north for the exit towards La Bisbal, where he then paid the charge with some euro coins he had.

The gentle contours of the Baix Empordà country-side glowed in the twilight, and signposts indicated that the route passed near to Púbol castle, where Salvador Dalí had renovated an abandoned fortress as a gift to his wife, Gala. Benjamin had been told that the home of the Marquès was on the outskirts of La Bisbal, and the instructions were to call a number he'd been given as he approached the old town in order to get precise directions.

Conscious that his iPhone hadn't properly recharged at the airport, he pulled up to make the call in the main thoroughfare of the old town of La Bisbal at around 9.30pm. The street was lined with antique and ceramic shops, many still open, with the late evening strollers dividing their time between the bars and perusing the shops' pottery displays spread out across the pavements.

The air was hot and humid, and Benjamin was sweating slightly in his corduroy jacket, aware that everyone else looked unhurried, far more relaxed than him, and dressed more appropriately for an early summer evening.

He headed into a bar, where he perched on a stool in the corner and used a socket near a slot machine to recharge his phone again. As the barmaid shot him a quizzical look, he asked for a small beer, drank it quickly and then ordered another, which seemed to placate her. Once the phone had rebooted, he searched for the aristocrat's number on the lecture leaflet, but soon noticed he had an incoming call.

'Hello, Walter,' he said, answering the phone.

'Hello, Benjamin, it's Walter Postlethwaite.'

'Yes, I know who it is.'

'I was just wondering if you'd spoken to your daughter. You said you were going to meet up with her earlier. It's just that the meeting with the other team is at noon tomorrow and I've been checking through the documents related to −'

'Walter, I have to stop you,' said Benjamin. 'I didn't get to speak to Sophie −'

'Oh.'

'− and I'm now travelling −'

'Again?'

'− and my phone's about to die, so I'll have to call you back, I'm sorry.'

He felt guilty for cutting Walter off again, but he had no option.

Minutes later, after finding the number of the Marquès on the lecture leaflet, he was finally connected with a woman who said she was his assistant.

She spoke enough English for Benjamin to understand that he had to turn left at the end of the street, immediately after an antique shop with old gramophones in the window, and to follow the sign up towards a hotel called Castell d'Empordà. Then he had to continue on the road all the way past the hotel, down a hill and winding track, for two kilometres in the direction of Peratallada, which is how he found the rambling old *masia,* with its ninth-century walls enclosing a second-century tower and a thirteenth-century Romanesque church.

The rich scent of Mediterranean pine hit him once he was out of the car, and he gazed up at sections of the stone building's façade that seemed to undulate like waves in the sea.

'I think we just spoke on the phone,' was all Benjamin said with a smile, after he was met at the front door by an elderly woman, and who he assumed was the housekeeper. She didn't say anything or smile back; she even looked surly. She had white hair and purple bags under tired eyes that avoided meeting his gaze.

From the front entrance, he could see a Gaudí-style staircase encrusted with coloured glass and ceramics, an elaborate fireplace and ornate, mosaic floor tiles. But there was also a shabby, grimy, unkempt feel to the house, with a musty odour hanging in the air.

Benjamin needed to use the loo but decided it would be polite to wait. He didn't want it to be the first thing he asked for.

He was led into an anteroom off the hallway and felt intrigued, knowing he was finally going to see the Marquès de Guíxols' supposed Dalí painting. As he stared at the walls, he was initially impressed with the art on display in what appeared to be a waiting room. There was even a painting similar to a Cézanne he'd once seen at the Barnes Foundation in Philadelphia. It was smaller, but with many of the same visual elements, and solid groupings of parallel, hatched brushstrokes. Suddenly the Marquès appeared at the doorway.

'Ah-hah, I see you're admiring my –'

'Copy of a Cézanne,' said Benjamin, turning to the very tall aristocrat entering the room.

'A *copy* of a Cézanne, you say,' the Marquès replied, somewhat playfully, and in excellent English.

'It's in the manner of Cézanne, after Cézanne, but certainly not Cézanne,' Benjamin said, studying the canvas again. 'In fact, I'd say it was painted by some crafty genius who's not only a clever artist and historian, but also a material scientist. It's easier to prove that a painting is a replica by finding anachronisms than it is to authenticate it.'

The Marquès moved closer.

'Y-e-s,' he said, in three syllables, looking at the painting, then at Benjamin. 'Well, we never believed it really was genuine, which is why it hangs in here.'

The aristocrat had a slight stoop and a ruddy, almost beetroot complexion. He had a snobbish sneer, a lecherous glint in his eye, and literally managed to look down his multi-veined, barnacled nose at Benjamin, through the gap between his half-moon spectacles and flying eyebrows.

'Guíxols. Jaume Guíxols,' he said, offering a hand that poked out from the cuff of his bottle green velvet jacket. 'You may call me Jaume. Your name, of course, is –'

'Benjamin.'

'But no one else knows you're here, do they?'

'No one,' said Benjamin, returning his stare.

'Good. We must keep it that way. This is a very delicate situation. I will explain, but not in front of Montse. Come, come …'

As Benjamin followed Jaume across the hallway towards a reception room, he tried to recall the last time he'd encountered a bottle green velvet jacket. It must have been on a poet or a theatre director some-where, or some other chain-smoking *bon vivant*. Jaume clearly wanted to give the impression that he was a lovable old toff, an upper-crust charmer, but Benjamin was not one to be impressed.

The housekeeper was still in the hallway and the aristocrat muttered something to her in Spanish, or maybe it was Catalan. She looked annoyed, shrugged, seemed to complain about something, but then disappeared. Jaume turned his attention back to Benjamin.

'You must be hungry. You must be thirsty. How was the journey? Were the directions easy to follow? Come through, come through,' he insisted, giving Benjamin no chance to reply to anything.

Jaume seemed to have a strange habit of smiling broadly and then quickly withdrawing it, like a momentary fixed grin. Benjamin wondered if it was a twitch or a nervous tic; it was difficult to judge if he was being friendly, cynical or simply taking the piss. Maybe it was the norm in the circle of sycophants that probably surrounded him, or maybe he just felt obliged to produce a token smile for plebs like, well, Benjamin.

Once in the reception room, Benjamin was invited to sit on one of the deep sofas, facing a tiny, elderly woman with wide, feline-like eyes. He guessed that Jaume had the slight stoop due to years of bending down to converse with her. She was painfully thin and appeared lost and abandoned on the sofa opposite, until Jaume sat beside her. She was introduced as Montse and she shook Benjamin's fingers, while keeping a steely, almost permanent gaze upon him.

They started conversing in what Benjamin finally realised was Catalan, as he failed to grasp anything that was being said. Montse spoke in a very high-pitched tone but was soon conscious that Benjamin didn't understand a word, eventually offering to involve him in the discussion.

'*Parla espanyol o català?*' she said to Jaume, before

turning to Benjamin and asking in perfect yet piercing English: 'Do you speak Spanish?'

'Very little. Just art vocabulary, really.'

'Of course, we must speak English,' said Jaume, followed by another short-lived smile. 'So, tell me, are you a close friend of Sir Anthony Hughes?'

Benjamin was about to explain that he'd only met Hughes once, when the stony-faced housekeeper reappeared, abruptly leaving a tray with three flutes of cava, and a half-empty bottle. Glancing at the label, he could see it was a *Marquès de Guíxols* – from the aristocrat's own vineyard, perhaps, if that was his line of business. Benjamin had a passion for wine and a great interest in learning more about grapes and winemaking, but he was here on a mission and needed to focus.

He was also starving. He checked his watch. He hadn't eaten anything since leaving the lecture in England, and already felt the happy and numbing effect of the two swift beers he'd downed in the bar in La Bisbal. As if reading his mind, another maid entered, shorter, Filipino, also looking annoyed. She was carrying a tray of something resembling tapas, which she practically slammed down onto the low table between the sofas.

Jaume and his wee wife appeared oblivious to the mood of their staff. As the Marquès raised his flute of fizz and took a healthy sip, Benjamin decided to do the same. He watched as a little cava escaped from Jaume's glass and dripped onto his velvet jacket.

'*Salut,*' Jaume said, wiping his mouth. 'I'm afraid

we ate rather a lot at a friend's luncheon today, but we can offer you some … how do you say it, *nibbles?*'

Montse picked up her own glass, momentarily waved it, but failed to take a sip. Instead, she replaced it on the low table alongside the canapés. The moody Filipino maid stayed in the room, waiting, Benjamin assumed, to see if anyone was going to eat anything. Famished, he didn't want to let her down, but decided he should wait his turn.

'Have you been to Barcelona before?' Montse asked.

'Many times, yes. And Figueres, of course.'

'Of course,' Jaume said, turning to explain matters to his wife. 'Anthony told me that our visitor is not just a qualified appraiser but a forensic art detective, a top scholar, lecturer, a rare academic, a specialist who investigates the authenticity and provenance of any painting from any period. Drawings, prints, sculptures, anywhere in the world. And we have him all to ourselves.'

Benjamin started to glow, but he didn't know if it was the bubbly or flattery. Jaume had given his work a glossy varnish, as many others often did, painting over the forgers and con artists, the cut-throats and thieves he had to deal with. For a moment, he felt relieved. It was as if the death threats, bribes, extortion and intimidation never existed.

Before he knew it, he'd taken another swig. Whatever complaint the Filipino maid had with the Marqueses, at least she could see he was thirsty. She filled up his flute again, then picked up the plate of miniature tapas and placed it nearer to him, before disappearing.

Benjamin was a foodie. He loved gastronomy, not just for the flavour of food but for the same reasons he loved art – for its look, colour, form and texture. He'd been pushed from an early age towards academia, eventually leading to forensic science and the fine arts, otherwise he believed he would have gone for the culinary arts and tried to become a chef. As he was constantly travelling, he didn't cook as much as he'd like ... and both those facts probably contributed to Claire walking out on him for someone else. Right now, he craved a big meal, but he was still intrigued to hear little Montse describe what lay in front of him.

In her high-pitched tone, she explained that what looked like bite-sized croissants to Benjamin were anchovy-butter canapés, meticulously baked using the egg yolk of the French Catalan coast. But it was all wasted on him, as he'd already scoffed his.

He then sat there for several minutes before anyone else ate. Eventually Jaume indulged, while Montse merely cut her own canapé in two, leaving half of it on the tray. Benjamin was about to devour it when the maid reappeared and replaced the tray with three new bite-sized treats, again slamming it down. Once again, Montse simply tickled her own, but before Benjamin could contemplate snatching her leftovers, the tray was removed.

Which was when the aristocrat asked what Benjamin had studied.

'Pretty much everything,' he replied. 'Diplomas in history of art, Spanish art, Flemish art, Italian and French Renaissance, American abstract expressionism, a diploma in biochemistry, then a bachelor's in chemistry, a master's in restoration and conservation, and finally a PhD in forensic science –'

'So, you're a Doctor –' Jaume said.

'No, I don't use that term.'

'A Doctor,' he insisted. 'It's fascinating, *fascinating* –'

'How long have you known Anthony Hughes?' Benjamin asked, trying to change the focus.

Within minutes, he had the old aristocrat sussed.

Jaume Ignasi Guíxols, seventh Marquès de Guíxols, was, it transpired, an 'Old Gregorian', just like Anthony Hughes, the name given to those educated at Downside in England. The Catholic boarding school was where many other wealthy Spanish families sent their children. And, yes, he assumed that Jaume could have called the Dalí Foundation in Figueres, and he probably could still involve them once Sotheby's had taken their first look, depending on Benjamin's appraisal report. But Jaume clearly owed Hughes a favour. From what he heard, Hughes had helped to enrol the aristocrat's daughter on a Sotheby's Fine Arts course in Paris, then gave her a job at Sotheby's in Geneva where she'd probably met her filthy rich fiancé.

Benjamin took a longer, irritated sip.

'Have you heard of that course?' Montse asked. 'The course that she did in Paris –'

'I have.'

There was a silence. Benjamin assumed that Montse, who clearly revelled in having a whirlpool of connections with social status and savoir-faire, was trying to ascertain if he also knew anyone who could further her daughter's career. Fortunately, she didn't ask.

Benjamin decided to then make a point of twisting his head from left to right across the room, as if looking for something. He wanted Jaume to show him the canvas they'd discovered, instead of enquiring after his experience and credentials. He was ravenous and couldn't handle much more of the Guíxols fizz, especially if he was going to drive. He also needed to pee.

Taking in the dust and the somewhat shambolic state of the room, he thought about the sullenness of the housekeeper and maid. Had they been paid? Were they owed money? Benjamin wondered whether the Marqueses really had been to a friend's luncheon, or whether it was just a show, and their minuscule tapas a cover-up for a bare larder. Why? Hughes said the Marquès had some personal and financial issues, but he had a cheerful, keeping-up-appearance demeanour, and he was clearly in no rush to acknowledge any problems, at least not in front of his little wife.

The aristocrat took the hint. He stood up and strolled over to a bookshelf. He selected a heavy, glossy art book, flicked to a specific spread, and returned to place it on the low table in front of Benjamin.

'Dalí's *Hallucinogenic Toreador*,' said Jaume.

Benjamin waited for the inevitable fleeting grin

from the Marquès and was duly rewarded. He then glanced at the image in the art book in front of him. He knew the painting so well; he didn't need to look twice. Hughes had insinuated that the canvas his friend had found resembled a study for Dalí's masterwork. But where was it? With Montse leaning forward to examine the image in the art book, Benjamin wondered how much they both knew about it. Were they also testing him again?

'Look for the green tie,' he said. 'The tie is your first clue. The bullfighter, Dalí's *Toreador*, can be seen by finding the green tie in the middle of the painting.'

Montse said something in Catalan to Jaume.

'Some say it was painted in twelve panels, with the depiction of the bullfighter being the secret thirteenth panel,' Benjamin said, still glancing around the room. 'But actually, his portrait isn't so hidden once you see that the repeated depictions of the Venus de Milo form the facial features of the toreador. A green skirt is his tie, a white skirt his shirt, and the bullfight arena his hat.'

'Yes –' Montse said.

'You'll see,' Benjamin continued, 'that the left breast of the central Venus forms his nose, her abdomen his mouth and chin, and the red robe of the Venus on the right becomes his cape, as if slung across a shoulder. The head of a dying bull can be seen near the bottom left corner. It's a tragic scene –'

'Yes, yes, I see.'

'You'll see how Dalí deliberately incorporated

several different styles of modern art to demonstrate his mastery of them all,' Benjamin said. 'Pop art in the solarised face of Venus at the upper left, cubism in the Venus at lower left, and op art in the dots of the toreador's cape ...'

'Benjamin –' Jaume started.

'You see Dalí was an expert in invisible images,' Benjamin said. 'On first glance, the bullfighter is invisible. But if you look carefully, he is there. Or at least you can *will* him to be there.'

'Yes, I see him again now,' Montse said, clapping her tiny hands together.

Benjamin hadn't expected Montse to be so interested. As he spoke, he'd even wondered where his pedantic tone had come from, but he put it down to his hunger, impatience and wanting to see the painting that the aristocrat had uncovered.

'You'll see the face of Dalí's wife, Gala, painted as a cameo-like apparition in the top left corner,' he decided to continue, 'and she's looking on disapprovingly because she frowned upon bullfighting. She's actually returning the young Dalí's gaze, who is in the bottom right corner. And they meet exactly midpoint in the canvas ...'

'Benjamin, *Doctor* Benjamin, that section is just like the study we've found.'

Benjamin wondered if he'd heard a sarcastic inflection in Jaume's tone. Squinting at where he was pointing to in the book, he felt curious.

'We must show you my painting,' the Marquès said.

'You must,' said Benjamin, noting the possessive 'my'. Whatever he'd found, the old aristocrat was clearly laying claim to it. 'Where is it?' he added, checking his watch again. 'More importantly, where was it found?'

'We discovered it in an old trunk in the cellar here,' started the Marquès, with another quick, cold smile. 'Our housekeeper, Lucía, helped me to bring the trunk up. I don't think —'

'How big is the painting?' Benjamin asked.

'Less than a metre square. I don't think it will take you long to authenticate it.'

'Is it framed?'

'No.'

'Is there a signature?'

'No, I didn't see one. But as I say, I really don't think it will take you long to authenticate it.'

'Any markings on the back?'

'Benjamin —'

'A date?'

'No, I don't think —'

'Any inscriptions?'

'No.'

'Any initials, or even a label? Any markings on the back at all?'

'*Benjamin* —'

'Any paperwork?'

'Benjamin, let's show it to you. Let's do it now.'

'Let's,' he said, getting up, but not before nimbly

polishing off the fizz. 'Do you mind if I just wash my hands?' he then asked. 'The bathroom, you know …'

Just moments later, Benjamin felt his phone vibrating in his jacket pocket. Checking it, he tried to ignore another call from Walter Postlethwaite, but finally caved in.

'Walter, I'm having a pee,' he said quickly.

'Hello, Benjamin, it's Walter Postlethwaite.'

Benjamin cut him off and put the phone on silent mode.

≈

Seven hours later.

Monday 4 June, 5.55am – near Girona-Costa Brava Airport.

Benjamin could now see the airport terminal in front of him as the lane finally met the slip-road off the motorway.

As he hurried ahead, he had a strong feeling that the housekeeper, Lucía, or the Filipino maid had tipped off someone to follow him. If they'd helped the aristocrat bring the trunk up from the cellar, were owed money or held a grudge about their employment conditions, they might have felt resentment seeing him drive off with the painting. But why savagely beat someone else to death at the service station?

Think, Benjamin, *think* …

9

Elena

Monday 4 June, 3am – city of Girona, northeast of Barcelona.

Elena was finding it hard to sleep but she knew she had to. It didn't help being on the sofa. While his foot was in plaster, her father was using her bed, the only bed in her small apartment. She could hear him snoring and it was also keeping her awake.

The wooden shutters in the living area were wide open, with the moonlight and warm night air filling the room. She drew her knees up to her chest, locking them with her arms. Perhaps she should simply give up, get up, then continue to work on her final dissertation. Besides, she didn't have much time left to grab any sleep thanks to her brother's slurred call.

He'd rung a few hours ago from some nightclub to plead with her, saying he'd be unable to do the morning taxi shift for their father. Something had come up, he'd said, trying to block out the loud music and a girl's laughter in the background. His dick had come up, that's what, Elena was sure of it. She stretched out again, aggressively kicking away a sheet just thinking about him. He was so unreliable. Deceitful.

She knew it would be a busy week ahead with the G20, however, and that business could be good. She knew her father needed the money. She did, too, and so she'd agreed to do the shift. She checked the time.

Shit, it was already 3am …

10

Isabel Bosch

Monday 4 June, 5.30am – Plaça Sant Jaume, Barcelona.

Everything about Isabel Bosch was prim, strict, straight, almost clinical. Even today's outfit with the white stilettos, a white two-piece suit, the boxed jacket with no cuffs, no collar, just three huge buttons and a square brooch, and the tight skirt, short, starched, taut: *clinical.* She'd wear huge, power-hungry shoulder pads if they were back in vogue. Shoulder pads like armour to intimidate adversaries, attract attention, or simply underline the fact that she'd take zero bullshit from anyone.

With her frosty and aloof expression framed by short, elegantly cut brown hair, Bosch was a career politician. She was hot-tempered, ambitious, authoritarian, very, *very* demanding, often speaking in a patronising way to subordinates or journalists as if to a five-year-old with learning issues … but she was also nervous right now.

With international flags being hung from every monument and lamppost, Barcelona was beautifying itself for the week ahead. From Tuesday to Friday, the city would be hosting its first G20 summit and a parallel UN Climate Change Conference. Lively, stylish, bright and eclectic, with its enthusiasm for vibrant architecture and design palpable at every corner, the city was revelling in being the focus of the world's media yet again, just as it had been over thirty years ago, for the 1992 Olympics.

Responsible for home affairs in the Generalitat, the Catalan government, the success and safety of the summit fell largely on her unpadded shoulders. Bosch had been working all weekend and every weekend for the past six months, and she was already at her desk at 5.30am on this Monday morning, still anxious if all scenarios had been covered. There was just too much at stake, especially the next step on her career ladder.

After studying another confidential G20 report, she gazed out the window of her office, tapping her blood-red painted claws on the desk, momentarily alone with her doubts and troubled thoughts.

The solid security umbrella that was about to unfold had been months in meticulous rehearsal, planned and implemented from the very top. That had meant coordinating the Generalitat's security plan with Madrid, the Spanish Interior Ministry and the Secretary of State for Security.

The coordination centre in Barcelona was code-named CECOR, the *Centro de Coordinación Operativa*, which controlled three separate command centres, a task force method that had worked very effectively for the Olympics. In collaboration with the city council, each command centre had the ability to mobilise all emergency resources, be it for firefighting, VIP protection, anti-riot or bomb disposal squads. For the build-up and duration of the G20, Isabel Bosch was part of the elite committee holding the all-powerful 'C4I': Command, Control, Communications, Computers and Intelligence.

But she still wasn't sure if it was enough.

She feared that even with the participation of fifteen thousand agents from Catalonia's Mossos d'Esquadra, the state's Policía Nacional and Guardia Civil, as well as Barcelona's own local police force, the Guàrdia Urbana, that fanatical jihadists and Al-Qaeda terrorists could still slip through the net. It had happened in La Rambla of Barcelona in August 2017, with the Madrid train bombings in March 2004, and it could happen again.

Over the past months, high security meetings had been held with staff at foreign embassies in Madrid and consulates in Barcelona, as well as with counter-terrorism experts from the CIA, MI6 and Interpol. Spain's intelligence service, the CNI, had participated in the drawing up of all plans, together with CITCO, the Intelligence Centre for Counter-Terrorism and Organised Crime. The Spanish Army and Air Force would be providing land and air security at the French border and at Barcelona, Girona and Reus airports. And NATO had emergency military units on standby to reduce the risk, at least to G20 delegates, from any chemical, biological, radiological or nuclear attack.

But was it enough?

In a sense, Bosch was less concerned about the G20 heads of state. Over the next forty-eight hours her team had to coordinate the safe arrival and transfer of world leaders, accompanied by their spouses and their economic and foreign ministers, to their virtual bunkers in hotels and consulates, but she was certain that nothing could go wrong there. If the usual anarchists smashed shop windows and cash machines, then she had her riot-clad police ready and waiting. They'd force back protesters with high-tech sound blasters, pepper spray and foam bullets, if required.

No, it was the unknown that unsettled her.

A recently radicalised convert or a solitary fanatic, capable of carrying out an atrocity at a supermarket, school or shopping mall in another area of the city where security was lax. Or anything else that might disrupt her rise to the very top.

She stood up to check her heels, peering down from left to right. Were they high enough? Sharp enough? There would be so many photo ops over the next twenty-four hours alone, and she wanted to get it just right.

11

Benjamin

Monday 4 June, 6am – Girona-Costa Brava Airport.

Benjamin found two Internet booths, red and yellow 'e-Point' machines that resembled old payphones, on the ground floor of the airport terminal. People were already queuing at check-in desks for early flights, while police teams with sniffer dogs were patrolling from one end of the concourse to the other. He was aware that he'd probably been staggering and swaying, and he needed to remain inconspicuous.

With the loose change he still had, he kept his head down and pushed a couple of euros into one of the machines, then opened the browser to search for his iCloud homepage. Once he'd logged in, there it was, the green tab for 'Find iPhone'.

At first, he wasn't sure if it would work. Late last night, when he was preparing to leave Jaume's home, he had the painting safely enclosed in a thin, flat port-folio case that the aristocrat had found in his daughter's old room, and Benjamin had then placed it alongside his backpack in the boot of the hire car. The house-keeper Lucía had been standing near the Marqueses, watching him do so.

When he'd finally left the Guíxols' home, he'd reached to extract his phone from his jacket pocket on the back seat, saw that the battery was almost dead again, and had then tossed it across the passenger seat, where it bounced and rolled down the side and under the seat.

He'd put it on silent mode after the last call from Walter, so whoever had stolen the car and the painting might not have discovered it if anyone had since called him. But he had no idea if the phone still had enough battery, or was connected, or could even be traced.

He waited for his log-in details to be recognised, then clicked on the green tab, watching the compass dial start to swivel, until, *yes*, there it was. A green dot on a map somewhere in central Barcelona. But then he lost the connection.

'*Shit*.'

He shoved another couple of coins into the machine, and eventually the dot showed the location of his phone again, but this time it stated it was the last known location. It didn't matter, it was all he had to go on.

He squinted at the screen, wondering whether the last known location was when he'd had the phone with him – but it couldn't be – he hadn't even been in Barcelona in the past few hours. He'd gone straight from this airport to the Guíxols home, so it had to be not only the last known location since the car had been stolen, if not the location right now, even if the battery had finally died …

He saw the clock running out on the coins he'd stuffed into the computer – *fuck*, there was nowhere to print out the map showing the green dot – so he dug into a pocket for his pad and pencil, then scrawled down the street name, quickly adding a diagram of the cross streets, more or less where the green dot was showing – *thirty seconds left* – he clicked on the standard, satellite and hybrid versions of the map, zoomed in as far as it would go – the green dot looked like it was near a railway line or something – was the vehicle in a car park? – it looked stationary, which was a good sign – and then the connection was lost again …

He just needed to get there.

A few minutes later, he was splashing cold water over his face and swabbing the back of his head with paper towels, which he tossed towards a bin with his eyes closed to avoid seeing the damp red stains.

Then he was pacing out of the airport, out to the front of the terminal with the sun now rising, then striding towards the taxi rank, trying not to stagger or sway.

12

Lieutenant Trias

Monday 4 June, 6.15am – service station near Girona-Costa Brava Airport.

It didn't take long for the chase to start, nor for the Catalan police, the Mossos d'Esquadra, to want to question and eliminate Benjamin from their enquiries. Not that they would identify him as such.

Soon after 6am, once morning activity was starting to pick up at the service station, now glowing in the warm light of dawn, a truck driver who'd pulled up to snooze for a few hours caught sight of a body slumped near a badly parked van. It was a luxury Chevrolet with blacked-out windows and the name 'Rafael Pérez' stencilled on its side. Once the truck driver had alerted the confused cashier in the shop, a Mossos patrol car arrived just five minutes later.

Catalonia's citizen protection policy was already at

high alert, as it was during any spring or summer weekend, with the cities and coastal towns already filling with tourists. Now, with the G20 and climate conference about to take place in the city of Barcelona itself, Catalonia was probably the safest place on earth.

At the Mossos Comisaria in Travessera de les Corts, central Barcelona, a call concerning a black Chevrolet had already been logged on the system.

The call had come through at 11.15pm last night, from Nîmes in the South of France, nearly three hundred kilometres northwest of Girona. The call had been made by a Spanish gentleman, claiming there'd been an incident at around 10pm outside the French city's Roman amphitheatre, the Arènes de Nîmes, which had been used for a bullfight. Regular reports of scuffles outside bullrings in Spain or southern France between pro- and anti-bullfighting groups were routine, especially since the bullfight prohibition in Catalonia.

But the caller had claimed to be the manager of Rafael Pérez, affectionately known as Rafa, the forty-five-year-old, five-foot-one Andalusian legend, the world's most famous living bullfighter. He said that not only had the vehicle been driven off by someone who wasn't the chauffeur, but that neither the chauffeur nor the bullfighter had responded to his calls or from any of the assistants who'd been planning to meet up with them in the morning in Valencia.

Although the call was conscientiously logged, the Mossos d'Esquadra were inundated with G20 work, and not a spare officer had been available to investigate or intervene in what appeared to be a squabble within a bullfighting entourage. The caller was told to also report the incident to the local Nîmes gendarmerie.

Police activity was already overstretched around Girona airport, but once the agents in the first Mossos patrol car verified there was a dead body alongside the abandoned Chevrolet and with the appearance of a vicious attack, two other patrol cars quickly arrived. Within minutes they'd secured the service station perimeter, blocking the exit and entry from the motor-way, so that the few visitors and staff currently on site could be interviewed as possible witnesses.

Lieutenant Trias was the first senior Mossos officer to arrive. He was sturdy and diligent, his eyes hard yet honest, and with a nose that had been hit more than once. He was already irritated that the incident would divert resources from his team patrolling Girona airport on the eve of the G20. Squinting at the scene in the low, morning sun, Trias was told that the body was not the famous bullfighter but possibly his driver, and that agents were already searching the area for potential clues or discarded weapons.

What Trias quickly concluded was that here was the abandoned Chevrolet, with the number plate confirming it was registered to Pérez SL, the company that managed the famous matador. His bullfighter's hat, a deep skullcap of black woven fabric with his name embroidered in the lining, had been left on the back seat of the Chevrolet, currently being examined.

Whatever happened in Nîmes would be a matter

for the French police. Whatever happened at the service station meant that it was now a murder scene, and a homicide squad and forensics team were already on the way.

Had the bullfighter killed his own driver and left? Unlikely. An abduction? If so, Trias knew that the early hours were crucial, and the rules were clear: immediately call in the kidnap and extortion division of the Catalan police. That meant one man, one expert, a veteran specialist in kidnap investigation and hostage negotiation.

Detective Inspector Vizcaya was contacted at 6.25am but was not at the scene until almost an hour later.

13

Benjamin, Elena – and the Marqueses de Guíxols

Monday 4 June, 6.45am – Girona to Barcelona.

Benjamin was trying to focus in the back of a taxi. He was gazing out the window at the cloudless blue sky with its rosy hue from the rising sun, but he couldn't get it out of his mind … *paranoiac-critical* … the concept of double imagery, where an object or figure is both what it may appear to be, and what it simultaneously transforms itself into.

Paranoiac-critical.

He often explained it whenever he was asked to give a lecture: 'Dalí's paranoiac-critical method was rooted in the notion that true paranoiacs often see double images and hidden images …'

However hard he tried, he couldn't separate the image of the painting that he'd seen at the Guíxols' home with what he'd seen at the service station, and not just the grotesquely disfigured corpse.

Something wasn't right.

There was an image he'd seen, a double image, and then something on a van, a *word* – 'bug, bug, bug, *bugger*,' he mumbled – well, it was a word like that.

He thought he'd seen it when he was out the front of the airport terminal, too, looking for the taxi rank. Something had caught his eye. But as his head was spinning and everything was in slow-motion, he assumed it was the concussion or that he was imagining things. When he tried to focus on it again, it had gone. What was the word and what else had he seen? Why had it reminded him of something he'd seen in the aristocrat's painting? He tried yet again to recall everything that happened last night …

∾

Eight hours earlier.

   Sunday 3 June, 10.30pm – La Bisbal d'Empordà.

The Marquès had been impatient, irritated, and had put pressure on Benjamin before he'd even had a chance to view the painting.

'This really should be very simple,' he'd muttered, taking Benjamin to one side as they made their way from the reception room to an adjoining library. 'How long before you can give me a certificate of authenticity?'

'Jaume,' said Benjamin, 'I want to warn you that it's highly unlikely that it will be a study for Dalí's *Hallucinogenic Toreador*.'

'No, I'm sure that this is.' His tone was clipped.

'All studies for the *Toreador* have been accounted for, at least those painted by Dalí himself,' said Benjamin. 'It turns out he painted just two. One of them, often referred to as *The Face*, belongs to the Dalí Foundation and hangs in the museum in Figueres. The other one sold for over a million dollars in New York back in 2007. I believe it is now owned by an Italian billionaire. It is highly unlikely, almost impossible, that he would have painted a third.'

'Why?'

'Because he was even late finishing the original masterwork itself.'

'How? What do you mean?'

'Look …' Benjamin took a deep breath. 'Reynolds and Eleanor Morse, the founders of the Dalí Museum in Florida, first saw the painting on the easel at Dalí's studio in Port Lligat, here in Spain in 1969, while he was still working on it. Then they saw it again, still unfinished, at an exhibition in New York, in March or April 1970. When they saw it in New York, they nego-tiated to acquire it. But Dalí said it was unfinished and that he needed to transport it back to his studio in Port Lligat to finish it, which wasn't until November 1970.'

'And?' said Jaume, coldly.

'Well, the Morses were even surprised that it still wasn't finished when they arrived in Port Lligat a month before, in October,' said Benjamin. 'The two studies for it, *The Face* and the one owned by the Italian billionaire, had already been identified by 1970, but there wasn't a third. It's highly unlikely that Dalí did further studies because he was anxious to get the masterwork finished. There was a lot going on in 1970. They were also reforming Gala's castle and Dalí was painting murals for the ceilings of the Figueres museum …'

'This is genuine,' the Marquès said, his voice hardening, 'and I'll need an authentication certificate immediately.' Any earlier playfulness had now been tossed to one side like a discarded cloak. There was spittle on his lips.

'I'm afraid it's not as simple as that,' said Benjamin, calmly.

Jaume ignored him. Instead, he swung open the doors to the library.

'Benjamin, *Doctor* Benjamin,' he said, suddenly producing another short-lived grin. 'Meet my Dalí study for *The Hallucinogenic Toreador* …'

Benjamin came face to face with a simple, rectangular canvas propped up on a bureau. He kept his distance at first, twisting his head to view it from different angles, before narrowing his eyes and trying to distort the image, shifting from one foot to the other.

'Come closer, come closer,' Jaume said.

Benjamin was unsure if the aristocrat was

addressing him or little Montse, who he suddenly realised had followed them to the library almost unnoticed. Benjamin shuffled a little closer towards the canvas.

It certainly looked like a replica of the oil study, *The Face*, which he knew was on permanent display in the Figueres museum, with its image centred around the main figure in the Venus de Milo and the face of the bullfighter.

'Well?' said Jaume, impatiently. 'What do you think?'

'What do I think?'

'Yes, yes. What do you think? It's genuine, isn't it?'

'Well,' said Benjamin, 'all the imagery is clearly there, the green skirt is his tie, a white skirt his shirt, the bullfight arena his hat.' He paused. 'From here, it's very similar to *The Face* —'

'What face?'

'*The Face* in the Figueres museum … the one I've been telling you about.'

'There's another?'

'There's only one *Face*, Jaume,' Benjamin said, as softly as possible, not wanting to anger the old aristocrat.

'One face?'

'Jaume, as I explained,' Benjamin said, moving even closer to the canvas, 'all known studies for the *Toreador* have been accounted for, at least those painted by Dalí himself. He painted two …' He paused. 'And it's highly unlikely he painted a third … but …'

Benjamin was right up against the canvas. He wanted to touch it, to hold it, yet asked for permission first. 'Do you mind? I should have brought gloves.'

'Go ahead.'

Benjamin picked up the painting. It was unframed and as always, he could feel his heartbeat accelerating. There was always that possibility, the discovery of something new, lost or unknown. He examined the back, front and sides, and ran his finger gently along the edges of the canvas and the old studs that pinned it to the wood. Then he closed his eyes and started to sniff it.

'Benjamin,' Montse squeaked.

'Where exactly did you find it again?' Benjamin asked, between sniffs.

'In a trunk in the cellar,' Jaume said.

'Yes, yes, of course, you mentioned that. But what else was in the trunk?'

'Nothing. Just old blankets.'

'Blankets? What type of blankets?'

'Old blankets. We can show you.'

'Yes, yes, but not right now,' said Benjamin. 'Was there anything else? Any paperwork? Any notes?'

'Nothing.'

Benjamin replaced the canvas to its position on the bureau, then took a few steps back to squint at it again.

'I have to admit that there's something,' he said. 'There's *something* that's … not quite right.'

'Not quite right?' the Marquès snapped.

'I hate to disappoint you, but my initial reaction is

that it's a good copy of *The Face* hanging in the Figueres museum.'

'A copy?' Jaume snarled.

'Yes.'

'A *copy*?'

'Yes, a copy. A reproduction. But by someone else, not by Dalí.'

Benjamin was wary of how much he might be able to explain to the Marquès, without enraging him. He'd already told him that his Cézanne was after Cézanne, or in the manner of Cézanne, and he was already pretty convinced that his Dalí was not a Dalí. At the very most it was in the circle of Dalí or by a follower of Dalí, possibly a work executed in the artist's style but not necessarily by a surrealist pupil, nor in the same period of the artist. But he would have to make sure.

'Not by Dalí?'

'Jaume,' said Benjamin, 'Dalí's enemies always claimed that he repeated himself, that he plagiarised himself. He often copied himself, so it's not absurd to imagine a third test for the *Toreador* might, but only *might*, exist. Look …'

He indicated to the bottom right of the canvas, then continued:

'A prime example of the way Dalí copied himself is the figure of the little boy in a sailor suit, with a hoop, looking at something. This little boy is in the lower right-hand corner of the masterwork, too. What is he watching, this boy, who is in fact Dalí himself?' Benjamin allowed himself a brief smile. 'He is looking at everything: at the Venus de Milo, at the bullfighter's face, at the cliffs that become the skirts of the Venuses which, in turn, form the bullfighter's cloak, green tie and shirt … you see? All that part is sketched out over here –'

'Benjamin –'

'Well, the boy in the sailor suit, this self-portrait that Dalí is so fond of, appears in many of his earlier paintings. The most widely known is *Spectre of Sex-Appeal*, painted in 1932, some 38 years before the *Toreador*. So, what I'm saying is that he often copied his own images …'

He squinted at the canvas again.

'Benjamin?'

'Time, image … *location*,' Benjamin muttered to himself.

'Benjamin?'

'Location,' he mumbled again.

When Anthony Hughes had said that a possible Dalí had been found 'outside Barcelona', Benjamin hadn't initially registered that the location would be in the heart of the artist's Empordà 'triangle', the Dalí Museum at Figueres, Dalí's home at Port Lligat, or the Púbol castle, the resting place of Dalí's wife, Gala. Careful to hide a sudden surge of excitement, he could also recall the signposts to Púbol on his way towards La Bisbal earlier.

Location …

Púbol was about ten kilometres from the Guíxols' home. But surely Dalí hadn't painted another test before finishing the masterwork? Even if he had, why would the painting end up in a trunk in Jaume's cellar? He knew he would need to investigate and establish the painting's journey, its provenance, not just the quality and details of the oil and canvas. But it had certainly started to intrigue him.

'Doctor?' the Marquès said.

Benjamin knew that the catalogue raisonné of all Dalí's paintings was considered as work in progress. Should Jaume's painting be examined further for it to even be considered for inclusion?

'I admit that right now,' Benjamin said, as if answering his own thoughts out loud, 'I can't say for sure …'

The Marquès clapped his hands. 'So, it is genuine,' he roared.

'I didn't say that, Jaume.'

'But you're not sure.'

'Right now, I'd say it was a reproduction, a good copy.'

'But a copy by Dalí himself –'

'No, I didn't say that, either –'

'But you're not sure.'

'It will take time.'

'What else do you need?'

'Look, I'd really like to help you if I can, but don't build up hope –'

'What else do you need?'

'I can give you my opinion based on this first look,

but one has to carefully document why a work is authentic or not –'

'What else do you need?'

'– because while authentication is an art itself, it is also based on scientific principles –'

'What else do you need, Benjamin?'

'I'm sorry?'

'What else do you need?'

Silence.

'Benjamin?'

'Let's have a look at the trunk and the cellar where you found it,' said Benjamin.

∾

Eight hours later.

Monday 4 June, 7am – Girona to Barcelona.

'Bug, bug, bugger,' Benjamin was now mumbling in the back of the taxi again, still trying to recall the word he'd seen on the side of a van screeching away from the service station last night, just before he'd been attacked, as well as an image he'd seen that had reminded him of something in Jaume's painting.

The young taxi driver was eyeing him in her rear-view mirror.

He'd found her at the front of the taxi rank outside the airport terminal, leaning against her vehicle, a gleaming, silver-grey Citroën Jumpy people-carrier.

Slender, in tight jeans, a loose top and with dark curls, she'd smiled at Benjamin as he'd hurried towards her. For a moment, it had almost floored him, probably because it was the first person who'd genuinely smiled at him for hours, possibly days, and a contrast to the gory image at the service station.

There was something about her – the way she was leaning, weight on one hip, maybe just the mystery of her smile – but he was immediately struck by her beauty. There was no discernible make-up, but her face was simply exquisite. In fact, Benjamin thought it might be the most beautiful face he'd ever seen, but he couldn't be sure because it was unlike any other. Her eyes were gleaming. What colour were they? Almost multi-coloured. They were both dark and light brown … like speckles … sparkling speckles …

He'd tried to smile back, and he'd quickly shown her the scrap of paper with the location and side streets that he'd sketched from the 'Find iPhone' screen, which she then keyed into the Sat-Nav on her taxi. When she'd spoken, she'd done so with a short, snappy, fiery undertone, as if she was also in a rush. She'd spoken very good English, even though Benjamin had politely tried some Spanish, and they'd managed to agree a hundred and fifty euros in cash to be driven to where he'd indicated in Barcelona, plus tolls.

The significance of the tolls hadn't dawned on Benjamin until moments later. It was when the taxi was pulling out of the airport complex, after the driver had called through to someone, probably to explain where she was off to, and then slowed to a halt at the toll booth. One direction said France, the other was Barcelona/Girona South. She took a ticket, tucked it into the sun-visor, and Benjamin sat up.

The toll ticket.

He remembered taking one when he'd joined the motorway back from the Guíxols' house last night. It was all coming back to him.

He'd first put the portfolio case with the painting in the boot of the hire car, alongside his small backpack, witnessed by the Marqueses and their housekeeper, Lucía.

He'd then set off towards La Bisbal, and where he'd again passed the sign to a hotel called Castell d'Empordà. He'd even pulled up, wondering if he could stay there, or at least grab more to eat. He could do neither. The hotel looked great, but it had been full, and there'd been nothing that he could realistically take away to scoff in the car while driving. He'd picked up one of their leaflets and tucked it into a pocket, then set off again. About fifteen minutes later he'd taken a ticket from a toll booth to join the motorway south towards Barcelona, and he'd also tucked it into the top of the sun-visor and flipped it back flat, just as his taxi driver had now done.

After the cava and coffee consumed last night at the Guíxols' house, he'd needed the loo again, which was why he'd pulled into the service station to also grab a sandwich, signposted as the exit for Girona airport at where he'd arrived just hours earlier.

Did whoever attack him before taking the car and the painting know there was a toll ticket in the vehicle? Had someone followed him from the toll booth? Surely whoever stole his car would have also needed a toll ticket to pay at the next tollgate in order to not raise any suspicion, unless they just crashed through the barriers …

'*Estás bien?*' the taxi driver was now saying, still eyeing him in her rear-view mirror. 'Okay?'

Benjamin was conscious that he'd probably been mumbling to himself.

'Not great, no,' he said, rubbing the back of his head. It felt good to be able to speak to someone. Before he could stop himself, he added: 'My car was stolen.'

'*Cómo?* Car?'

'Stolen.'

'Someone stole your car?'

It wasn't the intention, but this garnered sympathy from the driver. She appeared to want to pull over, insisting, it would seem, that Benjamin inform the police if he hadn't already done so. As he quickly shrugged off the suggestion, the driver took it upon herself to agree that the police would probably do nothing, that they were useless, *inútil*, and wherever he needed to go, she could drive him.

Benjamin nodded, in gratitude. His thoughts drifted back to the service station and the body. He'd wanted to do more, but there wasn't much else he could have done. By finding the painting, he'd also find the killer and his own attacker, he was sure, and that was the best option for now. He knew he'd have to call his contacts in due course, but he just needed some time to secure the canvas.

'G20?' the driver was saying.

'I'm sorry?'

'Your visit here. G20?'

'No, no,' he said. 'Not the G20 …' He caught her eye in the mirror. She was stunning. She looked away and he did, too.

He recalled Anthony Hughes saying that finding a hotel had been difficult because of the summit. He dug into a pocket and pulled out the lecture leaflet with the scribbled address in Barcelona where he was supposed to have stayed last night, a hotel called Splendido. He showed it to the driver and asked her if it was also near where they were heading.

She keyed it into the Sat-Nav, but then waved her hand and shrugged her shoulders. They were tanned and almost bare, with her loose top scarcely covering a tattoo on one of her shoulder blades. She said the address was possibly in the same area, but she wasn't sure.

'If not, no problem,' she said. 'I can also take you there. And if you want to come back to Girona, I take you, too, okay? It's good for me, a fare back, you understand?'

'I understand.'

There was a pause.

'Elena,' she said. 'My name is Elena.'

'Benjamin,' he said.

'Benjamin?'

'Yes.'

Elena took a business card from a plastic holder stuck to the dashboard and handed it to him. The card had 'Carmona Taxis – Girona' and a phone number printed on it. He tucked it away, catching her eye again in the mirror. He then wriggled out of his corduroy jacket while she put on a pair of sunglasses against the low, bright sun.

'Is the air conditioning okay?' she asked. 'Tell me if not, okay? They say today is going to be very hot.'

'It's okay … it's great, thanks,' said Benjamin.

Her phone bleeped and she briefly took off her sunglasses to check a message. He felt he had to stop ogling the back of her head, in case she caught his eye again. He sat back and tried to recall exactly how he'd left things with the Marquès last night.

Eight hours earlier.
Sunday 3 June, 11.30pm – La Bisbal d'Empordà.

It was Jaume who'd insisted that Benjamin take the painting with him. The plan was for him to examine it more closely first thing in the morning at one of the labs he trusted in Barcelona – 'but, yes, in secrecy and strict confidence', Benjamin had assured him.

Before leaving, Benjamin inspected the cellar and trunk where they'd discovered the painting wrapped in blankets, but he'd found nothing unusual. Nor had he found any papers, documents, receipts or further clues, but at least Jaume could vouch that the trunk itself had been in his family for years, possibly generations.

The cellar was dry, but not too dry, and so the temperature and humidity levels were stable. Nor would there have been any direct sunlight hitting the canvas, although Benjamin had no idea how long the painting had been kept down there.

'Direct visual examination is fine up to a point, but it won't tell the whole story,' said Benjamin, as he finally prepared to leave the Guíxols' home. 'There's vital information hidden beneath the visible surface of every painting, buried by the very process of creation. I need to study every aspect of a painting's materials and methods of production. I still think this is a good copy, but not by Dalí, although I admit that it's worthy of further examination.'

His comments were not well received by the old aristocrat. As he was escorted to the door, with Montse and the housekeeper hovering in the distance, Benjamin didn't like Jaume's tone, which had become almost threatening.

'Listen,' he said, 'I need a certificate of authen-tication.'

'If it is authentic, yes, but as I explained –'

'I don't think you understand –'

'I need to carry out the tests –'

'I said that I need a certificate –'

'I heard you, but –'

'I *need* a certificate.'

Benjamin stared at the ruddy-faced aristocrat.

'Jaume,' he said, 'even if it is possible, a certificate of authenticity without a flawless provenance, particularly for a work of art supposedly by Dalí, would be worthless.'

'I need a certificate.'

'Jaume … Salvador Dalí's work is one of the most varied and extensive collections of the twentieth century. The data listed for each painting currently in the catalogue raisonné includes the title, the date –'

'I need a certificate –'

'– the technique, support, dimensions, signature, inscriptions, current location, historical provenance, as well as observations, all backed up by a comprehensive exhibition history and bibliography, for every single painting –'

'I need –'

'Just wait, Jaume, *please*. You need to understand that as well as comparing visual examination with any photographic documentation, all other sources of information will need to be cross-referenced, too, from exhibition and auction catalogues, old press cuttings, the archives of the Dalí Museum in Florida and the museum in Figueres, including books in the library of the Foundation, and also from the artist's private library, even from his very own handwritten texts and diaries.'

'But you clearly know everything there is to know about the painting,' the Marquès said. 'You know the period. What else do you need?'

Benjamin stared at him. He realised the aristocrat wasn't undermining him or trying to belittle his work, he was challenging him.

'Are you incapable of examining this work?' he said.

'Of course not.'

'Should I ask Anthony Hughes to send someone else?' He flashed another one of his instantaneous grins.

'No.'

'Then I need a certificate.'

'*If* it is genuine, then, yes, but it will take time.'

'I need a certificate.'

'If you want me to falsify a document, I'm afraid that's not what I do.'

'I need a certificate. How long will it take?'

Silence.

'How long will it take?'

Benjamin waited, still staring at Jaume to make sure he wasn't going to repeat his demand yet again.

'I need to see if anyone made any preparatory outlines or alternative drawings for the painting below its visible surface,' he said. 'As *The Face* was a study for the masterwork, there are several drawings below the surface. The same should apply to this work, if it is genuine, and if those outlines are by Dalí. If there are no underdrawings, then it will be easier to dismiss it as a fake, or at the most, a straight copy of *The Face*.'

Jaume sneered.

'If there are preparatory drawings in charcoal, I'll be able to see them with infrared reflectography,' Benjamin said. 'I suggest we start there.'

'I want a certificate by noon tomorrow,' Jaume snapped.

'That's impossible.'

'And I want you to call me first thing in the morning to update me on your progress,' the aristocrat said, handing Benjamin a card with his cell phone number on it. 'And no one at all must know about this … is that clear?'

'Of course,' Benjamin nodded. 'As I've already said, no one will know anything. You have my word on that. I will call you in the morning.'

And then he left, with the painting in the boot of his hire car.

∼

Eight hours later.
Monday 4 June, 7.15am – Girona to Barcelona.

In the back of the taxi, Benjamin glanced at his watch, conscious that he would have to contact Jaume at some point.

Elena, meanwhile, had checked her messages while also keeping her eyes on the road. Her father had still been snoring when she'd left the apartment earlier, but she'd since left him a voice message to say that all was okay, and that she was standing in for her brother and had a passenger. Then she'd put the phone on silent mode, so as not to be distracted from the motorway again.

She glanced at the passenger in the back. How old was he? Older than her, definitely ... but how old? Forty? He didn't look very well. He looked a mess, as well as agitated. There was a red mark like a bloodstain on his collar, too, and something strange or different about him. Not bad, not good, just ... *different.*

14

Detective Inspector Vizcaya and Officer Soler

Monday 4 June, 7.30am – near Girona-Costa Brava Airport.

Detective Inspector Vizcaya of the Mossos d'Esquadra's kidnap and extortion division was a gruff, heavyset, walrus-moustached man with a weathered face and square head. Only in his early fifties, he looked older and had the air of a man who'd lived a full life.

Barrel-chested, with slightly puffy jowls and swollen eyelids that betrayed his fondness for a tipple, his style of investigation was based more on old-school intuition and observation than hard evidence. Often dressed in a rumpled suit and a tie that was never knotted properly, he was also balding, with the surviving hair always on end, askew and uncombed, making him look constantly startled.

The fingers of his left hand were missing, shot off

in a hunting accident twenty years ago, and how he gripped on to his old motor scooter was anyone's guess. He'd been born and bred in the Basque Country, growing up in a village east of Bilbao. After years of travelling across Spain as one of the country's most celebrated kidnap investigators, he'd finally settled in Barcelona for one simple reason. He'd married a Catalan.

Vizcaya had been snoring happily at their apartment in the Gràcia district of Barcelona when he received a call at 6.25am from the Mossos Comissaria. He wasn't a fan of new technology, and only had a smartphone because the police force insisted.

Roused from a deep sleep, he was informed about a possible high-profile abduction and told that his presence would be required at once. With a permanent tetchiness that often escalated into a foul temper, his initial reaction was to grunt that he'd get there on his Vespa after he'd enjoyed a good breakfast. He was told that the crime scene was on the motorway near Girona, and that he'd be picked up within five minutes in a squad car, together with his Missing Persons Officer, Marta Soler, a strong woman with short, spiky blonde hair and several studs in both ears.

Travelling flat-out from Barcelona with blue flashing lights clearing the motorway ahead, Vizcaya was briefed by Soler about the brutal murder of a chauffeur, already being investigated by a Mossos homicide squad, and the possible abduction in Nîmes of the famous Spanish bullfighter, Rafael Pérez. When

Vizcaya asked about the bullfighter's manager, agent or entourage, Soler said that they had all remained in France, adding that she had a team liaising with the French police to locate them for questioning.

'Do the press know yet?' asked Vizcaya. 'Anything on social media?'

'Not yet,' said Soler, constantly checking her cell phone.

As always, the Basque separatist terror group, ETA, was immediately at the forefront of Vizcaya's thoughts. True, it had declared a permanent ceasefire well over a decade ago now, but there was always the possibility of a new offshoot or faction group, more hard-lined and intransigent than before. Most of ETA's victims had been Basque industrialists, kidnapped for ransoms to help finance the group's war against the Spanish state. There'd also been kidnaps for political rather than financial objectives, for the exchange of ETA prisoners, propaganda, or the extraction of political intelligence. But why kidnap a bullfighter?

'Where exactly are we heading?' Vizcaya asked.

When he was told that the crime scene was adjacent to Girona airport, he ordered Soler to request passenger data on all departing private jets, information that often slipped under the radar.

Forty minutes later, he was pacing around the abandoned Chevrolet at the sealed-off service station, getting an update from Lieutenant Trias on what the homicide team had so far unravelled, as well as reports from Nîmes. Two photographers were taking shots of the body and surrounding area, as well as of the Chevrolet, inside and out, while others were meticulously combing the entire area, placing items into evidence bags, including the matador's hat found on one of the back seats of the vehicle.

Vizcaya had seen enough corpses in his career and took just a cursory glance at this latest one, before they zipped up the body bag in the presence of a duty judge to transport it off to a morgue in Girona for an autopsy. But from what he could see, death had been brutal.

The low, rising sun beamed over the shoulder of a forensics officer and into Vizcaya's face as he was given the gist of it.

'The man's skull had been split open, and he'd been tied and presumably gagged, as a ball of vomit-stained cloth was found on the ground next to his pulped face,' explained the officer.

'Did one of your team remove the gag?' asked Vizcaya.

'No, not us,' came the reply. 'Perhaps the victim was forced to answer questions before execution. Blood trails suggest that he'd either crawled from the back of the vehicle to where he was found or had been dragged.'

Officer Soler, who'd been exchanging messages with the French police, said that descriptions and photos being sent from the entourage in Nîmes appeared to confirm that the body was the bullfighter's driver, but official identification would be required from his family or next-of-kin.

For Vizcaya, what was clearly a murder scene added another dimension to his own task of resolving a kidnapping, assuming there'd been one. His kidnap and extortion division would need to work in parallel with the homicide squad, but all missing person investigations were an immediate race against time. With a murder already committed, how safe was the person abducted? It made matters much more precarious, as the kidnappers had nothing else to lose. They'd have no qualms about carrying out a second killing.

Soler had confirmed during the journey that no ransom demand had yet been received, and Vizcaya knew that the matador could be anywhere in Spain or elsewhere, possibly still in France, with the border just seventy kilometres away. All they had here was a dead driver and an abandoned vehicle. With no specific witness reports, it wasn't even certain that the bullfighter had been brought here, was still alive, or whether the Chevrolet had stopped anywhere else after leaving Nîmes.

'Does the vehicle have GPS?' Vizcaya asked Lieutenant Trias.

'No,' came the reply.

'Keys?'

'Not in the vehicle.'

'Any money? Driver's wallet? Phone?'

'Nothing.'

Trias gave more details, that CCTV at the service station only monitored the fuel pumps and not where the Chevrolet was parked, but there was basic video surveillance in the shop that they would analyse, and they were already interviewing the night staff and checking till receipts. He also said that a police truck was on its way to cover, seal and tow the Chevrolet away for further examination.

'Test it for traces of tranquilisers or anaesthetics, too,' said Vizcaya, holding up his fingerless left hand to make a solitary thumb up and show that he no longer needed information, or to halt Trias in mid-sentence so that he could rattle off observations to Officer Soler at his side, busy making detailed notes herself.

'What do we know about the dead chauffeur so far?' asked Vizcaya. 'Do we know if he was forced to drive here or if someone else did?'

He didn't wait for a reply. Barking instructions to Soler, he made it clear that he wanted to know about the chauffeur's whereabouts before, during and after the Nîmes bullfight, who else had access to the vehicle, who serviced it, cleaned it, put fuel in it, who else had keys and where are they now? When and where did the chauffeur last pay for anything? Where was he first attacked, when, how, why, and with what?

'Any papers, insurance documents, motorway receipts or toll tickets still in the vehicle?' he asked, turning quickly back to Trias. 'What about CCTV at any tollgates? ANPR?'

Even without watching Trias shaking his head,

Vizcaya guessed the answer. Years of investigating abductions, he knew there was no automatic number plate recognition at any of Spain's tollgates.

There were certainly CCTV cameras that monitored the flow of traffic during peak hours, but whether they'd been working at night and caught images of the Chevrolet and its passengers was doubtful. One thing was certain: they knew the time that the vehicle sped away from Nîmes, and so they'd also know the approximate times that it would have travelled through tollgates and the French border to arrive at where it did. Officer Soler was immediately despatched in a squad car to investigate all payments made during the relevant hours at any tollgates between Nîmes and Girona, and Girona on to Barcelona.

Vizcaya was also keen to play the secrecy weapon. Not easy, though, with several people already aware of what might have happened, and a helicopter now circling above. If he could just contain it for twenty-four hours, it would help. He didn't want the media to announce that the bullfighter was missing. As always, he wanted the kidnappers to make the first call, which often gave a vital clue; how they made contact often helped to trace where they were hiding.

With a high-profile abduction, Vizcaya was confident that his division within Catalonia's Mossos would already be sharing intelligence with the state's Policía Nacional and Guardia Civil, as well as with the French border police. Strict security controls were already in place for G20, but any further checks carried out on major routes surrounding Barcelona, including from the airports, port and mainline stations, would help. But it was never enough and was probably too late.

The entourage ...

The first group to be questioned had to be the bull-fighter's entourage. He also had to delay them from speaking to the press or making any noise on social media. How many were there? What was their itinerary? All their prints and DNA would also need to be checked against anything found in the Chevrolet. But where were they? Every question Vizcaya asked, the answer came to the same: Nîmes.

France.

Not only had Spain and France forged an excellent relationship in their fight against ETA, but Vizcaya had a better relationship with the French police than most other investigators. As ETA had traditionally used France as its logistical base to prepare attacks across the border, the cooperation between the two countries in cracking down on terrorist hideouts, helping to track down and free kidnap victims, had been immense.

He was unimpressed with the reports coming in from the Nîmes gendarmerie, however, and decided to take matters into his own hands. He called his old friend, Gilles Clémenceau, Director Régional de la Police Judiciaire for the city of Montpellier, under whose jurisdiction fell Nîmes, and told him he was on his way. Lieutenant Trias instructed an unmarked Mossos car to drive Vizcaya at top speed across the border, while he and his team stayed on at the service station.

Within minutes of Vizcaya leaving, they got a possible breakthrough. Agents who'd been interviewing the service station staff now had a report that a man had been banging on the shop window at around 5.30am, asking for directions to walk to the airport. He was described as 'odd', 'probably foreign', with thick curly hair. A full report was being compiled and the shop window checked for prints.

Officer Soler, meanwhile, was being driven back towards Barcelona, to the *Autopistas Concesionaria Española* in the Zona Franca industrial area of the city, the centre for all data related to the motorways and toll system across Catalonia, when she received an urgent call from a colleague at the Mossos Comissaria.

'There's been a call to *La Vanguardia* newspaper,' the agent said. 'They suggest you head there immediately.'

It was 8.15am.

15

Benjamin, Elena and Séverin

Monday 4 June, 8am – Sants station and Les Corts district, Barcelona.

In the back of the taxi approaching the centre of Barcelona, now bathed in sunlight, Benjamin started to question if it really was the Marqueses' housekeeper who'd targeted the painting. Lucía had spoken enough English to give him directions from the bar in La Bisbal to the Guíxols' house last night – so if she'd overheard his later conversations with the old aristocrat, she would have known that he highly doubted the painting's authenticity.

It seemed illogical to have sent someone to chase him along a motorway to steal the painting before he'd even had a chance to authenticate it. Had the Filipino maid ordered someone to follow him? Why? They could have stolen it from the house, or just as he'd left.

Art theft was big business, worth over five billion dollars a year, putting it among the top international crimes after drug trafficking, money laundering and arms dealing – and from Benjamin's experience, there were several motives for carrying it out.

Some crooks targeted masterpieces to be used as collateral, for bartering and bargaining, like 'get out of jail' cards, or in the hope of ransoming the art back to its owner or securing a pay-off from an insurance firm. Some stole with the aim of flogging it on to a dealer, and there were others who were paid to swipe a specific painting or received a commission.

Some even snatched works of art to keep for themselves, or to gain kudos in the criminal fraternity, often linked to underworld trading in drugs. Art used as a commodity to ransom back for cash, then cash for drugs ... and drug deals regularly involved extortion and violence. Again, Benjamin thought of the body at the service station with the shattered skull.

There were also incidents of stolen art that were a consequence of another robbery or residential heist. In those cases, the thieves normally had zero knowledge about art and would simply offload the extra loot without realising its true value – which is why precious missing art could sometimes be found at car boot sales or flea markets. So, did the person who attacked him and who stole his hire car know there was a possible Dalí in the boot? If not, it was just as worrying, as they could have tossed it away or destroyed it by now.

Benjamin knew for certain that art theft was rarely

an isolated incidence. Priceless art snatched and bartered as a valuable commodity meant that something else was usually involved, be it drugs, weapons, money laundering, prostitution, even human trafficking.

Images swirled in his head again as he tried to recall the word that he'd seen on the van that had sped away, just before he was attacked. He wondered if Jaume might have already received a ransom call for the painting, but it was unthinkable. He had to recover the art before the aristocrat knew it had ever been lost. He had to locate his car …

Elena asked to look at the scrap of paper again where Benjamin had scribbled down the cross streets in central Barcelona, near Sants station. She'd been driving around in circles for five minutes, yet finally pulled the Citroën halfway up onto a kerb. Car horns blared behind and she was quickly waved on by traffic police.

As she steered her taxi around the station's plaza, past a hotel Victòria, then round the back of the hotel to try and circumnavigate the entire railway complex yet again, Benjamin noticed there weren't any cars parked on any street close to those that he'd scribbled. He thought it might have been for the G20 security, but realised it was a drop-off point for cars and taxis. No parking was allowed anywhere.

Taxis were unloading passengers for the station and

then being moved on. Was there any point in asking her to stop, so that he could snoop around inside the station itself? For what? He'd seen plenty of bars and fast-food outlets as they'd continued to drive around in circles, but was there any point in finding a computer to log on to his iCloud account again to see if the last known location of his phone had been updated? No, not really, he was sure it had been drained of battery now.

He was feeling despondent, maybe the car had been driven to the station to drop someone off, and maybe the battery had then finally died, and maybe the vehicle was somewhere else now, anywhere – it could be *anywhere* … or, maybe …

Maybe it was at the hotel itself … in the car park of the hotel.

The hotel Victòria was next to a public car park, exactly on the corner of the cross streets they'd passed three times already as they'd circled the station, alongside some rental car offices for Avis, Budget, Europcar, Hertz and the Goldcar brand he'd rented his car from. Had they returned the hire car? Surely not …

He needed to at least check the car park, floor-by-floor, just to see if the vehicle had been dumped there – and so he instructed Elena to pull up wherever she could, to give him ten minutes, to keep circling if she had to. She was reluctant at first but finally agreed, and so Benjamin then ran into the car park and up the circular ramp, round the first level, row-by-row, row-by-row – searching for a VW Polo with a yellow

Goldcar sticker – then up to the second level – row-by-row – sweating now, feeling nauseated again with the pain in his head – then up to the third level, row-by-row – but there was nothing, *nothing at all*. By now he felt sick, so he staggered over to the open side wall to get some air, which is when he looked out, down and across, and he saw his hire car in a side-street, half on a kerb and half blocking the entrance to the back of the hotel – its hazard lights flashing, car horns going off behind it. It looked like it had been abandoned and was blocking the narrow road …

'*No, wait,*' he yelled, to himself more than anyone else, and then he was off again, charging down the car park's spiral ramp until he was down at street level and then racing out past the exit barriers, which is when he saw Elena in the taxi.

He waved frantically at her, then jumped in the front passenger seat as she pulled up, asking her to drive as fast as she could in the direction of the street he'd seen from the car park. She started shouting at him in Spanish but Benjamin wasn't listening – because once they reached the narrow street and pulled up about fifty metres from his hire car, Benjamin could see him: a hefty lout in a red hoodie, staggering back towards the vehicle from the back of the hotel's 'goods delivery' entrance, waving aggressively to other motorists sounding their horns in their blocked vehicles, threatening to cut their throats, before quickly jumping into the car. In the distance, sirens could be heard …

'Just drive, please, just follow that car – I'll explain,' Benjamin said to Elena, who started shouting again in Spanish, something about the *policía* – but all Benjamin was thinking was that not only could he get the car and painting back, but he'd pin down the possible killer, too, or at least the bastard who'd attacked him. And as the road became unblocked, they managed to keep the hire car in sight, right up to the district of Les Corts, where it slowed down in a narrow, pedestrianised street, signposted for authorised vehicle access only.

That didn't concern the thug at the wheel of Benjamin's hire car. He continued to drive around the lanes encompassing the Plaça de la Concòrdia, scattering pedestrians like startled ducks, and finally came to stop outside the entrance to a parking lot, adjoined to another hotel, off a street called Deu i Mata.

'Got you, you bastard,' muttered Benjamin, still sitting in the front passenger seat of Elena's taxi.

They'd now come to a halt about a hundred metres from where he'd pulled up, and Elena was still yelling in Spanish – *Qué pasa? Qué pasa?* – and then also in English, demanding to know what the hell was going on, telling him that he should call the police if this was his stolen car.

Benjamin looked at her. She was right, of course, but he knew he couldn't call the police – at least not the police she'd probably want him to call. Not yet. Not until he'd returned the painting safely to the aristocrat, with or without an appraisal.

'I will,' he said. 'But later …'

Looking back towards his car, he could see that the driver had so far made no sign of getting out of the vehicle but appeared to be eyeing the parking entrance to the hotel. Why? Benjamin's head was spinning. Was that what he'd been doing at the last stop, too? Eyeing the hotel's parking lot, or its 'goods delivery' entrance? *Why?* Benjamin waited, but then when the red-hooded oaf got out of the hire car, he couldn't stop himself.

He leapt out of the taxi and headed towards him, faster now, calling out as he ran across, and then he was upon him, tapping his shoulder, asking him what the fuck he was doing – who sent you to steal the painting? – you killed someone and attacked me last night, you *bastard* – which is when the thug turned to face him.

'You what?' snarled Séverin, glaring at Benjamin, and taking in the mad hair.

Who the hell was this guy? Where had he seen him before? Why had he touched him? He'd had more angel dust, so he wasn't totally sure what was happening, or where he was right now. All he knew was that he'd come to central Barcelona to find the Dutch motherfuckers who'd left him stranded at the service station, and who owed him eight thousand euros. He'd been trying to find the hotel they'd used for meetings. He also had a job to finish … someone to carve up. But now here was a fucking nutcase talking about a painting. Then he suddenly remembered where he'd seen him before …

Séverin immediately pulled out a hammer from his tool belt, swinging it to connect with Benjamin, who just managed to lift his forearm to block the first impact. But not the second one, *no*, he was far too slow – as Séverin swung it again and caught Benjamin's left shoulder – *fuck, that hurt* – so Benjamin doubled up and tried to ram his head into his attacker's chest as Séverin stumbled back, lost his balance, and fell. Benjamin went for the boot of the car instead of pursuing the fight – he wanted the *painting*, the portfolio case, if it was still there – yes, it *was* – but as he struggled to open the boot, the psycho came at him yet again, swinging the hammer against Benjamin's back – but he'd got the boot open now while trying to fend off the next hammer blow with his forearm again. He turned, tried to land a punch on the thug's jaw but missed, just before the hammer was swung towards his face. He managed to duck, letting it smash through a rear window of the car instead. Benjamin had the portfolio case and his backpack now, even though his phone was still in the car, but he still had to fend off a new attack from the madman who'd pulled out another hammer from his belt, this time swinging it against Benjamin's legs – *shit, he was trying to kneecap him*. As he buckled to the ground, his attacker suddenly lumbered away, up one of the pedestrianised streets and momentarily out of sight – leaving the dazed and battered Benjamin free to stumble back across the square to where he hoped Elena was still parked.

She was ... but only just.

She'd considered filming the fight on her cell phone for a possible news story, or just driving off. In fact, she was going to do both, but her passenger hadn't yet paid her the hundred and fifty euros they'd agreed for the journey from Girona airport to Barcelona, so she'd decided to hang around just a little longer.

Whatever argument he was having with the red-hooded guy in the hire car, it was none of her business, at least that's what she tried to tell herself. Her client – *Benjamin*, that was his name – was old enough to handle himself.

But the brawl started to get vicious, a car window was smashed, a weapon was being swung, so she yelled across, but the thug in the red hoodie trudged off. Then she saw him pull a man off his motorbike, snatching his crash helmet before starting to ride away – so Elena quickly edged her taxi forward to try and cut him off at the corner of the square. Their eyes met, the freak sneered and then spat at her windscreen, making a gesture as if to cut her throat, then he rammed the bike's front wheel hard against her door, twice, before he squeezed through and away, which made Elena *really* angry ... and it also meant that by the time Benjamin had finally staggered back to her stationary taxi, she was yelling at him again –

'*Qué coño está pasando?* What the fuck is going on? What just happened? What did you take from the car?'

Benjamin climbed into the back seat and quickly checked that the painting was safe in the portfolio case, before looking to see if the maniac was still around. It was already stifling in the vehicle with the engine and air-conditioning off, and he was sweating after the fight with the thug.

'Where is he? Where did he go?' he said. 'We need to find him. Did you take a picture of him?'

'Did I take picture of him?' said Elena.

'Did you?'

'Why would I take a picture of him?'

'I need to find him.'

'*Why would I take a picture of him?*'

'I need to identify him –'

'He's gone,' she shouted. She forced her driver's door open, then jumped out to point at the huge dent. 'And have you seen what he's done?'

Benjamin got out of the vehicle to look at the damage.

'Okay, I'm sorry,' he started, 'but we'll sort it out –'

'*We?*'

'I can sort it out.'

'How?'

'I'll explain things … but where did he go?' he asked again. 'Did you see where he went?'

He watched as she waved her arms around, at the same time as shrugging in a way that only southern Europeans could pull off. It was rather theatrical, and he assumed it meant 'How the fuck should I know?' – but then she finally pointed to a side street that led off the square.

'He stole a motorbike,' she said. 'And he went that way …'

Benjamin looked towards where she was pointing. The square was dominated by a church and bell tower, but there was also a news kiosk, several cafés, a fountain and an old pharmacy, all set amid ornate lampposts. People were peering down from wrought-iron balconies, curious as to who was disturbing the tranquillity of their neighbourhood. Benjamin couldn't see anyone who looked as if he'd had his bike stolen, and he didn't want to hang around.

'Did you get the number plate?' he asked, getting back into her taxi.

'*Qué?*' she said, returning to the driver's seat.

'The number plate of the motorbike.'

She didn't reply. Instead, she was looking into the distance, across the other side of the square, where his hire car with the smashed window had been abandoned, and where there was now a police motorbike and a tow truck with its orange light flashing.

'Fuck,' said Benjamin, following her gaze.

'You should speak to that policeman –' she started.

'No.'

'You have to –'

'*No.*'

Benjamin noticed that for a moment she looked surprised, even shocked at his refusal to involve the police, but then she shrugged and half-nodded again, as if she had her own doubts about them. He could recall her saying earlier that the police were useless when he'd first told her that his car had been stolen.

'Well, it's a city council truck,' she was now saying, 'and they're going to tow your car away …'

Benjamin quickly considered his options. If he went over to reclaim the vehicle in the right way, what would he need? A passport? It was in his pocket. The car hire paperwork? It was all in the car, he was sure – but *shit*, he didn't even have the car key, and he doubted it was still in the car. It would be one thing dealing with the tow truck workers in their yellow visibility vests, but another matter explaining things to a Barcelona traffic cop. Things could get complicated, there would be too many questions, and he couldn't risk it until he'd delivered the painting elsewhere, so that it was safe, secure, secret and still confidential – which he could do right now.

The red-hooded bastard had looked berserk, possibly on drugs, Benjamin thought, but he'd seemed too out of it to have orchestrated the theft of the painting on his own. Who was he working with? Had someone sent him to steal it? Benjamin was determined to find out. He was the killer from the service

station, he was sure of it. He had to track him down …
but there was no way he wanted a traffic cop involved.

He devised a plan. Once he'd delivered the painting, he would call his own police contacts to file a
report about the body at the service station, while
keeping the painting and the Marquès out of the equa-
tion. As for his cell phone still in the car, he'd lock it via
the cloud and erase all his details. If and when they
found it, he would have reported the car stolen, as well
as everything he'd seen at the service station, so all
would be fine.

'Let's go,' he said. 'Quick.'

'What?'

'Let's go. Please.'

'Where?'

Benjamin was sifting through his backpack and had
started to scribble on a scrap of paper.

'Why did you ask if I'd taken a picture of that
man?' insisted Elena.

Benjamin didn't reply but continued scribbling.

'Answer me.'

'He's dangerous,' he said.

'So, you should tell that policeman –'

'No –'

'You have to –'

'Not yet –'

'You must tell the police –'

'*No.*'

There was a silence.

'I *am* the police,' he said, finally.

From the darkness of an alleyway just off the Plaça de la Concòrdia, Séverin watched the couple in the taxi as he sat astride the stolen motorbike.

His breathing was rapid, his eyes somewhat red and glazed, but he could clearly now recall that guy from the service station, the one he'd whacked, and whose car he'd snatched.

How had he followed him here? How had he found him? And that taxi driver bitch … who were they?

After grabbing the bike, then scaring its owner shit-less and away from the area, Séverin had doubled back to the plaza to keep an eye on them.

He was keeping out of sight while the traffic cop was still around. His victims over the years had been despatched in isolation, clinically and without witnesses. He'd never been suspected of anything, as far as he was aware. He couldn't risk being detained for a street fight or stolen vehicle, and then having his identity or DNA checked against unsolved murders across southern France.

Things weren't going right for him, and the PCP angel dust wasn't helping matters.

That couple in the taxi knew something, he was sure.

He'd have to eliminate them, but could they first lead him to where Jürgen was, with all the cash and the hostage? Séverin could then finish the job properly. He hated leaving things half done.

16

Officer Soler

Monday 4 June, 8.45am – Avinguda Diagonal, Barcelona.

Officer Soler made it to the offices of *La Vanguardia* by 8.45am. As the newspaper had received a call from possible kidnappers, she'd delegated the investigation into tollgate data to another agent and diverted her driver to the media group.

Soler had often visited *La Vanguardia*, as a close friend had once been a crime correspondent for the paper. She knew the ground floor security guards, too, because as part of Vizcaya's abduction and extortion squad, she'd spent time at the British Consulate on the thirteenth-floor of the same building, after a young child went missing on the Costa Brava during a family holiday.

She flashed her badge to the concierge before she was escorted up to the seventh-floor editorial offices by two Mossos agents, who'd come to meet her there. The paper's editor, Alfredo Rodríguez, greeted them all at the lift, together with Carles Roig, a reporter, and a woman who was introduced simply as Inma.

They were led to a conference room with a flat screen on one wall, looking out at the open-plan offices with staff huddled at computers, their screens showing pages of the newspaper online. Above the desks, TVs were displaying news and sports channels.

'We're working around the clock on the G20 summit,' said Rodríguez, as if to answer Soler, gazing out at all the activity. 'With the US delegation already here and other world leaders arriving today, it's chaos.' He paused, as an assistant came in with plastic bottles of water and cups. He then invited Soler to take a seat at the boardroom-style table, but she raised her hand to indicate that she'd prefer to stand. They therefore all remained standing.

Rodríguez was bald, with an intimidating frame that hinted at the physical power he once might have had, unless it had always been just flab. Soler had always noticed that he looked well-lunched, even before lunch, with his business belly betraying too many corporate freebies and institutional galas, and not enough journalism. She'd never really got on with him but had to pretend that she did. Newspaper editors could be nasty, spiteful individuals, at least while holding the power.

'What have you got for us?' she asked, jumping in

as soon as the assistant had left. 'I'm very busy, too, Señor Rodríguez.'

'We knew something had happened,' he replied. 'We have a freelance photographer in Nîmes. We don't cover bullfights, we never really did, even before the ban in Catalonia –'

'What have you got for us?' insisted Soler. She looked at her watch. 'We were told you received a call. What call? When?'

The editor nodded towards Inma. Soler studied her with a level gaze, taking in the frizzy, corkscrew mane of red hair, the tasselled suede ankle boots, large hoop earrings and the bracelets and bangles jangling around her wrists. Exactly the kind of neo-hippie that got Soler's goat.

'At 5.45am,' said Inma. 'There were around six of us here at the time, all working online, and the call came through to my extension.'

'What is your job?' asked Soler.

'Night newsdesk,' said Rodríguez. 'But she's not alone. They all field night calls. It skipped through to her extension, that's all.'

'What call?' said Soler. 'What was said? Is it recorded?'

Inma sighed and started to unfold her notes.

'Is it recorded?'

'No,' said Inma. 'Why would it be?'

Soler looked at Rodríguez, who shrugged back.

'I have my notes,' said Inma. 'I can tell you exactly what was said. It was recited slowly: *Tenemos el torero* ...

We have the bullfighter. We don't want money. We demand that Spain's central government bans all bull-fighting immediately. If any more bullfights in Spain take place today, we will cut off his ears during the G20. There will be mayhem in Barcelona. We demand world peace for animals, not just the human race.'

There was silence for twenty seconds ... a very long time. Soler had winced, noting the symbolism. They cut off bulls' ears in bullfighting.

'Do you want me to read that again?' asked Inma.

Soler could feel her cell phone vibrating in her pocket. She pulled it out to take a photo of Inma's notes but was then distracted by the messages popping up on her screen. She now feared the worst.

'The call lasted for less than half a minute, then he hung up,' said Inma. 'I believe it was a foreign voice. He spoke Spanish but the message seemed practised, as if he was reciting it or disguising his voice. It also sounded like it was pre-recorded. I mean, there was no chance to hold a conversation. As soon as the last word was spoken, the call ended. I couldn't ask anything. It seemed like a voice bot or something, which is why I was suspicious of it ... at least at first.'

'Did the caller's number show up?' asked Soler.

Inma shook her head.

'I need all the phone records,' said Soler. She didn't wait for any permission from Rodríguez. She muttered instructions to the agents who'd accompanied her to the meeting, and who quickly left the room.

'Then what?' said Soler, turning back to Inma. 'What did you do after the call?'

Inma glanced at her editor. He nodded.

'I conferred with my colleagues,' she said, 'but we didn't take it too seriously, I admit. I then passed it on to Carles here, to see if he wanted to follow it up.'

Carles Roig, who hadn't said anything up to that point, now took out his notebook and arched an eyebrow at Soler. His mouth seemed to be permanently on the brink of a sneer.

'So, what's happened?' he said. 'We've told you about the call. It was less than three hours ago. Have you found anything? The vehicle? Our Nîmes photographer says it was driven away very quickly.'

Soler's phone was vibrating again.

'Señor Rodríguez, I need to speak to you in private,' she said.

The editor waved at Carles and Inma, who both left the room.

'Alfredo –' she started.

'Look, Marta –'

'– we've collaborated very well in the past –'

'– I'm well aware –'

'– the hostage investigation five years ago –'

'– of course –'

'– the abduction from the cruise ship, remember?'

'Yes, Marta, and we kept our word,' said Rodríguez, starting to raise his voice. 'We kept specific details out of the paper because we didn't want to jeopardise the investigation –'

'So, we can count on you again. We'll need a delay on this story –'

'It's too late, Marta.'

Soler stared at him.

'What?' she said.

Rodríguez opened the door again to beckon Inma and Carles back in. They stood in the doorway. Behind them, Soler could see even more activity than before. Phones were ringing non-stop, and staff were adjusting the TVs above their desks.

'We're not the only news organisation to have received the call,' said Rodríguez. '*The Guardian*, the BBC and *The Washington Post* got the same call, but in English. Some have already Tweeted it as breaking news. The agencies have picked it up, it's on the newswire, it's going viral, it's everywhere … and it's being updated on our digital edition right now.'

Soler looked at the screen on her phone. She went cold. She couldn't imagine how Vizcaya would react.

'Remember the day of the bullfight prohibition vote in Catalonia?' said Rodríguez, as he started fiddling with the remote control to turn on the flat screen in the meeting room. 'Every single news organisation in the world latched on to the story. This is going to be even bigger, especially with the G20 on here.'

At that moment the screen came to life on the wall and after a couple of clicks, Rodríguez got through to CNN's 24-hour news channel. Soler, now ashen faced, couldn't quite handle what she then saw.

'*We have breaking news coming in from the city of*

Barcelona, where the G20 and UN Climate Change Conference will be held this week, and where the President will arrive on Tuesday,' a sincere-looking anchor-man was saying on screen. *'A top Spanish bullfighter has been kidnapped by animal rights extremists and there are unconfirmed reports of at least one fatality. We'll give you more on this just as soon as we have it.'*

'They didn't have his name, or at least they didn't have it confirmed,' said Rodríguez. 'They had the same call we received – simply, "we have the bull-fighter" – but no name.'

He then flicked to other news channels showing similar breaking news, and finally to aerial photos of the service station alongside the AP-7 motorway, and an abandoned Chevrolet van.

'But they *do* have his name now,' he said finally. 'And can you confirm that his chauffeur has been murdered, Marta?'

Monday 4 June, 9.20am – Montpellier, France.

Inspector Vizcaya was apoplectic. His unmarked Mossos car was just pulling up outside the Police Judiciaire in Montpellier, southern France, when Soler called. At first, he screamed at her to not even speak. He'd already heard it, and, worse, he'd heard it on French radio.

Animal rights extremists?

115

After he'd calmed down enough to allow Soler to explain more, she confirmed that the kidnappers had not only threatened mayhem in Barcelona during the G20 if Spain continued bullfighting, but to also cut off their victim's ears – something that the French media had already broadcast as 'sensational breaking news'.

With no monetary ransom demand, it was going to make Vizcaya's job even more complicated. Kidnappers usually became inept when picking up ransom money, and it was at that point most got caught. It was also a key factor in the negotiation process, being able to talk money, to try and trace the gang's background, their calls, to wear them down, persuade them to give up, to bargain with them and understand their psyches.

Rafael Pérez was Spain's most famous bullfighter, and although Vizcaya had since learned that he also had two ex-wives who'd both drained him of a fortune – he'd assumed the killers would still demand a cash pay-off. But now that money wasn't the ransom currency, what was? Animal rights? They were murderers themselves, he noted.

As for the calls to the media, they were going for maximum international exposure on the eve of the G20. If they'd guessed the Spanish authorities might have tried to suppress the story for a few days, they'd guessed right. They'd gone global with their calls, and then social media had taken over from there.

'Set up an incident room in Barcelona right now,' Vizcaya shouted down the phone to Soler. 'Get Trias and the homicide squad there. I want the reports from

Girona airport. Do you have the tollgate data? I want details of every single animal rights activist in Spain and France –'

'*Bonjour* –'

'*Bonjour* –' said Vizcaya, holding up his fingerless left hand towards Gilles Clémenceau, in apology. 'Marta, can you hear me?'

'Yes.'

'Their news photographer, therefore ... did he get anything?'

'He got what everyone else got, I think,' said Soler. 'Shots of Rafael Pérez jumping into the Chevrolet, but no clear shots of the driver.'

'How did Pérez leave the Nîmes bullring?' asked Vizcaya.

'On the shoulders of a fan,' said Clémenceau, greeting Vizcaya with a pat on the back.

'On what?'

'On the shoulders of an *aficionado*.'

'Jesus Christ,' said Vizcaya, pulling at his walrus moustache. He wasn't a bullfighting man. He'd never seen one, except on TV. He wasn't necessarily for or against it. It was just that he didn't really understand it, so he didn't have any feelings about it one way or another.

But he was about to have a crash course.

17

Benjamin and Elena

Monday 4 June, 8.30am − Les Corts district, Barcelona.

'*Policía?* What do you mean you *are* the police?' said Elena.

Benjamin stared at her from the back of the stationary taxi.

'*Policía?*' she repeated. 'You?'

He gave a slight nod of the head, still thumping badly.

'Sort of,' he said.

Just moments before, Elena had been on the point of ordering him to get the hell out of the taxi and report the thug and stolen car to the policeman on the other side of the square − although she had no intention of reporting that her taxi door had been rammed by the same thug. The police had never helped her in the past, so why would they now? Two years ago,

118

they'd done nothing about a sick pervert who'd assaulted her, and she knew why; they'd clocked he was a serving officer, 'one of their own'. She'd felt violated, ignored, judged, even *blamed*, and it had haunted her. She didn't trust the Spanish police and had vowed to one day expose the bastard who believed he was untouchable. Could she trust her passenger? At that precise moment she felt she could, but whether she should, was another matter.

'If you're a *policía*, show me your card,' she said.

Benjamin had started to scribble on a scrap of paper from his backpack again. He realised that for now, he'd missed the opportunity to pursue the thug. He'd wanted to pin him down, and he still intended to, but at least he'd retrieved the aristocrat's painting.

'Show me your *policía* card,' Elena insisted.

He stopped what he was doing and looked up.

'I don't have one.'

'Are you lying about being a *policía?*'

'No, but it's not like that. I don't have police ID.'

'Are you a *policía* or not?'

'I investigate things, often for the police, yes, but it's mostly art.'

'Art?'

'Yes, art. But it's not glamorous –'

'*Qué quieres decir?*'

'I mean, I don't go around with a Sherlock Holmes pipe and magnifying glass, if that's what you're think-ing.' He smiled, trying to break the tension, but the shape of her mouth showed that he'd clearly failed.

'*Sherlock pipe?* What the hell are you talking about?'

He started scribbling again.

'How can I trust you?' she said, raising her voice.

'Trust me? Of course, you can trust me –'

'You haven't even paid,' snapped Elena. We agreed a hundred and fifty euros for me to bring you to the centre of Barcelona and now the taxi door is damaged, and I don't –'

'Wait, stop,' said Benjamin, digging into his jacket pocket for his wallet. 'I'll fix your taxi and I can pay you more. Here, take all this for now.'

Elena glared at him as he tried to thrust a wad of notes into her hand.

'What are you doing?' she said.

'Here, take it.'

'*No*, you can't buy me.' She pushed the notes back at him.

'I'm not trying to buy you. I'm trying to settle the taxi fare up to now, and to show that you can trust me.'

'Okay,' she said finally, 'but it's too much.'

She took some notes, leaving the rest in his hand. Benjamin waited, then showed her a scrap of paper. She glanced at what he'd scribbled.

'MNAC?' she said.

'Yes. It's where I need to go.'

'Are you crazy?'

'No.'

'You are crazy.'

'I'm not crazy. It's the Museu Nacional d'Art de Catalunya.'

'I know what it is —'

'It's a museum —'

'*I know what it is.*'

'— and I need to go there.'

'It's Monday,' said Elena. 'It's closed.'

'Not the office,' he said. 'I have a contact at the office, in the lab. In the department of restoration and preventive conservation, to be exact.'

'If you're police, why aren't you chasing that man?'

'I will, once I've been to MNAC,' he said. 'After that, we'll also fix the taxi.' A pause. 'I promise.'

Elena took a deep breath. She'd calmed down, but she caught his stare. 'What is it? What are you staring at?' she said.

'Nothing.'

She started searching for the best route to the museum on the Sat-Nav. 'And your hotel?' she said, seeing it was the last address she'd keyed in.

'Is it near?'

'Show me the details again.'

Benjamin dug back into his pocket for the name and address, and then they set off.

Keeping a prudent distance, Séverin, the savage thug, followed on the stolen motorbike.

18

Inspector Vizcaya and Gilles Clémenceau

Monday 4 June, 9.30am – Nîmes, France.

Gilles Clémenceau, the suave police chief for the French city of Montpellier and nearby Nîmes, was far more knowledgeable about bullfighting than Inspector Vizcaya would ever want to be, almost to the point of being an *aficionado* himself.

They were now travelling around Nîmes in an unmarked police car, with Clémenceau giving the Spanish detective a quick tour of the area surrounding the amphitheatre where the top bullfighter Rafael 'Rafa' Pérez was last seen at 9.15pm last night, after emerging from the bullring in triumph – or '*triomphalement*', as Clémenceau described it.

In contrast to Vizcaya, the French officer seemed quite relaxed. He was teak-tanned and in uniform, but he wore it with such panache that it looked like a designer suit, topped with trendy sunglasses that he pushed up over his wavy, catalogue-model hair. The shabbily attired Vizcaya opened his passenger side window to take the edge off a strong whiff of cologne.

Clémenceau was explaining that most bullfights see three matadors take on two bulls each, but tickets for yesterday had sold out for the rare opportunity to see Rafa face all six bulls in the closing event of the Nîmes festival. For that feat alone, he said, the kidnappers would have known that the *'maestro'* was going to be carried out shoulder-high through the amphitheatre's main gate, the *'puerta grande'*, whether he'd been awarded any trophy ears from the six bulls or not.

With international news buzzing with reports of the kidnapped matador and the brutal murder of his chauffeur, Francisco 'Paco' Chillado, and with the tabloids already running wild on social media about the threat to cut off the bullfighter's ears, Vizcaya and Clémenceau knew they had to work together. Their respective bosses would soon be pestering them about the progress of the investigation on the eve of the G20 in Barcelona, and neither wanted to look incompetent.

Clémenceau told Vizcaya that an elite hostage unit in Paris had also offered to help, that all available images and eyewitness accounts in Nîmes were already being analysed, as well as CCTV in and around the amphitheatre, the surrounding bars and streets, and out on the A9 motorway from Nîmes towards the Spanish border.

They agreed that the priority was to interview the

bullfighter's assistants, all still at their hotel in Nîmes. Vizcaya wanted to understand how they travelled, while Clémenceau's agents were already questioning the hotel staff and other guests for details of who had checked in and when.

The majestic Hôtel Imperator was one of the *grande dame* retreats of Nîmes; an old haunt of Ernest Hemingway, Ava Gardner and Picasso in its heyday. By the time Vizcaya and Clémenceau arrived, the bull-fighter's assistants were gathered in the bar area. While they were being interviewed, their rooms were also being searched by forensic officers, swabbing for DNA.

As Vizcaya made his way through the foyer towards the bar, he took in the glass cabinets with bull-fight artefacts. The bar had framed photos of Hemingway at various bullfights, and there was even a bullfighter's costume with the fading, yet clearly blood-stained leggings on display in a glass case. Vizcaya had always assumed bullfighting was just a Spanish tradition, yet it was also alive and kicking here in Nîmes.

Before interviewing the entourage, Vizcaya and Clémenceau were briefed by French officers on the schedule of the bullfighter and his chauffeur prior to Nîmes, and on the day of the bullfight itself.

Vizcaya learnt that Rafa had done three bullfights in as many days, with his season in Spain so far including Valencia, Seville and Madrid, as well as other cities and towns. After Nîmes, he'd been scheduled to appear in Valencia again tonight, en route back to Seville for yet another bullfight on Tuesday. Immediately after last night's appearance, his driver had planned to kill the seven-hundred-kilometre journey to Valencia in just over six hours, with a short break for a late meal at a transport café.

Vizcaya quickly realised that those among the bull-fighting fraternity were creatures of habit, easy to stalk, easy to target, and he was surprised that a matador hadn't been a kidnap victim until now. They didn't fly from bullfight to bullfight in Spain or France, he gathered, because flights were costly and unpractical, and a vehicle would still be required to take the men and all their equipment from airport to bullring. They travelled at night because nights were cooler, roads were empty, and it saved money on hotels if everyone could grab part of their required sleep in a minibus.

So, bullfighters didn't use hotels the way others did. They checked in early in the morning, checked out late at night, yet paid for only one night's accommodation. Just prima donna animal-killers trying to live like rock stars, mulled Vizcaya ... but at least they left the hotel furniture intact and paid for the mini-bar.

The luxury Chevrolet abandoned at the service station near Girona airport was ideal for the thousands of kilometres a top matador had to travel to each bull-ring across Spain and the South of France. The two rows of seats in the back flipped down to create a flat surface, where Rafa could sleep comfortably. Like other star matadors, he would travel alone with his driver while his assistants used a ten-seater Mercedes minibus that followed the Chevrolet across the country with all their gear.

Vizcaya learnt that Paco Chillado had driven the famous bullfighter across Spain and beyond for twenty years. Yesterday, he drove for the last time.

Rafa's team was comprised of eight individuals, excluding his chauffeur. There were five men who'd enter the bullring with him, on foot or horseback. Then there was Nico, who looked after all the gear and drove the minibus – currently being inspected by agents in the hotel's parking lot – as well as Felipe, Rafa's manservant, and Lorenzo, his manager, with whom Vizcaya now spoke.

Lorenzo was in his late fifties, dressed like an executive in a dark suit, stripey shirt and pink tie, with his hair gelled into a thick blob at the nape of his neck. A red handkerchief was artfully folded in the breast pocket of his jacket.

'Tell me about yesterday,' Vizcaya said. 'What time did you all get here? Who visited you?'

'Rafa arrived here at four in the morning, the rest of us an hour later,' said Lorenzo. 'We'd had a bullfight near San Sebastian on Saturday, then Rafa and Paco set off afterwards, just as they were supposed to do last night for Valencia. Nobody visited us, except a bull breeder and a photographer. We slept most of the morning, had lunch here, then Rafa spent the afternoon resting, stretching, and preparing physically, mentally and spiritually for the *corrida*, before getting dressed with Felipe's help.'

'Was he carried out of the bullring near San Sebastian, too?'

Lorenzo nodded. 'Except in Madrid, it's a rare bullfight if Rafa fails to cut at least two ears from two bulls,' he said.

'You always allow strangers to carry him out to his vehicle?' asked Vizcaya.

'They're not really strangers to us,' said Felipe, a thickset man in his late twenties. 'You get to recognise them. That's the success we seek, getting him carried out through the main gate. We have to allow the fans to get close for that part.'

'So, do you think you can help identify the regular fans in the photos and videos that the French police are analysing?' Vizcaya asked.

'I can try.'

Vizcaya conferred with Clémenceau, who'd already instructed his officers to set up a laptop to show the many images they'd collated. Waiting for them to do so, Vizcaya asked about the chauffeur's routine.

According to Lorenzo, Paco had been a gentle, loyal, chubby character, but he never watched a bullfight himself. After delivering Rafa from hotel to bullring at around 6pm, Paco would then park the Chevrolet somewhere in the shade, away from the crowds, to enjoy a cigar and a drink in a bar nearby. He'd then snooze in the vehicle, waking up in time to steer it back to collect Rafa at around 9pm. While doing so, he'd listen for the cheers from the crowd, or check his phone for a message from the entourage inside to know which gate he would exit from – which was nearly always the main gate on the shoulders of a fan.

Again, Vizcaya conferred with Clémenceau, who told him that he had agents doing the rounds, interviewing bar and bistro owners near the amphitheatre, trying to find out where the chauffeur had been.

'We knew something was wrong when the Chevrolet accelerated away,' said Lorenzo. 'Rafa knew he'd see me in Valencia, so I didn't need to follow them out of the arena. There was cash to collect and papers to sign. So, I went with the others to the minibus within the compound.'

'Within the compound?'

'Nico always parks within the bullring compound to unload and load up all the gear, and hand out photocards to the fans.'

'Why did you not all set off for Valencia, too, in the minibus?' asked Vizcaya.

'We never set off immediately. Only Rafa. He would have tugged off his costume and changed into a clean tracksuit –'

Vizcaya glanced at the faded, bloodstained costume in the glass case again. It was a bullfighter's 'suit of lights', so-called because the sun would reflect off the dazzling gold filigree, tassels, baubles and beads. He knew a tracksuit had been found in the

Chevrolet, as well as the bullfighter's hat. So, wherever Rafa was, he was still in his 'suit of lights'.

'We always come back to the hotel first, to shower, change and eat – and Nico needs to reload our minibus,' continued Lorenzo. 'But we couldn't make contact with Rafa. I called the police in Spain last night, and we spoke with the gendarmes here. We're sure it wasn't Paco in the driving seat of the Chevrolet, and one of our men says he saw someone in the back wearing a red hoodie …'

Five minutes later and they were all reviewing a video on the computer set up by one of Clémenceau's officers. For Vizcaya, the grisly symbolism of the kidnappers' threat to cut off their victim's ears became loud and clear. He didn't want to see it, but he knew he had to, as it immediately preceded the moment when Rafa was carried out of the amphitheatre.

The video first showed the crowd cheering Rafa as he pirouetted with the last bull of the evening, at one point dropping to his knees and passing the animal with a one-handed flip of the cape over his shoulder. He seemed to twirl around the bull every which way, spinning as it hurtled by, passing it while staring up at the crowds, and then standing in front of it with his cape folded, teasing it with the sword.

Before the killing, he lined himself up in profile to the bull, then almost leapt over its horns, pitching the sword into its body, sinking the blade deep between the animal's shoulders – and leaving it there. The bull stood still, then staggered backwards, with its mouth wide open and tongue hanging out. As the bull swayed, Rafa also swayed, with his arms outstretched and his pelvis pushed forward. The animal's head then slumped onto the sand of the arena, followed by the weight of its carcass. On screen, Rafa spun around, acknowledging the cheering crowd.

Vizcaya felt repulsed.

As the video continued, it showed the crowd waving white handkerchiefs. Lorenzo explained to Vizcaya that the president of the bullfight was signalling for Rafa to be awarded one of the bull's ears, but as the cheering continued, he was awarded both.

One of the warders knelt over the bull's carcass and cut off both ears, chopping at the skin and gristle to detach them from the skull. Rafa then held up the ears like trophies and started to walk around the ring, occasionally bowing in gratitude at the applause. Finally, he threw the severed ears into the crowd.

When the bullfight ended, he was gathered up on the shoulders of two fans who came onto the sand to carry him out through the main gate of the amphitheatre, directly out towards his vehicle.

By now, Clémenceau had paused the video a few times for Lorenzo and Felipe to focus on the men carrying Rafa out of the arena, but who they identified as simply regular fans.

The images continued outside the bullring where there was also a small yet vociferous crowd of anti-bullfight protesters. The police had kept them behind a barrier and were making sure that Rafa's Chevrolet could pull up directly outside the main gate. On-lookers and fans were pushing up alongside it, taking photos. There was no clear shot of the driver, other than a dark baseball cap pulled over his eyes – but Lorenzo and Felipe insisted that it wasn't the chauffeur Paco.

Then the images showed the crowd spilling out of the amphitheatre. There were stewards and police among all the spectators pacing alongside Rafa, still being carried out shoulder-high by the same men, waving his matador's hat to the crowd, with his gold and green 'suit of lights', white shirt and tie all stained with bull's blood. As he was lowered to the ground, his entourage started pushing away the fans.

Then it happened: there was a crash of glass as a bottle suddenly landed near Rafa's feet. He seemed desperate to get away, pushing ahead to his vehicle where the side door had been swung open, then jumping inside as the police held back the crowd, giving the Chevrolet the space it needed to speed away.

In the hotel bar, Rafa's assistants were shouting and pointing at the screen, where a red-hooded man could be seen in the back seat of the Chevrolet, just when the side door had swung open and closed. As the video ended, a French officer assured Clémenceau and Vizcaya that further analysis was being done on other images at the Nîmes police station.

. . .

Moments later, still unable to get the image of Rafa in a bloodstained costume out of his mind, Vizcaya finally turned his attention back to Felipe, the bullfighter's personal assistant.

'Last night,' Vizcaya asked, 'what was he wearing – precisely? What clothing? What fabrics? Anything at all that could help our investigation?'

Even though Vizcaya had already seen images of Rafa in his costume, there was a logic and purpose to his questions. For any missing person, there was a checklist that his squad stuck to. They had to register details about birthmarks, scars, physical anomalies, medications taken or needed to be taken, and a detailed description of the clothing believed to be worn at the time of disappearance or abduction. So, what exactly had Rafa been wearing?

Felipe started to describe the traditional socks, salmon-coloured with an arrow design over each calf, then how he'd helped Rafa put on his full costume, holding open the knee-length breeches so he could carefully step into one leg at a time, then a white tuxedo shirt, green tie, and the heavy waist-length jacket with wide epaulets and holes in the armpits for greater mobility …

'Marvellous, Felipe, thanks very much for all that,' Vizcaya said finally, flipping shut his notebook.

He wasn't sure at what point his concentration had wandered during the detailed description, but by the end, he'd become transfixed on the image of the bloodstained costume in the glass cabinet.

19

Elena, Benjamin and Séverin

Monday 4 June, 8.50am – El Raval neighbourhood, Barcelona.

Elena found Benjamin's 'Hotel Splendido' in the *barrio* of Raval. It was tucked away behind a row of dilapidated buildings. But it wasn't a hotel, it was a hostel, or maybe even a brothel, making her doubt the credibility of her passenger yet again.

Benjamin also looked surprised at the state of the building, saying that he wouldn't be staying there and that they needed to head straight to MNAC. But with Elena stopping the taxi and insisting, he agreed to dash in to see if there was a reservation for him.

After he left the taxi, she lowered her window to take in some of the balmy morning air, switching off the engine and air conditioning. She propped her elbow halfway out of the open window, then twisted herself around to look across through the passenger side, watching him head towards the run-down building in the deserted street.

Slowly, eerily, she sensed she wasn't the only one watching.

Someone else was breathing next to her.

She turned and screamed – it was *him* – the red-hooded freak sitting on the stolen motorbike next to her driver's door, at first just leering at her, before suddenly reaching into the vehicle to stroke her hair.

'Hey,' he said. 'You and me, huh?' He was frothing a little at the mouth.

She pulled away, striking his arm with her own, and struggled to turn on the ignition to close the window.

'No, no … don't be a bad girl,' he said, licking his lips. 'I'm giving you a chance.'

He came at her again, more aggressively, grabbing her hair instead of stroking it, but she quickly managed to free herself and shove his arm away, finally closing the window in the process.

He signalled as if to cut her throat, just as before, and then she heard him cursing her through the glass, with the words: 'You gypsy bitch.'

It incensed her. She forced open her already damaged door to push it hard against him, which nearly made him lose his balance.

'*You bastard,*' she cried.

He sneered, then revved the bike's engine and rode away, practically doing a wheelie as he accelerated down the street before turning back and stopping in front of her taxi again, still revving his engine, and still making a sign as if to cut her throat.

Which is when Benjamin reappeared from the building across the road.

He could see a guy in a red sweatshirt sitting astride a motorbike next to Elena's taxi, but he didn't immediately realise it was the thug from earlier, not until he accelerated and made a beeline directly towards him.

He jumped out of the way, only just, as the thug screeched the bike to a halt outside the hostel. Then the bike turned, swerved, and came at him once more – with Benjamin leaping to one side again as the maniac spun the wheels around for another attack.

Benjamin ran at him, aiming to barge sideways into the bike and shove him to the ground, but the thug took off at full throttle and shot down an alleyway alongside the hostel. Benjamin squinted in vain to catch the bike's number plate. He wanted to chase him, to grab him, but at that precise moment in time his priority was the painting in Elena's taxi. Was the psycho targeting it after all? Benjamin needed to get it *and* them safely out of the area. As the bike disappeared from sight, he jumped back into her vehicle.

'Let's go,' he said.

'*Qué coño,*' Elena was yelling in Spanish. 'What the fuck. Don't you want to go after him? Let's go after him.'

'*No, let's go.*'

135

'What the fuck, what a maniac,' Elena was still shouting, but she started driving slowly down the street all the same, shaking her head.

Looking back in the distance through her rear-view mirror, she caught sight of the thug again. He was now getting off the bike and heading into the run-down hostel himself. She saw that Benjamin was busy checking his belongings in the back of the taxi. Something was up. Something wasn't right.

'Did you have a reservation there?' she said.

He didn't reply.

'I'm asking a question. Did they have a room for you?' she insisted.

'It was full,' he said.

Something wasn't right.

Séverin watched them leave, then got off the motorbike and lurched towards the hostel.

Thanks to the angel dust, he felt detached, distant and estranged from his surroundings once he was inside. A pierced slob was sprawled out on an old armchair, behind a desk. Was Séverin having auditory hallucinations, or did he hear the prick say something about it being full – '*fucking full*' – '*and I just told the last guy*' –? That wasn't very polite … and now images were getting distorted, too.

'Where's Jürgen?' said Séverin.

'Who?'

'Where's Jürgen, where's my money, and where's the sinner?'

'Sinner?'

Séverin grabbed the scumbag by the hair, slamming his face against the desk, and then pulled out the pruning shears from his leather tool belt.

'Tell me where the sinner is, or I'll have one of your ears instead.'

'I don't know what you're talking about —'

Séverin wrenched the punk's head back up, placed the cutters at the very top of his left ear, and then started to snip downwards, as blood squirted up and splattered onto his sleeve. The slob twisted and squirmed, and the pruning shears jolted away. Séverin dug in again, cutting down to the middle of the ear now, half-severing it away from its stem of tissue and gristle, then snatching at it with his other hand, trying to yank the bloody wet, slippery chunk of flesh loose from his head. It wouldn't come free, not at first, so he tugged harder, twisting it left and then right in order to rip it off, causing more jets of blood to spurt over his sleeve, until finally he got the fleshy lump safely into his thick fist, and then into the pocket of his red hoodie, which was just what he needed.

The jerk fled from the building, screaming, with blood pouring from the side of his head. The hostel fell silent.

Séverin decided to stay. It was Jürgen's Dutch activist group who'd contracted him, and who owed him money – and he still had a job to finish.

Surely, they hadn't just hired him for his knowledge of Nîmes and to erase the chauffeur? They'd shown him the van they had access to, how it would work, and who they supplied. There was another Dutch hippie – Herman, Henry, Hendrik or someone. They'd done some PCP together, and it was him driving the van that had sped away earlier, leaving Séverin stranded. The bastards had conned him.

Where did they both work? Where was it? Who did they drive for? Was this hostel one of their hang-outs? He tried to focus. If Jürgen returned, he'd be ready.

That angel dust was strong. He was seeing things again. People were plotting to kill him, he was sure. In fact, it was the only thing he was sure about.

20

Inspector Vizcaya

Monday 4 June, 10.15am – Nîmes to Barcelona.

In a helicopter on his way back from Nîmes to Barcelona, Inspector Vizcaya perused the messages and reports he'd received. As expected, Isabel Bosch, Catalan home affairs minister, had requested an urgent meeting with him, and was already preparing a press briefing. In the message, she underlined the urgency to resolve things before 6.30pm that evening, the time of the next bullfights across Spain.

CCTV images from the service station were being matched with reports from the staff witness who'd said a man had been banging on the window of the shop, asking for directions to walk to the airport. The only news from Girona airport so far, however, was that bloodstained paper towels had been found in one of the men's toilets.

More significantly, there was a report that the dead chauffeur's credit card had been used for payments at tollgates from Nîmes to the Girona service station, and for two further payments at tollgates between Girona and Barcelona, presumably from a transfer or getaway vehicle.

Vizcaya slapped his thigh. *Of course.* You didn't need to key in a pin number at the tollgates; you simply tapped a card to pay or slotted it into a machine and the barriers opened. It was the kidnappers' first mistake. If they could match the time of the transactions with images from cameras monitoring early-morning traffic approaching the city centre, it would be a start. With luck, they should be able to narrow the time, image and location down to just a handful of vehicles.

Part Two - Time

21

Elena, Benjamin and Pedro Pardina

Monday 4 June, 9.30am – Museu Nacional d'Art de Catalunya, Barcelona.

Elena had driven in silence, eyeing Benjamin warily in her rear-view mirror as she weaved the taxi up towards Montjuïc, finally parking in the visitors' car park opposite the office entrance of MNAC. Benjamin then jumped out, clasping the portfolio case. Elena also got out and started to check her phone for messages.

She trusted her instincts and she wanted to trust her passenger, too, but she couldn't stop thinking about his fight with the thug who'd supposedly stolen his hire car, and who'd then grabbed a motorbike to ram her taxi door, first threatening to cut her throat before trying to grope her while calling her a gypsy bitch. She'd then seen him entering the hostel where Benjamin had first claimed to have a room himself.

She was now convinced it was dried blood on Benjamin's collar, in his hair, and even on the headrest in the back of the taxi. Who was he? He'd insisted that he didn't need to go to the police. He said he was some sort of *policía* himself, but that he investigated art. Art?

Getting out of the taxi, Benjamin noticed Elena checking her phone, and she appeared to quickly hide it from view when she caught his eye. She then put on her sunglasses while standing alongside her vehicle, but he could sense her distrust.

He was also thinking about the thug, cursing himself for not having pinned him down at the first opportunity. Was he just a carjacker or had he really been after the painting? Benjamin was still unsure, especially after being threatened by him for a second time outside the hostel. Images of the body at the service station flashed through his mind. He knew he had to report it, but he had to safeguard the painting first, and that could happen right now.

He didn't have a hotel, and he didn't want to lose his only means of transport. Whatever room had been booked for him at that Splendido pit, it no longer existed. As he hadn't arrived to claim it last night, they'd given his bed, or his bunk, or maybe his stained mattress, to someone else. If he was honest with himself, which wasn't always, he was also smitten by his driver, even though she'd spent most of the time yelling at him. Surprising himself, he asked her if she'd like to also come into the museum.

Her eyes were unreadable behind her shades, but he could see a flicker of surprise or hesitation in her mouth and jaw. She finally shook her head. He told her that it wouldn't take long, and it didn't.

It had been a few years since he'd visited the museum. He headed into reception, through a metal detector, placed the portfolio case through a scanner, and then asked the female guard for Pedro Pardina, from the department of restoration and conservation.

'Is he expecting you?' she asked.

'No.'

'Your name, please?'

'Is that necessary?'

'It would help.'

'Sorry, yes. Of course. It's Benjamin …'

'Sir?'

'Benjamin. He'll know.'

'Do you have any identification?'

'No.'

The guard gave him an odd look but picked up the phone. Five minutes later, a very cheerful Pedro Pardina appeared, wearing a white lab coat, with his neat, black hair greying at the temples.

'Benjamin, it's been a long time,' he said, in perfect English, slapping his visitor on the back. 'How are you?' Then: 'Oh, *God*, you look like shit.'

'I'm not here,' muttered Benjamin, taking Pedro to one side. He tried patting his hair into place. He wasn't aware he looked so bad.

'I understand,' said Pedro.

'But I have something,' said Benjamin, tapping the portfolio case.

'Let's take a look. Come. Follow me.'

They'd first met six years ago, at a conference in Oxford. Pedro, who specialised in MNAC's Renaissance and Baroque collections, had called upon Benjamin to ascertain whether works that had been lost in transit for forty-eight hours while on loan to an exhibition at the Tate, were still the originals. Benjamin had also advised MNAC on its potential acquisition of a Venetian painting purportedly by Giorgione. He then managed to save the museum considerable expense and embarrassment once he'd attributed the work to someone else, and its ownership to a small-time crook.

They didn't need to say much to one another; there was a mutual respect and understanding. While Pedro guided Benjamin up to his office adjoined to a lab, not once did he question his visitor's sudden presence in Barcelona, nor why he wanted it to be kept secret. As soon as Benjamin had extracted his Dalíesque painting from its case, Pedro knew what he'd come for.

Even art connoisseurs like Benjamin, those with the ability to make reasoned assessments about artistic authorship, to distinguish between originals and copies, or to identify forgeries, still needed to get under the physical surface of a canvas. Where else would an art detective start?

'IRR?' said Pedro.

Benjamin nodded. He knew all there was to know about infrared reflectography, so much so that he could have set up the apparatus on his own if he'd been allowed. He also knew Pedro's department had a camera capable of high-resolution, high-speed infrared imaging. It could quickly reveal layers of the painting not visible to the naked eye – if Pedro hadn't said it was being used by another department.

Pedro said he was busy, too, and that staff had been late coming in after the weekend. So, he told Benjamin to leave the painting and give him an hour or two, asking if there was a specific section of it that he wanted to examine, or if it was the whole surface area.

Benjamin was well aware there were several ways to detect whether there was something below the paint, but it would depend on how it was sketched or painted, if at all. If Dalí had drawn anything with pencil, charcoal or carbon, then it should be visible using IRR, which was ideal for studying underdrawing, cracks, *pentimenti*, hidden signatures, or the initial laying out of a composition. But if anything under the surface was created with paint, then it wouldn't show up. He told Pedro that five or six images to cover the entire surface would suffice, and they shook hands.

'Benjamin,' said Pedro, despatching him with a series of back pats before he left. 'Go and wash somewhere. *Por favor.* I'll see you in a few hours.'

22

Isabel Bosch

Monday 4 June, 10.30am – Plaça Sant Jaume, Barcelona.

A press briefing had begun at the Catalan government's headquarters in the Plaça Sant Jaume. Isabel Bosch strutted in her stilettos towards the podium in a room packed with Spanish and international media.

'*Bon dia*,' she said, tapping the microphone. 'Good morning. *Buenos días*. I will be brief. We have a lot to do with the start of this historic week, with our international friends arriving in Barcelona for the G20 and the UN Climate Change Conference. We welcome you all and hope you enjoy your stay in our beautiful, and may I stress, *safe* city.'

She paused before reading out a statement.

'We confirm that the Andalusian *torero*, Rafael Pérez, was abducted at just after 9.30pm last night, in

Nîmes, France. His vehicle was found abandoned close to Girona airport. His driver, Paco Chillado, was officially pronounced dead at 7.30am this morning at the Hospital Universitari in Girona, and our thoughts and prayers go out to his family and numerous friends. A murder investigation is underway.'

She let this sink in before continuing.

'As many of you already know, several national and international news organisations received calls in the early hours of this morning from a group claiming responsibility. They demand that Spain stop all bull-fights scheduled this week with immediate effect …' She paused, before adding, '… and indeed, stop bull-fighting altogether.'

There was muttering among the press.

'If the demands are not met,' continued Bosch, 'the group has threatened to maim the hostage and provoke mayhem in Barcelona during the week.'

Another pause.

'Rest assured that we will be hosting the G20 and climate change conference in safety. The citizens of Barcelona, of Catalonia, and the people of Spain, will never be held to ransom. These criminals, these murderers, seek publicity when the world's eyes are on this great city. They will not win. The Mossos d'Esquadra in Catalonia are working closely with the Spanish National Police, the Guardia Civil, and liaising with police in France. As soon as we have further updates, we will let you know. Thank you very much. I will take just one or two questions …'

Hands shot up. A CNN reporter got the first nod.

'When is the next bullfight scheduled in Spain, ma'am?' asked the reporter. 'Who is heading up the investigation? Do they have any leads?'

'There are bullfights scheduled in Andalusia at 6.30pm this evening,' said Bosch, instinctively checking her watch. 'Also in Valencia, in which I gather Rafael Pérez would have participated,' she added. 'Leading the investigation is Detective Inspector Vizcaya of the Mossos kidnap and extortion division, jointly with the homicide squad. I am not able to give further details at this stage.'

More hands went up. This time it was the turn of an Agence France-Presse journalist.

'As bullfighting has been banned in Catalonia since 2012, and also in the Canary Islands, do you now think that other regions of Spain will –'

'I won't make any comment on that,' cut in Bosch.

'But will the rest of Spain now consider stopping the bullfight? At least for the duration of the G20 week?' insisted the journalist.

There was an abrupt, stunned silence in the room among the Spanish press and officials.

'The Spanish state will never stop the bullfight,' said Bosch, before leaving the podium.

23

Santiago Quintana

Monday 4 June, 10am – El Raval neighbourhood, Barcelona.

Santiago Quintana from Chile, a part-time employee-cum-pimp at the hostel Splendido, had just been checked in to *urgències* at the Clínica Raval. He hadn't wanted to be checked in. He didn't have the right paperwork to be living or working in Spain. But he'd been unable to stem the flow of blood from his severed left ear, so he didn't really have much choice.

He'd staggered into a pharmacy first, clutching a towel to the side of his head. The pharmacist took it upon herself to call an ambulance. Santiago then had to give his name and his address, which was his place of work. Minutes later, he was being attended to by emergency staff.

24

Jürgen

Monday 4 June, 9.45am – El Poblenou neighbourhood, Barcelona.

Jürgen felt more than nervous as he slowly made his way back from Sants railway station, across the city, towards the depot in the neighbourhood of Poblenou. The area was one of the coolest in the city, popular with hipsters and start-ups, full of old warehouses that had been converted into co-working spaces and creative offices, with a few craft beer breweries, brunch hangouts and vintage markets.

But Jürgen was dreading going back there …

Murdering the bullfighter's driver had never been part of the plan. The threat of cutting off the bullfighter's ears was also supposed to be just that: a *threat*. As far as Jürgen was concerned, they'd already achieved their objective – they'd brought world media attention to the fact that barbaric bullfighting still existed in Spain and the South of France, as well as South America, and it had to be stopped, once and for all.

But things had gone seriously wrong because Séverin was a depraved, fucking psychopath, and he feared Hendrik was no better. He was convinced they were both taking weird, violence-inducing drugs.

The Dutch hippie Jürgen knew enough about most drugs, but he'd never trusted Séverin. Over the past two months, ever since the group had known that Rafael Pérez would headline the closing bullfight of the Nîmes festival, Jürgen had visited the French city twice to meet and plan things with the Frenchman – but on each visit he'd witnessed him turn increasingly agitated and then enraged.

Yesterday, on his third and final visit, monitoring the entrance of the bullfighter's hotel, taking it in turns to check the chauffeur would do what was expected of him right up until 6.45pm and beyond, the French thug seemed schizophrenic. Jürgen hadn't trusted him at all, but he had no choice. Séverin knew the streets of Nîmes, and he'd been instructed to work with him.

They'd watched the chauffeur park his Chevrolet in the quiet, narrow street of Trois Maures, very close to the Nîmes amphitheatre, once he'd delivered Rafa to the bullring. They'd waited while he had a drink and a cigar in a nearby bistro, then swiftly approached him as he returned to his vehicle, just as he was unlocking it.

Jürgen heard the first crack from the hammer blow that Séverin delivered to the back of the chauffeur's head, but he had no idea how bad it had been. His own job had been to grab the keys off the ground and get into the driver's seat. Within minutes, Séverin had tied the hands and feet of the slumped chauffeur with electrical cord in the back of the Chevrolet, before gagging and blindfolding him.

Later, once the bullfighter had jumped into what he hoped was the safety of his vehicle outside the amphitheatre – thanks to the chaos and bottles being hurled by other anti-bullfight protesters in the vicinity – Séverin also gagged him tightly from behind, before ramming a claw hammer against the side of his head.

Then the French psycho started ranting non-stop at the bullfighter all the way from Nîmes, calling him a 'sinner', and threatening to hack off his ears and carve him up because 'you must suffer in the same way you make animals suffer'. After prodding him hard with the hammer, he then held a knife under his nostrils while wrenching his tie to throttle him.

'What's the saying?' Séverin kept muttering loudly in the ear of the bullfighter. 'In suffering, animals are our equals. In suffering, animals are our equals. What's the saying? In suffering, animals are our equals … so, suffer this, *you fucking piece of shit* –'

In between, Jürgen could hear the chauffeur groaning in the back of the vehicle, but the Dutchman feared that he was as good as dead – and worse, he feared for his own life. It was while driving towards Girona that Jürgen decided he had to ditch Séverin. The stunt had become attempted murder, at the least, and that hadn't been the plan. He had to distance himself from the maniac, and it was now or never …

Just before midnight, precisely as planned, Jürgen had steered the Chevrolet into the El Gironès service station alongside Girona airport. It was where they'd planned to meet Hendrik.

Séverin, starting to stagger, had helped to bundle the bound and gagged bullfighter into the back of the transfer vehicle, just as soon as it rolled up nearby. While doing so, he'd jabbed a knife against the victim's throat as they'd dragged him between the vehicles, throttling him by the tie, slicing it and ripping his shirt.

Jürgen had then cursed him and shoved him away, before jumping into the front seat of the other vehicle alongside Hendrik and locking the door – giving Séverin no time to get in. Séverin, screaming obsceni-ties, tried to pull open the door, but the van screeched away.

Hendrik went berserk, not wanting to leave his narcotics pal behind, but Jürgen yelled at him to keep driving, and once they were out on the motorway there'd been no turning back.

Jürgen had taken the Chevrolet's keys with him. He had all the cash owed to Séverin for planning things in Nîmes, but he also had a clear conscience. As far as he was concerned, the chauffeur had still been alive when he'd left him at the service station.

He hoped the French savage would give up and flee, but he couldn't be sure.

And now, on his way over to Poblenou, he would have to remove all evidence of his own presence at the depot, and then deal with Hendrik …

25

Benjamin and Elena

Monday 4 June, 10.30am – Passeig Marítim, Barcelona.

Amid the morning sunbathers, council workers were cleaning weekend debris off the beach along the Passeig Marítim in the Barceloneta neighbourhood, as skateboarders and joggers in headphones whisked along the promenade, mostly drenched in sweat. Old men played dominoes in the shade near the board-walks, while nearby, groups of African immigrants laid out rows of Chanel handbags and Nike trainers for sale on blankets spread out across the pavement, easily transformed into sacks if they suddenly had to run from the local police.

Many would say that the city's former fishing quarter had lost its soul decades ago. It was now full of tourist apartments with few locals able to afford to live there anymore, but the property developers, seafood restaurant owners and some corrupt politicians had made a killing from the tourism surge over the years.

After MNAC, Benjamin had asked Elena to drive him to the seafront, but she'd been reluctant at first …

While Benjamin had been in the museum, Elena had seen the headlines on her phone about a kidnapped bullfighter. The Catalan government was about to hold a press conference, but she'd been more focused on two voice messages from her brother, Pablo.

Pablo had said there was an issue with their father's taxi insurance, but he was trying to sort it out with the taxi licensing authority. *What the fuck*, she cursed him … the vehicle was already damaged.

In his next message he'd promised to resolve it and would call back to confirm. So, she'd re-examined the huge dent on the driver's door, and the mess inside – it was definitely dried blood on the headrest in the back – which meant that when Benjamin returned from the museum, she'd yelled at him again.

'Please, Elena,' Benjamin had said. 'Just let me clean myself up, then I promise we'll sort out the damage …'

Which is how they'd ended up on the Passeig Marítim seafront.

As the taxi criss-crossed back down from Montjuïc and then along the traffic choked Passeig de Colom towards

Barceloneta beach, Benjamin had tried to weigh up his options and next steps. How, precisely, he might file a report regarding the body at the service station and his run-in with the thug, while keeping his prior visit to see the Marquès and the possible Dalí painting out of it all. That was if he couldn't track down the thug himself and discover if he really had been after the painting. Either way, he first had to wash, find somewhere to stay and grab something to eat. He was starving.

He first asked Elena to drop him within a stroll from the beach, in sight of a pharmacy and cafeteria – and she stayed with her taxi to further inspect the damage and make some calls.

On the beachfront, he found some taps designed to wash sand off one's feet, and he crouched down to try and spruce himself up. He hadn't realised that the back of his hair was still matted with dried blood, but he stuck his head under the water, careful to avoid sight of the pink liquid that rinsed away.

He knew it wasn't the right way to combat his phobia, but right now he couldn't face trying the psychodynamic psychotherapy he'd received in London. It was all part of his cognitive behavioural therapy course, deliberately and systematically exposing himself to things he feared, or at least *the* thing that made him feel faint, but which had absolutely nothing to do with logic or common sense. He had to separate the sight of blood from the thought of what it might induce in him – but he couldn't confront it right now.

Moments later and with Elena's taxi still in sight, he was sitting outside a cafeteria with a glass of water and black coffee, having swallowed two ibuprofen tablets purchased from the pharmacy. While the mix of painkillers and caffeine was finally helping him focus on the task ahead, he'd also asked for a couple of croissants with his coffee, but they hadn't arrived and it was making him even more ravenous.

Seeing the tourists in their T-shirts, shorts and flip-flops, Benjamin could feel the sweat trickling down the back of his polo shirt, despite having removed his corduroy jacket. There was a thick heat to the sea air, an intense humidity, almost tropical; it already felt like a heatwave and it wasn't even the height of summer yet.

He kept having to shield his eyes and squint if he looked out to the glimmering, dazzling sea, and where rows of small yachts with white sails drifted near the horizon. Close to the cafeteria, small, noisy, bright-green parrots flashed from one palm tree to another, while police sirens whined in the distance, and heli-copters circled continuously over the nearby port.

He pondered briefly about the calls that he'd cut short from his divorce lawyer, Walter, who was due to meet with the 'other team' this morning. What did he need to speak to him about? Benjamin felt bewildered and baffled by Claire's anger, exorbitant demands and viciousness towards him, when she was the one who'd had an affair. He didn't want to dwell on it, and nor could he contemplate her demands until he'd spoken to Sophie, his daughter. Walter would just have to wait, and besides, Benjamin had work to do.

Closing his eyes against the bright light, he still couldn't separate the image of the painting from what happened to him at the service station last night. But what was it? What had he seen? Was it just déjà vu? Still waiting for the croissants to arrive – *where the fuck where they?* – his thoughts turned to location, time and image again …

Location?

Púbol.

The *location* of where the painting had been found in Jaume's cellar, just ten kilometres from the Gala-Dalí Púbol castle, had intrigued him. Even with the infrared examination of the canvas being done, he would still need to speak to the aristocrat again. Location was good … yes, location was … plausible … but it was the date, the timing that had also begun to fascinate him.

The Hallucinogenic Toreador masterwork was painted between 1969 and 1970, finally completed at the end of 1970. It was exhibited, still unfinished, in March 1970, at a gallery in New York – that much he'd even told Jaume yesterday evening – and he also knew that Dalí then had the painting returned to Port Lligat after the exhibition to finish specific details.

The negotiations to purchase the abandoned

Gothic fortress in the village of Púbol began in 1969 – that was well recorded. He also knew Dalí and his wife gave the owner of the castle an advance payment, then settled in Paris for a while, wanting the building ready on their return. The following April – so, yes – after the exhibition in New York – *after* the original painting was returned to Port Lligat to be finished – they also returned to Spain, once the castle was ready and the deeds signed.

Dates … it was the same time that Dalí's museum in Figueres was taking shape – April 1970 – still before the *Toreador* was finished – when Dalí announced that his own 'theatre museum' would shortly be opening in Figueres, and that he'd bought the castle for Gala.

Benjamin was aware that Dalí then devoted the summer of 1970 to painting the two canvases he wanted for the ceilings of Figueres and Púbol at his studio in Port Lligat. Work on the museum began that October. Dalí followed it all meticulously, as well as the restoration of Púbol, so he was going backwards and forwards with no end of canvases and works … but surely, he hadn't secretly painted another test, perhaps in spring or summer 1970, before finishing the *Toreador?*

Even if he had, all tests would have remained at Port Lligat. Why would a painting end up in Jaume's cellar? Was it possible that Dalí visited the Guíxols' home while inspecting the restoration work at Púbol? Could he have taken a canvas with him? Why? Surely the provenance – that crucial chronology of owner-ship, custody or location of a work of art – didn't only extend to the painting being wrapped in a blanket in Jaume's cellar for over fifty years?

Opening his eyes, he searched his pockets for the card that the aristocrat had given him with his number. He needed to speak to him urgently if he could perhaps now borrow Elena's phone. The croissants hadn't arrived and he was pissed off. He couldn't function properly without food. He'd had nothing to eat since the tiny tapas from little Montse last night, and then he'd been attacked by that ape in a red hoodie at the service station, before he could stuff down the sandwich he'd bought. He tried to wave over a waiter to pay for his coffee, but instead got up, put on his jacket and headed inside the cafeteria to settle up.

So ... there was a good argument for the location of the painting, near enough to Púbol, and if the dates of its creation and movements could be established, then even better, although he still had to examine the *image* ...

Inside the cafeteria, Benjamin tried in vain to remonstrate with the barman about the missing croissants.

On the bar there were various baguettes filled with tortilla or ham. He asked for two – no, make it three – maybe Elena will want one – and then he rolled his hands around to show that he wanted them wrapped to take away. Which is when he caught a glimpse of the image on the TV above the bar, just before Elena suddenly appeared and grabbed his arm.

26

Inspector Vizcaya, Isabel Bosch and Beltrán Gómez

Monday 4 June, 11.15am – Plaça Sant Jaume, Barcelona.

Inspector Vizcaya arrived at the Catalan government's headquarters some forty minutes after Isabel Bosch's press briefing. He was still feeling upbeat about the reports of the dead chauffeur's credit card being used after the Chevrolet had been abandoned – a feeling that was quickly quenched once he entered Bosch's palatial, mahogany-panelled office.

'Where's the bullfighter?' yelled the Catalan home affairs minister, tapping a high-heeled foot.

There was a weaselly-looking young man hovering near her desk, but she didn't appear to be in a hurry to introduce him. Without being invited to, Vizcaya sat in one of the chairs facing Bosch. The sly chap remained standing and seemed unsure what to do.

'He can't just disappear – matadors don't disappear – you can't hide a bullfighter,' Bosch was shouting.

Vizcaya was about to say that he agreed, but he didn't get a chance.

'I've got everyone calling me non-stop, wanting answers now – *now* – so what have you got?'

Vizcaya eyed the silver picture frames on the immense desk, all positioned strategically so that visitors could see the ambitious Bosch at endless ceremonies, shaking hands with other dignitaries.

'The investigation is still very early –' he started.

Bosch silenced him with a wave of her hand.

'Do you have any idea what is about to happen? Well, I'll tell you,' she said, before anyone could utter a word. Not that the other person in the room looked like he dared speak.

Vizcaya glanced across at him. He was dressed in a black suit, white shirt and dark tie. He wore it as if it was a uniform, but it made him look like an undertaker. He was fidgeting, rubbing his hands in a peculiar way, as if drying them. Every now and then he'd use a single finger to scratch a different area of his scalp, as if attacking a nit with precision targeting, yet being careful to not spoil his perfectly slicked-back hair. Balding Vizcaya proudly stroked his own walrus moustache after observing just a tuft of bumfluff in the middle of the youngster's upper lip.

'Arriving at the airport right now,' said Bosch, glancing at her diamond bracelet watch, 'we have the Sultan of Brunei, the Chinese Minister of Foreign

Affairs, the Egyptian Prime Minister, the Indian Minister of External Affairs –'

'Okay,' said Vizcaya.

'– and their ambassadors are all asking *how* is it possible that a bullfighter has been kidnapped, his chauffeur murdered, *and*, more importantly, is there going to be mayhem during the G20?'

'We're making progress, the homicide squad and my own division –'

'What progress have you made, exactly?'

Vizcaya remained silent, waiting for Bosch to calm down. He wasn't going to reveal anything about his investigation until he knew who was listening. He stared at Bosch and then rolled his eyes towards her guest, who was still fidgeting. Taking the hint, Bosch beckoned for him to also sit, introducing him as 'Beltrán Gómez de Longoria, from Madrid, from CITCO'.

Vizcaya took an instant dislike to the young man just hearing his pretentious surname. The name reminded him of an old Francoist henchman, but he couldn't recall which one. He shook Beltrán's hand. Not only was it limp but it was also damp, almost wet. He appeared more like an intern on work experience than an agent from Spain's Intelligence Centre for Counter-Terrorism and Organised Crime. The agency reported directly to Spain's Secretary of State for Security, who in turn reported to the Minister of Interior in Madrid.

Vizcaya doubted Bosch was very happy that they'd sent someone over from Madrid to keep an eye on her, which was probably why she'd been slow to introduce him. But at least he was satisfied that he could discuss the investigation.

He said they were awaiting forensic results from evidence found in the Chevrolet, the service station and at Girona airport, as well as CCTV analysis against credit card transactions at tollgates, while in Nîmes there was a team of experts examining images of the crowd outside the amphitheatre when the bull-fighter was being carried out to his vehicle, in which a red-hooded man could be seen in the back seat.

'What are the animal rights groups saying?' Bosch barked.

'As a murder has taken place,' said Vizcaya, 'all animal welfare groups, national and international, are trying to distance themselves from it. The *Prou* move-ment has said that it achieved the bullfight ban in Catalonia over a decade ago through a parliamentary vote, that its members would never resort to violence –'

'The others?' cut in Bosch.

'PACMA and ADDA have both issued statements to deny this has anything to do with them. They've been targeting the UN on the eve of the summit to make a universal declaration on animal welfare, and so the abduction of a bullfighter, let alone a murder, is bad publicity for those seeking change by political lobbying. PETA have also denied that their members would be involved, as have the Animal Alliance, the Animal Protection Party, the Friends of Animals –'

'Animal rights extremists … what have we got?'

Finally, Beltrán spoke. Rather too softly and precisely, and with a bit of a lisp, but he spoke. From then on, too, he barely stopped. He may have looked timid, Vizcaya mused, but he was full of himself. He'd clearly been waiting for his grand introduction.

Beltrán said that they were running checks on the obvious hardliners such as ALF, the Animal Liberation Front, its copycats and spin-offs, the Animal Rights Militia, the Animal Liberation Army – but in every corner of the globe there were animal rights brigades, squadrons, legions, battalions and vigilantes.

He then went on to make a bit of a speech, explaining that a handful of the groups were highly organised, totally obsessive, and eager to resort to violence, bombings, arson attacks and terror tactics in their crusade to end all animal suffering, with many of their supporters shrouded in some 'green party mystique'. They were unable to see the moral incoherence of acts of violence against humans made in the name of animals, he said.

To conclude, at least temporarily, he said that he doubted any of them had managed to infiltrate a gang into Barcelona on the eve of the G20 amid all the security measures in place, especially as most of the hardcore extremists were already on international terrorist watchlists, as well as on 'his own' CITCO lists.

There was a brief silence. Vizcaya was already convinced it was more likely to be a new radical group, so far unknown yet turning impatient, a group that believed Spain would take decades, if ever, to eliminate bullfighting and bull-running events nationwide, but he decided not to voice it.

'The calls to the media?' said Bosch. 'What have we got there?'

Again, Beltrán spoke – and again, he found it hard to stop.

He said that fifteen national and international media groups had come forward to confirm they'd received calls, including Reuters, CNN, the BBC and Al-Jazeera. The automated robocalls were made in both English and Spanish using a foreign-sounding voice, pointing to an internationally planned or funded operation. Either way, he said, 'my men' were already on the case.

'What do you mean, *your* men?' snorted Vizcaya.

'What do I mean?' came the reply.

Beltrán didn't clarify who 'his men' were, but Vizcaya soon discovered that whoever they were, they'd been liaising overnight with CIA agents in Barcelona as part of the US advance delegation for the G20. They'd been investigating if any SIMs were linked to the computerised, auto-dialling that led to the calls to the media. Beltrán said they were applying state-of-the-art technology to analyse the logs from telecoms groups corresponding to what their cellular towers had recorded at the time of the calls in the Barcelona area – a process they'd used successfully on several occasions in the States, including when he'd been stationed over there himself.

He paused after dropping that last bit into his

speech, perhaps hoping to impress Vizcaya, or for the Inspector to implore him to explain where he'd been stationed in the States. But Vizcaya kept his mouth shut. Beltrán used an index finger to scratch something on the top of his head again, yet without ruffling his plastered-down hair, and then continued.

'I was trained at START,' he said, answering a question that no one had asked.

'Start?' said Vizcaya.

'University of Maryland,' said Beltrán, 'near Washington DC.' He turned towards Bosch, somewhat perplexed that the Catalan minister had not briefed Vizcaya more fully.

'START,' said Bosch, finally helping out, 'is the National Consortium for the Study of Terrorism and Responses to Terrorism.' She gazed briefly at some scribbled notes on her desk, before adding: 'A Department of Homeland Security Centre of Excellence, based at the University of Maryland. But he's now based in Madrid.' She looked across at Beltrán. 'Correct?'

'Correct,' came the reply. 'I was with START for five years, specialising in prevent and deter programmes, before returning to CITCO.' He unbuttoned his jacket and then buttoned it up again.

'Five years?' mumbled Vizcaya, stroking his moustache again while trying to estimate Beltrán's age. Early to mid-thirties at the most, he figured, even though he looked fourteen or fifteen, max. He assumed that he'd landed his job at CITCO thanks to Spanish nepotism.

That surname … *Gómez de Longoria*. The chinless wonder was the son of a diplomat, judge or state prosecutor, Vizcaya reckoned, and the grandson of some old fascist.

He wondered how much Beltrán and his CITCO men were going to depend on the CIA. He was also concerned why he'd been summoned to Bosch's office together with this START-trained upstart, although he had his suspicions. They were soon to be confirmed.

'As we know,' Beltrán was now saying, clearly delighted that they'd clarified his credentials, 'animal rights extremists over recent years have been adopting more personal and dangerous terrorism tactics, from firebombing the homes of biomedical researchers who use animal testing in their experiments, threatening their families, to sending letter bombs to the employees of meat processing plants, fur and leather companies, university research labs and some pharmaceutical companies. The groups also consistently announce their responsibility for these actions, these *crimes*, via social media with communiqués and press releases.'

As Isabel Bosch was now calm and nodding, Vizcaya decided it was wise to simply let Beltrán continue.

'Very few animal rights extremists participate in legal protests prior to committing their crimes,' he said. 'Most are haphazardly organised into groups. They come together usually through personal contacts, and function without a hierarchical organisational structure, committing offences as small working cells. Such tactics make the collection of intelligence and the investigation of such activities very challenging.'

'Quite,' said Vizcaya, beginning to feel he'd heard enough. 'But this is also a kidnap and murder investigation, let's not forget.'

'Wait,' said Bosch, indicating for Beltrán to carry on.

'The facts are,' said Beltrán, addressing Vizcaya directly, 'that animal rights extremists are individuals or groups that support biodiversity and biocentric equality. They believe humans are no greater than any other form of life and have no legitimate claim to dominate earth –'

'Yes, but –'

'They believe animals are in imminent danger, that governments and corporations are responsible for this danger, and that this danger will ultimately result in the destruction of the whole species. They believe that the political system is incapable and unwilling to take actions to protect the environment or to defend animals –'

'This is a kidnap and murder investigation,' said Vizcaya.

'This is terrorism,' said Beltrán, almost simultaneously.

From across the desk, Bosch glanced from one to the other.

'This is terrorism,' she said finally.

Vizcaya avoided meeting Beltrán's eye, but he

assumed the smug little creep was giving him a know-it-all, told-you-so look.

From then on, Vizcaya was ordered to share all details of the investigation with the smarmy youngster from the terrorism and organised crime agency in Madrid, the smart ass with wet palms who used 'state-of-the-art theories and data to improve the under-standing of the origins, dynamics and social and psychological impacts of terrorism' – yet looked like he was just old enough to join a boy band.

Although Vizcaya was regularly called out across the country to assist with abduction cases, he was employed by the Mossos d'Esquadra and therefore the Catalan government, which meant Bosch was boss. Beltrán, however, reported to the Interior Ministry in Madrid, which also controlled Spain's Policía Nacional and Guardia Civil. Vizcaya didn't even question whether he would still be in overall charge of the investigation. If the young brat didn't get in his way, then he was also okay about sharing the investigation with him, especially if it kept the ball-busting, stiletto-tapping Bosch off his back.

Vizcaya believed that one of his key strengths as an investigator was that he rarely believed a single word anyone ever said, and he certainly had his doubts about Beltrán. But with the presence of international security agencies in Barcelona for the G20, he had to accept that this was no longer just a matter of freeing a kidnap victim or tracking down a murderer, but a rush to avert any wider threat.

The message from Madrid was clear: extremists were not activists. Environmental and animal rights extremists had to be categorised in the same way as any other extremists who carried out serious crime in the pursuit of an ideology or cause. Extremists who pursued bombing or arson tactics, or who committed murder, kidnapping and threatened carnage were *terrorists*, period.

Once Bosch was satisfied that Vizcaya and Beltrán would work together, the CITCO agent tried to give more details of his plan to work with the CIA on cell phone technology.

'You see if the CIA can help us to trace a digital pattern for the calls made to the media,' Beltrán said, 'then it would be a great step forward. It might take time, but –'

'We don't have time,' said Bosch, scanning messages on her phone.

'Have you seen the Tweets? The image of Barcelona is at stake. They should be writing about our city and Catalonia, not about bullfights ... *for Christ's sake*, we've already banned that barbarism here. The King is hosting a reception at Pedralbes Palace at 9pm. The US Secretary of State is already here, as is the UN Secretary General – and they'll both be attending. All other leaders, including the US President, will be here by tomorrow afternoon. So, I don't give a damn about any bullfights starting at 6.30pm in Andalusia or anywhere else this evening ... just kill the fucking story, Vizcaya.'

Vizcaya glanced at Beltrán.

'You heard me, kill the story. Make an arrest before 6.30pm, before any bullfight starts and before the royal reception tonight. Then the story will swing from incompetence to how clever we are.'

'Look –' started Vizcaya.

'Don't tell me what we can and can't do, Inspector,' said Bosch, sharply. 'We don't have to release the name of who you arrest, at least not until after the G20. Within twenty-four hours of the arrest, make a request for a forty-eight-hour extension of the first seventy-two-hour police custody period – it'll be approved, you have my word – and by then, the summit will be over.'

Up to a point, Vizcaya couldn't question her strategy. Spain's anti-terrorism measures meant that detainees suspected of membership of any armed group could be held in 'incommunicado detention' for up to thirteen days, despite all efforts by Amnesty International to change things. It was thirteen days if suspected of terrorism-related offences – and up to five days in all other cases, which could still be extended by five more days in preventive imprisonment ... so either way, the G20 would be over.

Whether Vizcaya would be able to find the kidnappers and killers before 6.30pm, however, was another issue, with or without Beltrán getting in the way.

'Arrest anyone,' said Bosch, as if reading his mind. 'You have seven hours, Vizcaya. Maximum.'

27

Benjamin and Elena

Monday 4 June, 10.35am – Passeig Marítim, Barcelona.

'What?' said Benjamin.

'What happened at Girona airport?' hissed Elena.

They were back on the Passeig Marítim now, walking fast, with Benjamin trying to stay in the shade as Elena urged him in the direction of her taxi. She was angry, suspicious, asking him what happened at the airport, what really happened to his car – tell me the truth – *tell me*.

Just seconds earlier, Benjamin had been squinting at the TV screen in the cafeteria. Other customers had been glaring at the screen, too, as had the barman and waiter, even while Benjamin had been handing over some coins for his coffee and the baguettes that he was waiting to have wrapped to take away.

They'd all been mumbling to one another, some

shrugging, others just staring at the TV in disbelief. At first, he'd seen images of a woman giving a press conference, probably linked to the G20, but then it cut to a news bulletin. Benjamin hadn't understood what was being said by the newsreader, but he guessed it was something about a bullfighter since they kept showing images of one.

Images … images of a *toreador* …

Then there was a black Chevy van – and more images of a bullfighter – and then they were showing aerial shots of the whole scene, a crime scene cordoned off by police alongside the motorway, a *service station* – something looked familiar – and then Benjamin could see it was the service station where he'd been attacked and had his car stolen that very morning – where he'd seen *the body* – and he was just about to ask others in the bar if they could translate what was being said before Elena suddenly appeared, grabbing his arm, telling him that she'd seen the news on social media, and it was time to go.

'*Wait*,' he said. 'I've ordered us some food. I'm starving –'

'Forget it,' she snapped.

'*For fucksake*,' he muttered, being pulled away from the bar and out of the cafeteria.

Elena had received more messages from her brother, her father, and from friends in Girona, while Benjamin had been buying pain killers and having a coffee.

They'd wanted to know where she was. Had she heard the news? What with the famous bullfighter missing and his chauffeur murdered, the police were all over Girona airport and hunting the kidnappers and killers. So, wherever she was, and whoever she was with, she had to be careful, very careful, and perhaps she should return to Girona at once.

'What happened at Girona airport? she insisted, once they were standing alongside the taxi.

'What?'

'What happened to your car? Who stole it?'

'I don't know his name,' said Benjamin. 'But it was that maniac in the red hood.'

'Why?'

'Why what?'

'Why did he steal your car?'

'I don't know. At first, I thought –'

'Do you know him?'

'No –'

'Why did he follow us? Is he your colleague?'

'No, of course not.'

'So, you're not involved?'

'Involved with what?'

'*Qué pasó con el torero?*' she shouted.

'I don't understand –'

'They killed … *asesinaron a un chofer …*'

'Tell me what you mean –'

'*Un secuestro –*'

'I don't understand –'

'The bullfighter.'

'What bullfighter?'

'*Han secuestrado a un torero –*'

'*Torero?* The Toreador? The painting?'

'What?'

'The painting?'

'*No, un torero. Qué pasó?* What else did you see? *What else did you see?*'

Benjamin felt giddy as Elena repeated it, over and over again. *What else did you see? What else did you see?* Then she started to key in something on her cell phone. He briefly closed his eyes.

A double image?

Luis Romero ...

... that was him. Benjamin had researched it as part of a thesis. He had a long friendship with Dalí and was with him during the time he painted *The Hallucinogenic Toreador*. It was in the summer of 1969 when Dalí had first shown Romero an unfinished painting. Two huge Venus de Milos stood out boldly against the background of an arena. Dalí had told Romero to stand at the far end of the studio, and then asked the same question that he'd asked about other pictures: '*What else do you see in it?*'

It had taken time for Romero to work it out, and in the end Dalí had to help him see that the picture also represented the head of a bullfighter, whose face, hat and tie were incorporated in the canvas as the result of other elements. It was another example of his paranoiac-critical method … of double imagery …

'Kidnapping,' shouted Elena, showing Benjamin the translation for the word *secuestro* that she'd keyed into her phone.

'Kidnapping?' he said.

They were alongside her taxi now, with Benjamin waiting for her to calm down. What he'd seen on the TV in the bar had already unsettled him. If, as he hoped, the worker at the service station had notified the emergency services about the body, why were they showing aerial shots of the area when surely there was more important news with the G20?

He needed to borrow Elena's phone and make some calls, but she'd pulled him away from the cafeteria so quickly and had then started gabbling in Spanish, he hadn't had a chance to ask her.

'Yes, kidnapping,' she said. 'There's been a kidnapping of a bullfighter – his driver was murdered – and they found his van near the airport.'

'His van?' said Benjamin. 'His *van?*'

Elena was yelling again, demanding that Benjamin tell the truth – what happened to your car? – what else did you see? – you said you were *policía* – *you need to tell me.*

Benjamin narrowed his eyes. *A bullfighter.* They'd kidnapped a bullfighter and found his van near the airport, and his driver was dead ... possibly the body he'd seen, which might explain the images on TV.

He dug deep into his pockets and could feel the small button he'd found on the ground at the service station. But there'd been something else ... a piece of fabric that he'd seen when he was bludgeoned to the ground. There was also a word on the side of the other vehicle that had sped off ... but what was it? He was desperate to recall precisely what he'd seen.

He couldn't tell Elena about the body, not right now. She'd go crazy. But, yes, he now had to report how he was attacked, and that his car was stolen – although the Spanish police would ask why he'd delayed telling them. It wouldn't look good. The only option was to first call his own contacts, to cover himself until he'd spoken to Jaume and returned his painting. He needed Elena's phone.

'Elena –' he started.

'Who are you?'

'What?'

'Who are you?'

'I told you,' he said. 'Benjamin. Benjamin Blake.'

'Why did you need to get something from the hire car?' she asked. 'What is it? What is it ... this ... this *painting* you took to MNAC?'

'Elena,' he said. 'I tried to tell you ... it's my job ... I investigate art. But I can't tell you anything about this specific job. I'm sorry.'

She stared at him.

'I don't believe you,' she said. Suddenly, her phone

bleeped. She checked the screen to read a message. '*Joder*,' she cursed.

'What is it?'

'There's still a problem with the insurance.'

'What?'

'The insurance.'

'Insurance?'

'*Yes* – how many times do I have to tell you? The *insurance*. I don't know if I'm insured to drive the taxi, so if you call any of your *policía* friends, I'll blame you. *You* made me drive here. Got it? *Fuck* –'

Benjamin stared at her. It would seem impossible, he thought, but she was even more gorgeous when she was angry. She was now shouting something about the taxi being her father's – that the taxi licence didn't allow for just anyone to drive it – that her brother was trying to sort it out, but he was useless – and now the vehicle was damaged and she wasn't sure if the insurance would cover it as she wasn't a taxi driver, she was a sportswriter, training to be a journalist …

'Stop,' he said. 'You need to trust me.'

'Trust you?' she yelled. 'Trust you?'

Benjamin glanced around.

'Yes, me,' he said. 'But I need to use your phone.'

Silence.

'Please?'

Elena finally handed him her phone. Benjamin tugged out the card he'd been given by the Marquès, and then he called him.

28

Jaume, Marquès de Guíxols

Monday 4 June, 10.40am – La Bisbal d'Empordà.

Jaume had been obsessively checking his Patek Philippe watch, inherited from his grandfather, ever since he'd awoken at 6am that Monday morning. The antique wristwatch was one of the only treasures he still owned, or at least it hadn't yet been earmarked for confiscation. But how long before they took it away from him?

He was about to return to Barcelona with his wife, Montse, as he had delicate matters to attend to and she had meetings with florists and caterers about their daughter's wedding. She knew they had a debt to clear, but she didn't know the extent of it. Jaume hadn't yet mustered the courage to tell her that they couldn't afford flowers or food, let alone a wedding.

His brief, secret, catastrophic affair with the gold-digging Lisette Dijckhuijsen was also worrying him –

especially as she was threatening to expose him in front of Montse, should he decide not to follow through on promises that she claimed he'd made. She was also demanding to meet him at midday in compensation for not being his companion to the pre-G20 reception at the Pedralbes Palace.

Jaume had many problems, but it was his association with Spain's former finance minister, recently arrested on charges of money laundering, that was haunting him. The politician had become chairman of one of the country's major banks that collapsed back in 2020, pushing the government to seek a bailout for several other ailing banks.

Jaume's business empire, indebted to his old friend's bank, had crashed with it. Executives and associates of the bank had also clocked up over sixteen million euros in personal expenses using special black credit cards – 'black', as the owners never declared the credit as income. The cards had all been confiscated in the on-going corruption investigation, while the tax authorities were still busy scrutinising the financial affairs of each cardholder, Jaume included.

He'd made many mistakes in his life, but he knew he was innocent, and he had a clear conscience. The case had been dragging on for over three years, and many of his assets had been frozen. His lawyers had filed an appeal, and in the meantime, he'd been allowed to retain his two homes. But he awoke each morning in a cold sweat, wondering how long before a judge might call for his remaining bank account to be closed and for him to be finally led away in handcuffs.

He still clung to the hope that he could stand bail for himself if he was put in custody, which is where the only new asset not yet listed as part of his estate could prove to be his lifeline: the Dalí painting.

Jaume urgently needed to know when and where he could meet up with Benjamin, once he'd carried out his tests on the painting. He had said he would call first thing, but he hadn't – and it was infuriating him.

He'd already heard the morning news on the radio: Rafael Pérez kidnapped by animal rights extremists and his chauffeur murdered; 'Save the Planet' banners hanging from Gaudí's Sagrada Família cathedral; European airports being targeted by climate change activists, with flashmobs rioting against runway expansion plans, all on the eve of the G20. What was the world coming to?

Jaume had never been a bullfight fan, but he had friends who were – not that any of them still spoke to him. His former affluent circle had included bull breeders among all the wine and sherry barons, and the last thing they needed were more activists seeking to ban bullfighting further than the ban in Catalonia. As for climate change ... who cared? He'd already lost a fortune with disastrous investments in Catalan grapes and Californian vineyards, and no change in the weather would ever bring it back.

His cell phone started ringing, and he rushed to answer it.

29

Inspector Vizcaya, Beltrán Gómez and Officer Soler

Monday 4 June, 11.40am – Mossos Comissaria, Les Corts district, Barcelona.

Inspector Vizcaya's vast expertise in abductions had served him well up to now. Despite the terrorism paranoia he'd encountered in his meeting with Isabel Bosch and Beltrán Gómez de Longoria, the typical kidnap gang that he'd encountered in the past had been small, normally no more than five people: three to take turns guarding the victim, one to negotiate (usually the ringleader), and one to organise the vehicles and buy provisions – often the same person responsible for any ransom pick-up.

Other than fanatical, guerrilla-style hostage-takers, most kidnappers didn't have criminal records up until the point of abduction. Kidnapping was a complex and sometimes personal crime, and it certainly didn't follow that a thief or murderer could also be a kidnapper.

The brutal killing of the chauffeur, however, put a different spin on things. From Vizcaya's experience, previous fatalities during the act of kidnapping had been unintended, or 'no choice' scenarios where body-guards had forfeited their lives defending the target. The fact that the chauffeur was apparently unarmed yet still beaten to death meant they were dealing with a cold-blooded gang and would need to tread carefully.

Following the meeting with Bosch, the pedantic, pubescent-looking Beltrán was now installed at Vizcaya's incident room at the Mossos Comissaria, with full access to the investigation.

He'd been allocated a desk and computer in the far corner of the room, behind a glass partition, on which he was already sticking up details about terrorist organisations and methods of radicalisation, alongside rows of different coloured post-it notes.

'Comfortable?' barked Vizcaya, as he made his way past.

'Comfortable that we have seven hours to track down and dismantle an eco-terrorist cell?' said Beltrán.

Vizcaya stopped and stared at him. He'd noticed in the meeting with Bosch that the kid from Spain's counter-terrorism agency had an irritating habit of answering a question with another question.

'I meant with your desk,' he said. 'If you need anything, you know who to ask.'

'Do I?' came the reply.

'I assumed you knew everything,' said Vizcaya. 'We're about to get an update on the Chevrolet, so you should listen in … and I'll introduce you.'

Vizcaya had been quietly obsessing about how and where the kidnappers had concealed a bloodstained bullfighter. From what the entourage said in Nîmes, it wasn't the chauffeur at the wheel of the Chevrolet outside the amphitheatre at the end of the bullfight, but his bludgeoned corpse had still ended up at the service station near Girona airport.

So, the gang first targeted the bullfighter's vehicle by attacking and later murdering his driver, whether he was forced to drive it for them, or whether he was killed because he refused to do so. They'd snatched the Chevrolet to snatch the matador, before using another vehicle to move him on … so they were *vehicle* savvy.

What other vehicle was used after abandoning the Chevrolet at the service station? Vizcaya hoped his team had identified it.

The incident room was heaving with activity. A huge map was now pinned on the wall at the front, and silence fell among the Mossos agents as Vizcaya approached it, alongside Officer Soler.

'That,' said Vizcaya, first pointing to a figure hovering at the back once he'd got everyone's attention, 'is Beltrán Gómez de Longoria from CITCO. He's here to, er … help us. So, also help him.' The silence continued until he turned to Soler. 'Okay, Marta, what have you got?'

'It is three hundred kilometres from Nîmes to El Gironès service station, just before Girona airport,' she said, pointing at the map. 'The Chevrolet travelled there in about two hours, twenty minutes, not arriving before 11.45pm. The vehicle took a toll ticket at 9.17pm in France for the motorway to the border. Ten minutes later, it was paid for using the chauffeur's credit card – a cost of five euros. At 9.44pm a ticket was taken at the next tollgate and, just before the border, it was paid for at 11.05pm. Sixteen euros.'

It intrigued Vizcaya. Records from the chauffeur's credit card had shown that the vehicle's fuel tank had been filled in Nîmes on the morning of the bullfight. It had no need to stop for gas, not even where it was abandoned at the service station near Girona airport. So why stop there? If the intention was simply to get to Spain, why not stop at any other service station?

'There's a service station at the first tollgate, after the border at La Jonquera, where the Chevrolet took a ticket,' Soler continued. 'There's also a service station midway to Girona. But it stopped at neither.'

Vizcaya assumed the kidnappers had transferred to another vehicle as the Chevrolet would have become more conspicuous the nearer it got to Barcelona, especially with the bullfighter's name emblazoned on its side. But why stop at El Gironès?

His initial theory had been the proximity to Girona airport, but the Chevrolet had already passed the French airport of Béziers Cap d'Agde, soon after Nîmes. There were also airports at Cannes, Nice and Montpellier, so he was now convinced that the bull-fighter hadn't been stowed away by plane. The kidnappers had wanted to bring him to Barcelona, to the G20 media circus, and they'd almost confirmed that with their calls to the press.

There were reports of a man at the service station seeking directions to Girona airport at around 5.30am that concerned him, however, but then Soler delivered her final report …

'The toll ticket that the Chevrolet collected after the border was finally used and paid for by another vehicle on the periphery of Barcelona. We've calculated that the waiting time at El Gironès service station was therefore minimal – just enough time to transfer to the other vehicle. Traffic cameras at that last tollgate near Barcelona have identified it as a VW Polo, a Goldcar rental car, hired from Girona airport at 8.45pm yesterday evening. It was paid for in cash, in the name of Brandon Bartholomew …'

'Brandon Bartholomew?' said Vizcaya. 'What do we have on him?'

'Not a lot,' said Soler. 'In fact, nothing.'

'Obviously a lone wolf …' Beltrán mumbled to himself at the back of the room. 'Classic.'

30

Benjamin and Elena

Monday 4 June, 10.45am – Passeig Marítim, via MNAC, to Les Corts, Barcelona.

Benjamin handed the cell phone back to Elena. He'd made three calls but had only managed to speak to Jaume Guíxols. Benjamin had told him there were some other issues he was having to deal with in Barcelona, but the old aristocrat had simply barked down the phone at him.

'Have you got the painting?'

'Of course,' Benjamin had said. The Marquès didn't need to know that the canvas had also been in the possession of a crazed carjacker and murder suspect for several anxious and lost hours.

'Have you done the tests?'

'They're being done right now,' Benjamin explained, before Jaume once again cut in to say that he needed an authentication certificate immediately. Benjamin said that he needed to ask some questions, but Jaume snapped back, saying he didn't have time, he just needed the painting and the certificate. He ordered Benjamin to bring everything to him at a restaurant in a hotel called 'arts' at one o'clock, or he'd call Anthony Hughes to 'get someone else to do the job'. Then he'd abruptly ended the call.

'Fuck,' said Benjamin, sweltering in his jacket again, thinking the only consolation was that the cantankerous old bastard hadn't mentioned receiving any ransom call for the canvas. The savage who'd attacked him had clearly not targeted the painting.

'Thanks,' he now said, after handing the phone back to Elena and watching her check her messages. 'Do you know where there's a hotel called *arts*?'

'Hotel Arts?' She pointed to a tower block across the port. A helicopter was hovering over it. 'Why?'

'After we've been back to MNAC, I need to –'

'I'm not taking you anywhere,' she said, raising her voice. 'I told you I don't trust you. Where was your car stolen? *Where*, exactly? If you work for the police, why didn't you arrest that maniac? Why?'

He stared at her.

'Tell me,' she insisted. 'Why didn't you stop him?'

'I'll get him,' he said.

'I don't believe you.' She pulled open the taxi's

dented door while also checking her phone. 'You missed your chance,' she said.

Benjamin stood still. Moments earlier, he'd considered telling her about the body at the service station, but then decided against it. He thought she'd drag him to the police before he was ready, or even go herself.

Elena sat in the driver's seat, the door open, and before long she was ranting in Spanish to someone on the phone. Benjamin assumed it was to do with her vehicle's door, as she kept gesticulating towards it. He decided to get into the seat beside her, which more than surprised her.

'I'm not taking you anywhere else,' she told him again, in between speaking in Spanish on the phone. 'Get another taxi.'

Benjamin waited for her to end the call. When she did, he quickly and calmly said: 'My car was stolen at a service station near the airport.'

'*Dónde?*'

'A service station. I saw it on TV in the cafeteria.'

Elena frantically scrolled through the news reports on her phone.

'*El Gironès?*' she said, still eyeing him with distrust.

'What?'

'The name of the service station … *el Gironès?*'

'I've got no idea. It was next to the airport, which is why I then walked there.'

'*Oh, my God,*' she said, jumping out of the taxi and immediately trying to call someone again.

This time she wasn't having any luck getting

through to whoever she was calling. Instead, she started reading out a news report to Benjamin.

'The bullfighter was kidnapped somewhere between Nîmes and Barcelona, and his vehicle was abandoned at a service station near Girona airport, where his chauffeur was found dead ...'

She stopped reading and glared at him.

'But you already know this, don't you?'

'What?'

'You were there.'

Benjamin didn't reply.

'What else did you see there?' she said. 'Were you involved?'

'Look, I just need to get to MNAC,' he tried once more, 'then that hotel, then we'll go to the police –'

'Hotel? What hotel?'

'I told you –'

Elena suddenly took a picture of him with her phone.

'No, don't – what are you doing?' he said, holding up a hand. 'I told you, we'll go to the police together –'

But Elena had no intention of going to the police. Since the press conference earlier, the murder and kidnap story had gone global, helped by the fact that half the world's media had descended upon Barcelona for the G20. She realised she had news to report. She'd already tried to call a journalist friend for advice, but she hadn't picked up. She knew what she had to do, though; she just had to write it herself. She'd been trying to get some bylines to attach to her final dissertation, and now she had a real opportunity.

It would show she could report news and wasn't trying to 'use her looks' to land a job as a TV sports presenter – like that pig of a lecturer had suggested.

Her passenger had been at the service station where the matador's vehicle was found, she was sure. He was a possible witness, at the very least, if not involved in it himself. She'd ask more questions, she'd record him, she'd video him, but she had to be careful.

Did she trust him? No. Well, yes and no. He'd shown no signs of leaving to get another taxi, despite her saying she wasn't going to drive him anywhere else. But what if he drove? Well, if *he* drove, she could jump out if she felt unsafe. As for any doubts she had about the taxi's insurance, then he'd have to explain things himself if they were stopped by the police …

'Elena?' Benjamin was saying. 'Look, I'm starving, so why don't we –?'

'If you want to go back to MNAC, then you drive,' she said, marching round to the passenger side. 'I need to send messages and check the reports. *You* drive …'

So, he did. Elena quickly set up the Sat-Nav, put the meter on again, told him where and how he had to drive, and before long he was steering the taxi back towards Montjuïc, initially in silence. The only thing he asked was how to turn on the air conditioning. She checked the news reports, then discreetly used 'voice memo' on her phone to record their conversation.

'Where are you from?' she started, trying to sound friendly enough.

'London,' came the reply. 'You?'

'Girona, but my parents were originally from Andalusia.'

Silence.

'So, why are you over here?' she said.

'Working. I told you.'

'Of course.' She paused, then asked him what time his car was stolen at the service station.

'What?' said Benjamin, focusing on the traffic.

'What time was the car stolen?'

'I don't know ... it was around midnight, I think.'

'Midnight?'

'Yeah ...'

'But I picked you up from the airport at six in the morning, right?'

He gazed at her. She was fiddling with her phone.

'I guess,' he said. 'Why?'

'So, what were you doing between midnight and six in the morning?'

'Elena –?'

'What were you doing? Why didn't you call anyone or tell the police?' she tried again.

'My phone was in the car. I thought I'd told you.'

'What were you doing for six hours?'

'I was concussed, and then it took me a while to walk to the airport ...'

'Who else was at the service station?' she said. 'Why were you there? Was there no one there to help you? What else did you see there? *What else did you see?'*

What else do you see, Benjamin?

Look at the crime scene. Look at it like a work of art.

He was squinting now, yet careful to keep his eyes on the road.

Look at it like a work of art.

The disfigured body, the images on TV, the toll ticket, the murder, the kidnapping, a missing bullfighter – Dalí's *Toreador* painting – Jaume's painting – a piece of green fabric he'd seen fluttering on the ground as he was struck and then collapsed – everything started swirling as one hallucinatory scene again. He tried to recall the word he'd seen on the van speeding away from the service station. What was the word?

The aerial images of the service station that he'd seen on the TV in the bar had unsettled him. From what Elena had since said, he now knew that the bullfighter had been fighting, or performing, or competing, or whatever it was that bullfighters did, in Nîmes, and he'd been abducted between there and Barcelona, with his vehicle abandoned near Girona airport – clearly at the service station where he was attacked last night.

That explained the images on TV.

The bullfighter's chauffeur had been found murdered – he was sure it was the body he'd seen – and he knew it was his responsibility to now tell the police. Seeing patrol cars drive past, he even considered stopping the taxi to wave one down – but having to explain his prior whereabouts and break client confidentiality would be complex and very damaging.

If he went to the Spanish police right now, he would have to explain that the painting had initially been stolen, and his reputation as an art detective would be in ruins. He'd be crucified by Anthony Hughes, sued by the Marquès de Guíxols, and he'd probably never work again.

He also wondered what information he could give the Spanish police that they didn't already have. He'd seen the body but not the murder. He had no idea that the corpse was the bullfighter's chauffeur, but the police had already deduced all that. True, he believed he'd seen the killer, he'd been attacked by him twice himself, but he was also sure he could track him down before the police. The van he'd seen screeching away from the service station was almost certainly linked to the kidnappers, and if he could recall the word on it then he'd find the bastards sooner than the police …

So, that's what he resolved to do. Now the painting was safe, he'd find the killer and the kidnappers himself. And he'd find the bullfighter, the *toreador*, too.

Because that's what he does. He helps the police solve crime.

'What else did you see?' Elena was still asking. 'Did you see the kidnapping?'

'No.'

'Did you see who attacked you?'

'It was that psycho in the red hoodie, I told you. I remember the pattern on his trainers. He'd been kicking me.'

'Kicking you?'

Benjamin was still squinting. 'When I was down,' he said. 'And there was something else …'

'What was it?'

'I'm trying to remember. I need to focus …'

Elena started writing notes on her phone, irritated that he hadn't explained why he was at the service station in a hire car at the time, or where he'd been beforehand. And the hostel? She was still suspicious that he knew the thug. Something didn't add up.

'*No, turn left,*' she suddenly said, having to divert her attention away from her phone to give him directions on where to drive.

Her arm brushed against his as she gestured at him to take a left at some traffic lights. She could sense him glancing at her.

'Just follow the Sat-Nav,' she said.

Before long, she was back reading the news feed on Twitter. As for any reports about the climate change conference, forget it. It seemed the world's media had adopted a collective obsession not just with the murder and kidnap story, but the so-called bullfighting 'debate'.

What debate?

As far as Elena was concerned, there was no debate. Some claimed that when Catalonia banned bullfighting, it was just an anti-Spain and anti-Madrid action. Well, Elena wasn't Catalan, nor was she a Madrileña. Her family came from Andalusia, a stronghold for bullfighting, but she still believed there was no debate. Bullfighting was simply evil.

She felt sorry for the bullfighter's dead driver and his family, but she was finding it hard to have any sympathy for the kidnap victim himself. Reporting on it, however, she would have to be neutral and balanced. Some jerk had once told her that she could never become a reporter because she was *unbalanced*. Unbalanced? The bastard.

'*Qué cabrón,*' she muttered to herself.

'What?' said Benjamin.

'*Nada* … it's just what they're writing about bullfighting …' Anger had crept into her voice.

'Is it still popular?' asked Benjamin.

'Is what still popular?'

'Bullfighting. I thought it was a dying sport −'

'It's not a sport,' she snapped.

'I understand that. I didn't mean *sport* sport. They never call foxhunting a sport, either. It's a *blood* sport −'

'Bullfighting's not a sport or blood sport, okay?'

'Okay.'

Benjamin didn't want to get into a debate with her about bullfighting, but he also didn't want her to think that he approved of it.

'Look, I'm not −' he began.

'Don't say the word *sport*.'

'I'm not going to say that word. I'd never go to a

bullfight, but I guess it's given a lot to Spanish culture in the form of art, literature, opera, ballet, flamenco –'

'Are you mad?'

'– and, you know, Goya, Dalí, Miró, Picasso, even Vincent van Gogh, they all painted the bullfight –'

'You're saying that because Picasso painted the bullfight, bullfighting should be allowed to continue?'

'*No*,' said Benjamin. 'I'm not saying that. In fact, Picasso only explored the mythology of bulls and bull-fighting because for him, the bullfight was a tragedy –'

'Are you, what do you call it, *mansplaining* to me?'

'In bullfighting Picasso saw a symbol of suffering, grief and rage. The drama of ferocious struggle became a recurring theme in his work –'

'I don't want to know.'

'Fine. But I'm just saying.'

'*I don't want to know.*'

He drove on in silence, while she went back to writing notes on her phone. Soon afterwards, he was trying to find a parking space in the visitors' car park of MNAC. His head was throbbing, and he was begin-ning to feel dizzy. Images had started taunting him again, the disfigured corpse, a missing bullfighter, the *Toreador* painting, the fabric he'd seen on the ground, that word on the side of a van that had sped away – which is when he found a parking space only to find it half-occupied by a tiny Smart car.

'Bugger,' he said. Then: '*Bugaderia*,' he added, instinctively.

'*Cómo?*' said Elena.

'*Bugaderia* … what does it mean? What's *bugaderia* mean?'

The engine was still running. Elena shrugged, started touching her clothes, rubbing them …

'Gorgeous?' said Benjamin.

'*Qué?*'

'Clothes?'

'*Sí* … clothes.'

'Fashion?'

'No … clothes … washing.'

'Washing clothes?'

'Yes.'

'You mean laundry?'

'Probably, yes.'

'So, a van with *bugaderia* on its side … a laundry van, right?'

'Yes,' said Elena. 'Why?'

Benjamin stared at her in silence for ten seconds, then he jumped out of the taxi, leaving its engine running, and ran up to the office reception of MNAC, where the female guard was still at the front desk, giving him another odd look. He asked to see Pedro Pardina again.

Moments later, an assistant from Pedro's department came down, and handed Benjamin the portfolio case with the painting, and a memory stick wrapped inside a compliment slip from Pedro, on which was written: 'Nothing visible.'

Then Benjamin was out the front again, running towards the car park, with the word '*bugaderia*' still pounding his brain. As he approached the taxi, he saw that Elena was now in the driving seat, with the engine still on, and she appeared to nervously hide her phone as he climbed into the seat next to her. It looked like she'd been about to reverse the vehicle to leave. He propped the portfolio case on the floor in the back, alongside his backpack on the back seat. He asked her if she was okay to drive and she nodded, and so he said let's go and she asked *where* and he said back to the first place we saw my car, near the station, and she said are you crazy and he said no and she said you *are* crazy and he said no, no, no, I am *not* crazy, Elena …

She drove in silence, discreetly checking her phone for messages. She took them back to the area around Sants railway station first, and then past the Hotel Victòria, near where Benjamin had seen his car on the kerb – outside the goods delivery entrance of the hotel. Traffic cops were still everywhere, so they weren't allowed to stop. Not that Benjamin needed her to. He saw what he was looking for, and it was just as he recalled. The hotel looked like it was part of a chain, a group called *IB*, and if he was right, the second hotel where they'd followed the thug to, and where they'd first had a fight, was part of the same chain.

It was.

Very soon they were back there, near the Plaça de la Concòrdia. The abandoned hire car had been towed away, the area was back to normal, and he told her to park up for a few minutes. He wanted to ask a few questions at the IB Hotel Concòrdia. He grabbed his backpack and got out of the taxi, thinking he might even be able to reserve a room there or pick up something to eat as he prepared to stroll across.

'What are you doing?' asked Elena.

'I'll explain,' he said, standing on the pavement. But then when he turned to face her, she was taking another photo of him. 'Don't, please –' he said.

'Don't you like having your own photo taken? Why did you ask me to take a photo of the thug?'

'Elena –'

'*Why are you here?*' she shouted.

'Jesus Christ,' he said. 'Do you have anger issues or something?'

'*Qué?*'

'I mean, all you've done is shout at me. I just need a taxi driver to –'

'*I'm not a taxi driver, I told you. Why are you here?*'

'Because this is where the maniac had been hanging around, possibly for –'

'*But he's not here,*' she yelled.

'*But I'm going to find him, Elena,*' he also finally shouted. '*For fucksake.*'

Silence. They glared at one another.

'I'll find him first,' she then said, suddenly revving the engine before accelerating away.

'No, wait,' he said, but it was too late.

She'd driven off … and with the painting in the back.

31

Jürgen and Hendrik

Monday 4 June, 11am – El Poblenou neighbourhood, Barcelona.

From a squat in The Hague, via a commune in Utrecht, and then a campsite within a derelict factory on the outskirts of Barcelona, Jürgen had initially been happy to meet and hang out with a fellow Dutchman, Hendrik, when he'd first arrived in the city.

They had a lot in common. They both had temporary jobs driving for a group in Barcelona, linked to a Dutch conglomerate. It was seasonal work for the summer months. Neither spoke much Spanish, but their fluency in Dutch and English was useful for the group whose clientele included many establishments catering for tourists and business travellers.

Hendrik, with his Mohican-mullet haircut matching his long, narrow face, was a member of

Extinction Rebellion back in the Netherlands, a movement that used non-violent civil disobedience to seek social reform. Jürgen, meanwhile, had joined protests for Animal Rebellion, an animal and climate justice movement pushing for a plant-based future worldwide.

Jürgen had gone for the seasonal job in Barcelona to escape a failed relationship back in Utrecht, and because a contact in Amsterdam had said he could earn extra cash from a stunt being planned to coincide with the G20. Having concluded that the whole livestock industry was at fault for its contribution to greenhouse gases, Jürgen believed that the planet had to stop eating meat. Arriving in Barcelona, he felt respect for Catalonia having banned bullfighting over a decade ago, but it shocked him to learn that towns still held bull-running events – and it sickened him to discover the extent of bullfighting still taking place across Spain and in parts of southern France.

While in Barcelona, he resolved to join the crusade to stop bullfighting elsewhere by joining an offshoot rebellion group, believing that it carried out non-violent direct action. Thanks to his contact back in Amsterdam, he was then recruited to participate in the Nîmes mission. He had no idea that the group had been infiltrated with ruthless extremists linked to animal front terror organisations, who also hired the likes of Séverin ... and Hendrik.

Ever since they both met Séverin to finalise the plans, Jürgen had seen Hendrik undergo a personality change. He'd become unpredictable and threatening, and his blank stares in the middle of any conversation were unnerving. Recently, he'd been muttering about chemical detergents, and how they could remove any stain or 'sinner' known to man. He'd been listening too much to Séverin and snorting the same powder.

Jürgen was in trouble. He was in serious danger.

He'd been naïve to go on the mission. It wasn't enough to have just left Séverin behind at the service station. And it was one thing still having all the cash, but he didn't trust Hendrik – he'd been far too close to the Frenchman. As he reached the depot to remove all evidence of his own involvement, he knew he would have to also remove Hendrik ... but peacefully so.

Yeah ... Hendrik wasn't ... really ... all there ...

He was high.

He was feeling enraged, yet also fucking powerful.

Séverin would forgive him for driving off ... at least he hoped so.

They had a deal ... they'd shared angel dust ... Séverin had become a mate. It was Jürgen who the Frenchman would be chasing.

Hendrik had got the matador in front of him now, bound and gagged, and that was all that mattered.

It had taken longer than expected for the bull-fighter to come round from the needle they'd jabbed into him. When he did finally stir, his breathing was rapid, his eyes red and glazed, and Hendrik was unsure if he could even focus. He was groaning under the gag, opening and closing his eyes, then opening them for good when he finally registered Hendrik sitting opposite, glaring madly and wielding a knife.

'We're gonna cut off your fucking ears,' said Hendrik.

Rafa, the bullfighter, slayer of a thousand bulls, was now as helpless as a trussed lamb. He tried to shout from beneath the gag, wriggling and twisting in the wooden chair he'd been strapped to.

Hendrik spat at him, then rammed his fist hard into his throat. Rafa choked under the gag, and the chair started to topple backwards. Hendrik grabbed him by the collar, pulling him forwards again before waving the knife under his nose.

Rafa writhed, quivering in the chair, watching in horror as Hendrik picked up a jerry can of industrial bleach off the ground, and opened it.

'You thirsty?' he said.

No answer.

'You thirsty?' he said, louder now.

Rafa shook his head.

'*You thirsty? You thirsty?*' he yelled … until Jürgen kicked open the door.

32

Jaume, Marquès de Guíxols

Monday 4 June, 12.30pm – Pedralbes to the Port Olímpic, Barcelona.

The thick heat from the midday sun had evolved into a fierce humidity. The air-conditioned Mercedes carrying the Marquès and Marquesa de Guíxols was approaching central Barcelona, heading along the ringroad towards the uptown *zona alta*, the name for a series of smart neighbourhoods including Sarrià, Pedralbes and El Putxet, stretching out across the lower reaches of the Collserola hills. Gazing out the back window, Jaume could see police helicopters above the hills, keeping a G20 eye on the city's telecommunications infrastructure.

What could still be termed the Guíxols home in Barcelona, before any imminent visit from the bailiffs, was in the Carrer de Monestir, in the heart of

Pedralbes. Jaume always quipped that it was a white stone's throw from the Pedralbes monastery itself. White, because Pedralbes stemmed from the Latin *pedras albas* – white stones.

Hurl another white stone and you'd hit the nearby Royal Tennis Club, where Jaume's father had been a former president in the good old days. Even nearer was the United States Consulate, where helicopters were landing and taking off from its lawns, with dignitaries toing and froing from the US HQ in the Port Olímpic.

Unlike Jaume's other disgruntled staff, his elderly driver, who nowadays was paid in cash whenever there was any cash, was simply happy to still be allowed to drive. They'd been warned that traffic might be heavy from roadblocks on the approach to this affluent corner of the city, but they'd encountered just one security check. A quick look at the vehicle's residential badge meant they were swiftly waved through, then on towards the ornate gateway to the Guíxols' mansion – possibly soon to be expropriated.

After dropping Montse off at home, in time for her appointments with wedding caterers, florists and then her pedicurist, manicurist and spray-tan guru, Jaume had put on a clean shirt, tie and sports-jacket, before setting off with his driver yet again.

He had agreed to Lisette Dijckhuijsen's demand to meet up at the new restaurant in the Hotel Arts, where she was involved with the PR, and to clarify matters once and for all about their brief affair. A wine connoisseur by nature (if only he had the funds to sustain it), Jaume had also been pestered by the hotel manager to visit the new restaurant, even though it would mean a trek back across the city from Pedralbes to the Port Olímpic. Besides, he had to keep up appearances; it was all he had left.

He was grateful to still be on Barcelona's VIP invitation lists that included the so-called elite public figures from Catalan society, such as ... well, such as himself. Those who compiled the lists, the PR-mafia in the city, were still unaware of his precarious financial situation, or the fact that his name was still included in the banking corruption investigation. He simply had to enjoy the taste of freedom while it was still possible. As for the Dalí painting and authentication certificate, the PhD-qualified art specialist, Doctor Benjamin, could simply deliver it all to him at the hotel.

Once Jaume's driver had made it over to the port, they encountered a security checkpoint of concrete blocks and armoured SWAT trucks, some two hundred metres from the hotel.

A quick check by Mossos agents, with Jaume leaning out of the Merc to explain that he'd been personally invited by the manager – and the radioing through to confirm soon turned into apologies. After sniffer dogs circled the car, the vehicle's windscreen was slapped with a sticker allowing it to park adjacent to the port. From there, it was a short stroll to the hotel's front entrance security check, visible to a swarm of curious locals and tourists lining the harbourside. Across the hotel's concourse, a pool of official G20 photographers and TV crews kept their focus on the comings and goings of the hotel's guests and conference delegates.

Once inside, the Marquès was stopped by security, and his phone and empty wallet put through an X-ray. He was saved from any pat-down because the hotel's guest liaison manager was also there to receive him, greeting him gushingly before guiding him out to the terrace restaurant, overlooking the pool and Mediterranean. The only reminder that it was G20 week came in the shape of numerous burly agents, all mumbling into invisible mics with wireless earpieces, but all failing to look inconspicuous with their dark suits, shades and essential buzz cuts.

'My apologies but security is beyond maximum,' enthused the guest liaison manager, almost bowing in front of Jaume as he guided him along. 'It's an honour to have you here with us today. Come and enjoy a glass of our special G20 vintage champagne. I believe the Señora Dijckhuijsen is waiting for you …'

33

Benjamin

Monday 4 June, 11.45am – Plaça de la Concòrdia, Les Corts district, Barcelona.

Benjamin sprinted down the road in pursuit of Elena and her taxi, but it was impossible. Seeing the vehicle turn right in the distance, he dashed down an adjacent street to see if he could keep track of it, but it had already disappeared. He then ran back to wait on the pavement outside the IB Hotel Concòrdia again, cursing her, but at the same time praying she might have just been fooling around, and that she'd soon return after driving around the block.

But she didn't.

He waited five minutes … but she never returned.

'*Fuck.*'

He still had her 'Carmona Taxis' card in his pocket, so he rushed into the hotel to explain he was in a spot of bother – no, actually, it was a *fucking emergency* – and he needed to make a call, waving the card at the girl behind the reception desk.

She took the card and dialled, but eventually shrugged, saying that nobody was answering the phone. Seeing that the card was for a taxi service, she told Benjamin that if he needed a taxi, she could call him one – any taxi – to go anywhere he wanted.

Benjamin could feel the memory-stick from the MNAC museum in his pocket and considered his options. What did he have? A psychopath, possibly the killer, presumably involved with the kidnapping, who'd been eyeing the goods delivery entrance of two IB hotels. He glanced at one of the leaflets on the reception desk; it said they had a hundred hotels across Spain, including an 'IB Collection' chain.

What else did he have? He'd seen that '*bugaderia*' word on a van leaving the service station, just before he was attacked, around midnight. Was the timing significant? He hadn't a clue, but he'd told Elena that he'd find the thug and he would ... even if she said she'd find him first ...

What he didn't have was the fucking painting.

He suddenly remembered using Elena's cell phone earlier, when he'd called the Marquès. With luck, her number would still be logged on the aristocrat's phone.

'Yes – yes, thanks,' he said to the receptionist. 'I need to get to the Hotel Arts.'

Five minutes later he was on his way ...

34

Inspector Vizcaya, Beltrán Gómez, Lieutenant Trias and Officer Soler

Monday 4 June, 12.15pm – Mossos Comissaria, Les Corts district, Barcelona.

Inspector Vizcaya was not a happy man. He never really was, but the pressure was already starting to get on top of him and he didn't like it. It didn't help that social media was buzzing with theories about the murder, the kidnapping, and the gang's ultimatum: that if any more bullfights went ahead in Spain that evening, they'd be cutting off Rafa's ears and causing mayhem in Barcelona during the G20.

Each media report was more critical of the authorities, trying to be one step ahead of the investigation team, yet at the same time demanding official updates and more press briefings, as if the police had the obligation to solve all crimes live on Twitter, in 'real time'.

Vizcaya hated social media and he wasn't used to

such pressure. His speciality was kidnap negotiation, which took time, patience and secrecy. This was different, with the G20 about to start and government ministers breathing down his neck, as well as the counter-terrorism agency in the slimy shape of Beltrán Gómez de Longoria.

With the tabloid media having a field day about the kidnapped bullfighter, the Spanish police were also grappling with several anti-G20 protests across the country, yet with their resources already stretched.

In addition to activists rioting against runway expansion plans at European airports, 'art attacks' had also been carried out at museums in Paris, Rome, Berlin, London and The Hague – and the first attack in Spain had now taken place at the Prado Museum in Madrid. The acts of vandalism across Europe had seen protesters gluing themselves to the frames of famous paintings, after pouring fake blood or tomato soup over the protective glass. In Madrid they'd used gazpacho.

Vizcaya couldn't quite comprehend why eco-activists would glue themselves to the frames of two Goya paintings to raise awareness about the need to save the planet, but he was certain it was unrelated to the kidnap and murder case he was handling, which centred on an animal liberation demand.

The paranoid Beltrán from CITCO, however, who called them eco-*terrorists* and not activists, was already searching for a connection with events in Barcelona, using his top-notch, super-sized smartphone that he thought put Vizcaya's old model to shame.

They were both now in a meeting at the incident room with Lieutenant Trias and several Mossos agents, while a screen on the wall displayed various images: the bullfighter's abandoned Chevrolet; the dead chauffeur; Rafael Pérez being lifted out of the bullring; his clothing and 'suit of lights', as well as CCTV images from the service station and tollgates. Vizcaya was also waiting for Marta Soler to re-join them. He wanted an update on the vehicle hired from Girona airport yesterday evening, paid for in cash by a Brandon Bartholomew.

The atmosphere was tense, since Vizcaya had relayed Bosch's instructions to the team to make an arrest by 6.30pm, before the start of the Valencia bullfight in which Rafa would have participated, and before the start of the evening's G20 royal reception.

Trias explained that the examination of the Chevrolet, the chauffeur's clothes, shoes, fingernails, hair, the gag and electrical cord used to bind him, as well as footprints and tyre marks in the vicinity of where the vehicle had been abandoned, was well underway – but it was all going to take time.

Updates from Nîmes confirmed that the bullfighter's entourage had identified nothing unusual in the images of fans carrying Rafa out of the amphitheatre – in that most were regular *aficionados*.

Due to the blacked-out windows on the Chevrolet, combined with chaotic crowd movement and reflections from flash photography, no clear images had emerged of the suspect driver, other than a baseball cap and dark glasses. His hands gripping the steering wheel were also gloved, so any prints would be scarce, if there were any at all.

It was on the side of the vehicle, however, just when the sliding door of the Chevrolet had been opened and Rafa pushed inside, where it had been confirmed that a figure in a red hoodie could be seen – coinciding with what members of the entourage had witnessed. There was no face, no clear shot of the figure, it was just someone in the back of the vehicle opening and then slamming shut the sliding door. There was even the glint of something that shone in their hand, possibly a knife. It was enough; they had a suspect in a red hoodie, and it was a clothing fibre they were also searching the Chevrolet for.

As for the bistro in Nîmes that the chauffeur had visited during the bullfight, the French police had discovered it was a stroll from where he'd probably parked the Chevrolet – but there were no CCTV images of the vehicle parked nearby. He'd had a tapa and cognac, which would be confirmed by the autopsy, as well as any sleeping pills in his bloodstream.

The bistro's staff recalled that he was alone, and that he'd left soon after 7.30pm. So, unless the figure in the red hoodie had been hiding in the Chevrolet all day long, it was while the chauffeur had been at the bistro that his vehicle had been broken into, or he was attacked while returning to it.

Each member of the entourage had given finger-prints and root hair strands for DNA testing, if only to corroborate their statements of who travelled in the Chevrolet from time to time or had any access to it. But then matters became more complex …

'The Chevrolet is covered with blood spots and hair strands,' Trias said. 'Both human and animal … they're everywhere.'

Vizcaya rolled his eyes. If forensics had to eliminate each strand of animal hair to find what human hair was also in the vehicle, it was going to take forever – and the more types of hair recovered, the less value as evidence in a criminal investigation. It was a minefield, and he now feared that the blood spots might be equally hard to analyse.

How many bleeding bulls had Rafa brushed up against or killed in the last year? How much blood had dripped onto the vehicle's seats or floor, either bull's blood or from his own wounds? Too much, it seemed … which brought them back to the hire car from Girona airport, just as Marta Soler rushed back in.

'Brandon Bartholomew,' she said, flicking through her notes. 'We now have a copy of his British driving licence from Goldcar rentals, and we're checking passenger lists on flights that arrived prior to the rental time. As we know, the hire car was paid for in cash. A swiped credit card taken to cover excess insurance gives the cardholder's name simply as ALC Inc, but which was later confirmed to be a void card.'

'ALC?' said Vizcaya.

'We're searching European company registrations for anything resembling ALC linked to the name of

Bartholomew,' continued Soler. 'So far, there's nothing. CCTV at Girona airport doesn't cover the Goldcar rental desk, but we're scanning other video surveillance, including passport control. The London address on the driving licence is false, *and* – for now, at least – neither the British police nor Interpol have come forward with further information.'

'Why?' spat Vizcaya.

Soler shrugged and moved swiftly across to the other side of the incident room, where she started to sift through a pile of reports with other agents.

Vizcaya thumped a desk. He looked up to see if Beltrán might answer him, but he was now on his phone, while busy checking that his hair was still greased flat and to perfection with his other hand.

'Because they've fucked up?' he yelled. 'Because an extremist from ALC has slipped through Interpol's net? It doesn't surprise me. ALC? What is that, anyway? Animal Liberation *what* ... Corps? Coalition? Cell?'

Suddenly the door of the incident room burst open.

'They've found the vehicle,' called out an agent from the special operations division. 'It was abandoned in Les Corts this morning, its rear window smashed, and it was taken to the compound.'

'Let's go,' said Vizcaya, halfway out the door.

But Beltrán stayed put and continued his call, while Soler's attention had suddenly been diverted to a computer screen and a message with new images to analyse.

35

Jürgen and Hendrik

Monday 4 June, 11.30am – El Poblenou neighbourhood, Barcelona.

It happened quickly, in the end. He didn't really have much time to think it all through. On reflection, he probably would have done things slightly differently, but the panic churning inside was far too intense at the time.

Jürgen had always considered himself a pacifist. He only wanted to save the planet. He'd never really hit anyone before, not properly, let alone half-kill them.

Once he'd made it back to the *barrio* of Poblenou, confident that he hadn't been followed, he walked across the adjoining aparthotel's forecourt, then on towards the depot's storerooms where he'd agreed Hendrik could hold the hostage for up to forty-eight hours.

As he reached the loading bay, he heard a noise like a cat screaming. It was faint, it was eerie, but he soon realised it was someone yelling. He knew how to get through to the sealed off area, the cellar, because Hendrik had once shown him – it was just below the loading bay. Hendrik had told him how he'd once spent two nights in one of the spare storerooms when he'd been kicked out of a hostel for lack of funds. As Jürgen made his way along the narrow corridor, the yelling was getting louder and louder … it was Hendrik yelling.

Jürgen grabbed a wooden pole as he kicked open the cellar door, only to see Hendrik waving an open can of bleach in the face of their hostage tied to a chair, while screaming, '*You thirsty? We'll cut off your fucking ears.*' It was the last thing he would say for a long time, because he turned to face Jürgen at precisely the moment he swung the pole hard – *really* hard against Hendrik's jaw – which split open, blood spouting now, teeth slamming against tongue, and the bleach splashing up into his face and eyes as he screamed in agony …

The effect of just a drop of sodium hypochlorite, liquid bleach, on the eyeball, can be excruciating. Poured all over the eyes, however, and it's utter hell. As Hendrik fell backwards, the jerry can of bleach then fell onto his chest, tipped sideways, and the liquid simply spurted out all over his face and into his eyes, and it kept on spurting. The pain was so severe, he was in utter agony, writhing and yelping, but he couldn't see Jürgen or the bound and gagged bullfighter, Rafa, watching him in a state of shock and relief.

He couldn't see Jürgen kick the jerry can away from his chest, either, or pick up his knife to force Rafa, under threat, out of the cellar – nor could he see or hear Jürgen use his cell phone to make a rapid call to security, reporting an accident.

Later, once the depot's security guard had finally arrived to find Hendrik alone, semi-conscious, and trying to crawl out towards the loading area in search of water to wash out his eyes, he was in relatively good hands.

An ambulance team arrived and rushed him to Barcelona's Hospital Laforja for emergency treatment, consisting of washing the eyes with saline solution and administering analgesic and anti-inflammatories. A demulcent agent and hydroxypropyl medication were applied to the eyes' conjunctiva, which were then bandaged for twenty-four hours while he remained in hospital.

36

Mitch Gibson, US State Department Spokesman

Monday 4 June, 12.15pm – Port Olímpic, Barcelona.

A former Princeton University boxer, stocky, intense, with thinning hair and a deep stare from small brown eyes, 'muscles' Mitch Gibson, the US State Department's spokesman, took in the panoramic views of Barcelona and the Mediterranean Sea from a conference room on the forty-second floor of the Hotel Arts. Earlier, he'd held a G20 brunch briefing and planning session with senior staff from the US delegation, but he was still in a tetchy mood.

The top three floors of the hotel had been transformed into the US HQ for G20 week, the culmination of the White House Advance Office carrying out site survey missions for the past three months. Mitch himself had arrived in Barcelona yesterday evening with his boss, Secretary of State Chuck Patterson Jr., together with his wife Pamela Patterson, and all their staff. The President himself was scheduled to arrive tomorrow afternoon.

The advance team had spent weeks looking at every possible venue that might become a stopping point for the presidential party. They'd taken shots of each potential storyboard, the background scene that might frame the President as he spoke, focusing on what might be a mediagenic image, but at the same time acceptable to the security experts.

Military office staff had worked out arrangements for Air Force One and the Marine One helicopters at Barcelona airport, as well as holding rooms for the White House communications gear. The medical unit had ensured that a supply of the President's blood type would be placed in each major Barcelona hospital, while the Secret Service had reviewed all motorcade routes, vetoing those deemed too vulnerable.

The hotel advance group had scrutinised the public and non-public routes that both the President and Secretary of State might take within and around the building, and then drawn detailed diagrams for the presidential footsteps. As the veteran Secretary Patterson still liked to jog, the surrounding area of the Olympic port and Parc de la Ciutadella had also been mapped out for possible kidnap or sniper threats.

'Jeeeez,' sighed Mitch, taking in the views, on his own now that everyone had left the conference room.

While Mitch didn't officially speak for the White House, many of the issues that the administration faced had an international focus, and regularly involved Patterson and the State Department. He'd scheduled the earlier meeting as a pre-summit breakfast get-together to gauge the mood in Barcelona, so that nothing blindsided him at press briefings and 'haggles' during the week.

He was irritated because the mood was clearly one big, beefy animal rights debate – a subject that he feared would remain on the table until the kidnapped bullfighter was found, dead or alive. He knew the CIA had offered to help Spain's law enforcement agencies, but they needed to solve things now, right *now*, goddammit.

The kidnap was dominating the headlines and providing fodder for chat shows both sides of the Atlantic. The French President had been asked if he would now ban bullfighting in the South of France. The Italian Prime Minister had been quizzed about bareback horseracing in Siena. Then there were the 'special relationship' Brits being grilled about loopholes in their fox-hunting ban ...

As for the USA, they'd been grouped with any other nation that permitted animal testing, fur farms, zoos and circuses – but the fact that they also ate half the world's meat together with the Chinese seemed to put the two countries to shame on a par with their combined CO_2 emissions and responsibility for global warming.

For 'muscles Mitch', the right to eat three burgers a day was as much an American right as driving an SUV and carrying a firearm. He was all prepared with briefings and speeches on almost every other issue that existed, from the planet's green energy debate to global fiscal responsibility … international civil rights, human rights, gay rights, transgender rights, foetal rights … *jeez*, Mitch had comments prepared for all the rights you'd ever need, other than friggin' animal rights.

On top of that, he would now have to keep Pamela Patterson's presence here in Barcelona under control. It was enough having the outspoken environmentalist speaking at the climate change conference and heading up the G20 spouse programme, also referred to as the first wives' club. He now had to minimise any references to her former patronage of the US Humane Society and past aggressive lobbying for animal welfare issues. He couldn't afford to have Pamela making stray remarks, going 'off-message', or ranting to journalists about goddamned bullfighting.

There was no way he could allow her to take the spotlight away from her husband, not with his post-summit retirement imminent, and his plans to hit the circuit of Manhattan and Hollywood fundraisers with the launch of the Patterson Foundation, a multimillion-dollar global foundation, just like any other ex-statesman …

He checked his watch. His boss would be off for a jog now. It was the only time Mitch had to himself.

37

Elena

Elena had no idea that Benjamin's portfolio case with the painting was still in the back of the taxi when she drove off − not that it would have stopped her from doing so.

Maybe she shouldn't have left him stranded on the pavement, but she still had her suspicions about him, and if he really was a *policía* then he could handle himself.

She'd taken photos of him, she'd recorded him − and he'd confirmed that he'd been at the service station around midnight when the maniac in the red hood had attacked him and stolen his hire car. He'd even recalled the pattern on the thug's trainers as he was being kicked.

But Elena knew where the thug had gone, or at least the last place she'd seen him go, and it wasn't where Benjamin had asked her to stop.

No, she'd seen him heading into the hostel Splendido where Benjamin had supposedly had a reservation. So that's where she was heading, that's where her story, her report, her *instinct* was leading her. The dilapidated building could be where the bullfighter was being held hostage. And if she uncovered that, then she'd have the scoop of a lifetime …

38

Inspector Vizcaya

Monday 4 June, 1pm – Parc de Joan Miró, Barcelona.

Inspector Vizcaya paced around the hire car in the municipal compound, taking in the smashed back left window. There was nothing in the boot, but a forensics team had been summoned after agents had found a hammer on the back seat. There were blood spots and strands of hair on the handle of the hammer, something to test for a match against the DNA of the dead chauffeur and the missing bullfighter.

Vizcaya knew that the matador was slight, light and short – five foot one, if that – so he could have been bundled onto the back seat easily enough, even if there was no visible evidence of stains or smears from the bloodstained costume. He could have been drugged and covered with a sack, or perhaps he'd tried to kick his way free – which could explain the smashed glass –

and forensics would check for any traces of fabric to match to the 'suit of lights'.

He'd also get them to search for anything else that could link the hire car to the abandoned Chevrolet. Fingerprint analysis would take time, though, and hire cars were complex to check. If the rental company hadn't polished the interior after each client, there could be dozens of prints all over it.

After they'd received a report on where the car had been abandoned in the district of Les Corts, Vizcaya had ordered a search of nearby premises and for any eyewitness accounts. Reports had already come back of a scuffle near to where the car had been abandoned, as well as a motorbike stolen, although little else.

However, they did have a suspect – the man who'd hired the car. It was something to report back to Isabel Bosch, if the shifty Beltrán hadn't already done so, while also taking the credit. The vehicle had been involved in some kind of attack – the smashed glass and bloody hammer proved that. It was also the vehicle in which the dead chauffeur's credit card had been used at two tollgates between Girona and Barcelona. It had been hired with false or forged documentation. It was enough to bring Brandon Bartholomew in for questioning ... if they could find him.

After he inspected the car, Vizcaya ordered for it to be sealed until the forensics team arrived. It meant that no one found the battery-drained iPhone under the front passenger seat for two hours, or the toll ticket tucked in the sun-visor.

39

Benjamin, Jaume and Lisette Dijckhuijsen

Monday 4 June, 1pm – Port Olímpic, Barcelona.

What with last night's attack and losing the painting again, Benjamin's blood was up and he was now ravenous. With his head still pounding, he made it to the Hotel Arts just in time for his meeting with the Marquès de Guíxols, without any idea why Elena had driven off, other than her saying that she'd find the thug first. *Where was she?* Earlier, he'd called the Marquès using her phone. He now had to locate her number to retrieve the canvas again, before delivering on what he'd resolved to do … track down the killers and kidnappers himself.

Roadblocks meant that his new taxi driver had to pull up a good distance from the hotel, across the other side of the port, leaving Benjamin to complete the journey on foot. Fifty metres from the hotel's main entrance, he was stopped by security and told he couldn't enter the hotel lobby. He said he had an appointment at a restaurant adjoined to the hotel, and was ordered along to another checkpoint, complete with an airport-style X-ray scanner.

A security guard ordered Benjamin to put his jacket and any keys, coins or phone on a tray to go through the scanner, as well as his small backpack. All was fine, but then the bag wasn't handed back.

'*Consigna,*' said the guard. 'The bag must stay in the luggage lockers.'

'Okay, hang on …'

After Benjamin had taken his wallet, passport and some notes out of the bag, the guard put it in one of the rows of lockers outside the hotel, before handing a plastic token back to him. Then he was free to head up some steps and across to the terrace area of the restaurant, overlooking the hotel's swimming pool.

He stopped dead once he caught sight of the Marquès, who was standing and sipping champagne. Benjamin wondered what else he did all day. This time there was no sign of his wife, but he looked uncomfortable, Benjamin thought, alongside a tall, curvaceous blonde, mid-thirties, possibly half Jaume's age.

Benjamin took in the red stilettos and Louis Vuitton handbag. She looked identical to others he'd encountered on the periphery of the art world, all with their permanent tans, bleached-white teeth, all trying to get close to the private collectors. If she was after Jaume's money, however, she'd be disappointed.

Benjamin doubted he had much, judging by his disillusioned staff and urgency to sell what he hoped was a Dalí. In those brief seconds he caught sight of them both, he quickly figured she was Jaume's mistress, or at least a romantic complication.

As he hurried towards them, anxious to check Jaume's phone, the aristocrat also noticed Benjamin and moved towards him – with his eyes searching from side to side as if looking for the painting. He was next to him now, pulling him to one side, and then they were standing in a passageway that led out to the terrace, while waiters had to squeeze past, carrying trays of drinks and canapés.

'Jaume –' started Benjamin, so hungry that he instinctively helped himself to a canapé from one of the waiter's trays, and then stuffed it into his mouth.

'Where's my painting and certificate?' snapped the Marquès.

'I couldn't bring the painting *in* here,' said Benjamin, with his mouth full. He felt the token for his backpack in his pocket, alongside the MNAC memory stick. He felt chuffed about his quick reply. It seemed to briefly placate Jaume, too … but then the blonde was also approaching.

'Jaume,' she called out, before she was immediately upon them, stopping a passing waiter to hand over two flutes of champagne to them both, and already introducing herself to Benjamin with, 'I'm Lisette Dijckhuijsen, but call me Dixie. And you are?'

With his mouth still half-full, Benjamin watched as

call-me-Dixie held out her hand.

'Lisette … Dixie, dear … if you'll just excuse us,' said Jaume, with one of his momentary fixed grins.

She had no intention of doing that. Benjamin was about to shake her hand, but she pushed her botoxed top lip forward to give him two air-kisses instead. There followed an awkward silence while she eyed him curiously: his bruised, dishevelled state and wild hair.

She seemed to be involved with the restaurant, simply clicking her fingers to get the waiters to arrange a fresh table for them, to bring more champagne and some shiny black olives. Benjamin tried to work out if she was Dutch, Danish, French or German, certainly not Spanish – while she continued to size him up as if he might be worth something.

Did Benjamin look as if he was worth something? No. And now he just longed to be with Elena again. *Where the hell had she gone?*

'What a morning, I must look absolutely exhausted,' were the next words call-me-Dixie said to Benjamin, after the air-kissing. She then perched on a nearby stool, crossed her legs, leant back, stared at him, and waited for him to contradict her.

He didn't. Instead, he asked to use Jaume's phone.

'I beg your pardon?' said the old aristocrat.

'I called you earlier,' said Benjamin. 'I need to see the number I called you from. It's urgent. Later, I'll explain …'

Jaume pulled out his phone, as Benjamin snatched another canapé from a passing waiter.

40

Chuck Patterson Jr.

Monday 4 June, 12.45pm – Parc de la Ciutadella, Barcelona.

Just a mile from the Hotel Arts and with his tracksuit sodden with sweat from the intense humidity, Chuck Patterson Jr., the seventy-four-year-old US Secretary of State, was jogging painfully slowly in the Parc de la Ciutadella, which encompassed Barcelona Zoo and the Catalan Parliament.

A tall man with short, Brillo-pad hair and a long, corrugated neck, he was accompanied by a large group of security aides walking quickly alongside, followed by a posse of press photographers. He puffed and panted as he tried to chat to an aide striding alongside.

'Beautiful … park … huh?'

'Sure is,' said the aide. 'And great fountains.'

'*Fuck*,' barked Patterson, suddenly stopping and clasping his chest.

41

Inspector Vizcaya, Beltrán Gómez and Marcos Constantinos

Monday 4 June, 1.45pm – Mossos Comissaria, Les Corts district, Barcelona.

'Findings show that the cell number used to trigger the robocalls to the media is a unique configuration number, issued to a new brand of phones that have limited numbers and life,' said Beltrán. 'It appears to be an internationally coordinated attack, and not one that was masterminded from within Spain.'

'Is that it?' asked Vizcaya.

'Is that what?' said Beltrán.

Immediately after inspecting the hire car at the municipal compound, Vizcaya had returned to the incident room for further updates. He'd been hoping for some news about their suspect – the Brandon Bartholomew who'd hired the car in which the dead chauffeur's credit card had been used at two tollgates between Girona and Barcelona. Thanks to help from his 'CIA friends', young Beltrán had instead started to give his analysis of the calls made to the media. Annoyingly, he was also still answering every other question from Vizcaya with another question.

'Is that all you've got?' said Vizcaya.

'No,' said Beltrán. 'We believe the SIM and cell phone used to trigger the robocalls were not purchased in Spain. We've also run checks on international data and found a recurring code that matches cell phone data from yesterday's European airport expansion protests on the eve of the G20.'

'So, it could be a coordinated attack by the usual G20 green activists after all,' said Vizcaya.

'Could it?' said Beltrán. 'Or something more specific. The cell number used in central Barcelona to send automated calls to the media this morning was also used for the first time to make a call to a London number on Sunday afternoon, from southern France. Crucially, the number it called was also logged on various cell phones from airport expansion activists arrested during yesterday's protest at London Gatwick.'

'What number received calls from the same cell?' asked Vizcaya. 'Are you on to it?'

'Are we?' said Beltrán. 'Not only are we on to it, we've found it's a number registered to *Cell Conscience*, a foundation run by tycoon Marcos Constantinos.'

'Who?'

'Constantinos runs a law collective providing a legal defence fund for green protesters who end up in court,' said Beltrán, referring to his notes. 'In the past year, he's spent a fortune backing hundreds of enterprises ranging from anti-capitalist websites to a guerrilla gardening movement, whose members descend on derelict urban spaces to cultivate them, as well as Plane Crazy, which campaigns against airport expansion.'

'Plane Crazy?'

'Correct. Constantinos is passionate about non-violent direct action. He feels that people who get involved in direct action put themselves at risk to look after others, and he likes to help them.'

Vizcaya was getting impatient.

'What has this got to do with my, *our* kidnap and homicide investigation?' he said.

'You mean terrorism investigation?' said Beltrán, checking his hair was still immaculately slicked-back again.

'Look –'

'Plane Crazy activists broke into Gatwick airport yesterday and delayed thousands of passengers by chaining themselves to airline apparatus close to the runway,' said Beltrán. 'When similar protests were held at Heathrow last year, Constantinos paid the legal fees of fifty-six so-called *activists* who were arrested. Yesterday, all protesters arrested at Gatwick asked to make calls through to a cell number registered in the name of his Direct Aid fund. The same cell used to trigger calls to the media to boast about the bullfight kidnap, also made a call to that same number during Sunday … *before* the kidnap.'

'Do you think Constantinos organised it?' asked Vizcaya.

'Do I?' said Beltrán. 'No, I doubt it. He normally insists on peaceful protests. But it's possible the kidnappers, the extremists – *terrorists* – will try to seek support from his law collective. Either way, Scotland Yard officers in London are knocking on his door right now. We're also running checks on all the recent eco-terrorism at airports and museums to see if there's a Barcelona connection –'

Before he could finish, Vizcaya was already barking instructions to Marta Soler, who was in the far corner of the incident room. He wanted information about the passenger lists at Girona airport, and for any news on Brandon Bartholomew ...

In leafy Hampstead, London, the eco-eccentric, goatee-bearded tycoon, Marcos Constantinos, had been catching up on the news in his luxurious, self-sustaining, prefab-pod.

He'd been genuinely shocked to read about the violent death of a driver caught up in the kidnapping of a bullfighter in Spain.

'*Brigitte,*' he called out.

Then his front door had been smashed down by agents from Special Branch, and his foldable, eco-friendly bicycle flattened as armed officers stormed into his home.

42

Benjamin, Jaume, Lisette and Chuck Patterson Jr.

Monday 4 June, 1.30pm – Port Olímpic, Barcelona.

There was no answer from Elena's phone. Benjamin tried again. Still no reply.

He scribbled the number on a paper napkin that he took from a waiter's tray, but then instead of handing the phone back to Jaume, he propped it up on the table that his blonde companion had guided them to, keeping his eyes on the screen for a returned call. He desperately needed to find Elena to retrieve the painting. One way or another, he'd track down the psycho, too – with or without her help.

'Where's the painting?' the Marquès snapped again, as soon as call-me-Dixie's attention was briefly diverted by having to greet other guests, after which she wandered off to apparently 'powder her nose'.

'I told you. I couldn't bring it *in* here,' Benjamin whispered loudly.

'Then where is it?'

'It's safe.'

'Where's the certificate?'

'That will take time, if it warrants one.'

'How long?'

Benjamin decided not to reply.

They sat side by side, with Benjamin still keeping his eye on the phone, and they continued to converse in hushed, urgent tones.

'Are you okay?' said Jaume, peering at Benjamin. He flashed another one of his weird, tic-like grins that quickly vanished.

'I'm sorry?'

'You look ill.'

'Yeah, well, you know …' His voice trailed off.

'Have you been in a fight or something?'

'No,' said Benjamin. 'Well, yes, but I'm fine now. One question: do you trust your housekeeper, Lucia?'

'Yes, of course. Why?'

'No reason.'

'*Why?*'

'Who else knows about us meeting at your home last night?'

'No one, other than Montse and my staff. Why?'

'I just wondered.'

'Look, I need that certificate.'

Benjamin took a deep breath.

'Jaume, I told you it's going to take time –'

'*I don't have time,*' snarled the Marquès.

There was a brief silence.

'I have little time … very little time …' he continued, more softly.

Benjamin gazed at him as he started mumbling to himself in Spanish. He wondered whether he was terminally ill, on the verge of bankruptcy, or possibly both. What was it?

'Jaume,' he started, 'I want to help you, I really do, but I can't carry out further tests on the painting if I don't have …'

He stopped.

'If you don't have what?' said Jaume.

Benjamin had only just managed to avoid saying the word 'it'. The fact that Pedro's infrared examination at MNAC showed nothing visible beneath the surface of the painting didn't necessarily rule anything out. But whether the Marquès would allow Benjamin the time to do a second radiography test, or better still, find a way to use an X-ray fluorescence gun, was another matter. And that was assuming he could even recover the painting from Elena first.

'More information,' said Benjamin. 'To examine the canvas further and determine how it came to be in your cellar, I really need more information.'

Jaume was silent. Benjamin managed to catch the eye of a waiter and then he helped himself to a couple of canapés from his tray. He beckoned Jaume to do the same, but the aristocrat simply waved him away.

'As I said, I want to help you,' said Benjamin,

between bites. 'When I called earlier, I tried to ask you if Dalí might have ever visited your home near La Bisbal.'

'Oh, it's quite possible, yes,' said the Marquès, perking up a little, yet still in a hushed voice. 'In fact, I believe we've uncovered a study for a painting that had eluded my father some fifty years ago.'

'*What?*'

'Keep your voice down.'

'You say it eluded your father … what did? The possible study, you mean?'

'No, *no*. Who knows? Perhaps my father never saw the study we've uncovered. No, he'd wanted to acquire the original masterwork itself.'

'Why didn't you tell me that? Are you serious?'

'Of course,' said Jaume. 'My father died twenty years ago. One painting that had eluded him was the *Toreador.* He privately followed Dalí's work for years, but as far as I know he never acquired anything. Apart from the painting we've uncovered, that is.'

Benjamin was now more than intrigued. He didn't know the Guíxols family had once had an interest in Dalí's original masterwork. As far as he was aware, there'd only ever been one potential owner of *The Hallucinogenic Toreador* – Reynolds Morse, who acquired it over fifty years ago. The price was not public knowledge, although Benjamin knew that it was around \$150,000 – a huge amount of money at the time.

'Jaume, that might change things a bit,' said

Benjamin, trying to gather his thoughts to gain further time.

Deep down, he believed it was virtually impossible that the Marquès had uncovered a genuine Dalí oil study, but the fact that his father had sought to acquire the original masterwork now both excited and worried him, especially as Elena had driven off with the canvas. Of course, if the masterwork *had* eluded his father, it could have also provoked him to commission a copy, a fake, but Benjamin didn't have the heart to suggest this to the aristocrat, who he genuinely wanted to help.

'If you say that Dalí might have visited the property,' he continued, 'then we'll need to ascertain the possible year, date or dates, and I'll need to examine the trunk again –'

'We don't have any *time* –'

'– and we'll need to determine why this painting was left in the trunk, and by whom –'

'Yes, but –'

'– and when,' said Benjamin, 'that's very important. I'd like to know not only the year but the month, week, even the day if we can pinpoint it. Then we can work on the authentication of the date it was painted.'

'Look,' said Jaume, 'I appreciate what's involved with the work you carry out, but … well, I just need some sort of certificate … it's complicated … it's a financial matter … I'd rather not have to explain it.'

Benjamin waited. At first, he thought Jaume was about to sob, but he was just screwing up his eyes and shaking his head, as if trying to rid his mind of his personal issues or old memories.

'If you don't mind me asking, what is the family business?' said Benjamin.

'*Was*,' said Jaume. He gazed around, as if looking for words that wouldn't come. 'Various investments,' he added, finally. 'Mainly property, wine, vineyards –'

'Wine? My passion, alongside art and food,' said Benjamin. 'It's my dream to have a small vineyard. Who knows, maybe one day I will …' His voice drifted off.

Jaume glanced at him, nodding gently.

'Look, your financial affairs are none of my business,' said Benjamin. 'But I promise I'll find out if this painting is genuine or not, and if it *is* genuine, then it could be worth a fortune. It will help other issues …'

Benjamin hadn't expected it, but Jaume flashed a big and genuine smile. It was for real, not one of his lightning, twitchy grins. The aristocrat continued to look at him, smiling, then at his glass of champagne, then from side to side, and finally at Benjamin again. He also seemed keen to discuss Dalí's masterwork.

'I'd never really understood the original painting until you started to explain it all last night,' he said. 'And I still don't …'

Benjamin could see Lisette slowly making her away back across the restaurant, stopping to introduce herself to other guests along the way, no doubt telling them to also call her Dixie. She walked as if she were floating. He tugged out his lecture leaflet from yesterday, and on which an image of Dalí's masterwork was shown. It was part of the series of talks on 'deceptions and discoveries' in which he'd been participating when Anthony Hughes from Sotheby's had called him. He now used a menu as a support to scribble on another paper napkin, as he set out to explain sections of the painting to Jaume.

'Look,' he started, 'Dalí created the idea of the painting after seeing the face of a bullfighter as a double image in the body of Michelangelo's sculpture, the Venus de Milo, on a box of crayons.'

Jaume gazed down at the leaflet and nodded.

'The Venus de Milo is repeated numerous times from different angles in such a way that the shadows form the face and torso of a young toreador, creating a double image ...'

'Okay.'

'Look at the obsessive repetition of that double image of the Venus de Milo, from the front and back – *see?* – while its shadows form the facial features of the toreador –'

'Yes, yes, I see.'

'– and then a green skirt is his necktie, a white skirt his shirt, the bullfight arena his hat –'

'Yes, yes.'

'And it's a tragic scene,' said Benjamin. 'I mean, the whole setting is contained within a bullfight arena – you see?'

'I see,' nodded the Marquès.

'You'll see flies swarming over the arena to form

the pattern on the bullfighter's hat and cape, the shape of the dying bull – and even the teardrop that the bullfighter is shedding in one eye, having received a premonition of his own death.'

'Okay –'

'The only other study also came down to that central green tie image,' said Benjamin, scribbling specific words on the paper napkin. 'Which is what I always say when starting to explain the painting … *find the green tie*,' – he scrawled – 'and then *you'll find the bullfighter* …'

'Dixie, dear –' Jaume suddenly said, as Benjamin took the hint and quickly tucked the lecture leaflet back into his pocket, pushing the menu and paper napkin out of sight. The blonde was back.

She perched herself next to Jaume and they started talking in Spanish. Benjamin knew it was now critical to find Elena and the painting. He picked up the aristocrat's phone again and started to redial.

While praying for Elena to answer the call, he gazed around at the other guests. It looked like a snapshot of Barcelona's in-crowd or jet-set, with many glitzy and glam women looking bored stiff alongside identical men in light-blue suits and beards talking too loudly, all running their fingers through their hair or slapping one another on the back.

Overhearing Jaume's blonde companion greet others or introduce them to the old aristocrat, everything was 'super' and everyone was a 'darling'. Super this, darling, super that and super those-over-there, darling. Before he knew it, Benjamin was also a darling, having known call-me-Dixie for less than twenty minutes, and despite his cheeks being crammed, chipmunk-fashion, with yet another vol-au-vent.

'Try one of these, darling, you seem peckish,' she said, beckoning him to take a croquette from a waiter's tray. He was grateful, though. Nodding his thanks, he took two, while still holding Jaume's phone to his ear with the other hand.

Just as he did, there was a loud commotion near the entrance of the terrace restaurant, followed by several thickset bodyguards striding in. Directly following them, a tall, breathless, elderly man staggered in. It was the US Secretary of State, Chuck Patterson Jr., drenched in sweat and with one hand clutching his chest – and with even more bodyguards and photographers following him.

Hotel staff also rushed in, with an official photographer battling for space among other cameramen. Like other guests, the Marquès, Lisette and Benjamin – who was now enjoying the croquettes and still waiting for Elena to answer the call – all stood up, more out of surprise than anything else. As their table was near the commotion, it was quickly encircled by agents.

One of the bodyguards rushed over to a trolley, picked up a jug of iced water and filled a glass – from which Patterson gulped until it dribbled from the corners of his lips. He regained his breath, then indicated to his bodyguards to step back and relax.

Many guests wanted to greet him, and he looked

happy to meet them, almost eager to be flesh pressing. The thoroughbred veteran statesman started to work the room alongside his aides, with his wanting-to-know-all-about-you-eyes and smooth, seasoned tone. Despite sweating profusely, there was a purposefulness about him, and sincerity still shone from his eyes as he greeted one guest after another with a practised glance and raised eyebrow. Which is when he caught sight of the Marquès de Guixols, who was standing with his blonde companion and Benjamin.

Patterson moved more swiftly towards the aristocrat as the anxious aides followed closely at his side.

'I recognise you from a previous visit when there was a state banquet,' he said to the Marquès, stretching out a hand. 'I never forget a face.'

Benjamin quietly concurred that it would be very difficult to forget Jaume's flushed, scarlet complexion and barnacled nose, along with his nervous tic grins.

'Secretary of State, sir,' beamed Jaume, proudly shaking hands.

'And this is your daughter?' said Patterson, leering at the blonde.

'Oh, no, *no*, this is, er —'

'Lisette Dijckhuijsen,' said Lisette, shaking hands and prolonging it to make sure a photographer could catch her special moment.

Benjamin waited for her to tell the statesman to call her Dixie, but it didn't happen.

'Lisette,' nodded Patterson, before turning to Benjamin and expecting to be introduced.

'And this is —' said Jaume, looking at Benjamin, 'this is the, er …'

'The doctor … you know, with the PhD,' said Benjamin, through a mouthful of croquette and trying to help the Marquès. He shook hands with Patterson while still holding the aristocrat's cell phone in his other hand. 'How do you do?'

The Secretary of State's handshake was as firm as could be and his look told Benjamin that whatever the state of his tracksuit and Brillo-pad hair, glistening with sweat, it was the last thing on his mind.

'The doctor?' he muttered, eyeing Benjamin curiously.

The hotel's official photographer and a pool of other cameramen took more shots. The Secret Service agents were now shuffling impatiently. Instructions were to usher Patterson along as quickly as possible, but he didn't seem to be in a rush to leave the terrace.

'We really should be moving on —' started one of the aides.

'Good jog?' asked Benjamin, before he could stop himself.

'Great jog,' said Patterson, still perspiring.

The agents started pushing in again.

'Sir, we really have to —'

'Isn't it too hot out there?' said Benjamin.

'Sure is,' said Patterson. 'But there's this great park with fountains. It's the one that king built …'

Benjamin couldn't resist it.

'Which king was that, then?' he said.

The Secretary of State turned towards an aide.

'Which king built that park?' he asked.

More agents pushed in, determined to move Patterson on, and neither the aide nor anyone else from the US entourage could offer any clue as to who built the Parc de Ciutadella. They started to gently push back the photographers, clearing a path for Patterson to walk back through to the main foyer of the hotel, until Jaume tried to answer the question, perhaps keen to also prolong his brief audience with the statesman.

'That might have been the nearby park named after the original citadel of Felipe the fifth,' he suggested.

'The fifth Felipe?' said Patterson, grabbing a napkin to mop himself.

'That's right,' nodded the Marquès.

'How many Felipes are there?' quipped Patterson, but the Secret Service agents had had enough.

'We have a tight programme before the royal reception this evening, sir,' said one of the aides.

Patterson nodded and turned towards the Marquès.

'They're moving me on,' he said.

'You'll be at the royal reception?' asked Jaume. 'I'm also invited. I hope we can catch up again there.'

Then the agents hustled Patterson through to the hotel, just as Benjamin heard shouting from the other end of Jaume's phone …

43

Inspector Vizcaya, Officer Soler and Beltrán Gómez

Monday 4 June, 2pm – Mossos Comissaria, Les Corts district, Barcelona.

'Are you sure?' said Inspector Vizcaya.

'We now know that Brandon Bartholomew boarded a Ryanair flight from London Stansted to Girona yesterday afternoon, departing at 5.15pm UK time, yes,' nodded Officer Soler, pointing towards a series of CCTV images on the screen in the incident room, showing a man with thick, bushy hair.

'The flight arrived at 8.15pm,' she continued. 'Bartholomew travelled on a one-way ticket and did not check in any luggage. He then hired the VW Polo at 8.45pm, paying in cash. The flight reservation was booked through an entity with the reference ALC Inc, registered in London, matching the void card swiped at the hire car booth. We've requested further details from Scotland Yard and Interpol. You can see Bartholomew at Stansted here ... and here ...' she added, clicking through the images, 'and making a purchase here, again in cash, before departure ... and then again *here*, arriving through passport control at Girona.'

Exactly why there'd been an hour's delay in confirming the PNR data for passengers on flights from London to Girona yesterday had not been clarified. But Vizcaya put it partly down to incompetence, and partly down to the chaos incurred by the pre-G20 airport expansion protest that had delayed flights out of Gatwick, and its knock-on effect across all flights leaving London. He didn't have time to consider anything else, nor had young Beltrán, also sitting in on this latest briefing, offered up any conspiracy or scholarly explanations.

Matters were moving fast, with reports coming in from all angles, and they still had the pressure from Bosch and social media to resolve the case immediately. But he was confident that CITCO might now draw further evidence to link the law collective run by the Constantinos tycoon to Bartholomew's cell phone, if he'd used one, although no confirmation of this had come through.

Marta Soler then had more to report.

'Now compare these images,' she was saying, pointing to the screen.

Earlier, while Vizcaya had been at the compound to inspect the abandoned hire car, and then getting an update from Beltrán about the cell phone investigation, Soler had spent time narrowing down the CCTV footage from the service station, both at the fuel pumps and from inside the shop. Her findings focused on the period between 11.45pm and midnight, during which the bullfighter's Chevrolet was estimated to have arrived at the service station, and when the kidnap victim was possibly transferred to the hired VW Polo, paid for by Brandon Bartholomew.

'At 11.55pm last night, you'll see an image inside the shop at the service station,' said Soler. 'A man with bushy hair runs into the shop. Do you see him? He quickly uses the washroom then re-emerges to make a cash purchase of a sandwich. This again is Brandon Bartholomew. He is not seen on any CCTV covering the fuel pumps, so one might assume he has arrived on foot, or simply parked his vehicle away from the surveillance area …'

While everyone remained seated and continued to stare at the screen on the wall, Beltrán stood up.

'I've seen enough,' he said. 'He's our man –'

'I haven't finished,' said Soler, annoyed at being interrupted.

'He hired the car at 8.45pm,' continued Beltrán, ignoring her, 'but remained in the vicinity of the airport. He had no time to get to Nîmes. His alibi for the physical abduction in France is his own arrival time at Girona. Very clever. But he stayed around the airport service station for three hours to coordinate the transfer. He's the mastermind. He's holding the bullfighter, or at least he knows where he is. The red-hooded extremist from Nîmes made the delivery, then Bartholomew took over. He hired the vehicle, then abandoned it with a smashed window and blood-stained hammer on the seat. It's the vehicle from which the dead chauffeur's credit card was used at tollgates, and it was hired with false documentation. He's our man ...'

'But wait −' said Soler, preparing to click through to further images.

Vizcaya also stood up. He was about to state that *he*, Detective Inspector Vizcaya, and not some obstreperous little brat from Madrid, would decide if Bartholomew was 'our man' or not. But Beltrán was now at the door of the incident room, greeting a newcomer who he introduced as a 'forensic toxicology analyst' from CITCO.

Vizcaya knew that initial forensic reports had come in from tests done on the Chevrolet, but he wasn't aware that Beltrán had secured privileged access to the information, nor that he'd enlisted CITCO's help to analyse it all. It riled him even more. He'd agreed to share the investigation, however, so he made a huge effort to keep his anger under wraps in the presence of Soler and the rest of his team, and simply listened in to witness how the paranoia of a terrorist threat now seemed to be backed up by toxi-cology reports.

Not only had a hypodermic needle been found in the Chevrolet, but powder traces and residue analyses confirmed that a variety of potentially lethal chemicals had also been discovered.

'Can you, for once, be more specific?' Vizcaya asked, trying to maintain his composure.

'Can I? Yes …' said Beltrán. 'They've found traces of phencyclidine – PCP – possibly being used as a recreational drug, but the liquid form of PCP is dissolved most often in ether, which is a highly flammable solvent.'

The forensic toxicologist was allowed to take over from there.

'Although very slight, we've also found another powder trace that we believe to be pentaerythritol tetranitrate, or PETN. It's a highly explosive, colourless organic compound, related to nitro-glycerine …'

'Inspector,' said Beltrán, cutting in to add further emphasis to the threat. 'PETN ingredients have been used in Semtex explosives …'

Vizcaya knew what was coming next. In between Beltrán's textbook explanations, he tried to simplify the situation for himself. If shoe bombers, underwear bombers and syringe bombers could construct devices mid-flight, using a pack of combustible powder, a bottle of Lucozade, a touch of hair bleach, chapati flour and other materials, finally detonated via a battery and the flash of a disposable camera, then it could also be done in the back of a Chevrolet – combined with the kidnappers' knowledge of cell phone and SIM card technology. They murdered the chauffeur, so anything was possible. Quite where they might detonate explosives, however, was another matter.

'We can't take any risks,' Beltrán was saying, pulling out his cell phone. 'We can't delay any further. We need to make an appeal to the public and the media. We need to find Brandon Bartholomew and bring him in.'

Vizcaya had already decided that Bartholomew had to be questioned, but how they found him and brought him in would need careful consideration. With the safety and location of the kidnapped bullfighter still unknown, putting out a public appeal so early could endanger everything.

He was now further incensed how Beltrán was trying to call the shots and lead the investigation, and in front of his own team. He assumed the smug bastard was now trying to call the Catalan minister, Isabel Bosch, to give her an update and take all the credit.

'Just hang on a moment, señorito,' said Vizcaya. 'We need to be sure of the timing of this. And if it's okay with you, young man, *I'll* speak to Bosch.'

'Bosch?' said Beltrán, moving towards the door as he keyed in some numbers on his phone. 'I'm not calling Bosch. I'm calling Madrid.'

'*Beltrán Gómez de fucking Longoria, get back in here,*' yelled Vizcaya, thumping a desk.

But Beltrán had already gone.

44

Séverin and Elena

Monday 4 June, 1.15pm – El Raval neighbourhood, Barcelona.

'In suffering, animals are our equals,' Séverin muttered to himself, still slumped in the armchair that the punk had vacated at the Splendido cesspit – after he'd hacked off his ear, and which was still tucked safely in a pocket of his Nîmes Olympique red hoodie.

He'd been trying to think things through and remember where the Dutch hippies hung out, but the PCP angel dust wasn't helping matters.

Somewhat ironic that PCP was once used as an animal tranquiliser, a veterinary anaesthetic, in Séverin its effects would grow steadily from a stuttering, slurred speech and staggering gait, through disorientation and loss of balance, and sometimes on to a full psychotic, hallucinatory, out-of-body experience. He couldn't remember the first time he'd tried it. He wasn't sure he even enjoyed its full impact that much, but he needed to get his kicks from somewhere, and he'd become slightly addicted.

Séverin didn't need any assistance to turn violent, but intoxication by angel dust often mirrored schizophrenia, plus a fear that people were plotting to kill him. Sometimes, it provoked him to retaliate with excessive and frenzied violence in unnecessary self-defence, although he never enjoyed mutilating someone who'd done nothing wrong. It went against his code of conduct. Or so he told himself.

Jürgen and Heinrich or Hendrik, or whoever he was … well, *they'd* done more than enough wrong. Not only did they owe him eight thousand euros, but they'd driven off and left him stranded at that service station. What were they, anyway? Bunny-huggers? Yoghurt weavers? Greenpeace or Friends of the Earth luvvies? He hated hippies. Jürgen with the hipster beard had kept going on about *non-violent direct action*. What did that mean? Supergluing yourself to something? Fuck that. Bullfighters had to *die*. Bullfighters had to be carved up. Séverin had been hired for the job and he was determined to see it through.

'In suffering, animals are our equals,' he muttered again.

Late last night, when they'd left him at the service station, he'd felt his brain boiling. Just beforehand, he'd helped them bundle the bullfighter into the back of the transfer vehicle, jabbing his pruning shears against his neck while dragging him between the vehicles, throttling him by the tie and then cutting it and ripping his shirt. But then the van had simply sped away.

He could recall returning to the Chevrolet and taking his rage out on the chauffeur still lying in the back, repeatedly hitting his skull with a hammer before dragging him out onto the ground.

He'd then climbed into the driver's seat, grateful that he still had the chauffeur's wallet. On the way from Nîmes, he'd been handing Jürgen the chauffeur's credit card from the back seat at each tollgate, and Jürgen had always passed the card back to him. He'd vowed to find them and kill them, but then realised that Jürgen had taken the keys of the Chevrolet.

He'd punched the steering wheel, knowing he couldn't stay there, knowing he had to chase them. A car had pulled up, and it had been parked near the fence, just before the transfer van had driven off. That weirdo with all the hair had got out and had hurried inside the shop. Searching around the Chevrolet, Séverin had grabbed the toll ticket from the drink holder, then waited for him to return to his parked car.

His blood was boiling again now, just thinking about the Dutch hippies. He needed to cool down, and he needed to find them. It was time to move, although he felt comfortable here. No one had dared question his presence or disturbed him … at least not until the girl suddenly arrived …

Elena had miscalculated the distance, and with the G20 diversions and roadblocks, it had taken her much longer than expected to return to the hostel. She'd noticed the first missed call on her cell phone while searching for somewhere to park. She didn't recognise the number, though, so she didn't return the call. She'd been receiving so many messages and she already knew she had to be careful.

Once she'd finally parked the taxi just a few metres away, she strolled up to the hostel, clutching her car keys and phone. There were a few junkies on the sidewalk nearby, but that didn't deter her. She pushed open the front door and immediately saw the freak sprawled out on an armchair at a makeshift reception desk, which was splattered with blood. His sinister eyes appeared glazed as he looked up and finally focused on her, at first smiling and ogling her with his brown teeth and demented-looking fringe. Then he jumped up when she held up her phone to take a picture of him. He was enormous.

'You called me a gypsy bitch,' she snapped. 'Where's the bullfighter being held?'

'Er … that's what I want to know …'

'What is Benjamin's role?'

'Who?' said Séverin, now drooling. 'Have you come here for sex?'

Elena watched as he licked his lips. She noticed the sick, repulsive pig had a French accent, and she could see the blade of a knife or a pair of cutters in his fat fist, glinting from the light beaming through from the street.

'Answer me,' he said, almost slobbering. 'Sex, yes?'

Elena was silent.

'Don't be a naughty girl,' he said, starting to pant. 'You haven't done anything too bad yet, so I won't harm you. We'll just have sex. You'll still squeal, but with delight.'

He moved from behind the desk and towards her a little.

'Keep away from me.'

'Do you like flowers?' he said, edging closer. 'I'm going to open a florist's shop and I could give you a job. I can pay you a lot of money.'

Elena noticed he was wearing some kind of double holster around his waist, below his red hoodie. She thought he was carrying a gun at first, but instead it looked like a set of builders' tools and knives.

He was so near to her now that she could already smell his rancid breath, but then her cell phone rang again and this time she answered it, simply in a bid to shout for help.

'*Where are you?*' said a voice from the other end of the line – '*Who's this?*' Elena said back – '*Benjamin*' came the reply – and then just after Elena managed to yell, '*At your hostel*', the phone was knocked out of her hand.

Séverin had pushed himself against her, and she

barely had any chance to react, other than to scream. She used both fists to thump him, still with her car keys in one hand, then stepped quickly to one side and tried one of the moves she'd learnt in kickboxing. She thought she'd connected a decent enough kick to his left leg, but it didn't appear to hurt him – *no* – Séverin's ingestion of angel dust meant that he felt little or no pain at all. It was a useful side effect of the anaesthetic drug, that lack of pain, that feeling of strength, that sense of invulnerability – which enabled him to withstand her next kick, too. She screamed again, just before he slammed her hard against the wall, pinning her there with his immense arm, and waving his pruning shears under her chin with his other hand.

'I could gouge out your pretty eyes, but I won't if you do what I say,' he said. 'Rub your little hands against me.' He stuck out his slimy, foul tongue and tried to lick her face.

She retched, wriggled free and sprung back, gripping her keys to try and jab him in the face, but he grabbed her hand and squeezed it, harder and harder, until the keys simply fell to the ground. Someone was shouting, and Séverin quickly decided not to hang around. He already had a severed ear in his pocket, and he couldn't risk being questioned or detained. He had more important things to hunt down: where the Dutch scabs were holding the bullfighter, along with the eight thousand euros.

He put his cutters away, picked up the keys, tried to slash them against her face as a farewell shot, but she managed to jerk her head out of the way. He shoved her viciously against the wall again, and then spat in her face before staggering out.

She nearly collapsed, shuddering as she propped herself against the wall, trying hard to hold back her tears and her rage.

The earlier shouting had become louder, and Elena looked up to see that an old man had appeared at the top of a staircase. He was now yelling at her, asking her what the fuck she was doing in his property. She gazed up, asking him what he knew about the kidnap, but he merely shouted back that he knew nothing about anything, and to get the hell out of his building or he'd kill her.

No one helped her as she limped out into the street in search of the psycho. He'd gone, but she'd find him … she swore that she'd find him. She'd remember him anywhere, and he couldn't have gone far. Her taxi was still there, but he had the keys. She started to walk slowly down the road, looking in doorways, and down alleyways. She'd find the bastard …

45

Benjamin

Monday 4 June, 1.45pm – from Port Olímpic to the Raval neighbourhood, Barcelona.

Benjamin had been alarmed when he heard the shouting and screaming from the other end of Jaume's phone. Then he'd heard Elena yelling that she was back at the hostel before the phone went dead.

She'd sounded in trouble, and he was worried about her. She had the painting in her taxi, too, so he'd dashed out of the hotel restaurant, practically unnoticed amid the throng of security agents still hustling Secretary Patterson away. He'd first thrust the phone back into Jaume's hands, vaguely apologising and saying that he'd be back in touch later on, and then darted out of a side exit. Finding himself near the seafront, he waved down a taxi, all the time grappling in his pocket for the scribbled address of the hostel Splendido.

He was in luck, and the G20 traffic cops were keen to wave vehicles away from the Olympic port area as fast as possible, which meant that within minutes he was on his way towards the vicinity of the hostel in the *barrio* of Raval.

By the time his taxi arrived, however, there was no sign of Elena – certainly not on the street outside the Splendido slum. Rushing inside, he came face to face with a thin, wiry, old man, who looked like he was trying to clean the place up after a raid. He was shuffling and hobbling around with a broom, with his left leg rigid but which he eased into step at an angle. He also had a warty, dark eyelid, like badly applied mascara, or as if someone had just bashed him and then sprinted away to safety.

Benjamin asked if he'd seen a girl – a girl called *Elena* – but the man simply became aggressive, waving at him to get lost. He suddenly raised his broom handle and swung it in the direction of Benjamin's face, who grabbed hold of it and shoved him to one side.

'Don't be fucking silly,' said Benjamin, pushing past to check the area behind the reception desk.

He then bolted up two flights of stairs and banged on bedroom doors, calling out for Elena. Each door eventually opened to reveal users, winos, as well as some sex workers with their shocked clients – but there was no sign of Elena at all.

Once he was back out in the street again, Benjamin caught sight of her taxi parked nearby, the silver-grey Citroën with the dented side door.

He tried all the vehicle's doors, but they were locked. He looked up and down the street for her. A couple of junkies were watching him. He could hear police sirens, getting louder. After waiting a minute for her to return to the vehicle, he decided to act. He found a medium-sized rock in the gutter and within seconds he'd smashed open a back window of the vehicle, before reaching inside to take the portfolio case off the back seat.

A man was shouting in the street somewhere behind him, but Benjamin didn't look back. He ducked between the parked vehicles and then scurried down an alleyway. He then ran away from the area as fast as possible, clutching the painting to his chest.

46

Mitch Gibson

Monday 4 June, 2pm – Port Olímpic, Barcelona.

When news of the US Secretary of State's apparent seizure while out jogging came through to spokesman Mitch Gibson, he almost had a seizure himself. By the time he found his boss and the security entourage gathered in the hotel's new terrace restaurant, the breathless attack had been put down to acute indigestion.

The last thing Mitch needed was an image of the US delegation's key figure, second only to POTUS himself, clasping his chest in pain. The fact that the old statesman had taken it upon himself to then mingle among the guests, showing he was still fit, healthy and alive (or as near as dammit), was a welcome exercise in damage limitation, and suggested that Patterson was also conscious of the slip-up. Besides, Mitch had enough on his plate with the G20 spouse programme.

The Spanish Prime Minister's wife, as well as the wife of the Catalan President, were together hosting the spouse programme. They would be welcoming the wives, girlfriends and occasional husband of twenty heads of delegations attending the G20 summit in Barcelona, combining their cultural excursions over the next few days alongside a parallel theme of 'arts education for underprivileged children'.

The spouses included grandmothers and mothers, academics, economists, lawyers, businesswomen, an ex-actress, a former Olympic gymnast, an ex-girlfriend of a Rolling Stone and a former Miss Italy. But one of the key spouse guests – bearing in mind that POTUS was still a very happy, very single and very powerful bachelor – was the US Secretary of State's wife, Pamela Patterson, who was also scheduled to make a speech at the climate change conference. The wife of Mitch's boss was not your run-of-the-mill American society heiress, or an ageing Barbie in Washington DC. No, she was sharp, witty, talented, intelligent, cultured, outspoken and ... *ballsy.*

Mitch was determined that the Secretary's spouse should also receive positive press coverage. The Patterson brand was at stake, prior to the launch of the multimillion-dollar Patterson Foundation. He was already uneasy about the superficial reports ahead of the G20 spouse programme's inaugural event at the Picasso Museum. Every so-called 'style correspondent' on the planet was poking fun at the Chinese President's wife 'who has never said a word in public', and that it would be a 'miracle' if any of the four wives of the King of Saudi Arabia 'were seen, let alone heard'. He knew the media wanted to see and hear from Pamela, but he had to steer things away from her animal welfare lobbying, or comments about goddamned bullfights.

'Take Spain's geographic diversity and varied landscape, take its history of invasions, migrations, expansion, conquest, and what do you get? Art, with a capital A. Spanish Art was born of the ebb and flow of civilisations that has determined Spain's history since antiquity. New cultures with new ideas have always met, clashed, intermingled and been transformed in the great melting pot that is the Iberian Peninsula. Spanish artistic creativity has always been determined by the tension between what came from abroad and what already existed in Spain ...'

Thus begun one of the many PR handouts introducing the G20 spouse programme, perhaps with more prominence given to Spanish, Moorish and Al-Andalus art over Catalan art than the Barcelona authorities might have preferred. But it was a fair preamble to the surrealist and architectural marvels that lay ahead for the first wives' club over the next few days in the work of Gaudí, Picasso, Miró, Dalí and Tàpies.

And everything would have gone exactly to plan, too, if it hadn't been for Séverin ...

47

Benjamin

Monday 4 June, 2.45pm – near La Rambla, Barcelona.

Benjamin breathed in and out, closing his eyes for just a brief, beautiful, blissful few seconds. It was the only time he felt he could spare. He'd found an Internet café just off La Rambla, inside an Oriental Bazaar store selling everything – and where he'd installed himself at one of the desktop computers at the back, with the portfolio case wedged safely between his legs.

It was slightly cooler in here, but he was still starving, despite grabbing as much as he could from the waiters' trays earlier. Before finding the store, he'd roamed the streets around La Rambla that had echoed with cooking sounds, the clanking of crockery and cutlery, shouts and laughter. On every street corner there was a smell of fried garlic, coffee and tobacco, often blending in with a musty whiff from the city's drains. He craved something simple – what was that Catalan dish? – crusty bread rubbed with tomatoes, drizzled with olive oil and layered with some ham? A work of art on a plate, washed down with a cold glass of wine ... but he had no time.

There were a few other customers sitting in front of computer screens nearby – a middle-aged woman on Facebook, an old man reading sports reports, and a young Chinese lad in mammoth headphones playing a video game. Benjamin logged on to a PC, went directly to iCloud, then eventually selected his lost phone before clicking 'erase'. Once it was done, he also deleted the device from his account, then went back to Google and through to access his Gmail account.

He sent a quick email to his daughter, simply stating, 'In Barcelona, phone stolen, will call when I can, Bx' – and then started to draft another one to his main contact at Scotland Yard. Where to start? The confidential call from Anthony Hughes sending him off to Barcelona, of course ... but then he paused.

Look at the crime scene, Benjamin.

Look at it like a work of art.

You saw the body at the service station. You saw a laundry van accelerating away. *Find the killers.*

Before Elena had left him stranded, claiming she'd find the psycho first, he'd asked her to take him back to the area of two IB hotels, because that's where he'd seen the maniac hanging around. Who serviced the hotels? Who did their laundry? Was it outsourced, in-house, or both?

He Googled 'IB hotels' and within seconds he was on the English version of their corporate website. As a publicly listed company, it boasted a log-in area for shareholders, a press room, as well as a social responsibility section explaining how IB also helped the environment with its suppliers.

The statements and promises flashed up in front of him: 'We consider our suppliers to be key stakeholders for consolidating our commitment to sustainability ... ethical development ... and to promote *local purchasing* in each region where we operate ...'

When he finally found the hotel group's procurement page for Spain, he started to scroll down the list of different suppliers. He couldn't find any section for laundry, so he just clicked 'print', aiming to collect the sheets on his way out of the store.

Why had Elena driven off? Why had she gone back to that Splendido hostel – that brothel? Had she not trusted him?

She'd said that *she'd find the thug first* – but Benjamin had searched the hostel and there'd been no sign of him or her. Had she been abducted, too? Hearing her shouting down the phone had unsettled him, and he felt anxious for her safety.

He searched for her taxi card in his pocket again. It simply said, 'Carmona Taxis – Girona', and there was a phone number, the one he'd tried earlier … but nothing else. It wasn't much to go on, but he Googled the name and number. Other than a mass of recommended Girona taxis and Costa Brava airport transfers, nothing else showed up. There wasn't a specific entry or website for Carmona Taxis.

He keyed in 'Elena Carmona'. There were hundreds of suggestions to click through to Facebook and LinkedIn profiles, with many having a second Spanish surname, as well as several 'María Elena Carmonas'. Benjamin had long abandoned Facebook and nor did he use LinkedIn, opting for near anonymity instead.

He tried again: 'Elena Carmona + Girona' … and, yes, there was something, there was a blog. It was all in Spanish, he didn't understand any of it, but there were several sports images, and an article about Messi, Paris Saint-Germain and Barça, and something on women's football, too, but he wasn't sure if it was her page or not as there wasn't a photo of her.

He searched for a phone number or email address, but there was nothing. He finally found an '@' address – what was it? Instagram? Twitter? TikTok? *@elenacarmona30* … if this was her, how could he send her a message when he wasn't even on social media?

He scribbled it on her taxi card and then stuffed it

into a pocket of his khaki pants, where he could feel the small white button that he'd found on the ground at the service station, near the corpse ...

Focus, Benjamin, *focus* ...

He'd left his backpack in the restaurant lockers at the Hotel Arts – not that there was much inside it – but he felt he should go back to collect it and speak to the Marquès again, if he hadn't already left with call-me-Dixie. He could picture the old aristocrat foaming with rage and impatience about an authentication certificate – and he still had an obligation to give him a definitive report, one way or another. He'd given his word to find out if the painting was genuine or not, and he would keep his word, but he was still finding it difficult to separate the image of the painting from what happened to him at the service station.

Was it Joan Miró who once said that it should be possible to discover new things every time you see a picture? He was pretty sure it was Miró. *'It must have radiance. More than the picture itself, what counts is what it throws off, what it exhales ... as long as it reveals a world, something alive.'* Yes, it was definitely Miró.

He considered taking Jaume's painting out of the case to study it again. He glanced around. The middle-aged woman who'd been trawling through Facebook briefly looked at him, and so he turned his attention back to the computer screen.

From their conversation at the hotel restaurant, it

was clear that the aristocrat's urgency to ascertain the painting's authenticity had everything to do with a precarious financial situation, although Benjamin had no idea as to the extent of his predicament. He'd seen it all before, especially within the circle that the Marquès moved in. If a possible masterpiece, newly discovered, was confirmed as genuine, it was often hushed up for tax reasons, or to avoid ugly ownership disputes among heirs, ex-wives or with the artist's estate.

Benjamin still believed it was unlikely that the Marquès had uncovered a genuine Dalí oil study, but the fact that his father had sought to acquire the original masterwork and that Dalí might have visited his country home changed matters considerably.

If anything, it was a 'possible' study for *The Hallucinogenic Toreador* masterwork, not a finished painting. It was a possible study in the same way that *The Face*, hanging in the Dalí Museum in Figueres, *was* a study. But a study or not, Dalí's work had great value – and Benjamin had to tread very carefully. The highest price paid for a Dalí painting had been $21.6 million for his 1929 portrait of the French poet Paul Éluard, Gala's ex-husband, at a sell-out auction in 2011. He shuddered at the thought of having lost Jaume's canvas twice … first to the savage who he would track down, and then … well, to Elena.

He pulled out some notes from another pocket, and found Jaume's address near La Bisbal, scribbled on the back of the lecture leaflet. He wanted to check its exact proximity on Google maps to the Gala-Dalí castle in nearby Púbol – but then he was curious as to what he might find simply by searching for 'Marquès de Guíxols + Salvador Dalí'.

Nothing relevant came up, so he tried, 'Marquès de Guíxols + art' … but again, nothing came up that he recognised. Then he tried 'Jaume Guíxols + Marquès', which threw up multiple reports about misconduct involving a bank. Most of the links were in Spanish, but as Benjamin searched further, he could see a story had also appeared in the *Financial Times* and *Wall Street Journal*, with the words 'corruption investigation' and 'financial scandal' within the headlines and intro.

He reminded himself that the aristocrat's financial affairs were none of his business. His only duty to Jaume was to examine his painting, currently wedged between his legs in the portfolio case. Nothing more, nothing less.

From the moment he'd set eyes on the canvas yesterday evening, he'd noticed something different, something special about it … but he hadn't been able to pinpoint what it was, and neither had the initial examination at MNAC revealed anything.

He now Googled for images of *The Face* that he knew was hanging in the Figueres museum, aiming to compare it with Jaume's canvas – if only he could find the right moment to take it out of the case to scrutinise it again. He glanced at the others sitting at computers nearby, and then back to his own screen, which is when it hit him …

He shut his eyes, then opened them again.

In front of him, on the screen, was an image of *The Face* with the green tie of the bullfighter, very similar to Jaume's painting, and one of the only two known oil studies for *The Hallucinogenic Toreador* painted by Dalí … the grand master of ambiguous imagery … *double images* that could change the observer's point of view, images that could be read in multiple ways …

Every crime scene is a work of art.

It was coming back to him now … the service station, the *crime scene* … at first it felt like déjà vu again … but, no, he could now recall what he'd caught sight of last night, in addition to the disfigured corpse, just after being whacked on the back of the head and slumping to the ground.

It had looked like a thin green rag or ribbon, half-curled up, but flapping in the wind on the ground beside him, just before he'd lost consciousness. When he'd come to, it had vanished … perhaps blown away. But he now knew what it was, as well as that small white button that he'd found on the ground. The green fabric had been ripped or cut – threads of cotton had been hanging from one end where the seam had been torn – he could recall it very clearly now. It was the tail of a thin green tie that had been ripped. Was it the tie of the bullfighter, the tie of the kidnap victim who'd been held right there at the service station?

What had they done to him?

Where had they taken him?

He had to find out, but he also now realised it was the connection he'd missed in Jaume's painting yesterday evening ... something in the same green tie area of the canvas that contrasted with the version of *The Face* in Figueres ...

Benjamin lifted the portfolio case, opened it, and half-slid out the canvas. Within seconds he knew he had to carry out further tests on it, whether the aristocrat allowed him to or not. He'd promised to find out if it was genuine, and his sudden instinct was that it now could be.

He needed to move fast.

Even though nothing had been visible from MNAC's infrared reflectography tests, he could still try radiography, or even material analysis using an XRF gun. There was also someone who could help him – so he quickly Googled 'Conso Puig + Figueres' to see if she was still there – before scribbling her address on a scrap of paper and clicking through to Google maps to check if her studio was where it always had been. It was ... and then he eventually found himself back on a page displaying news, where he thought he saw a name he recognised ...

He squinted.

No, or maybe, yes … *yes,* there was something familiar … there it was again … breaking news reports … yes, *look* … he recognised something …

What. The. Fuck.

Was he seeing double images again?

Was he imagining things?

No, there it was … in *English,* too … the police were seeking 'a *Brandon Bartholomew* to help them with their enquiries over the murder of Paco Chillado and the kidnapping of Rafael Pérez'.

Oh, for fucksake.

He felt queasy as images of blood-soaked bulls with sharp sticks flapping from their backs filled the screen, alongside a bullfighter called 'Rafa' Pérez in his costume and green tie. Benjamin clicked away, back to the headline news in English, too. He read that Pérez was the bullfighter who'd been abducted from Nîmes last night, with his Chevrolet van and dead chauffeur found at the service station. There were more images, diagrams and *world* news – and then he came face to face with it … an *image* of himself …

Oh, Jesus Christ.

It wasn't a very clear image, which was a good thing – but it was also rather unflattering, taken from an angle and from above – and rather vainly, indeed *insanely,* Benjamin started to ponder that it wouldn't necessarily have been an image he would have chosen for himself … but it was definitely him.

Oh, for fucksake.

It looked like a CCTV image taken at the airport,

at passport control, while arriving at Girona yesterday evening. It said that it had been issued by Spain's Guardia Civil and the Ministry of Interior. They wanted to question a Brandon Bartholomew *and* someone else. There wasn't a name for the other person, just an image – it was a faint shot of a figure in the back of a vehicle – in Nîmes, it said – but it also looked familiar – *fuck, yes* – it was the red-hooded psycho.

Benjamin bolted upright and looked around.

Was this why Elena had driven off? Had she seen all this while scanning through all the news on her phone earlier? Had she even gone to the police herself? *Fuck.*

He looked at the email he'd been drafting to his contact at Scotland Yard. He deleted what he'd started, then simply wrote: 'Bartholomew is blown. Saw body at service station but couldn't go to police. Am chasing killer and will find him. Might need assistance to clear that name.' He pressed 'send', briefly contemplated also sending an email to his lawyer, Walter Postleth-waite, but instead logged off.

Benjamin had had enough of others telling him what to do. He'd helped the police with their enquiries before, in more ways than one, so he knew precisely what to expect and how he'd be received if he went to the Spanish police right now, without first making contact with Scotland Yard or Interpol. Like it or not, he'd be kept in detention for at least twenty-four hours, however innocent he was. As soon as he presented himself to a police officer or at a police station, his possessions would be taken away from him for examination, including the painting. He simply could not allow that to happen. There would be a language problem, too, and a convenient delay before he was allowed to call London or have access to a bilingual lawyer … and nobody would believe his version of events at the service station, or his run-ins with the maniac in the red hoodie.

He *would* help the Spanish police with their enquiries, but not in the way they might expect. He'd carry out what he'd already resolved to do: find the killer and the kidnappers.

And now he *had* to … if just to clear his own name.

He could see the till area of the store near the open door, where he could pay for the sheets he'd printed off and collect them on his way out … but he also needed to disguise himself. He jumped up and paced quickly around the aisles of the Oriental Bazaar, grabbing a cheap Barça baseball cap, some sunglasses, and an XXL lumberjack-style shirt. He carried it all to the till to settle up, before dumping his corduroy jacket and polo shirt in the nearest bin outside.

Time was against him.

He had to act fast. Very fast.

48

Séverin

Monday 4 June, 2.30pm – El Born neighbourhood, Barcelona.

It would pain him to ditch his red Nîmes Olympique football hoodie, but Séverin had come to a sufficient level of realism following his last psychotic attack to know it would be safer to do so.

Since leaving the hostel where that gypsy bitch had confronted him, he'd been perched on a stool in a crowded Irish bar in the city's Born neighbourhood. It was air-conditioned but he was still dripping with sweat and his heart was pounding. It could take up to six hours to wear off, but only if he wanted it to. He'd already downed four Cokes and a litre of iced water.

Fuck those Dutch hippies who still had his cash. He'd find them and beat them to pulp. *Fuck* the bull-fighter's dead chauffeur, too. He got what he deserved; he had no right to drive an animal-killer around in the first place. And just as soon as he located the bullfighter himself, he'd skin him alive.

In the Irish bar, Séverin had been staring at one of the TV screens, trying to stop himself from hallucinating. He didn't want to step outside his own body again or have conversations with objects around the bar that kept springing to life. But then the TV news showed clips of a police appeal, and there was an image of a faint, red-hooded figure in the back of a van.

Séverin knew who it was; he didn't need another PCP trip to see it. Whether anyone else in the bar realised it was him or not was another matter, but he had no intention of hanging around to find out. He waited for a potbellied man to waddle over to play on a fruit machine again, just as he'd done twice already, and then he snatched the leather jacket that he'd left on the back of a stool.

Outside, Séverin dashed across a narrow street and then into an alleyway leading to the Carrer de la Princesa. He rummaged through the pockets of the leather jacket, pulling the cash and credit cards out of a wallet, before tossing the wallet in a trash can. Next, he went through the pockets of his own hoodie, transferring the bloody lump of severed ear to the jacket.

Although he felt even hotter in the jacket, it fitted perfectly, just covering the top of his labourer's belt that held all his tools and the remaining claw hammer. He rolled up his hoodie and tucked it among a pile of cardboard in the street, which is when he heard the sirens and saw the motorcade approaching …

As a number of limos and people-carriers rolled slowly past, escorted by dozens of police motorbikes, Séverin paced further along the street, following the crowds and on-lookers. He heard some tourists say that it was the G20 spouse party, the wives of the heads of state who were already in Barcelona and about to visit the nearby Picasso Museum.

He was still sweating and shaking, but he made it down to the corner of the narrow street just as the motorcade stopped near to a side entrance of the museum about fifty metres away. One by one the vehicles dropped off their VIPs, who were all guided inside the museum, together with a pack of photographers. Security barriers were then rolled across to seal off the side street.

Séverin noticed that many other cameramen, those without access to the museum, were being directed around to the back entrance, to the Plaça de Jaume Sabartés, where there was more space. Each photographer then took up position behind a security barrier to take shots of the spouses once they emerged from the museum after their tour. A large crowd of on-lookers had also gathered there. Séverin nudged his way into the throng, as near to the front as he possibly could, blending in with the crowds as just another spectator.

He watched … and he waited.

49

Elena

The pain in her shoulder, where the savage had slammed her hard against the wall, had become more acute by the time she'd walked from the Raval to the Born area of the city. Striding in the searing, airless humidity, she'd followed the same direction that she thought he was heading in, or at least a figure that resembled him. Finally losing the trail, she lurched into the busy foyer of a four-star hotel just off the shaded Via Laietana, then headed straight to the restroom.

There, with the stench of the pervert still lingering in her nostrils, she felt something tighten inside her. She retched again, then splashed cold water over her face, pulling her top to one side to inspect an already bruised shoulder.

She tried to compose herself as best as she could,

but she felt sick, enraged and repulsed. He'd grabbed her keys, but she still had her bank cards and ID, all inside a leather holder tucked deep in a front pocket of her jeans. Once or twice she'd instinctively checked her pockets for her cell phone, too, forgetting that he'd smashed it out of her hand. Whether he'd taken it, or it was still on the ground at the hostel, she wasn't going back to find out.

The photos and audio she'd recorded earlier would be safe on her cloud, and who would she call, anyway? Her brother? Then what? Would he be sober enough, or even willing to come all the way to Barcelona with his own set of taxi keys? The *police?* She'd already seen many police agents as she'd staggered along Laietana; they were everywhere for the G20. Approaching them was the last thing on her mind. What would they do? Check their records, find that she'd accused one of their own of sexual assault two years ago … then laugh in her face and blame *her* for also being assaulted by a red-hooded thug. Fuck the police.

No, she had no intention of going to anyone until she'd written her story and sent it off, although she still needed some help getting it to the right person ….

She could cope without a phone for now if she could just get online. Once she was back in the foyer of the hotel, she asked if there was a computer with Internet she could use at the crowded reception. The concierge pointed towards a 'business zone' at the far end of the foyer and said that the computer accepted coins or cards.

Minutes later, she'd sent an email to her brother and father to say she'd been attacked and had lost her phone and taxi keys, but that she was 'okay'. She then went on to her Twitter account and sent a message to a colleague from the journalism course: 'I have a story. Can you help?'

While waiting for a reply, she scrolled through the news feed, thinking again about her near escape from possible rape at the hostel … and about her passenger, Benjamin. The psycho hadn't flinched when she'd mentioned his name; he didn't seem to know him. It was weird, but she suddenly felt she could have done with Benjamn's company right now.

That was until she clicked on a news report and saw a picture of him. She felt her face flush as the shock and anger started to surface.

He'd lied.

He'd fucking lied.

He'd lied about his name, so he would have lied about everything else. He *was* involved. The police wanted to question him …

Suddenly a message came back from her friend: 'Sounds cool. Let's meet. Where r u?'

50

Benjamin

Monday 4 June, 3.15pm – from Sants Station to Figueres.

Benjamin Brandon Bartholomew Blake had two British passports.

It was as simple as that.

It was totally innocent, too, at least for now, until the one he shouldn't really have had in the first place expired. Which would be quite soon if London hadn't expired it for him already. One passport was in the name of Benjamin Blake. The other passport was in the name of Brandon Bartholomew. For reasons of the dates that they were taken, the photos were different in the two passports, and there was no reference to one in the other. So, he simply had two identities, as and when he ever needed two identities. He had two driving licences, too.

It had sometimes worked well, but he'd always worried that one day it could backfire, like right now.

He had two passports because … because *he did*. It was almost an 'administrative error'. Nearly ten years ago (which was why the Brandon Bartholomew ten-year passport was about to expire), Benjamin had been travelling regularly on a series of assignments for an international art insurance company, way before he'd set up his own art loss detective agency. As the destinations included China, Russia, Saudi Arabia, India and Israel, he needed to lodge his original Benjamin Blake passport for periods at various embassies for visa purposes, yet while still needing to travel … and even more so after Scotland Yard's Art and Antiques Unit suddenly called upon his services.

At the time it was all rather mysterious, but the money being offered was excellent. According to Scotland Yard, Benjamin had been chosen or 'recruited' by someone whose full details had to remain anonymous, but who was a former Home Office Permanent Secretary still advising the UK's Minister of State for Crime and Policing. They wanted Benjamin to participate in an urgent undercover assignment being coordinated with Europol across the Continent. He briefly even wondered if he'd be able to introduce himself as, 'Blake. Benjamin Blake. Art squad.'

His Benjamin Blake passport, however, was still in a visa pile at the Chinese Embassy, and so the Home Office fast-tracked, or created, what was supposed to be a temporary second passport for him, together with a matching driving licence, using his middle names. Then somehow, after the assignment was successfully carried out, they forgot to cancel the documents.

Several years went by, during which he renewed his Blake passport, but whenever he mentioned the other documents to the small team running the Art and Antiques Unit, they feigned ignorance.

Then there was a change of government and some civil servants at the Home Office were reshuffled along the way. The few times he tried to explain things to anyone, nobody wanted to take responsibility. So, he continued to use the second passport and driving licence for discreet work on behalf of key clients, yet only across Europe. A handful of clients (Anthony Hughes' PA at Sotheby's included) had even made bookings for him under the name of Brandon Bartholomew, linked to his agency. As far as Benjamin was concerned, Brandon had never done anything illegal. His second, 'temporary' passport was still valid because the Home Office had never told him otherwise, and nothing had ever gone wrong … until now.

But Brandon Bartholomew was now dead.

He was finished.

At least for this Dalí job.

Benjamin Blake, however, was on a slow, regional train to Figueres, dressed in an XXL lumberjack shirt, Barça baseball cap and sunglasses – and with the painting in its portfolio case propped up safely on the seat beside him. He'd dumped his corduroy jacket and polo shirt nearly an hour ago. He didn't know it would be a slow train before jumping on board, but it was definitely slow. *Too* slow.

The green fabric, ripped and frayed, that he'd seen flapping in the wind at the service station – like a patch of the bullfighter's green tie in Jaume's painting – and the small button he'd later found on the ground near the corpse, had set his mind searching for clues as to the fate of the kidnapped bullfighter. Had he also been at the service station when his driver was murdered? Where had they taken him? Had he also been killed? Had they strangled him, perhaps with his own tie?

The image that the police had released of himself, 'Brandon Bartholomew', was grainy enough, but the image of the thug in the red hoodie was even more obscure. It had looked like he was sitting in the back of a vehicle. What vehicle? It wasn't Benjamin's hire car, surely? Nor could it have been the van that sped away from the service station, that *bugaderia* laundry van, as Benjamin had seen it accelerating away *before* he'd been attacked. And why had the maniac been waiting around the goods delivery entrance of two IB hotels in Barcelona? For what?

Benjamin had scanned through the pages he'd printed off about the hotel group at the Internet store, but he had no idea what to look for. How could he track the psycho down? It had stalled him, and he didn't like it. If he was to find the killers and clear his own name, he would need time to dig deeper. He didn't have time, and so right now he needed instinct.

Instinct had also led to his decision to temporarily get out of Barcelona. He'd drawn a parallel between the torn green fabric and button at the service station with something he'd missed in the aristocrat's painting. But what was the connection? He'd decided to take the canvas to his old contact, Conso Puig, in Figueres. If anyone could help, it was her. She'd be able to get under the surface of the painting where MNAC had failed. She'd be able to trace *pentimenti* … those alterations made by an artist during painting, or any image that preceded the visible one.

This slow train wasn't helping matters, though, and he was still ravenous. He hadn't bought anything at Sants station for lack of time, and he couldn't risk searching for a buffet carriage now.

Security at the station had been at a maximum, with sniffer dogs and armed police carrying out random bag searches. As Benjamin didn't have any luggage other than the portfolio case, it had been easy enough to enter the huge glass-fronted concourse without much bother.

As far as he could recall, Figueres was a '*media distancia*' destination and not '*larga distancia*' – but there'd been long queues for tickets at every counter. In his baseball cap and shades, he'd finally paid cash for a ticket, asked what platform the next train to Figueres departed from – *any train* – and had then rushed down the escalator to board a near-empty carriage.

As the train pulled out of Sants, all he could initially focus on was the flashing sign in the carriage. It was hypnotic, conveniently letting him know what the next stop would be, the current hour and the temperature outside. '*Propera parada*' it said in Catalan, then '*próxima parada*' in Spanish.

First stop was Passeig de Gràcia, where the temperature was twenty-nine degrees Celsius. Second stop, Clot-Aragó, announced with a buzzing bell jingle, which was fine for a stop or two, but began to irritate after a few more.

Up to that point the train had still been underground or in pitch-black tunnels, but then shortly after Clot-Aragó they emerged into bright sunlight, and all the snazzy graffiti on railway sidings, under bridges and derelict buildings came into view.

As the train continued slowly north, at the third stop, St.Andreu, four Scandinavian-looking tourists got on and sat behind Benjamin – but he still had his own four-seater space. Across the aisle, a woman with two toddlers suddenly occupied the adjacent four seats. They also looked like tourists, certainly not Spanish. She was wearing headphones and seemed engrossed with videos on her cell phone. One of the toddlers, the eldest, was also wearing headphones, and was playing a game on his Nintendo.

Benjamin noticed that the other kid, with bubbles

of snot inflating sporadically from his nose, was holding a big white sandwich of Nutella, or something else that was brown and viscous – the little shit. He took just the occasional bite, while alternating between staring at Benjamin and whingeing at his brother to get his attention. He wanted to play on the Nintendo.

'Theo?' he said, more than once within minutes of sitting down. 'Theo? Theo? It's my turn, Theo. Theo? Th-e-o …'

Oh, Jesus Christ, no, thought Benjamin.

Neither Theo nor his mum could hear the snot-bubbler, and they were probably wearing headphones to ensure they couldn't. Benjamin tried to ignore the little brat and gazed out the window instead.

Apartment blocks, pylons, cement works, car dealers and a beer factory all flashed past, then the buildings and construction sites thinned out as the train rolled further away from Barcelona towards the Empordà countryside, with old *masias* scattered within the hills on the horizon, replacing the ugly edge-of-city commercial parks and shopping centres.

Propera parada … próxima parada …

Benjamin's head was spinning again as the chaos of the past twenty-four hours started to catch up with him. With the soft rocking of the train, he started to think about Elena and the Marqueses, his daughter Sophie, his ex, Claire, and his divorce lawyer, Walter Postlethwaite, and how the hell he was going to explain everything about Brandon Bartholomew …

'Theo?'

51

Elena, Nicole and Séverin

Monday 4 June, 3pm – Picasso Museum, Barcelona.

The inaugural event on the G20 spouse programme was well underway at the Picasso Museum in the heart of the Born neighbourhood. The spouses had been divided into separate groups while being escorted through the galleries displaying Picasso's Blue Period paintings and a specific gallery for 'Cubism to Classicism'.

The US Secretary of State's wife, Pamela Patterson, had arrived in the motorcade with a full contingent of Secret Service agents in her wake. Together with the Spanish First Lady and the Catalan President's wife, she distributed hugs and handshakes with other spouses wherever she moved, exuding warmth, familiarity and chattiness – a woman clearly trained in the art of being the centre of attention.

As far as Elena, now positioned outside, was concerned, the news coverage of the G20 spouse tour was so far inane. The organisers had claimed that the spouses visiting museums and performing arts schools was to show young people that 'they have a place in our world, in our museums, our theatres and concert halls', and that 'through music, art, literature, drama and dance, we can tell the story of our past and express our hopes for the future'. But so far, the Twitter hashtag feed of #G20Spouses only described each spouse's outfit, and in such detail that she wondered if anyone was interested in the art on display at all, let alone arts education for underprivileged kids.

'Mrs. Mexico', apparently, was 'resplendent in green and turquoise', the Spanish First Lady in a 'lavender silk suit with matching shoes', while 'Mrs. France', an ex-model, looked stunning 'in a taupe, pink and green patterned cocktail dress with straps'. By the time Elena had read that 'Miss Italy' was 'displaying the first cleavage of the tour, in a black suit with a low-cut top and five-inch stilettos', she'd had enough.

Perched on a press photographer's stepladder alongside an outside broadcast truck near the back of the museum, in the Plaça de Jaume Sabartés, Elena's shoulder was still throbbing, but she felt privileged to have been squeezed in among the media throng. It was thanks to Nicole Fugère, a friend she'd met on the journalism course. Nicole had since qualified, and as she spoke good French, she'd landed some work during the G20 with the AFP news agency. The area where they were standing was packed with cameramen and a large crowd of on-lookers, all strategically positioned to take shots of the spouses when they emerged from the museum after their tour.

It wasn't what she'd planned after leaving the hotel where she'd sent a message to Nicole. But she'd heard the police sirens and seen the motorcade heading down towards the museum, and so she'd followed it, knowing that's where her friend had said she'd be working.

As soon as she'd located her, Elena told her that she had a story, and she needed help in getting it to the right person. There was so much noise, Nicole could hardly hear her, and she beckoned her towards the side of the OB truck instead. They'd get a better view while perched on one of the ladders, she said.

Elena tried again to explain that she had a story, but Nicole was instead showing off the AFP tablet she was using – giving full access to the entire online G20 media portal, with links for all the resources, including all transcripts, photos and all the live video content.

'Look,' she told Elena. 'We can see what's going on inside.'

It temporarily distracted Elena, watching the spouses now ending a final Q & A session with the museum's director and curator, and it started to anger her, too. She wondered why the press were so obsessed with the spouses' wardrobes, and what the spouse tour was really for, what it had to do with the millennium development goals, for example, like eradicating extreme poverty, or reducing child mortality, or helping to fight climate change. They'd all flown to Barcelona in private jets, the *hypocrites* …

'Nicole, I have a story,' she said again, louder.

'What?'

'*I have a fucking story.*'

'Okay, you need to speak to Jérôme,' said Nicole.

'Who's Jérôme?'

'My boss.'

Elena had no time to ask how to contact him, because by then the G20 spouses had filed outside the back of the museum for a group photograph – and she suddenly caught sight of a hefty figure in the crowd who she recognised. He was pushing his way towards the front, swaying and moving in the same manner that she'd seen before. He wasn't wearing a red hoodie anymore, but he had that demented haircut and fringe; it was clearly him. As he reached into a pocket, she tried to point and shout out, but it was too late.

While smiling, waving and fanning herself in the heat alongside Pamela Patterson, Spain's First Lady, still resplendent in her lavender silk suit with matching shoes, suddenly recoiled and screamed in horror as a bloody lump of flesh slapped into her chest. Then there was utter chaos as security agents scrambled to push each spouse back into the waiting limos, while police agents dived in among the crowd in search of the culprit.

But Séverin had already fled.

Elena, too. And she was trying to keep him in sight as she sprinted up the road …

Part Three - Image

52

Benjamin

Monday 4 June, 4pm – Barcelona to Figueres.

Image … a representation or likeness of a person or thing; an optically formed reproduction of an object, such as one formed by a lens or mirror; a person or thing that resembles another closely; a mental picture or idea produced by the imagination; a double or a copy. Or perhaps just a simple case of mistaken identity?

Mistaken identity.

Benjamin was still on the slow, regional train to Figueres, and still rattled by the snivelling toddler with the Nutella sandwich in the adjacent seat, whining at his brother, Theo, to have a go on his Nintendo. Theo, with headphones on, was still ignoring his little brother – as was the kids' mum, who was also wearing headphones and watching videos on her phone.

'Theo?'

A pause.

'Theo?'

Another pause.

'Theo?

Ditto.

Benjamin waited, dreading the inevitable.

'Theo?'

Benjamin was about to reach over and rip off Theo's headphones, then scream in his ear: '*Answer your fucking brother, you nasty little shit*' – but decided against it.

'I don't think Theo can hear you,' he said to the toddler instead, removing his sunglasses and forcing a smile.

This probably wasn't the best idea, either. The snot-bubbler didn't smile back. He glanced at his mum, probably to check that she'd defend him if it came to it, although she hardly seemed aware of his existence. Then he simply stared at Benjamin, scowling while nibbling slowly on his sandwich.

He was like Damien in *The Omen*, the son of the Devil and the Biblical Antichrist with the triple-six birthmark, probably plotting to have Benjamin impaled by a church spire that would crash down after being hit by lightning in Figueres. But at least the railway carriage was silent again and there was air-conditioning, even though the train was still too slow.

Benjamin tucked his sunglasses into one of the chest pockets of his huge lumberjack shirt, placed the portfolio case onto his lap, and then shut his eyes to concentrate.

Go away, devil child.

Thank God that Sophie was never obsessed with Nintendo. Only singing. Always singing. And dancing. He had to call her. He had to explain a few things. And Walter, his lawyer … what would he say? Shit, what would *Claire* say? She knew nothing about his second passport. Would it now fuck up all Walter's negotiations?

As the image released by the police of Brandon Bartholomew at Girona airport had been almost unrecognisable, Benjamin believed that the damage to his professional reputation was minimal – but it still put an end to him using his middle names for any undercover work. He would also have to be extremely careful how he finally cleared his name, *all* his names. There were some Italian and French mobsters who only knew him as Brandon Bartholomew. Some of them were doing time. If they discovered his real name then they'd have him dismembered, well before the devil child could have him impaled by any church spire.

Focus, Benjamin.

Mistaken identity … *double imagery.*

The masterwork of *The Hallucinogenic Toreador* was, of course, an oil painting *à clef.* The bullfighter, about to die, represented the painter's dead elder brother, the Salvador Dalí Domenech who was born, and died, before Dalí himself was born. Dalí's parents liked to think of him as a reincarnation of his dead brother, seeing a close spiritual and physical likeness in their two sons. But to feel regarded, in the eyes of others, as someone else, and someone who was dead, was a problem that exercised a strong influence on the formation of Dalí's character.

To be regarded, in the eyes of other people, as someone else.

Benjamin started to tap his fingers on the portfolio case. *Anamorphosis*, that was it. Encrypted images that appear only when we concentrate our focus on a picture, or a *scene*, in a certain way.

Just like a crime scene.

He reminded himself that Dalí was fascinated by optical illusions and experimenting with hidden or ambiguous imagery. He had the ability to see things in an entirely different manner from those around him. But the ability of the viewer to see double images depends on his degree of *paranoia*, Dalí also said, meaning his ability to organise hallucinations produced by dreams …

Was Benjamin paranoid? No. *No.* He could admit to often being suspicious, certainly mistrustful, but not *paranoid* … definitely not paranoid.

He sat up.

'Art is not what you see,' he mumbled, opening the portfolio case and sliding out the painting. 'It is what you make others see.'

He studied the canvas.

Something wasn't right.

53

Inspector Vizcaya, Isabel Bosch and Beltrán Gómez

Monday 4 June, 3.45pm – Plaça Sant Jaume, Barcelona.

With the media speculating that the severed ear hurled at Spain's First Lady during the inaugural spouse event belonged to the kidnapped bullfighter, the Catalan police refused to confirm or deny it, as they simply hadn't a clue. Not at first, anyway.

In the chaos outside the Picasso Museum during the immediate aftermath, police moved rapidly among the crowd of onlookers, dispersing them as they went, while holding back all possible witnesses. Within minutes the entire area had been under lockdown to search for the culprit. An urgent appeal to the media for images of anyone hurling the chopped-off ear – finally retrieved for forensics after being scraped off the sole of a Manolo Blahnik shoe worn by a horrified Miss Italy – proved fruitless. All cameras had been focused on the G20 wives at the moment of impact, which meant the images they did have were spectacular.

When Inspector Vizcaya heard that a bloody chunk of ear had been thrown at the spouse party, he felt that his worst fears had been confirmed.

He was still incensed that Beltrán had gone over his head to issue a grainy image of Brandon Bartholomew arriving at Girona airport to the media and public, even though he was fully aware they had to track down and question the suspect. The little bastard from CITCO had released the image via the Ministry of Interior in Madrid and the state's Guardia Civil, which meant the Catalan police had no other option than to also share it.

Vizcaya and his boss, Isabel Bosch – also alarmed by Madrid's interference – had so far avoided making any further comments about the investigation to the media. But when news of the bloody ear thrown outside the Picasso Museum reached the incident room, Vizcaya assumed that the kidnap gang had exacted revenge and had finally followed through on their threats.

They'd threatened to cut off Rafa's ears at 6.30pm *if* bullfights went ahead in Spain, however, so the timing wasn't right … which made him feel something else wasn't right.

He decided to head to the scene outside the museum, yet not before ordering a team to visit all emergency wards across Barcelona to see if anyone had suffered serious ear injuries. He needed to know whether the severed ear matched the bullfighter's DNA, but it would take time.

In the meantime, social media was swamped with memes of the ear-splattered Spanish First Lady, some even comparing it to shoe throwing. The Greek, Australian, British and Turkish Prime Ministers, even the Pakistan President – they'd all endured or dodged shoe throwing over the years, but never ear throwing.

Amid the cynical posts, more serious commentators were starting to question Barcelona's G20 security measures, and whether the authorities were really up to the task. First a bullfighter had been kidnapped and his driver murdered just as world leaders were arriving, and now a slashed ear had been thrown at the spouse party.

How was it possible, they asked, for the police and security personnel escorting the spouses, to have not been alert enough to prevent someone lobbing a lump of flesh? How far away had the culprit been standing? How far could one accurately throw an ear? Ten metres? Fifteen metres?

Not one single report focused on the spouse programme's objectives of promoting arts education for underprivileged kids. But every 24-hour news channel, every daytime chat show, radio and podcast had their own theories of the supposed trajectory of the flying ear missile, some even backed up with online diagrams and maps of the possible position of where the culprit had been standing, or how he or she had fled.

International security agents were irate and nervous, too. The message emanating from G20 delegates was, 'Thank God it hit the Spanish spouse'. What if the ear had hit, say, the Chinese, Indian or French spouse, or Pamela Patterson herself? In fact, what if it had hit any of the other spouses instead of Spain's First Lady? Each country's armed security contingent had been entrusted with protecting its own leader, spouse and ministerial entourage. Nothing could be allowed to obstruct or put that mandate at risk, but they also needed to work closely with the Spanish and Catalan law-enforcement agencies.

So, what the hell was going on and who was in charge?

At the very top it was the Interior Minister in Madrid and Spain's Secretary of State for Security, but the woman on the ground in Barcelona taking the brunt of it all was the power-hungry Bosch – and she was having the worst day of her life. Her job was now on the line, even before the G20 had officially begun.

US Secret Service agents in Barcelona were demanding a review of security plans for all remaining spouse programme events, while the intelligence services representing most other G20 nations had requested a reinforced police presence for all public appearances or group photos involving the spouses.

Bosch's only response to date had been to order the

arrest of anyone with links to anarchists or animal rights extremists. Six social squat centres in the city were stormed and searched, arresting an entire group whose alleged aims were 'the destabilisation and collapse of the system'. No weapons or explosives had been found, let alone a kidnapped bullfighter with an ear missing. Only yoga mats.

Beltrán Gómez de Longoria had been summoned in front of Bosch to give an update on whether his appeal to the public via the Guardia Civil had thrown up anything about the suspect Bartholomew.

He found her marching around her vast office in her stilettos, barking instructions and berating any member of staff who dared to poke their head around her door. She'd had enough of the reports accusing her department of incompetence, as if *she* and the Catalan police were incapable of resolving the crisis on their own, and she had every intention to off-load the blame on others – Beltrán included.

The young CITCO agent first tried to draw parallels with the eco-terrorism taking place at museums and art galleries around Europe, including at the Prado in Madrid, and that the incident outside the Picasso Museum could have been the same 'climate change catastrophists, part of a radical environmental terrorism movement that –'

'*Get on with it*,' yelled Bosch.

Beltrán paused, just briefly, but then started to

explain that the ear throwing was probably just an isolated incident, a 'misdemeanour disorderly conduct charge' to quote the term they used while he'd been stationed in the States, often resolved in a federal court with a one-year probation sentence, with the accused agreeing not to own a weapon or come within five hundred metres of the residence or workplace of any person protected by the Secret Service …

'*Fuck your time stationed in the States,*' cried Bosch. 'What have we got on the red-hooded figure seen in Nîmes, and on Brandon Bartholomew?'

Beltrán was about to detail his theory that Bartholomew was either an operational mastermind with advanced doctrinal training, a key player working as a document forger or as a trusted travel or financial facilitator for other operatives, yet all the time using an alias or name variant, possibly as a previously watch-listed person − when an urgent call came through to Bosch's office from Vizcaya, who claimed to have 'relatively good news'.

Bosch put him on speaker.

'What is it?' she said.

'Am I still leading this investigation or not?' started Vizcaya. 'I've been trying to speak to you since that dickhead Gómez de Longoria approached his pals in the Guardia Civil to release that image −'

'He's sitting right here,' said Bosch.

'Is he now?' said Vizcaya, raising his voice. 'I'll tell the señorito myself, then. Beltrán, you're a total and utter −'

'What have you got?' snapped Bosch.

There was a pause, while Vizcaya calmed down.

'It was a left ear,' he said, finally.

'What?' said Bosch.

'The severed ear – it was a left ear.'

'So what?'

'It's not the bullfighter's ear, therefore,' said Vizcaya.

'How do you know?'

'The left ear that was thrown had been pierced several times, although the earrings were missing. The bullfighter's entourage confirm that Rafael Pérez has only one piercing, in his right ear – none in the left ear – and we have photographic evidence.'

Bosch then yelled instructions to release a statement confirming that the severed ear 'did not pertain to Rafael Pérez' and was instead being treated as an 'isolated, separate incident'. There was a pause. 'Then whose ear is it?' she said, finally.

Vizcaya told her that he couldn't say for sure, but that he was about to find out.

Indeed, while Beltrán had been summoned in front of Bosch, Vizcaya had been slightly cheered by news from agents visiting emergency hospitals across the city, and who'd reported back from the Clínica Raval. A young man had apparently checked himself in to *urgències* that same morning, with a serious ear injury, after first staggering into a pharmacy near Rambla del Raval, clutching a towel to his head. It was unfortunate for the young man, of course, but it possibly meant the bull-fighter was still unscathed.

The patient's name was given as Santiago Quintana. He claimed that he'd been robbed and attacked at his place of work, an unlicensed brothel called the Hostel Splendido, and that he'd been unable to stem the flow of blood from his severed left ear, which had been cut off in an attack. Medics at the hospital recalled that he was heavily tattooed. After being stitched up, the incoherent, semi-deaf patient had limped away from the hospital.

Vizcaya's team was now searching records for a Santiago Quintana, and it had become a priority to find him. Vizcaya himself was already on his way over to the rundown brothel to find out what might have happened.

As soon as Bosch ended the call with Vizcaya, Beltrán's own cell phone started buzzing. He answered it. There was news of an unattended bag that might require a 'controlled explosion' at the Hotel Arts, and where his own presence would be appreciated immediately.

54

Jürgen

Monday 4 June, 3.30pm — El Poblenou neighbourhood, Barcelona.

Jürgen was shaking. He'd been shaking since moving the gagged and bound bullfighter to the boiler room, behind the industrial machines, using Hendrik's discarded knife to threaten him along the way. It was noisy in there, deafening at times, and any employee with access normally had to wear earplugs. But it was a place where no one would find, let alone hear Rafa, or at least that's what he hoped.

The bullfighter's hands and feet were tightly secured, so he couldn't escape, and he had no choice but to stay close to Jürgen as he shuffled him along.

Jürgen was certain that Hendrik wouldn't go to the police. How could he? What would he say? That he'd been attacked while keeping guard on the hostage?

Nor would he be returning here for any driving or delivery work again, not until he recovered from his eye injuries … if he ever recovered.

No, it was only Séverin he worried about.

Which was more than enough.

Jürgen would have to organise the bullfighter's release, but it couldn't happen until he was safely out of the country himself, back in Amsterdam and at the Ruigoord commune.

He couldn't stay here any longer, not with Séverin surely looking for him. There was too much linking him to it all; he could be charged with accessory to murder. He had all the cash to escape, to change his appearance and lie low for months, if not years, but it was crucial to contact Brigitte about the clean-up operation first. If only she'd pick up the phone …

55

Elena and Séverin

Monday 4 June, 4pm – From the Picasso Museum to Sants, Barcelona.

The distance from the Picasso Museum to Barcelona's Sants railway station is approximately four kilometres, about a fifty-minute walk, cutting back through the old city and part of Eixample. As the narrow, labyrinthine streets and alleys finally turned to broad, geometrically precise roads, mostly clogged with traffic, the pain in Elena's shoulder was getting worse. She'd had to jog a few times to keep up with him in the unbearable heat, but she'd managed to keep the thug in sight from a safe distance, all the time trying to keep in the shade.

He was moving swiftly and methodically through the city in search of his next prey, she assumed, or hopefully to the kidnappers' hideout. He clearly knew the streets of Barcelona, but it was only once they'd reached the Avinguda de Roma that she guessed he was heading towards the station.

She knew what she was after, and what she had to do. She wanted to track the bastard until the end, to get her story. It was too good an opportunity to miss. If he was heading to Sants, that was also where Benjamin had asked her to drive to earlier. Maybe the savage was trying to reunite with him ... *Brandon Bartholomew* ... that impostor sought by the police. She'd started to feel angry for finding him interesting, curious, *different* ...

If the thug was planning to jump on a train from Sants, then she could do the same, and later she'd find time to post her report, with or without Nicole's help via the AFP news agency.

But when Séverin finally reached Sants station, he didn't enter the concourse itself. Instead, he headed round to the back, to the Plaça de Joan Peiró, where young skateboarders were practising their moves, rolling and swerving near small groups of winos and junkies who were sprawled out on benches around the square.

56

Beltrán Gómez

Monday 4 June, 4.15pm – Port Olímpic, Barcelona.

The champagne reception had long been cleared away at the new terrace restaurant within the Hotel Arts at the Port Olímpic. Security staff had also combed the premises to prepare it for another event to be attended by US and UN delegates resident at the hotel. Sniffer dogs had prowled around, and all appeared to be secure within the restaurant itself, but not at the left-luggage lockers outside. All lockers had been emptied, and each locker's token had been returned, except for one. That locker had therefore been opened by security to reveal a small backpack left inside.

While sniffer dogs reacted with disinterest to the bag, an extra cautious agent, diligently following instructions that everything had to be double-checked, insisted that hotel security show him the CCTV images covering the restaurant entrance to the hotel and lockers.

It wasn't the clearest of images, but with closer scrutiny the agent felt that the man with bushy hair who had tried to enter the restaurant with the bag before it was put through X-ray and then placed in a locker, looked like the man sought by the police in connection with the murder and kidnapping.

The restaurant manager was also asked to view the CCTV images to see if he might recall the unidentified guest. Not only did he recognise him, but he said it was the same man who'd introduced himself to the US Secretary of State when he'd arrived with his entourage after a jog. The agent made a couple of calls, and seconds later the hotel restaurant was swarming with more security personnel.

Beltrán was driven over there in a blue-flashing Seat that screeched to a halt at one of the checkpoints outside the hotel. He'd initially wondered why his precious time was being wasted on an unclaimed bag, until he was fully briefed on the situation.

Agents from the Mossos and US Secret Service were already arguing with one another and with the head of security at the hotel, but Beltrán was keen to avoid a full-on security alert. He didn't want it publicised that their suspect – or at least a guest resembling Brandon Bartholomew – had simply breezed in, amid what should have been the tightest ever security at one of the key hotels reserved for G20 delegates. If Bartholomew was still in the area, then he also didn't want to scare him away.

The restaurant had already been sealed off and was again being meticulously searched. Satisfied that the backpack contained no explosives, it was opened and examined by agents, yet nothing of particular interest was found, apart from an art book, scribbled notebooks, a plug adapter, and an iPhone cable. There were no weapons, knives or severed ears, but it was still bagged and sent off to forensics for analysis.

Interviewing the restaurant manager, Beltrán was quickly able to confirm that the suspect had been seen conversing with an elderly aristocrat, as well as shaking hands and introducing himself to Secretary of State Patterson as 'the doctor'. Shortly afterwards, he'd left the restaurant in what appeared to be a great hurry.

Beltrán didn't even stop to think that there might be any innocent explanation. Already playing with the authorities under their noses, he assumed this was now the mastermind's cynical, fanatical, self-styled alias: *the doctor.*

He demanded access to all photos taken during the champagne reception, with the aim of putting an embargo on any images of the suspect shaking hands with the US statesman. He was told that it was too late. There were already pictures on social media, the restaurant manager explained, because his PR expert, a Barcelona socialite known as Dixie, had already seen to it. In addition, many other photographers had also followed Secretary Patterson into the restaurant, just after his jog.

'There are hundreds of images out there already,' the manager said. 'Haven't you seen them?'

He didn't have much time to respond.

One of the waiters had recalled 'the doctor' grabbing some paper napkins off his tray, and then scribbling on them while using the back of a menu card. He'd shown agents where the man had been sitting, chatting with the aristocrat. Next to a pile of menus stacked on a nearby shelf, they'd found a discarded napkin with some words scrawled on it:

'Find the green tie … you'll find the bullfighter.'

57

Benjamin

Monday 4 June, 5pm – Barcelona to Figueres.

No one had checked Benjamin's train ticket as the fourth stop, Granollers, came and went.

By now, he'd replaced the canvas safely back into the portfolio case and put his sunglasses back on, while images of Dalí's *Toreador* still flashed through his mind. His thoughts had drifted back to the service station and the corpse again, and a possible connection between the torn green fabric and button that he'd seen there with something that had struck him about the aristocrat's painting.

He thought about Elena and the psycho, the *killers*, and how the hell he could track them down and clear his name, just as soon as he'd delivered the canvas to Conso Puig in Figueres … if only the train would hurry the fuck up.

Theo's snivelling brother with the Nutella sandwich was still scowling from across the aisle, but with the gentle rocking of the train he was also starting to look drowsy, which was a relief. After the fifth stop of Sant Celoni, Benjamin could see some mountainous peaks on the horizon out of the left side window, but he assumed it was too soon for it to be Pyrenees.

A sixth stop, Gualba, and a seventh, Riells i Viabrea-Breda, then an eighth, Hostalric, then a ninth, Maçanet-Massanes, all followed – and Benjamin wondered whether he'd ever get there, or if he was even heading in the right direction. Every time he peered out at the platforms, however, there was the same 'Girona/Portbou' sign, pointing in the direction the train was heading, but it was just *too slow*.

Gazing around the carriage with his shades on, he could see the four Scandinavian-looking tourists were still sitting behind him, and there was Theo, the snot-bubbler, and their mum across the aisle, but other than that, it was empty – and it was empty, he deduced, because it was a *crap* train.

Where were they now? As if in response, an inspector started to saunter through the carriage. Benjamin dug into a pocket of his khaki pants for his ticket, where he could still feel the small button that he'd found at the service station. He then pulled his Barça baseball cap further over his forehead as the inspector checked his ticket, not even meeting his eye.

'Figueres?' said Benjamin. It was a risk, but he wanted to know.

The reply came in the form of some hand chopping, as if the inspector was cutting vegetables – indicating, Benjamin assumed, that it was a few stops yet.

It was. In fact, it was another eleven stops. First there was Caldes de Malavella, then Fornells de la Selva, and then Girona appeared, and where everyone else, the Scandinavians and Theo's family, all disembarked – with the devil child himself sticking his phlegmy-Nutella tongue out and a middle finger up at Benjamin as he was ushered off the train. Charming.

As no one else got on, Benjamin wondered whether this was the end of the line, and whether they all had to change – but then the train started moving again.

Alone, still starving, and realising that the toddler wasn't holding his sandwich when he got off, Benjamin went in search of it. Even if the kid had been nibbling at it while bubbles inflated from his nose, it would do. Maybe the crust was still intact and germ-free. It was something to look for, something to cheer him up. He took off his shades, stood up, and then rummaged around where Theo's family had been sitting, only to suddenly stop and take stock of his situation.

How had it come to this? Here he was, still recovering from concussion after losing his car, iPhone, backpack and even the aristocrat's painting a couple of times, wanted for questioning by the Spanish police, mid-divorce, still with a job to finish and a psycho to track down in order to clear his own name, yet scavenging for the remains of a snot-soggy sandwich in a railway carriage somewhere in Catalonia. It didn't help matters when he eventually found it squashed and stuck to the bottom of his shoe.

'At least that's one mystery solved,' he muttered, trying to stay positive, and scraping the semi-masticated lump off his foot.

After Girona came Celrà – where the doors didn't even open – then Bordils-Julià, then Flaça, then Saint Jordi Desvalls, then Camallera, St.Miquel de Fluvià and Vilamalla – until *finally,* Figueres – where Benjamin stole a bicycle.

He didn't mean to, he hadn't wanted to, but in the end, he felt he had no choice.

It was after the stop of Flaça when things had suddenly taken another turn. He'd gazed out and seen the sign that pointed towards the direction of *Frontera*, the French border, so he knew he was still heading vaguely in the right direction. At Saint Jordi Desvalls station, three lycra-clad cyclists got on the train with their bikes and stood in the area near the doors. They kept themselves to themselves as Benjamin sat back, rather concerned, however, with an elderly couple staring at him for the next two stops.

What the hell were they staring at? His oversized lumberjack shirt, his baseball cap, his shades? Whatever it was, they just kept staring and then abruptly got up and moved to another carriage. He picked up the portfolio case and patted his pockets for his notes and ticket again, assuming that if the screen at the end of the carriage was to be trusted, then Figueres would be the next stop, which is where he would get off.

As did the cyclists …

… and which is when Benjamin got the distinct feeling he was being followed by the couple who'd got on a few stops before – the couple who'd been staring at him, but who'd then moved to another carriage. It was obvious they were following him – *why move to another carriage?* – and now they'd got off at Figueres and it didn't feel right – so he followed the cyclists pushing their bikes towards the exit – simple enough, really – the ticket collector was just waving people through – even more so for the cyclists who had to go through that special gate – and Benjamin followed behind them, clutching the case under his arm, yet glancing back to see the elderly couple now talking to a guard on the platform – *about him?* – he didn't want to hang around to find out – and so he jogged ahead, faster now, wondering whether they'd recognised him – *impossible,* surely? – and then as he finally made it out through the concourse there was a cafeteria and a TV on the wall showing a news bulletin – which is when he saw his image again, flashed up on the screen – and he thought he heard someone shout so he started to run – *sprint,* even – right out to where he saw the bikes propped up near the fountain in the little plaza, where the cyclists were replenishing their water bottles, and where, unnoticed, he quickly grabbed one of the bikes, balanced the portfolio case across the handlebars, and then set off, as fast as he could …

'Location, time, and now image,' he said, racing away.

58

Inspector Vizcaya and Officer Soler

Monday 4 June, 4.15pm – El Raval neighbourhood, Barcelona.

Images, locations and times were issues still puzzling Inspector Vizcaya as he rushed over to the Splendido brothel on his Vespa, having already instructed ahead for the nearest Mossos agents to secure the premises, as well as adjacent buildings, in case the hostage was being held there or nearby.

Running through his head in a constant loop were images of Rafael Pérez being lifted out of the bullring in France, the figure in a red hoodie in the back of the Chevrolet, and the CCTV images of Bartholomew arriving at Girona airport and also entering the service station shop before midnight.

He kept thinking about the locations where the bullfighter might be held, where the Chevrolet and murdered driver had been left, and where the hire car was finally abandoned.

Then there were the times when the kidnappers made calls to the media, having also called a London number providing a legal defence fund for green activists. Not forgetting the deadline set by Isabel Bosch, to kill the story and arrest anyone before sunset.

He was yet to learn about Beltrán's 'doctor' revelations over at the Olympic port, which was probably just as well. Vizcaya had had more than enough of the terrorism paranoia, although he knew he had an obligation to cover every possible theory.

Officer Soler had messaged to say she'd be meeting Vizcaya at the brothel, insisting she had urgent updates from forensics and CCTV analysis to share with him, as well as news from Lieutenant Trias, now back in Girona. Vizcaya responded by asking if there'd been any further developments on Marcos Constantinos, the tycoon running the legal collective who the kidnappers had called, and who the police in London were supposed to be questioning. He also wanted to know if Scotland Yard or Interpol had given them any further information on Brandon Bartholomew.

Nothing yet, came the reply.

Arriving at the Splendido before her, Vizcaya was first briefed by two Mossos officers, who said that if it hadn't been for his interest in the ear injuries sustained by a man who'd told medical staff that he worked there, they would have simply registered the case as another statistic of the city's vice or drug crime.

Inside, they'd been questioning the elderly owner. They'd found him shuffling around with a severe limp, due to a clubfoot defect at birth that had never been surgically corrected. His sallow complexion gave him the look of a drug-ravaged gangster, but he was also willing to cooperate, clearly worried that his joint would now be shut down.

He'd confirmed that Santiago Quintana, his 'cleaner and receptionist' from Chile, was a drug-pusher and user. Wherever he was and whatever injuries he'd sustained, he hadn't returned to work and was probably on the run or hiding. And *with one ear missing*, Vizcaya presumed – but until they could locate Quintana or confirm his DNA, they couldn't be sure.

With the old pimp still hovering nearby, the Mossos officers concluded their briefing by handing Vizcaya a torn, tacky journal, apparently used for reservations at the so-called hostel, or for appointments with prostitutes. As soon as Vizcaya flicked through the pages and saw a scrawled *'Bart'* reservation, as if the full Bartholomew name might not have been understood, things moved much faster.

The Mossos agents called for back-up, and very soon all rooms in the hostel were being searched – yet nothing was found, let alone a kidnapped bullfighter in a 'suit of lights'. When some of the sex workers were shown images of Bartholomew, however, they said they'd seen him on the landing, shouting and banging on doors. Minutes later, the police had the entire street under lockdown, with a forensics team called to help scour the premises, as well as examine the blood found on the reception desk.

The old owner claimed to not recognise the images of Bartholomew or the red-hooded figure he was shown by Vizcaya, and he swore that neither had stayed at the hostel last night. He said he lived on the top floor of the building and had come down to sort the place out, after hearing some shouting and scream-ing. He insisted he hadn't *seen* anything himself.

Vizcaya stared at the sad, slightly tragic figure, convinced he was hiding something. Beneath the lighting in the hostel, his skin looked yellow and hardly thick enough to cover his scalp, where a few locks of white hair clung to either side. What kind of life must he have led, he wondered – and not for the first time, from his past dealings with the Raval underworld.

Minutes later, after Mossos agents who'd been checking vehicles parked nearby found that the number plate of a silver-grey Citroën taxi with a smashed window was from Girona, Vizcaya got really heavy with the pimp, grilling him yet again and threat-ening to have him locked up.

He swore he knew nothing about the taxi, but it didn't take long before he'd handed over a cell phone with a shattered screen, claiming that he'd found it on the floor of the hostel when he'd come downstairs.

. . .

By the time Marta Soler joined Vizcaya, news had come through from the police in Girona. They'd made contact with the registered owner of the Citroën taxi, a man named Diego Carmona. He was laid up with a fractured foot and was initially concerned whether the police enquiry was related to his vehicle's insurance, because he said his lazy son had 'fucked up again'. His son had been planning to drive the taxi for him that day, but his daughter, Elena, had done so instead – and now he was panicking about her safety. She'd called after picking up a passenger from Girona airport at around six in the morning, to say she was heading to Barcelona – but where was she now?

'*What's happened?*' he cried.

The Girona police had been unable to give him any answers or placate him. They'd told him they would need to speak to his son to corroborate the sequence of events, and to urgently trace Elena. They'd asked for a photo of her, and several other details, and said they'd be back in touch.

A little later, while the taxi was being sealed outside the brothel and towed away for investigation, Soler had tried to get Vizcaya's full attention as they stood near the front entrance, but he barely gave her the chance.

'So, what have we got?' he said, before proceeding to answer his own question. 'Bartholomew arrives at

Girona airport at 8.15pm yesterday evening. He hires a car, yet supposedly hangs around the airport area until just before midnight –'

'No, wait,' said Soler, 'this is very important –'

'– when he's *then* caught on CCTV entering a service station shop –'

'Inspector, listen –

'– and possibly had a reservation or a safe house at this Splendido pit.'

'They found an iPhone and an unpaid toll ticket in the hire car,' said Soler.

There was a brief silence before Vizcaya acknowledged her.

'What?'

'An iPhone and toll ticket.'

'And?'

Soler said that the phone had been found under the passenger front seat and sent off for analysis. Whoever owned it had deleted everything, via a cloud account. The unpaid toll ticket was found in the driver's sun-visor. The vehicle had joined the motorway at junction six from the C-66, at 11.46pm, from anywhere as far as Palafrugell. She said that after Bartholomew hired the car at 8.45pm, he'd therefore headed towards the coast before returning to the service station at around midnight.

Vizcaya nodded but was unsure whether it changed anything. Bartholomew was still at the service station in his hire car during the period of the Chevrolet's arrival, probably at the time of the chauffeur's murder and presumably for the transfer of the bullfighter. A bloodstained hammer had been found on the back seat of his abandoned hire car in Barcelona.

'But what about the man seen outside the service station shop at 5.15am, banging on the glass and asking directions to walk to the airport?' said Soler.

Vizcaya stared at her.

'We have a witness report, remember?' she said, reading from her notes. 'A staff member who was starting the morning shift at the service station described the man as odd, probably foreign, with thick hair.' She paused. 'Same as Bartholomew? We checked with the witness again, and he thinks that, yes, it could be the same man caught on CCTV entering the service station shop to buy a sandwich just before it closed at midnight. So, Bartholomew was at the service station just before midnight *and* at around 5.15am.'

Silence.

'There's no CCTV covering the taxi rank at Girona airport,' she continued. 'But if Bartholomew was also the passenger being driven by Diego Carmona's daughter in his taxi from the airport at around 6am – and it's possible that he was – then it's highly unlikely that he was also driving his hire car towards Barcelona from midnight onwards.'

Vizcaya stroked his moustache, unsure how to respond. Once again, he quietly cursed Beltrán for putting out an appeal with the image of Bartholomew so soon, although they certainly had to eliminate him from the enquiry.

'We don't know if Bartholomew was the passenger in that taxi,' he said, finally. 'Even so, possibly he just supplied the kidnappers with their transfer vehicle. That was his job. He hired the vehicle but didn't personally drive it to Barcelona. He cleaned up while the rest of the gang headed there, then followed in the taxi after making the calls to the media –'

'The calls were made from central Barcelona, Inspector.'

'There would have been no room in the hire car for them all, so he followed on later in a taxi,' he said, mumbling now. 'There are many possibilities ...'

He stopped and stared at Soler. She was several steps ahead of him.

'Why was the unpaid toll ticket still in the sun-visor of the hire car?' she said. 'Why wasn't it used for the onward journey to Barcelona? We've since gone back to analyse the payments made with the chauffeur's credit card. We've reconfirmed that the ticket paid for at the last tollgate before Barcelona, *with* the hire car, was the toll ticket from the bullfighter's Chevrolet, collected near the French border. It wasn't the ticket in the sun-visor, from junction six of the C-66.'

Vizcaya shrugged. He knew it was an issue, and very hard to explain, but he still questioned whether it changed anything.

'As I said, maybe Bartholomew just supplied the transfer vehicle but didn't drive it to Barcelona. His job was to clean up. Maybe he instructed the gang to use their own toll ticket from the Chevrolet.'

'Or maybe the hire car was stolen,' said Soler.

'No, *listen* –'

'Well, we don't know.'

'We find kidnap victims and missing persons,' snapped Vizcaya.

The entire investigation was getting to him again, thanks to Bosch's urgency to make an arrest, on top of Beltrán's groundless and shitbrained terrorism theories.

'Let's just focus on where the bullfighter is being held,' he said, raising his voice. 'Not *here* at this slum, but we've picked up the scent, no? He was here, according to the hookers upstairs. He could be anywhere near here.'

Soler fell silent.

'Look,' he continued, starting to shout. 'Beltrán should *never* have undermined my authority, but the fact remains that Bartholomew hired a vehicle used in the transfer, from which payments were made using the chauffeur's credit card, and which was found abandoned with a claw hammer. Even if he'd hung around Girona airport and got a taxi to follow the gang to Barcelona, we still need to speak to him. Why haven't we heard anything from Scotland Yard or Interpol? Carmona thinks his daughter is in danger – a punk from here has had his ear sliced off – and we also have a possible reservation for a 'Bart' at this shithole. Whoever this Bartholomew is, we need to find him, because I believe it will lead us to the bullfighter. And that's what *we* do, Soler … we find missing persons.'

Soler kept quiet, but she still doubted Bartholomew

had stayed around the service station simply to clean up. Why wait until 5.15am? Why then ask for directions to the airport? It was true they didn't yet have proof that Bartholomew had been Carmona's passenger, nor that he was the man asking for directions. But it was bugging her, and it wouldn't go away.

Vizcaya, meanwhile, had started examining the cell phone that the old pimp had handed over, being careful not to contaminate any potential evidence. It was unlocked, but the smashed screen meant it was impossible to see any of the photos on the device. He checked the call register, though, and the 'recent' and 'missed' numbers were visible enough.

Before long, and with Soler's help in calling the Girona police, he discovered that the cell phone belonged to Elena Carmona, the daughter of the taxi owner, Diego. The WhatsApp calls confirmed her chats with her father *Papi*, and brother *Pablo*, and one or two others logged in the contact list, either friends or other taxi drivers.

The last incoming call was from an unnamed number, and it was the same number that appeared several times on the missed calls list, and once on the outgoing or 'dialled' list. Vizcaya took out his own phone and keyed in the number.

An irritated, pompous-sounding voice eventually answered.

'Who is this?' said the Marquès de Guíxols.

59

Benjamin and Conso

Monday 4 June, 5.15pm – Figueres.

Benjamin peddled away frantically to get away from the area near Figueres railway station. The humidity was intolerable with no breeze at all, and he was breaking into a sweat.

He could already see the roof of the Dalí Museum, a building as surreal as his paintings, topped by a huge metallic dome and decorated with luminous egg shapes. If he could just keep that in sight, he'd be able to get his bearings from there. He heard a police siren in the distance, but didn't care. As he pushed away at the peddles, carefully balancing the portfolio case across the handlebars, he tried to recall the last time he'd visited the museum. It was Dalí's last creation and a work of art in itself – proof of how he'd planned for immortality, seeing as he was also buried there.

That elderly couple on the train ... *had they recognised him?*

After cycling up to the main Rambla boulevard of Figueres, he reached a narrow lane that he remembered from years back, tucked away off Lasauca street, very near the 'Dalíland' square.

He searched his pockets for the scrap of paper where he'd scribbled the address of his old contact, then rolled the bike along the road, scanning the small townhouses with front patios amid the modern apartment blocks, some with a space to park a small car, others overgrowing with plants. He finally reached number ninety-seven, where there was a rusty, old yellow Seat car parked on the terrace. He propped the bike against the gate, then knocked on the front door.

She looked much older than when they'd last met, certainly more frail. But her luminous, excited eyes still sparkled, as ever the eccentric yet gentle character she'd always been, her face criss-crossed with laugh-lines and deep creases from a lifetime of squinting in the Catalan sun.

'Benjamin, *Benj-amin*. What have you got for me now? What *have* you got for me now?' the wonderful old Consuela – Conso, as she preferred – greeted him in her broken English, once she'd unbolted her door.

Benjamin noted how she still had the habit of repeating most things twice, the second time with more emphasis, and she'd always spoken to him very slowly and loudly, as if she was afraid he wouldn't understand.

She was wearing yellow espadrilles, a sky blue maxi-skirt with ruffles, huge red earrings, and a loud, graphic T-shirt with bold slogans all over it. She was a colourful character in every sense, and Benjamin envied the fact that she loved art and was *artistic;* she wasn't just an art connoisseur. He'd always pictured her being part of the flower power generation, or the equivalent of the swinging Sixties or Seventies in Barcelona or Ibiza, perhaps even hanging out with Dalí himself. She would have been stunning in her day, and still glowed with her foxiness and coolness.

Ten minutes later they were seated outside a quiet bar in the shade of the plane trees on the Rambla, the central rectangular avenue framed by two small squares surrounded by bistros and shops. Benjamin had his baseball cap and shades on again, after removing them to greet Conso.

They'd walked there slowly in the heat, but more slowly than Benjamin would have liked. He'd forgotten that a stroll normally taking five minutes could last half-an-hour with Conso.

The café was halfway from her house to where she'd moved her studio, she said, and it was her custom to rest briefly in the Rambla whenever she made the journey. She told him that she'd retired from lecturing, and that she spent her days mostly reading if there was no painting in for cleaning or restoration. She rejected the distractions of television and the Internet, and it was a miracle how Benjamin had managed to locate her, adding that she hardly ever used the new 'smarty phone' that her nephew had given her – 'or whatever this thing is', she said, laughing and waving it in front of him as they'd strolled.

A waiter came over to greet her in Catalan, bringing a small tumbler of white wine with ice and an ashtray, without even being asked. He then hovered near the table to see if her companion wanted to order anything. Benjamin still craved something substantial to eat, but he didn't think he had time. He opened and closed his hands, trying to ask for the menu – maybe he could finally grab a baguette – and the waiter nodded and sauntered off.

Conso was clearly a regular and also wanted to smoke, already tapping a cigarette out of a packet that she produced with a lighter from her straw bag. She never smoked at home or in her studio, she said, grinning, but did so while sitting outside all the bars and cafés around town.

She lit a cigarette and blew smoke out of one side of her mouth, before taking a sip of her iced wine. Smokers nowadays always seemed to be from the older generation, Benjamin pondered – the 'if it was going to kill me it would have done so by now' set.

'After a certain age, you can pretty much do what you like,' she said, as if reading his mind. 'No one tells you off, except your doctor or kids. As my kids now live all over the world, they don't really know.'

As well as many years spent having a ball, Conso was a highly qualified professor and a specialist in the restoration of art, having set up her own lab for the analysis of paintings. She didn't work for just anyone, but she had a soft spot for Benjamin, impressed by his fanatical research when he'd once spent time in Figueres, and his excellent thesis on Dalí that had also credited her own work.

She explained that her nephew had been getting involved with her business and had also set up a 'web-site thing'. He'd even installed some new equipment in his own studio in Cadaqués, about thirty-five kilometres away.

As the waiter hadn't returned with a menu, and without divulging any details about the Marquès de Guíxols, Benjamin slipped the painting out of the case and showed it to Conso. She immediately stubbed out her cigarette in the ashtray, narrowed her eyes and smiled.

He dug into a pocket and then handed her the memory-stick from MNAC. He told her that he'd become obsessed with the bullfighter's tie and collar area of the painting. He couldn't say why, but there was something that wasn't right, and he felt it deserved a radiographic examination, and possibly more, if she could help. He said that they'd tried IRR but that nothing was visible – although they both knew that only meant no outline drawings in charcoal were visible.

Conso nodded, checking her watch, and said that she could certainly examine the painting, but she'd need her nephew to help. She believed he was on his way back from Cadaqués but said that she would check – and she picked up her 'smarty phone' to call him.

Watching her make the call, waiting for her nephew to answer, Benjamin put the canvas back in the portfolio case. Her technique to examine it would be relatively straightforward, he thought – and he knew she had the experience. Whatever was under the surface of Jaume's painting, she could help find it.

With no answer from her nephew, she sipped her wine again, while Benjamin explained that the painting had been discovered in an old *masia* not far from Púbol. She lit another cigarette and grew attentive, starting to talk about Púbol and the surrounding area, saying that many friends of Dalí and Gala had helped them in their search to find a small castle to renovate, some even taking aerial photographs to help choose the best option.

Suddenly her phone started to ring very loudly with a heavy metal ringtone from Motörhead.

'*Jesus Christ, what's that?*' said Benjamin, genuinely startled.

'It's my nephew returning my call,' said Conso. 'He set the phone up for me and I don't know how to change it.'

She answered it, and then started conversing for

quite a while in Catalan, with her cigarette still alight but growing long with ash between her fingers. Benjamin craned his neck, trying to find the waiter, wondering why the hell it should take so long to bring a menu. Once she'd finished the call, she smiled at Benjamin while stubbing out her cigarette.

'My nephew Josep will be here soon,' she said. 'You'll like him.'

Conso was an '*Amic del Museu Dalí*', an association of 'friends' of the Dalí Museum, as well as a former consultant to the Dalí Foundation itself. Benjamin told her that before or after she carried out radiography on the painting, he wanted to take it into the museum to compare it with the brushstrokes on the original *The Face* – but she said it would be impossible, that the museum wouldn't allow him to take in a canvas, and he should know better. Then when she told him the museum was closing early, he started to panic.

'Early?'

'For security –'

'What security?'

'For tomorrow's visitors.'

'What visitors?'

'VIPs … something to do with G20 … so it's closing early today –'

From then on, things moved fast, with Benjamin jumping up, almost knocking over her glass on the table in the process, checking his watch again and asking how long it would take her to examine the canvas, *she* then telling him that it would depend on when her nephew finally arrived, but her studio was now very close – and so they set off – via the museum, with Conso using her Dalí 'friends' card to haggle with her contact at the ticket office who said the museum was about to close, yet who finally allowed Benjamin in quickly to see one specific work of art. Benjamin asked Conso if he could borrow her phone, then he took the painting out of its portfolio case again to take a shot of the canvas, before finally heading into the museum, with Conso setting off to her studio to meet up with her nephew, agreeing to rendezvous back at the bar in the Rambla in, say, an hour-and-a-half, maximum …

He knew it was a risk, but at last he was back at the Dalí Theatre-Museum, and he was *alone* … with all other visitors being ushered out for closing. He felt a surge of excitement deep in his belly and he wanted to see it all, *all over again*, the snail-infested occupants of a steamy old-fashioned black Cadillac, the driver covered in ivy, a man in the back in a mask with barnacles all over him and a hole for a stomach, the soaring totem pole of car tyres topped with a boat and an umbrella, the plaster nudes in the windows, wash basins on the wall – *what else do you see?* – paintings where two dimensions appear as three if looked at in a certain way – lips for arches, breasts as drawers, knots as nipples, knobs as navels, jokes with espadrilles, figures made of spoons – not to mention the Mae West room with giant nostrils, red sofa lips and hanging tresses. It was right then that he suddenly wished he could be sharing it all with Elena … but it was impossible.

He felt at home, even though he knew he should be rushing through. But here it all was, the evolution of Dalí's complete works – impressionist, futurist, cubist, pointillist and fauvist canvases, until arriving at surrealism, to his classicist and nuclear-mystical period … a provocative, mystical Dalí, impassioned by science and the Dalí of the final period … but what *else* do you see, Benjamin?

What else do you see?

As he headed through the Palau del Vent, a central hall with three smaller rooms off it, he gazed up at the ceiling mural, an oil painting on canvas pasted to the plaster of the roof, and then he finally found the 'Workshop', the room where the oil study, *The Face*, was exhibited by the right-hand entrance.

Benjamin took a deep breath and approached the work, framed in a glass case. A label on the wall described it as a '*Study for The Hallucinogenic Toreador*' and painted between 1968-1970. He counted the twenty pin nails on either side of the canvas, with fourteen on top and bottom, then took out Conso's phone to look at the shot of Jaume's version, holding it up to compare and squint at both paintings …

Which is when the phone suddenly rang with the loud Motörhead ringtone again, startling him to drop it.

60

Inspector Vizcaya, Officer Soler and the Marquès de Guíxols

Monday 4 June, 4.45pm – El Raval neighbourhood, Barcelona.

'Sorry, who's this?' said Vizcaya, waving at Soler to urgently trace the number he was calling and that had shown up on the cracked cell phone found at the hostel, while he continued the brief conversation from his own phone.

'No, who are *you*?' came the pompous voice from the other end.

'Well, you called Elena Carmona,' said Vizcaya, 'a taxi driver –'

'Who?'

'Carmona Taxis from Girona, perhaps?'

'No, I didn't.'

'I think you did.'

'No, I think you have the wrong number.'

'This is Detective Inspector Vizcaya of the Mossos d'Esquadra –'

'Who?'

'Of the kidnap and extortion division. Do not hang up.' Vizcaya could hear the man muttering something, and then also a female voice in the background. 'Did you make a call to Elena Carmona or Carmona Taxis earlier today?' he insisted.

'I have no idea what you're talking about.'

'Sir –'

'Everything has already been documented with my lawyers.'

'Excuse me?'

'I have nothing further to say. You must speak to my lawyers.'

Click.

'What the fuck?' said Vizcaya, turning to Soler.

'The number is registered to Jaume Guíxols, Marquès de Guíxols,' she said, quickly ending a call herself before calling the incident room. 'Hang on.'

Vizcaya waited.

'Find out what you can about the Marquès de Guíxols – it's urgent,' Soler eventually said down the line. A pause, then: 'Okay, I'll tell him.' She turned back towards Vizcaya.

'They want you over at the Hotel Arts,' she said. 'Apparently, Beltrán's already there. They say it's important. In the meantime, I'll find this Marquès …'

61

Elena

Monday 4 June, 4.45pm – Sants station, Barcelona.

Elena was puzzled as to what the psycho was doing in the plaza behind Sants station. He seemed to have a clear purpose in his stride, however, as he made his way towards one of the skateboarders. No more than a young kid, the skater looked nervous at the approach, but from the body language it was clear that they knew one another.

She watched the thug hand over some cash and receive something back, but then the kid pulled out his cell phone and made a call. After a few seconds, he simply held up the phone to the freak's ear, as if allowing him to reply or listen to a message. It happened so quickly, that Elena didn't have time to react when the thug glanced over in her direction before he hurried off. Perhaps he'd seen her – but either way, she'd lost him.

She knew she shouldn't be doing it, but someone had told her about the trick and so she decided to try it herself. Be calm, be confident, no one will question you. Just do it.

She marched over to the skateboarder and quickly flashed her leather credit card holder in his face, giving him no time to scrutinise it.

'I'm an undercover cop and you have two options,' she snapped.

He looked at her, grimacing. His friends had already scarpered.

'Tell me who you just called, or you're detained,' she said. There was a pause. '*Now.*'

He didn't say anything, but he held up his phone. Elena grabbed it and then called the last number.

Eventually someone answered: 'Yes, this is the Hospital Laforja, and this is Hendrik Oomen's phone. Can I help you?'

A few minutes later she was on her way.

62

Inspector Vizcaya, Beltrán Gómez and Mitch Gibson

Monday 4 June, 5.15pm – Port Olímpic, Barcelona.

Even before Inspector Vizcaya joined him at the hotel in the Olympic port, Beltrán's personal manhunt to track down Brandon Bartholomew, *the doctor*, had gone up a gear, albeit holding back images of him shaking hands with Secretary of State Patterson, in a rather futile attempt to avoid any accusations of incompetence.

As his suspect had been in direct physical contact with the highest-ranking executive of the US President's cabinet and the National Security Council, Beltrán had no choice but to liaise even closer with Secret Service agents and counter-terrorism experts from the CIA … but he was delighted to do so.

He'd also come into contact with the US State Department's spokesman – an irate, muscular, mouthy spin-doctor called Mitch Gibson, who'd been pestering Beltrán for explanations at the hotel, together with an array of other White House cronies.

Vizcaya arrived to witness it all. Despite the tense atmosphere, Beltrán seemed to be revelling in it. With an already overinflated ego, he now looked puffed up and full of himself, and still with his perfectly slicked-back coiffure; it was clearly everything he'd ever dreamed of while stationed at the University of Maryland with START.

Vizcaya could tell from the twisted body language of Gibson, however, that he wanted to throttle Beltrán. He could sympathise with the sentiment, too.

The image of the Pattersons had hardly been enhanced in the short time they'd graced Barcelona with their presence. Pamela Patterson, the statesman's wife, had had to dodge a bloody lump of auricular cartilage while posing for a group photo on the spouse programme. As for Chuck Patterson, the world's media had first reported that he'd suffered 'chest pains and a possible stroke' while jogging in the park. He'd also been followed by a mob of paparazzi, totally oblivious to the fact that he'd been placed, at least in Beltrán's opinion, in a 'compromising and potentially life-threatening scenario', face-to-face with the 'fanatical, cynical doctor'.

Were the Pattersons being specifically targeted by animal rights extremists? Had security been tightened for Pamela's next events on the spouse tour? Was everything in place for the Patterson double act to safely attend the eve-of-summit royal reception later that evening? These were questions that Mitch Gibson, horrified about any damage to 'brand Patterson', had fired at Beltrán – who didn't really know how to reply or appease him, but was simply delighted to be in the thick of it all.

Vizcaya immediately tried to intervene and convey the 'possible reservations they might now need to consider regarding Bartholomew', following the updates on toll ticket analyses – but it was too late.

Firstly, he was handed a forensics bag containing a paper napkin with the scrawled message of '*find the green tie … you'll find the bullfighter*'. Unsure how to interpret it, he was then informed that Beltrán had already issued a new public appeal via the Guardia Civil, with a clearer image of Bartholomew released to the media, showing the suspect caught on CCTV as he was trying to enter the hotel restaurant with a backpack.

Vizcaya desperately wanted to punch Beltrán very hard on the nose, and then remove a few of his teeth, but he quickly decided it wasn't the most sensible thing to do in front of the US security forces at the hotel. Instead, he slammed his fingerless left fist into the palm of his other hand, which was interpreted as a clap.

'Yes, thanks,' said Beltrán, as if acknowledging the applause. 'I've had instructions from Madrid to bring in Bartholomew by the end of the day at any cost.'

Vizcaya could only stand there and stare as the young CITCO agent then started to pore over a laptop displaying pictures taken at the reception, alongside

Gibson, a couple of Mossos agents, plus the hotel's restaurant manager. They were trying to identify the guests seen with Bartholomew while he was talking to Secretary Patterson, just after the statesman had staggered in with his entourage.

'That elderly gentleman is the Marquès de Guíxols,' said the restaurant manager, pointing at the computer screen.

'Who?' said Vizcaya, perking up.

'Jaume Guíxols ... the Marquès de Guíxols.'

'I spoke to him just a while ago,' said Vizcaya. 'And Soler should have tracked him down by now ...'

63

Benjamin, Conso and Josep

Monday 4 June, 5.45pm – Figueres.

'What happened?'

'I dropped your phone. You seriously need to change that ringtone –'

'Benjamin, can you hear me?'

'Yes, I can hear you. I said you need to change –'

'Where are you standing, Benjamin?'

'I'm sorry?'

'Where are you standing?'

'I'm in the museum.'

'But where, exactly?'

'In the workshop gallery.'

'What can you see?'

'*The Face,* and, as I suspected, there's a striking –'

'No, no, Benjamin, what else can you see?'

Silence.

'Benjamin, what *else* can you see?'

'There's an image I'm still missing, isn't there?'

'No, listen to me. Is there a door nearby? An exit?'

'No, I can't see a door –'

'Benjamin. Look towards the other end of the gallery. There's a fire exit. Do you see it?'

'Excuse me?'

'Do you or do you not see the fire exit?'

'Yes … yes, I do now …'

'Then run.'

'What?'

'Run.'

'Is there a fire?'

'Run, Benjamin. Just get out of the museum right now – through that emergency exit – we're outside – yellow car – *now*, Benjamin.'

So he ran, and seconds later found himself in an alleyway at the back of the museum, and he could hear an alarm inside the building at the same time as the phone rang with the Motörhead ringtone again, which he answered – then Conso was calling out, *'Over here'* – and he could see her waving at him from the passenger seat of her rusty old Seat, using a phone which she then handed to a guy in the driving seat, and then *he* got out – it was her nephew Josep, she said, as Benjamin approached the vehicle – with Josep then pushing him into the back seat while glaring at him …

'What the hell is going on, Benjamin?' cried Conso, after her nephew was back in the driving seat.

'Going on where?' said Benjamin.

'What have you done?'

'What do you mean?'

Squashed in the back of the tiny, mildew-smelling car, where he could see two crash helmets on the back seat, and where Conso had also propped the portfolio case, Benjamin tried to make sense of what she was saying. Her nephew was still open-mouthed, staring at him through the rear-view mirror. He had long hair and a beard, and was wearing a leather biker's jacket with some heavy-duty metal zips and studs.

Conso didn't know the full scale of Benjamin's work, and certainly not his undercover work with the British police or Interpol. So, they wouldn't, they *couldn't* have connected him to the blurred airport image of Brandon Bartholomew, surely? But he wasn't so sure.

'What have you done?' Conso was still saying. 'What have you done?'

Benjamin took a deep breath.

'I borrowed a bicycle,' he said. 'Okay, I stole it.'

'A bicycle?'

'Yes, a bicycle, but we can return it now. It's outside your house –'

'A bicycle?'

'It's no big deal. Have you started to examine –?'

'*A bicycle?*'

'Yes …'

'*Nobody wants to question you about a bicycle.* What about the bullfighter? *A murder and kidnap?* What's going on?'

64

Lisette Dijckhuijsen and the Marquès de Guíxols

Monday 4 June, 5.30pm – Passeig de Gràcia, Barcelona.

While Benjamin was in Figueres, matters had moved on rapidly in central Barcelona. The US security forces didn't need to ask how a suspect in a murder and kidnap investigation had got as near as he had to Secretary Patterson – because the world's media asked the question instead.

No one had an answer.

It was the photo that the State Department's spokesman, Mitch Gibson, would have done anything to avoid. Patterson, drenched in sweat from his quasi-jog, shaking hands with 'the doctor' and possible mastermind behind the killing and abduction.

Photos and videos taken at the launch of the hotel's new restaurant had first appeared on local online media in Barcelona, as well as on some Catalan influencers' Instagram accounts. But the fact that Patterson had also graced the opening with his perspiring presence had suddenly put an international spin on the story.

Photos of Patterson shaking hands with the restaurant manager and VIP guests, the Marquès de Guíxols included, were soon visible online as part of the global media coverage of the G20's sideline events. But then as soon as Beltrán released the CCTV image of Brandon Bartholomew trying to enter the venue, initially with a backpack, the world's picture editors took over from then on. Not only had the suspect *succeeded* in entering, but he was also pictured shaking hands with the Secretary of State, while holding a cell phone in his other hand.

There was video footage showing Bartholomew making a call prior to greeting Patterson, and then appearing to continue the call immediately afterwards. As the manhunt to find him was launched in full force, the priority was to track down the two other guests he'd been seen conversing with: the Marquès de Guíxols and Lisette 'Dixie' Dijckhuijsen.

And Officer Soler eventually succeeded.

Busting into Dixie's luxury apartment off the Passeig de Gràcia, the police finally found them half-naked, in flagrante …

65

Benjamin, Conso and Josep

Monday 4 June, 6pm – Figueres.

'What's going on, Benjamin? Tell me.'

Benjamin wasn't sure where to begin. While Conso continued to glare at him, squashed in the back of the old Seat, her nephew Josep had stopped eyeing him through the rear-view mirror and was instead scrolling for something on his phone.

'Look,' started Benjamin, 'if you're talking about an image of someone at Girona airport, then –'

'No, Benjamin, *no* –'

'– it's just a case of mistaken identity –'

'– *no, Benjamin* –'

'– a spot of bother, that's all … a bit of a pickle –'

'Benjamin –'

'I hired a car, which was stolen at a service station – the same service station where the vehicle of the bullfighter was abandoned. I can't go into all the details, but now that the painting is safe with you, I intend to speak to the police, just as soon as I've tracked down the thug who –'

'Benjamin, there's a picture of you with the American statesman.'

There was a silence, then:

'What?'

Josep held up his phone to show a clear image of Brandon Bartholomew shaking hands with the US Secretary of State. The same Brandon Bartholomew who the police wanted to question about the murder and kidnap.

'*Oh, for fucksake.*' Benjamin's mind flashed again to his divorce lawyer, Walter Postlethwaite, to Claire and his daughter Sophie, to the Marquès de Guíxols and Anthony Hughes at Sotheby's … to Elena … and to the ruthless gangsters who'd now certainly recognise him from previous undercover work, and with this clearer image surely putting an end to any future covert assignments. 'Oh, fuck.'

'*Benjamin,*' Conso was saying, 'who is Brandon Bartholomew? Have you committed a crime? They want to eliminate you from their enquiries …'

Benjamin had had enough. For a moment he felt astonishment, or maybe it was joy, but he suddenly reckoned he could kill someone … certainly the bastard who'd tried to kill *him* and who'd triggered this nightmare in the first place. He briefly wondered whether he was going off the rails, but *no*, it was just the simple realisation that he didn't have to be polite to anyone anymore, or at least not to everyone *all* the time.

He'd had enough of people telling him what to do, what was best for him, or what they were *expecting* of him. From now on, Benjamin decided, he alone would be responsible for his future. He had absolutely no idea what it would bring, but now that Claire wasn't going to be in it, at least he could control it.

As for eliminating people from police enquiries and then exposing the real criminals, well, that was normally *his* job – and he was good at it. Not just art thieves and forgers but all the other crooks exploiting the art world, using it for insurance fraud, money laundering, in exchange for drugs, weapons, or for blackmail and extortion. There were people who killed to simply get their hands on a masterpiece, and more than once he'd found himself in the middle of it.

He needed to return to Barcelona, to placate Jaume, call Anthony Hughes, liaise urgently with Scotland Yard, who he hoped had received his email – and he was now hell-bent on bringing in the bastard who'd tried to kill him. He wanted to explain things to Elena, too, if he could find her, or at the least send her a message. As the police still didn't have his name right, he believed he still had time ... but only just ...

He thought he would have to placate Conso and her nephew, but it wasn't necessary. After nudging

Josep to drive on quickly, away from the museum and the centre of Figueres, *she* was telling Benjamin that she trusted him, but that he had to clear his name.

In between waving her arms and muttering in Catalan with her nephew, Conso told Benjamin that he could leave the painting with them – as it was an indication to her that he had nothing to hide. He could take her old car, too – she never drove it, she said – adding that Josep had a motorbike to take her around. She also instructed Benjamin to hang on to her new phone so that they could call him once they'd carried out a radiographic test, but which they would now do in Cadaqués at her nephew's studio.

With that, after they'd zigzagged their way out of the centre of Figueres, she instructed Josep to pull up the car, just off a roundabout with a signpost indicating the AP-7 to Barcelona.

Conso got out, and her nephew followed, taking the portfolio case and the two crash helmets with him. He left the keys in the ignition and the engine running, before guiding Benjamin out of the back and into the driver's seat.

'Go, Benjamin,' said Conso. 'Go and clear your name.'

Nothing else was said.

66

Hendrik and Séverin

Monday 4 June, 5.45pm – Sant Gervasi-Galvany neighbourhood, Barcelona.

Lying with his eyes bandaged, all alone in the ophthalmology ward of the Hospital Laforja off Muntaner Street, Hendrik had no idea of Séverin hovering beside his bed, deranged and slavering at the mouth.

Not at first.

Séverin craved revenge. Earlier, he'd been scouring the streets of Barcelona in search of the spineless shit who'd left him stranded at the service station, after driving off with the other Dutch hippie, Jürgen. He'd figured that if he could locate the driver, he'd find where they'd hidden the bullfighter, and then he'd gouge out their eyeballs and collect all the cash he was owed.

Séverin thought the Dutchmen worked for a hotel group, but he'd tried the two hotels where they'd all met and found nothing. In the end, since controlling his psychotic palpitations after hurling the severed ear at the G20 spouses, he'd finally tracked down the driver without much trouble. He did so by going in search of his angel dust dealer, the young skateboarder who'd supplied them both and who used to hang out near Sants station.

The kid confirmed the driver's name: *Hendrik.* He also had his number. Séverin bought more angel dust, only after ordering him to call Hendrik. Eventually, a nurse who said she was at the Hospital Laforja answered the phone, asking if she could help, and whether he was 'family' …

Hendrik could hear the soft shuffle of footsteps near his bed, assuming it to be a doctor or nurse. The visitor was fiddling with something on the little table to his left. It was where they'd put his personal items, they'd said earlier, safely in the drawer. His eyes, covered by the bandages, were still itching and burning. He hoped they'd returned to give him more painkillers and anti-inflammatory medication.

'Nurse?' he murmured, with his busted jaw and teeth still shooting with pain. There was no reply. 'Doctor?' he groaned again. 'Do you have more painkillers?'

'Of course,' a voice said. 'Open your mouth wide.'

Hendrik instinctively opened his fractured mouth just a little, as much as he could without causing excruciating pain, and then jutted his tongue out just a fraction. There was something about that voice, the *accent*, however, that was different to the last doctor. It unnerved him, but he said nothing.

Nor would he say anything ever again.

Séverin clasped the steel claw end of his spare hammer and thrust its solid rubber grip handle into Hendrik's mouth, wriggling it to get it fully inside, much to the writhing patient's shock and horror, then forcing it between his shattered teeth and bleeding gums, prodding and pushing it further, wedging it deep inside, pinning his head to the bed, before ramming it *really* hard, right against the back of Hendrik's throat, with as much pressure as possible, over and over again.

Hendrik brought his hands up to try and wrench away whatever was being forced into his mouth, but it was impossible. The pain was beyond unbearable, worse than anything he'd ever experienced, let alone having liquid bleach poured all over his eyeballs earlier. If he could have screamed, he would have done so, but his tongue was trapped and he couldn't speak, cough, swallow or even breathe – especially once his attacker had squeezed and pinched his nostrils closed with his other hand.

It was hell.

That voice … that accent … it was *Sevi*, the maniac from France. The one they'd left at the service station after driving off. That had all been Jürgen's idea – he needed to explain that to Sevi – surely, he'd understand – they were mates, no? They'd got high together on angel dust ... Sevi? ... *Sevi?*

But he was starting to panic now, he was still writhing yet losing control, and the only thing spinning through his mind was the story he'd heard of someone dying in police custody after trying to hide a plastic bag of drugs by *swallowing it* – and then the cops trying to hook and dislodge the bag with a sharp object, only to push it down further, causing asphyxia – *what the fuck, Sevi, just let me go ... no?*

No.

Being unable to see while being choked and suffocated was a terrifying way to go. He was sucking and searching in vain for air now, kicking his way towards oblivion ...

Just one finger poked to the back of the throat gives you the feeling of needing to gag. Pushing it further, you feel an intense sensation of nausea. By the time the full rubber grip of the hammer had been repeatedly rammed and then wedged securely at the back of Hendrik's throat, he'd violently endured both those early stages.

With respiratory obstruction of the larynx and trachea, as well as being unable to breathe through his nose, he'd then shot rapidly from the gag reflex to a full laryngeal spasm in under a minute, starting to choke on his own vomit. It wasn't long before the blood, bile and puke was clogging his oesophagus, and from there, via reflex regurgitation, flooding into his lungs. At some point, after multiple convulsions, he lost consciousness, although his body continued to wriggle and squirm.

Séverin, meanwhile, felt ecstatic. He simply kept one hand resting on the steel end of the hammer, maintaining the downward pressure, while the other hand blocked his victim's nostrils. He had to stop himself from shrieking with delight as jets of bloody mucous eventually spewed and seeped out from around Hendrik's lips, semi-glued to the hammer's rubber grip.

Eventually, the writhing slowed, then finally stopped. Hendrik's body became still, lifeless. Séverin eased out the hammer, which popped like the sound of a plunger coming unstuck. He then wiped the handle's sticky mess on the bandages covering Hendrik's eyes.

He grabbed the wallet he'd found in the bedside table drawer, together with a plastic entry card for the depot where Hendrik worked.

That new batch of phencyclidine angel dust that his dealer had given him was having its effect.

He was hallucinating again.

He felt *invulnerable*.

A perfect yet paranoiac, psychotic effect …

67

Officer Soler, the Marquès de Guíxols and Lisette Dijckhuijsen

Monday 4 June, 6pm – Mossos Comissaria, Les Corts district, Barcelona.

The Marquès de Guíxols refused to say a word until his lawyer was present. He refused to say much thereafter, either, which would delay matters severely.

It had taken a while to locate the old aristocrat, despite Officer Soler swiftly collating some key facts about him. He'd inherited a rambling country house on the outskirts of La Bisbal, northeast of Barcelona, which had been in his family for generations. He also had a Gaudí-style mansion in the heart of the city's affluent Pedralbes neighbourhood – but he'd been unavailable at both.

Soler discovered that he was married to Montse Guíxols and had once been a permanent fixture among the old money brigade and elite circles of both

Catalan and Spanish society. He'd been a regular guest at most royal galas and glitterati jollies, but had recently fallen from grace, partly due to Spain's economic crisis, and partly due to many speculative investments that had gone spectacularly wrong.

The Guíxols wine and cava business had been forced into administration, and he was also under investigation by the tax authorities in the fall-out following the collapse of a major bank. But from what Soler understood, the Marquès was not one of the key suspects. He was neither a director nor shareholder of the failed bank, but it was his high-profile status and friendship with the bank's chairman – a former Spanish finance minister facing charges in Madrid for money laundering – that had served him no favours.

When Soler finally managed to get through to the Marquès, he still refused to cooperate. Even when she explained that her call had nothing to do with the bank case, but that Spain's counter-terrorism agency and the Mossos d'Esquadra's kidnap and extortion division had an urgent interest in talking to him, all on the orders of Spain's Interior Ministry … it made no difference whatsoever. He still insisted on having a lawyer present.

Even more so once Mossos agents had broken down the front door of Lisette Dijckhuijsen's deluxe apartment in the Eixample district, only to find the Marquès semi-clothed and still fielding Soler's calls.

· · ·

Following instructions from Vizcaya, Soler had been simultaneously trying to locate the Danish socialite, 'Dixie' Dijckhuijsen. Background research on the thrice divorcee revealed that since arriving in Spain just a decade ago, she'd managed to marry, quickly divorce, and drain the fortunes of a real estate entrepreneur, a tuna fishing magnate, and the owner of several Michelin star restaurants.

According to gossip magazines, the 'alimony-millionairess' who described herself as a public relations consultant, had even tried it on with a crypto-billionaire in Andorra and the King of Spain, yet she now had her eye on a Saudi prince. There was no hint of her slowing down the gold-digging, but she had no real interest in the financially crippled Marquès de Guíxols, other than flirting with him for his own contacts and network.

Dixie's own cell phone had been switched off while she was massaging the aristocrat's hairy back, so she was unaware that she was being sought by the police, let alone the counter-terrorism agency. Earlier, she'd received a couple of texts from the hotel restaurant, thanking her for the massive press coverage that the launch party photos had provoked – but she had no idea of the full impact.

When her front door was smashed open by Mossos agents, she'd screamed, while the red-faced Jaume struggled to quickly get dressed.

Highly embarrassed at being caught with his pants down, and distraught that his wife would find out, the Marquès immediately became indignant and bolshy, accusing the police of trespassing, even though it wasn't his property. Lisette watched as he berated everyone, remonstrating that he had 'nothing further to add', and that, sure enough, he had no intention of saying anything unless his lawyer was present.

The police were under strict orders to take no chances. The apartment was searched, Lisette and Jaume separated, and then they were individually escorted down to the Mossos HQ. The Marquès was allowed to call his lawyer to join him there. Lisette called a divorce lawyer, to see if he might want to earn another commission.

68

Benjamin

Monday 4 June, 6.30pm – Figueres to Barcelona.

Conso and her nephew had left Benjamin ideally positioned for the AP-7 towards Barcelona, but before joining the motorway, he stopped briefly in a lay-by on the outskirts of Figueres. He tugged all the notes and leaflets from his pockets, spreading them out over the front passenger seat beside him, including the list of the IB hotel group's suppliers that he'd printed off.

He checked Conso's phone, relieved it was fully charged – delighted, too, that it had a connection via its *Movistar* provider. He rustled through his notes on the passenger seat and found Jaume's cell phone number. He rang, and kept it ringing, but there was no answer. He waited and then rang again … no answer. He found Elena's taxi card, tried the Girona number on that, too, but it simply cut off, as if the line had been disconnected.

He turned Elena's card over and saw that he'd scribbled '*@elenacarmona30*' on it. He swiped back and forth on the screen of Conso's phone, looking for a Twitter, Instagram or TikTok app, but he found nothing – and even if he had, he wasn't sure what he would need to do to make contact.

He took a deep breath, then Googled for the Sotheby's office number in London, rang through, asked for the chairman's PA, but after being transferred to several further extensions, he eventually got through to an answer message. The chairman was at a conference in Beijing and wouldn't be returning until the end of the week. Benjamin had other calls he needed to make, especially to his contact at Scotland Yard, but he didn't have the direct line and knew he wouldn't find it via Google. He'd already sent an email, and he suddenly realised that maybe he shouldn't be trying to call anyone. He scrolled to the phone's settings and turned off the location services.

He panicked as he approached the first tollgate to get on to the motorway, but all he had to do was take a ticket from a machine, so that was okay. It got him thinking about the psycho again, how he must have had his own toll ticket if he'd come from the same direction, because by the time Benjamin saw the signs for Girona and the airport coming up at junction eight again – he still hadn't encountered a second tollgate to pay for the ticket he'd collected.

He could recall what Elena had told him, and the online news reports he'd read, stating that the bullfighter had been abducted in Nîmes. So, had the thug come from Nîmes? Had he been driving the bullfighter's van, before abandoning it and using its toll ticket after stealing Benjamin's hire car? It was possible … but what about the other vehicle … the laundry van?

With the window half-open for some air and with one hand on the steering wheel, he tried to shuffle the papers around on the passenger seat, searching for the print-out of the hotel group's suppliers.

He slowed down as he approached the Gironès service station near the airport, just before junction eight. He intended to pull off the motorway and return to the scene where he'd been attacked. He wanted to quickly re-enact where he'd parked the hire car, away from the fuel pumps. There'd still be enough time and light to search the ground where he'd come to at around 5am that same morning, and where he'd seen the battered corpse.

But the motorway exit to the service station was cordoned off. There were several police vehicles on the slip-road, traffic cones were blocking the exit, so he had no choice but to drive on past – only to pull up quickly on the hard-shoulder five kilometres further along the motorway, for a closer look at the papers he'd printed off.

He'd caught sight of the laundry van screeching

away from the service station at around midnight, just as he'd got out of his car to head into the shop. *Then* he'd been attacked. He didn't believe the laundry van had come all the way from Nîmes. It was a distinct, old-fashioned looking vehicle – it could have simply been making deliveries in the local area, maybe at the airport itself. He thought he'd seen a similar vehicle outside the terminal just before getting into Elena's taxi, but he'd put that down to the slow-motion double images he'd experienced after the attack ... an after-effect from the concussion. But then he'd seen the thug hanging around those two hotels in Barcelona, as if waiting for someone or something ...

The laundry van ...

Is that what he was waiting for?

A rendezvous with the laundry van?

69

Elena

Monday 4 June, 6pm – Sant Gervasi-Galvany neighbourhood, Barcelona.

There was a taxi rank on the crossroads of Laforja and Muntaner streets, just outside the Hospital Laforja. Elena was standing on the other side of the road, out of sight, when the thug finally emerged from one of the hospital's side exits. She had no idea what he'd been doing inside, but it hadn't taken him long. The person from the hospital who'd answered the skateboard kid's call earlier had said it was 'Hendrik Oomen's phone' – maybe it was one of their gang, or even a member of staff.

She wondered if the thug had been into the hospital to grab some drugs that he couldn't get from the skateboarder, or drugs that someone inside the hospital shouldn't be supplying him. She didn't know what to think, but as soon as he started swaying and staggering along the line of taxis outside, trying to get a ride somewhere, she knew she still had to track him.

He looked unsteady, and she watched as he was rebuffed by four of the taxi drivers waiting in line in the shade, each one sitting in their vehicles and either waving him away as he approached or indicating for him to try the taxi behind. Only when he reached the last taxi on the rank did he manage to get a lift, no doubt because the driver was willing to take him anywhere rather than wait last in line for another client.

As the taxi set off, Elena dashed across the road – but her plan was not to grab a taxi herself and follow him. Not yet. Instead, she strolled alongside the drivers, each one with their arm resting on an open window, casually telling them that she, too, was a driver, and that dickhead had also been trying to get her to drive him somewhere, and 'Where had the jerk been asking *you guys* to take him?'

One of the drivers got out and relit the remains of his cigar while admiring Elena's tight jeans and legs, as she paced up and down.

'Olimpia,' he spat. 'Olimpia aparthotel – other side of the Olympic port. Too many roadblocks over there. And he looked out of it, right?'

70

Benjamin

Monday 4 June, 7.15pm – Figueres to Barcelona.

Benjamin pulled off the motorway and parked on the edge of an industrial estate, some thirty kilometres from central Barcelona. He'd been using his knees and upper legs to control the steering wheel while struggling to unfold scraps of paper, but now he needed to use the map on Conso's phone to check through the IB hotel group's supplier details once again.

Images from the service station had been swirling through his mind … the ripped green tie and shirt button suggested that the bullfighter had been attacked there, perhaps savagely in the same way as his driver. Whether he'd also been butchered or was still alive, where had they hidden him? As the thug had been hanging around IB hotels in Barcelona, possibly to rendezvous with the laundry van that Benjamin had seen speeding away, is that how they'd moved him? In a laundry van? But where to?

Scanning through the IB hotel group's supplier list, Benjamin thought something was odd. Most of the suppliers were international firms based outside of Spain, despite it being a Spanish hotel chain – but then he realised that only the corporate head office of each one was listed.

Using Conso's phone, he Googled '*Textile Standard*', one of the suppliers that IB used for furnishings – but it was based somewhere in the middle of Holland.

Then he tried the '*Brycolen Group*', claiming to be 'the perfect pan-European partner in linen services for hotels, restaurants, holiday parks and wellness centres', *also* in Holland, as well as in Germany, Poland, Belgium and Luxembourg.

He read on to discover that *Brycolen* was 'a specialist provider of professional laundry services … rely on us to make sure all your bedding, towels, napkins, bathrobes, kitchen towels and chefs' clothing are ready for spotlessly welcoming your guests' … and then he saw that they *also* owned a subsidiary company in Spain … in Barcelona.

It was called Olimpia.

Olimpia Bugaderia …

71

Inspector Vizcaya and the Marquès de Guíxols

Monday 4 June, 6.45pm – Mossos Comissaria, Les Corts district, Barcelona.

Jaume Guíxols' lawyer had very strange eyes. They oscillated from side to side, and it was very difficult to focus on him or have any lengthy conversation. Not that Inspector Vizcaya wanted any lengthy conversation. He just wanted to know what the purple-faced aristocrat had been discussing with Brandon Bartholomew in the hotel restaurant prior to the US Secretary of State's arrival, and why the so-called 'doctor' had scribbled cryptic messages on a paper napkin about finding the missing bullfighter.

The eyeball-swivelling lawyer, however, simply shook his head or nodded at his client, depending on whether he was obliged to answer a question or not.

How much he'd been paid to sit there and roll his eyes was anyone's guess.

Officer Soler, meanwhile, was busy interviewing Lisette Dijckhuijsen in another room, where the Danish socialite had insisted on being called Dixie.

On arrival, the aristocrat's lawyer had first spoken to Vizcaya in a corridor at the Comissaria, out of earshot of his client. With his dark, laser-parted hair and revolving eyes, his hands fingering the neat and perfect knot of his blue silk tie, he'd asked the Inspector *what*, exactly, had the Marquès done wrong?

'Nothing, I hope,' Vizcaya had replied.

He told the lawyer that neither the Marquès nor his mistress, Dixie, had been formally detained or were under arrest, but they'd been asked to voluntarily help the police with their enquiries. Officially, they could be held for up to twenty-four hours before they had to be charged with a crime or released – 'But I hope it won't come to all that,' he said.

Without giving too many details about the investigation, Vizcaya said that because the Ministry of Interior and Guardia Civil (via the over-eager Beltrán) had issued another appeal to locate their 'mastermind suspect', Bartholomew, and because the Marquès was the last person seen talking to that suspect, in addition to the US Secretary of State, they had to question him.

'But my client had no idea about any suspect or manhunt,' said the lawyer, sharply.

'Look,' Vizcaya said, losing his patience. 'Your client also received and made several calls to a phone found at a brothel, and where a drug-pushing pimp and illegal worker from Chile fled the scene after being savagely attacked. So, if it comes to it, your client could be charged for being uncooperative with a police investigation, for obstruction or withholding information – but as I say, I hope it won't come to that.'

With all the other legal proceedings and tax fraud accusations wreaking havoc on Jaume's life, his lawyer advised him to cooperate. Vizcaya himself doubted that the whereabouts of the kidnap victim would be resolved with any information that the aristocrat might offer, but he decided not to mention it.

Now that they were all sitting comfortably in the interview room, Vizcaya tried once again.

'What can you tell us about Brandon Bartholomew?' he asked the Marquès.

'*Who?*' barked Jaume.

'Brandon Bartholomew,' said Vizcaya, showing him the images from the hotel reception.

'Never heard of him and I have no further comments,' came the brusque reply.

It was going to be a long evening. But at least Vizcaya knew he could leave the questioning to the nit-picking boy wonder, Beltrán Gómez de Longoria …

It was 7pm when Beltrán came into the room to take over. Vizcaya noticed that he looked even more puffed up and full of himself than earlier, with a sort of permanent self-congratulatory grin fixed across his smarmy face. His presence also seemed to be briefly welcomed by the cantankerous old aristocrat, who bizarrely started to flash a series of temporary, weird grins. Because Beltrán *looked* like a young toff, the Marquès probably thought he was 'his sort'. Beltrán, meanwhile, clearly longed to be a Marquès, yet without Jaume's financial woes, naturally.

Even the lawyer, whose hands had previously lay like dead fish on the desk in front of him, began to toy with his fountain pen, as if with Beltrán's sudden appearance he believed that some kind of business arrangement could finally be signed, or at least a hand-shake on a gentlemen's agreement.

Once Vizcaya heard Beltrán speaking in a different tone with the Marquès than he'd heard him speak in the incident room or in Bosch's office, more fawning and toadyish, he realised that his own scruffy, balding presence would no longer be welcome or required in the interview room.

He'd seen it all before among the upper-crust fami-lies, wannabes and social-climbers around Spain, and especially among the old fascist fraternity. There was always an instant chemistry or recognition between them, whenever they met up; like some kind of cult secret handshake – 'My father knew your father' or 'I was at law school with your cousin'. They would circle one another while sussing out their social credentials, oblivious to the fact that they were probably just a bunch of in-breds.

It always drove home to Vizcaya not only his own

humble origins, but that he didn't really feel Spanish. He felt Basque. One thing was certain in Spain, though: the so-called *pijos* or 'good families' all stuck together, from whatever part of the Iberian Peninsula they were from … and right now, he couldn't stand being in the same room as them.

'Inspector?' Beltrán was saying. 'Inspector?'

'Yes,' said Vizcaya, finally.

'I was saying that I can take over from here.'

'Yes, of course you can,' said Vizcaya, happy to be leaving them to it.

Back in the incident room, Vizcaya studied the autopsy update regarding the blunt force trauma homicide of the chauffeur. It showed that cranial imprints and fracture patterns on his skull revealed spider web cracks radiating outwards from the point of impact. They'd found several abrasions, contusions and lacerations on the head, with the back of the skull showing a square-shaped break with pieces of scalp missing, later collected from the back of the Chevrolet.

He read that there was a clear correlation between the skull's fractures and the square-headed claw hammer found on the back seat of Bartholomew's abandoned hire car. As bone tissue and skull architecture had the ability to preserve marks inflicted through blunt force trauma, the contours of the cranial imprint were consistent with the size and shape of the hammerhead, possibly struck at an angle, several times, and leaving V-shaped fractures and imprints.

Hair and blood samples found on the hammer also matched to the dead chauffeur. In short, the claw hammer was the murder weapon found in Bartholomew's car ... so it was important for the Marquès to divulge everything he knew about the suspect to the police, but Vizcaya was convinced it wouldn't be much.

He checked his watch. The 6.30pm deadline set by the kidnappers had come and gone without further incident. The bullfights scheduled in Valencia and southern Spain had commenced, but no more severed ears had been hurled at any G20 dignitaries, nor had any bombs been detonated in Barcelona – although the threat was still very real.

The kidnappers and killers were still at large, the bullfighter was still missing, and while the hunt to find Bartholomew was well underway, security had also since been strengthened for the G20 royal reception at the Pedralbes Palace, starting at 9pm.

Vizcaya was happy to leave Beltrán searching for his pseudo terrorist suspect.

He would now focus on what he did best: find the location of the kidnap victim before it was too late.

72

Benjamin

Monday 4 June, 8pm – Figueres to Barcelona.

Benjamin, meanwhile, had been going flat out in Conso's rickety old car since re-joining the motorway following his last stop, and after opting for the coastal ring road to guide him towards central Barcelona – specifically back towards the Olympic port area.

The location that he'd found using Conso's phone for *Olimpia Bugaderia*, the partner in Catalonia for the IB hotel group's European linen supplier, a Dutch conglomerate called Brycolen, was over in the Vila Olímpica-Poblenou area of the city.

With each kilometre that the rattling vehicle managed to accomplish, Benjamin wondered whether Elena had already gone to the police, or if the police had even caught up with Jaume. But what information would *he* divulge? Benjamin hadn't had time to read everything about the banking scandal he was linked to, but the old aristocrat had certainly been adamant about keeping his possible Dalí under wraps.

Dalí …

Dalí and *anamorphosis* … encrypted images that appear only when one concentrates on a picture, a *scene*, in a certain way … like a *crime scene* …

What was it that Conso had said about Púbol – the gift that Dalí had given his wife, Gala – a palace where she could get away from him and 'entertain her lovers' – the palace that he could only visit with her permission? That friends of Dalí and Gala had helped them in their search to find the perfect fortress to renovate? That one specific friend had a pilot's licence, enabling him to take photographs of possible places? As far as Benjamin knew, there was no documental evidence to confirm where else they'd looked – although Conso had mentioned two other small castles before they'd settled on Púbol. But surely they hadn't considered the Guíxols' country home?

The sun had dropped but it still felt as humid as ever by the time Benjamin slowed up to finally pay cash for the toll ticket on the outskirts of Barcelona. There were police checks after the tollgates, but they were waving down and checking random vehicles that were leaving the city. After a brief glance at Conso's old car coming the other way, it was waved on through with no problem at all.

73

Jürgen and Séverin

Monday 4 June, 7pm – El Poblenou neighbourhood, Barcelona.

In addition to its core laundry business, the Olimpia hospitality supplies group controlled various other ventures, all within the same complex, including a three-star aparthotel. It was a popular choice for business visitors, offering self-catered, short-let apartments. Guests used a simple card-key access system to come and go. There were hardly any staff, just occasional housekeepers, as well as delivery drivers such as Jürgen.

With Hendrik and other part-time drivers, Jürgen's seasonal job had been to deliver laundered towels, sheets and table linen to hotels, restaurants and serviced apartments across the city, and then return to the Olimpia depot with dirty laundry. But no longer.

Agitated, scared and hungry, he was now desperate to speak to Brigitte, but she hadn't answered his calls.

He had no idea if she was still in London or back in Amsterdam. Something had gone very wrong; he was sure of it.

He had finally decided that he couldn't wait for instructions about the clean-up operation. He had to get out of Spain and back to his Dutch commune. He couldn't stay around at the depot any longer, not with the risk of Séverin paying a visit. He couldn't keep watch over the bullfighter, either – the noise in the boiler room was deafening. He had to leave, and he had to do it now.

He grabbed the rucksack with all the cash from his locker. As he'd hoped at this time of the evening, the small reception desk was unattended, nor was there anyone near the vending machines. He had to avoid other staff, and having to come up with a reason for why he was still around or working so late. He pushed some coins into one of the vending machines in exchange for a bottle of Coke.

As he made his way to the exit, he didn't see the blow coming. It wouldn't have helped if he had. It was a vicious swipe, sweeping up from Séverin's right side and catching Jürgen low in the stomach. He gasped, then fell to his knees, dropping the rucksack. Coughing and wheezing, he gulped for air, with his arms folded in front of his belly.

Séverin snatched the rucksack. With his other hand, he grabbed a fistful of Jürgen's long hipster beard, then used it as a lead to drag him along the corridor.

74

Beltrán Gómez and the Marquès de Guíxols

Monday 4 June, 7.45pm – Mossos Comissaria, Les Corts district, Barcelona.

Once the niceties were out of the way, Jaume Guíxols soon decided that he trusted the young CITCO agent less than he trusted the Inspector who'd interviewed him earlier.

The balding Inspector with the walrus moustache and gammy left hand – what was his name, *Vizcaya?* – had at least been blunt and straightforward, despite looking oafish with his ill-fitting shirt scarcely concealing his beer belly. But trust this sycophantic Beltrán Gómez de Longoria from CITCO? *No way.*

CITCO existed to avert the threat of terrorism, which was fine, but they also investigated organised crime. Jaume was convinced that this whole charade was a further attempt to probe into his tax affairs and

390

assets following the collapse of the bank, and the arrest of its board directors on charges of corruption.

The more Beltrán asked about his conversation at the hotel event with the doctor, the so-called *Brandon Bartholomew*, and why he'd been writing about a bull-fighter on a paper napkin, could only mean that CITCO knew something about his Dalí painting and its true value. But there was no way Jaume was going to discuss *that*. So, he simply hushed up.

Beltrán, meanwhile, had been trying to show goodwill. He explained that his interest wasn't in the doctor's relationship with the Marquès, but why the suspect had been on his phone immediately before and after edging himself closer to the US Secretary of State.

It wasn't curiosity; he was seriously worried. Early tests on Bartholomew's backpack left in the hotel's luggage rack had shown that very faint traces of the components used for the self-made explosive, TATP, had been found inside. The three components of TATP were hydrogen peroxide, acetone and a strong acid, such as hydrochloric acid. Acetone could be found in nail polish remover, or in products for cleaning or thinning paint.

Beltrán had rejected the idea that the doctor could have been working with chemicals for paint cleaning, but that there was instead a much more sinister and terrifying scenario. TATP could be triggered by an electrical charge connected to a SIM card, detonated by calling or sending a text.

He feared it was what Bartholomew had been rehearsing with the cell phone in his hand, while he was standing next to the US Secretary of State. Having tried in vain to enter the hotel with a bag, had he been doing a trial run to see if he could ignite it with a call?

'Why did the doctor make a call while standing near to Secretary Patterson?' he asked.

'I have absolutely no idea what you're talking about,' said Jaume, with a fleeting grin, and while his lawyer's eyes continued to swivel.

In between questioning the Marquès, Beltrán had also been waiting for updates from the investigation team. Something was bugging him … something he thought the CIA should have already resolved. If Brandon Bartholomew really was the animal rights terrorist mastermind, how had he been allowed to fly to Spain?

As a suspect, Bartholomew's details had been run through TIDE, the US Terrorist Identities Datamart Environment – the catch-all list of known or suspected international terrorists. The fact that the report had come back as negative was perhaps irrelevant. The question wasn't whether his name was on any 'watch-list' or 'no-fly list'. It was: *should it have been?*

Beltrán had been waiting for his new buddies at the CIA to clarify the matter, but they were blaming the British intelligence agencies and Stansted airport, from where Bartholomew had flown. With anti-aviation activists causing havoc in London as an aperitif for the G20 in Barcelona, *how*, they asked, could the Brits have had preparations to deal with everything from airline crashes to hijacks, but not for flashmobs storming the runways? Their security failure, the CIA claimed, was how the doctor had also slipped through the net.

That complacency, Beltrán assumed, was probably also why Scotland Yard hadn't yet come up with any information on 'doctor Bartholomew'.

With Beltrán's training and paranoia, he was convinced that the animal rights fanatics were a cynical and manipulative bunch. They weren't romantic, penniless idealists working out of basements. They ran multinational, multimillion-dollar corporations, plotting ad campaigns and stunts from office blocks, and Marcos Constantinos was living proof of it. These green, vegan, millionaire lefties had nothing to do with saving the planet, but everything to do with power and self-importance. It was ecology *terrorism*, that's what it was.

CITCO had taught him to be in constant search of the next threat. There were always new recruits, individuals without any known terrorist affiliations, even aristocrats and diplomats' sons. Which is why he still had doubts about the Marquès …

Only as the hour for the start of the royal reception at Pedralbes Palace drew nearer, and to which the aristocrat and his wife, Montse, had been invited to, did Beltrán glimpse a tiny chink in the Guíxols' armour.

Montse's name suddenly illuminated on his phone. It was vibrating on the table between his lawyer and Beltrán – as it had done earlier, a few times, although it had then been left unanswered.

This time, however, Jaume muttered with his lawyer before answering the call. He was abrupt, telling her that something had come up, and he was unsure if he'd make it to the reception. There was some high-pitched shrieking from the other end of the line before the aristocrat quickly cut her off.

Even before Monste had called, however, CITCO had been monitoring the aristocrat's cell phone and relaying the information back to Beltrán. Earlier, when his phone had vibrated twice from another number, they'd tracked the location of the incoming call to Figueres, northeast of Barcelona. CITCO had found that the caller's SIM card had been recently purchased for cash in the name of 'J. Puig'. As it was a pay-as-you-go, no address or bank details had been given.

Nothing particularly sinister in that, perhaps, except that Beltrán had now also received news of a man arriving at Figueres train station that afternoon, bearing a resemblance to Brandon Bartholomew …

75

Elena

If there was one thing Elena had learnt from her sports journalism course, it was that an image, a photo, or preferably a *video*, often told the whole story, or at least most of it. Not that she wanted to specialise in photo-journalism. She loved her blog, she loved writing, and as soon as she'd qualified, she hoped to land a job that enabled her to continue writing regularly. She'd been trained in the instantaneous world of social media, however, and while pursuing the thug from the museum to Sants station and then to the hospital, she'd been reaching into her pocket for her cell phone to try and film him or send messages about him. *But her phone wasn't there …*

After making a mental note of what the taxi driver

had told her outside the hospital – that the psycho had asked to be taken to an aparthotel called Olimpia – she went in search of a Vodafone shop and found one halfway down the nearby Carrer de Muntaner.

Still in severe pain with her shoulder, she told the shop assistant that her old phone had been stolen, and that she wanted to cancel the number in case it had been hacked, and to replace it, right now.

The assistant started clicking away on her computer, asking for the old number, asking for Elena's DNI – *good,* that was all fine – checking her account, no problem there, either – while Elena kept insisting on the very best phone she could have – *right now* – there and then, even a pay-as-you-go if it had to be – but she needed it to be up and working with full data, the whole works. The assistant asked her how she would pay, whether she wanted to put it all on the existing account, or cash, credit card? Whatever was required, Elena said. It was no problem at all, and the assistant began to show her all the options …

'You don't also have some paracetamol, do you?' Elena asked, once the new phone was charged and fully functioning. 'My shoulder's killing me …'

A little later, she hailed down a taxi and was on her way across to the Olympic port.

In the back seat of the cab, she logged back on to her Twitter account, and there were several urgent and direct messages from Nicole at AFP.

'I'm back online,' Elena replied, before suggesting how they could work together.

76

Inspector Vizcaya and Marcos Constantinos
- Beltrán Gómez and Jaume Guíxols

Monday 4 June, 8pm – Mossos Comissaria, Les Corts district, Barcelona.

'Find the green tie … you'll find the bullfighter,' Inspector Vizcaya muttered to himself, sitting alone in the incident room.

It had been one of the longest and most trying days of his career, and it wasn't over yet. He was a highly experienced kidnap detective and hostage negotiator, but this, *this … animal rights extortion …* combined with the pressure from Bosch, Beltrán and all the international security forces in Barcelona for the G20 … this was something else.

This was a homicide, kidnapping and an abduction – the fine line distinction being that a kidnap was normally carried out for a ransom, while the latter was often to cause harm, and potentially murder. Eighty percent of abducted victims were harmed or killed by a member of their family or a relative. The grim reality was that they were usually killed quickly – and Vizcaya knew from experience that with every hour that passed, the chances of finding them alive decreased.

Was the bullfighter already dead? It was over twenty hours since he was abducted, and there'd been no sighting of him at all, nor any of his body parts, despite a pimp's ear being hurled at the G20 wives. What concerned Vizcaya more than anything was that there'd been no promise to release the victim at all, even if the demands were met, and even if they did go ahead and chop off his ears.

Vizcaya had tried to put all the terrorism paranoia to one side. He'd tried to *compartmentalise* the chauffeur's murder, the discarded bloody hammer and severed ear. And he'd returned to the root of every previous kidnap and abduction he'd ever investigated: location.

Where was the victim being held?

Where would you hide a bloodstained bullfighter?

And the clue, in fact the only clue – '*find the green tie, you'll find the bullfighter*' – had been scribbled by the main suspect himself. Was he even trying to *help* the police?

Just as he was wondering how the puffed-up Beltrán was getting on with the Marquès de Guíxols, Officer Soler returned to the incident room after interviewing the socialite, Lisette Dijckhuijsen.

'What a total bitch,' she said. 'We've let her go.'

'Nothing?'

'Nothing. She confirmed that she'd personally invited the Marquès to the event at the hotel, in the same way that she'd invited many others – because she was responsible for the PR,' said Soler, checking her notes. 'She admitted to, I quote – a *brief, unsatisfying fling* with the old man, but it *meant nothing because he was worth nothing*. Can you believe it?'

'I can, actually,' said Vizcaya, nodding.

'She said that she knew nothing at all of the so-called doctor who'd probably gatecrashed the function – nor had she ever met him before. She agreed, if required, to be a witness to the fact that the aristocrat had been speaking in *hushed tones* with the man, but she had no idea what about. That was it.'

She tossed her notes onto her desk and looked around.

'Where's the child prodigy from Madrid?' she asked.

'Still grilling the Marquès.'

'God help us,' said Soler.

They were then joined by Lieutenant Trias, looking cheerful with news of a breakthrough in the investigation.

'We've received a report from Scotland Yard about Marcos Constantinos and his legal aid fund,' he said.

'Go on,' said Vizcaya. 'Last we heard was that the cell phone used to trigger the robocalls from central Barcelona to the media about the kidnap *also* called a

London number registered to Constantinos – and from Nîmes in France.'

'Marcos Constantinos and his Dutch partner, Brigitte Mulder, to be precise …' said Trias, handing a file to the Inspector.

Vizcaya scanned the report, as Trias continued his update.

'Constantinos has denied any involvement in the murder or kidnapping,' he said.

'Obviously,' said Soler.

'He said that a cell phone number registered to his law collective *might have* received a call from southern France – but in the same way they received hundreds of other calls from those arrested at Gatwick airport for protesting against airport expansion,' said Trias.

Vizcaya, reading the report while listening to the update, stood up.

'His partner Brigitte, however, finally broke down,' continued Trias. 'It transpires that she never told Marcos that she'd given some money, *his* money, to another group. She'd handed over the cash, a lot of it, during a trip back to Amsterdam, to an ex-boyfriend called Jürgen. He said that he'd joined a vegan activist group in Barcelona and that they were planning a radical animal rights and climate change protest during the G20. He said they'd codenamed the operation as a *coming clean mission* to expose the true horror of animal cruelty, and that the bullfighter had to be treated like dirty laundry –'

'Laundry?' said Vizcaya, now gripping the file that Trias had handed him. *'Laundry?'*

Clothing, suits, shirts, ties and bloodstained costumes started flashing through his mind.

'Where would you hide a bloodstained bullfighter?' he said.

Trias and Soler remained silent.

'We have to search every launderette and laundry depot across the city ... *immediately* ...'

Beltrán didn't know how many people with the name 'J.Puig' lived in Catalonia, but he guessed it would be thousands. Puig was a common surname, and the 'J' could stand for any number of Jaumes, Jordis, Joseps, Joans or Joaquims – and that was just the men.

How many 'J.Puigs' had purchased a pay-as-you-go SIM card just a week ago from a shop in Figueres, however, and had called the Marquès de Guíxols twice this evening? That narrowed it down.

Seeing the aristocrat's reaction after asking him if he knew a J.Puig from Figueres had also made Beltrán suspicious.

'*Who* in Figueres?' he'd shot back, ignoring the advice from his lawyer, and instead taking it upon himself to answer directly.

Why had Figueres suddenly made him react?

'J.Puig,' Beltrán said again. 'From Figueres. Who is he?'

'I've never heard of him,' said the Marquès.

Figueres ...

Beltrán was chuffed that his media and public appeal to find Brandon Bartholomew had thrown up a possible sighting of 'the doctor' arriving at Figueres station, but it also worried him. Figueres was the next destination on the G20 spouse programme tomorrow morning – a cultural visit by motorcade from Barcelona to the Salvador Dalí Museum, to be followed by a luncheon in aid of a charity for under-privileged kids.

Beltrán knew that extra agents had been deployed to Figueres, but he now feared that the eco-terrorist attacks at museums across Europe and Madrid were more closely linked to events unfurling in Barcelona than first suspected. Was it first Picasso, and now Dalí? Was Bartholomew and his band of animal rights terrorists deliberately targeting the G20 wives on their art itinerary? Beltrán suddenly had the urge to get to Figueres himself, to oversee operations there.

Watching the Marquès whisper with his lawyer, he now also got the impression that he might even be looking for some kind of deal ...

77

Séverin and Jürgen

Monday 4 June, 7.30pm – El Poblenou neighbourhood, Barcelona.

Séverin now tightened his grip on Jürgen's neck. He'd already dragged him along the corridor by his hipster beard, then forced him to stand and lead the way across the empty inner forecourt, towards the laundry zone at the back of the Olimpia complex, which was the area where the Dutchman had finally revealed the bullfighter was being held.

Séverin's brain was frying. That last batch of angel dust was *way* too strong. PCP, originally a horse tranquiliser, *for fucksake*, yet taken off the market for its dissociative and hallucinogenic side effects … yeah, well, it was boiling his brain again.

Getting into the Olimpia premises had been easy enough, despite his unsteadiness. He simply used the plastic card that he'd found in the wallet of Hendrik or whoever he was, the other Dutch jerk now lying dead with vomit-clogged lungs in hospital.

He'd come here to punish Jürgen for leaving him stranded last night; to get the cash he was owed – and which he'd since discovered in Jürgen's rucksack; and to find where they were holding the *animal killer*, the bullfighter. Then, finally, he'd carry out his duty; he'd finish what he'd been instructed to do.

His body temperature wasn't helping his stability, though, and he was more than sensitive to sound, which meant that the humming noise he kept hearing was making him even more paranoid, and certainly more aggressive.

'*Show me, then. Where's the fucking bullfighter?*' He was foaming at the mouth and spitting at Jürgen. '*Show me. Where is he? Where's the animal killer?*'

As Jürgen was forced ahead and into the laundry facility, the intense noise from the industrial washing machines hit Séverin even more. It was yet another psychotic side-effect of the angel dust – sensitivity to noise, *noise*, *NOISE* – and he briefly let go of Jürgen's neck to try and block out the sound by covering his ears, which was when the Dutchman seized his half-chance to try and wriggle his way free … but failed.

Poor Jürgen.

Séverin yanked his beard to one side and slammed his head hard against the corner of one of the washing machines. He then took a different grip, ramming his head against the machine again but this time nose first, which burst open, with the blood spurting out left and right. Jürgen gulped and tried to yell, but Séverin jerked his head up and kept a rigid choke hold to keep it still, while fumbling in his holster belt for his spare claw hammer.

'Where is he? Where's the animal killer? Where's the bastard who gets awarded bloody ears?' yelled Séverin.

Jürgen was choking. He couldn't answer. He was trying to point at something but Séverin hooked the claw hammer over the top of his left ear, ramming it in hard before tugging it downwards – yet only half-ripping it from his head, as blood shot out from around the split cartilage.

Séverin then dug the claw in again, pulling it down harder, but the ear still refused to come free. It hung by a thread, a stubborn gooey tail of fleshy membrane. He was about to tug it off with his fingers, but as Jürgen was now pointing desperately to a row of store-rooms nearby, he finally released his grip.

As Jürgen crawled away to relative safety, back towards the forecourt while leaving a trail of blood behind him, Séverin turned his sadistic attention to where he'd been pointing …

78

Benjamin

Monday 4 June, 8.15pm – Passeig Marítim de la Mar Bella, Barcelona.

Benjamin squinted into the distance, southwest along the Barcelona coastline, as the sunlight slowly began to drain away. The shimmering Mediterranean Sea was now tinged with pink, and the lengthening shadows of giant palm trees deepened into blue and purple along the promenade. The lanterns of beachside bars and restaurants were flickering to life, while the sound of shrieking kids mingled with guitar music from street performers carried along the seafront.

Despite the faint sea breeze, it wasn't enough to break the relentless humidity, and if anything it had got worse as the day wore on. Roller skaters, skateboarders and joggers were out again, yet withering in the heat, perhaps longing for a thunderstorm to clear the air.

Benjamin had come off the ringroad soon after reaching the Diagonal-Mar corner of the city. Conso's old car was still alive, but only just. He'd used his knees to control the steering wheel again while struggling with the map on her phone, immediately after leaving the motorway. Despite having the accelerator pedal glued to the floor, the vehicle had simply trudged along – so as soon as he knew he was within walking distance to the Olympic port, he'd parked up outside a beach-side seafood restaurant. He'd decided it would be safer to complete the journey on foot.

He'd get there, he was determined – he'd find the *Olimpia Bugaderia* if he could find the street of Ciutat de Granada, which following the map led down to the Carrer del Taulat – and that street ran parallel to where he was walking now, towards the port – which is when the image of a bullfighter's breeches suddenly forced its way into his mind …

Why?

Was it because of the bloody images he'd tried to scroll away from when reading the news of the kidnapped bullfighter earlier? *Bloodstained breeches?* What was it with the kidnapped matador and Dalí's invisible *toreador* … and now a bullfigher's breeches?

'Dalí's bullfighter is only visible if you *will* him to be,' he muttered, as he paced ahead. 'He lacks a clear outline, this bullfighter, whose blood we neither see nor want to see …'

79

Beltrán Gómez and the Marquès de Guíxols

Monday 4 June, 8.30pm – Mossos Comissaria, Les Corts district, Barcelona.

It was starting to get late when the Marquès de Guíxols, after conferring with his lawyer, finally succumbed – or at least partially.

Beltrán had returned to the interview room after checking on other reports, when the lawyer suddenly said that his client could see 'a possible way out'. The police, he explained, clearly wanted his client to help them. His client, however, also wanted help on other matters.

'What other matters?' said Beltrán.

The Marquès glanced across at his lawyer. Beltrán couldn't tell if the lawyer glanced back or not. He couldn't tell where he was glancing, as his eyes kept oscillating.

'If I tell you what I know,' the Marquès said, 'then I want immunity in return.'

'Immunity?'

'From the bank investigation. Of which I'm innocent, anyway.'

'Look, sir,' said Beltrán. 'As was explained to you at the start, at the moment you have no obligation to remain here at all, but –'

'I have no obligation to help you, it's true, but I do have information that I could share with you. However, this is a personal, private matter, and I want assurances that if I do, then I will have immunity. And I also want no reference made of that Dixie Dijckhuijsen woman to my family.'

Beltrán said that he personally didn't have the authority to grant any immunity, that he would have to go higher, much higher, to the fiscal authorities, perhaps even to the Ministry of Interior or Justice in Madrid.

'Then do so,' said the Marquès, flashing a quick grin. 'I'm sure you have the contacts, young man.'

Beltrán returned the aristocrat's stare. He suddenly felt rather flattered.

'I certainly have the right connections,' he said, stroking his slicked-back hair. 'I'll see what I can do, sir,' he then added, pulling out his top-of-the-range phone with his other hand.

80

Elena and Jürgen

Monday 4 June, 8pm – El Poblenou neighbourhood, Barcelona.

Because of G20 roadblocks, it took Elena much longer than expected to get across to the area where she'd located the Olimpia aparthotel with the help of her new cell phone, in the *barrio* of Poblenou, the other side of the Olympic port. The taxi couldn't take her further than the corner of Avinguda d'Icària with Marina, but it was fine, because she could walk the rest. She knew the area, more or less.

Many of the old factory buildings in the neighbourhood had been transformed into co-working sites, trendy offices, concept stores and art studios, while the nearby seafront, once full of slimy rocks, sewage and rotting warehouses, had been filled with tons of golden sand, imported palm trees and landscaped promenades, all thanks to the 92 Games.

The streets were mostly deserted, probably due to the unbearable humidity. Elderly women sat listlessly on plastic chairs in the doorways of apartment blocks, fanning themselves, in contrast to some boisterous tourists in flip-flops returning from the beach, carrying cans of beer in plastic bags. It felt peaceful enough, apart from the distant whine of police sirens ... and the bloodied figure sitting on the side of the road, moaning and pleading for assistance.

Elena's immediate reaction was to help him, but when she saw that he was trying to hold the remains of an ear to the side of his head, she instinctively knew it had something to do with the savage she'd been chasing. She could see a trail of blood and assumed it was from the direction the man had staggered. She told him to sit him up, to explain what had happened and who'd done this to him – *where was he?* – but his face and nose had been smashed, his mouth was blood red, and he could hardly speak.

She waved down a passing cyclist, shouting for extra help. Two pedestrians coming from a side street also stopped to help, with one of them saying he'd call for an ambulance. The victim seemed to panic, groaning that he couldn't go in any ambulance – but they took no notice of him. Elena backed away from helping further. Without anyone noticing, she took some pictures on her phone, just as an ambulance arrived and the others helped him towards it.

Then she was off again, her adrenaline pumping, and very soon she'd found the Olimpia aparthotel ...

81

Inspector Vizcaya, Beltrán Gómez and the Marquès de Guíxols

Monday 4 June, 8.45pm – Mossos Comissaria, Les Corts district, Barcelona.

The police operation led by Inspector Vizcaya making enquiries at launderettes and laundry depots was underway – but it was going to take time.

There were hundreds of laundry businesses servicing the hospitality industry within the city's metropolitan area and beyond. Resources were limited due to the G20, and so a specialist team was trying to narrow down the search. They were targeting launderettes in the Sants area where the robocalls to the media were activated, the district of Les Corts where the hire car had been abandoned, and the Olympic port area where Bartholomew had been seen at the hotel restaurant. As for the Splendido brothel, it didn't use any laundry services and never had.

But it was the area near Girona airport and the motorway service station where Vizcaya himself had asked to be driven back to, precisely where the bull-fighter's Chevrolet had been abandoned. He'd left Soler in the incident room with the task of pinpointing any laundry companies that serviced the airport and nearby hotels, telling her to prioritise laundry depots that had laundry *vehicles* – potentially all tracked and monitored with delivery times and schedules, possibly some even having fleets of vehicles with GPS …

Back in the interview room and oblivious to the search being undertaken by Vizcaya's team, Beltrán sat opposite the Marquès de Guíxols and his lawyer.

A duty judge had just left the room, having explained the contents of a document that had been placed in front of the aristocrat. While immunity had been granted against any charges linking Jaume to the bank investigation, he would still have fiscal obligations for any personal tax discrepancies. He'd agreed to the deal, signed the document, and the judge had left.

'Well?' Beltrán then said, impatiently.

The Marquès glanced at his lawyer.

'Tell me what you really know about Brandon Bartholomew, the *doctor*,' insisted Beltrán.

'He's got my painting,' said Jaume, finally.

'What painting?'

'*My* painting. And I want it back.'

82

Benjamin

Monday 4 June, 8.45pm – El Poblenou neighbourhood, Barcelona.

There's no such thing as the perfect crime, Benjamin mused. All you need to do is ask the right question of the right person and look in the right place. Which is precisely what he intended to do right now.

Why had a laundry van sped away from the service station last night, moments before he was attacked? Who was driving it? What was inside the van? Who murdered the bullfighter's chauffeur? The thug? Why was there a ripped green tie and shirt button on the ground near the corpse? Presumably it was from the missing bullfighter … the *invisible toreador* … but where was he now? Where was he being held?

Benjamin had circled the Olimpia premises several times, discreetly from a distance, with his baseball cap pulled firmly over the top of his face. It looked like there were several businesses within the same complex – Olimpia 'hospitality supplies', a three-star aparthotel, and a laundry depot, the *Olimpia Bugaderia*.

He knew he was in the right place. He knew it because he could see a few vans … *identical to the van he'd seen at the service station …*

There were a couple of them inside the courtyard, and there was even one parked out on the road, with a special parking permit resting on top of its dashboard. They were distinct and there was no doubt about it – they were identical to the style of van he'd seen screeching away from the service station, just before he'd slumped to the ground.

They were old-fashioned Bedford CFs, almost vintage or retro-style, not unlike old ambulances or classic ice-cream vans – but without the open-glass side panels from where they'd sell the ice-cream. The *bugaderia* word he'd glimpsed before the attack was clearly stencilled on the sides, with *Olimpia* much smaller. A style of van to portray a traditional service of laundry and dry-cleaning, perhaps – and ideal for nipping around the old city's narrow streets to establishments like the IB hotels, where the psycho had been hovering outside.

Standing opposite and across the road, Benjamin could see that the gates to the laundry depot were locked with a chain at this hour, and the adjacent aparthotel was the only building with lights on.

He suddenly heard police sirens, and it jolted him.

With the G20, however, it was to be expected, he assured himself – as was the noise of helicopters circling above. There was a faint yet constant hum of chanting and drumming that he could hear, too. Possibly it was just the Catalan nightlife, or maybe G20 protesters.

He checked his watch and the screen of Conso's phone yet again. He hadn't received any call or message from her or her nephew regarding the test on the painting yet, but it would take time.

He buttoned up his lumberjack shirt to the neck, pulled the baseball cap on even tighter, and then strolled purposefully across the road and straight into the Olimpia aparthotel, hoping to get across to the laundry depot via the back, once he was inside.

83

Beltrán Gómez and the Marquès de Guíxols

Monday 4 June, 9.30pm – Mossos Comissaria, Les Corts district, Barcelona.

The Marquès hadn't exactly been forthcoming with more information about Brandon Bartholomew.

He declined to give any details about the painting he claimed that he'd run off with, nor did he have any intention of estimating its value. He simply said that the man, 'a doctor or professor', whose first name he thought was Benjamin, 'but it could have been Brandon', had visited his home near La Bisbal on Sunday to view the painting, and that he'd been recommended by an old friend, the chairman of Sotheby's. He'd then left with the canvas in his car to carry out tests.

Despite meeting again with the man briefly at the hotel event, the Marquès was now 'utterly distressed and distraught' – his lawyer's words – fearing that he'd been robbed of a 'priceless work of art'. When the aristocrat was asked to give a full description of the painting, he refused, and simply said: 'It's a Dalí.'

Shortly afterwards, from his glass-partitioned space at the back of the incident room, Beltrán managed to locate the chairman of Sotheby's, Sir Anthony Hughes, in Beijing, seven hours ahead of Barcelona.

'Do you know what time it is?' yelled Hughes.

Beltrán said that he did. He then asked Hughes if he knew the Marquès de Guíxols, and whether Sotheby's had booked a flight from London to Spain on behalf of a consultancy firm called ALC, under the passenger's name of Brandon Bartholomew.

Hughes barked that he had 'absolutely no bloody idea' what Beltrán was on about, and that 'Spain had no jurisdiction to call or question him on anything'.

After the call ended abruptly, Beltrán was surprised to see the incident room was nearly empty, with just Marta Soler and another Mossos officer manning the phones. He sat staring at his glass wall covered with post-it notes, deep in thought, before flicking through another report that had been left on his desk.

He read that Interpol had since confirmed that Bartholomew's passport and driving licence were both valid but 'perhaps shouldn't have been', whatever *that* meant. Scotland Yard was apparently still 'doublechecking its facts' with the UK's Passport Office on the matter, too – but the issue was becoming increasingly bizarre. Was it a stolen or forged passport?

He knew he'd been right in getting the Interior

Ministry to issue images of the suspect to the media, but something was bugging him about Bartholomew running off with the aristocrat's painting – 'a Dalí', he'd said. It brought Beltrán back to the connection with eco-terrorism at museums, and to *Figueres* and the Salvador Dalí Museum, the next destination on the G20 spouse programme.

He logged onto his computer to check for updates from CITCO. They'd since traced the unanswered calls made to the Marquès while he was in the interview room to a 'Josep Fèlix Puig', a resident of Cadaqués, thirty-five kilometres east of Figueres.

Puig had recently set up his own business; a studio dedicated to the preservation and conservation of art. CITCO had been trying to track the current location of Puig's phone, but after the calls made to the Marquès, the GPS location had been lost or disconnected. Whoever was using the phone was on the move and not wanting to be tracked. Beltrán sent a message to instruct the Cadaqués local police to keep a watch on his home and studio, then checked the next report.

The possible sighting of a man resembling Bartholomew who'd arrived by train from Barcelona to Figueres in the afternoon was also summarised.

Analysis of CCTV images in and around Figueres station showed the man as being dressed, or disguised, in a loud checked shirt and baseball cap, carrying a 'flat case' under his arm. It was not yet conclusive from the images if it was the same man who'd arrived at Girona airport on Sunday evening or seen shaking hands with the US Secretary of State at the hotel event – but there was certainly a likeness.

Beltrán immediately contacted the Dalí Museum in Figueres. Despite stringent security measures in place for the G20 visit, he wanted to know if anyone wearing a similar shirt and baseball cap had tried to enter the museum between the hours after the train's arrival and closing time. And, yes, sure enough, someone had …

Beltrán punched the air in the same way he'd seen FBI agents punch the air in a recent TV documentary. He suddenly realised why the suspect had taken the aristocrat's painting.

Bartholomew's interaction with the Marquès was a smokescreen. He was using the *identity* of an art expert to infiltrate the upper echelons of Catalan society, clearly to plan another attack, while leaving cynical clues to hamper the investigation.

Since orchestrating the kidnapping, the murder and the tossing of an ear outside the Picasso Museum, he was now targeting the Dalí Museum and he'd taken the aristocrat's painting as collateral, as a *way in*. What was he intending to plant there? A bomb? Beltrán had a duty to get to Figueres before the G20 wives arrived. He'd make a call and go straight to the top again.

Just think … one day *he* would be at the very top.

'God, you're good, Beltrán,' he muttered, stroking his plastered-down hair before picking up his cell phone. He'd known all along he was right. He'd always been right. But he now also wanted the credit, the *recognition*.

84

Benjamin, Elena and Séverin

Monday 4 June, 9.15pm – El Poblenou neighbourhood, Barcelona.

Benjamin had expected a reception area at the Olimpia aparthotel, with someone manning a desk at the least, but there was no one. Just vending machines for snacks, drinks, toiletries, fruit and breakfast packs. There were no guests or staff around; there was no bar. There wasn't even a reception 'desk' – it was a table.

He leaned over it to see if there was anything that might help him. Perhaps there was some information on the adjacent laundry premises that was closed off from the street, or some keys … anything. But there was nothing. Nothing at all.

He could understand aparthotel guests being self-sufficient, but it left him cold. The world was becoming a ticketless, staff-less, faceless journey. You could book train tickets without anyone physically checking your ticket or greeting you. You could shop or do all your banking online without ever talking to anyone ever again … and now here was a hotel without any staff.

Or was there? Was that a scream he just heard?

The noise was coming from behind a 'staff only' side door. As there were no staff around, and still hoping to reach the laundry premises via the back of the aparthotel, he decided to open it.

It led to a long corridor.

'Hello?' he called out. '*Hola?*' No response.

He walked along the corridor and heard a door slam at the far end. No one emerged to ask what he wanted, or what he was looking for – but nor had any alarm gone off, which was a relief. He edged further along the corridor.

Again, a door suddenly banged.

He glanced at the paperwork pinned to the notice-boards. It was all in Spanish and Catalan, employment and insurance certificates, health and safety instructions, housekeeping rules and timesheets. He kept on walking until he reached the far end, where a fire exit door had been opened but had not swung shut properly. He stepped out into a covered courtyard. It was darker here, so he waited a few moments for his eyes to adjust.

Squinting across the courtyard, he could see it was deserted except for two of those old-fashioned laundry vans. It was an area of the Olimpia complex that hadn't been visible from the street. There was another large building adjoined to what looked like two ware-houses, and he was now certain it was the laundry division.

There was still no one in sight, so he pushed the fire door shut behind him and started to stroll across, feeling a sudden beat of excitement, or maybe appre-hension. He peered into the two parked vans but could see nothing odd. He pulled out the phone, then jabbed it with his thumb to illuminate the screen. He wanted to check if anyone had called, but noticed that he now didn't even have a signal.

The far building was dimly lit from the inside. He stood still for some moments, listening to the sounds beyond. He could hear the rumbling of machinery. His nerves were starting to jangle, but he was determined to press ahead.

Suddenly, there was a noise behind him, precisely from where he'd come. He stopped and turned. The fire exit door had swung open again, and was gently banging against a side wall, back and forth. He thought he'd seen a figure by the door, briefly illumi-nated in the shadows. He squinted. Whoever, or what-ever it was, had now gone.

Turning back to face the building and warehouses at the far end of the parking lot, he walked on, more cautiously – even more so when a cat, or maybe a large rat, scurried across the gravel in front of him. The rumbling and humming noise got louder with every step he took, and then when he finally reached the side of the building, he stopped.

Peering through a side window, he could see a brick wall passageway with bare lightbulbs hanging from the ceiling, and rows of laundry carts. He followed the dim light that was coming from the other side of the building, slowly edging his way around the outside until he found a door.

He felt for the phone in his pocket again, to possibly use it as a torch. He wondered whether he should go back, but it was only a very brief thought; he knew it wouldn't happen. The voice of determination inside his head told him to simply keep going, and to resolve matters for himself, just as he'd always done.

The door was thick, heavy, and it took some effort to push it open. He soon realised why. It was a sound-proof door. The noise inside was extreme. On the wall was a sign illustrating that it was a non-smoking and high-visibility vest area, and it also indicated that he should be wearing ear plugs or headphones. He could detect a distinct smell of something wafting in the air. What was it? Bleach? Chlorine? Looking around, there were rows of containers of liquid and powder chemicals stacked against a wall. There were wooden pallets, too, some broken, with planks of split and splintered wood lying around.

He stepped over the debris and finally made his way into the main industrial unit, still dimly lit, but with rows of heavy-duty washing machines and tumble dryers rumbling away loudly. There were wide roller machines that he guessed were for ironing or folding all the linen, but there were no workers in sight. It looked like an automated production line, all tech and no staff, at least for this evening's shift, just like the staff-less aparthotel next door.

He moved on, making his way along a passageway that led down to a storage area … and then suddenly he stopped.

There she was.

It was *Elena*.

She hadn't heard him over the noise, and her back was turned towards him, so she hadn't seen him yet, either. It looked like she was struggling to open the doorway of a storeroom, but he wasn't sure. He wanted to call out to her, but he didn't get the chance. She turned and looked up, just as he was about to speak, and then she screamed. He could hear her scream, even above the noise of the machines, but he couldn't catch what she was then yelling. She was pointing, too. She was pointing to behind him …

He turned, just in time to see the psycho swinging a hammer at him.

The first blow, thanks to having spun round, half-caught Benjamin on the lower left side of his face instead of the back of his skull, which was fortunate, all things considered, because any further cerebral injury leading to an intracranial haemorrhage might have killed him.

His baseball cap dropped off as he fell to his knees, and he didn't know what shocked him the most, seeing

Elena, or the hammer colliding with part of his jaw, or the fact that the psycho had suddenly appeared from behind. The pain was immediate, but he tried to find some comfort in the knowledge that he was obviously in the right place. Glancing up, he realised the humungous freak was no longer wearing a red hoodie, but a leather jacket with a rucksack on his back. There was also a tool belt around his vast waist, containing knives and screwdrivers.

Suddenly, he was swinging the hammer again, so Benjamin sprung up and lurched headfirst towards his crotch, trying to ram him to the ground. The maniac toppled backwards but remained upright.

The hammer then struck Benjamin's left shoulder, but he kept fighting, he kept trying to defend himself, grabbing the thug's legs to try and pull him down and minimise the space he had to swing his hammer.

Again, the thug swayed, but still remained upright, and then he started to kick and stamp on Benjamin, eventually freeing his legs to clamber over him, before moving on towards the girl …

'Leave the fucking bullfighter to me,' is what Benjamin heard, or so he thought, and then something about 'suffering' and 'equals' and the Bible.

He was aware that blood had started to seep from his nose and around his mouth. He could already taste it, but he didn't want to see it; it would only make matters worse. All he could hear was the psycho yelling something about the bullfighter, Elena screaming, and then things became very hazy. The only thing he could think about before virtually passing out was whether he had a simple dislocated jawbone – a *temporomandibular* joint, they called that – or maybe it was a broken lower jaw, a full *mandible fracture* ...

Elena knew she could come across as argumentative at times; she knew she had a snappy, combative attitude. She'd been told she could be impulsive, and prone to finding herself in risky situations. But it was never going to stop her. Not right now ...

Earlier, by following the trail of blood left by the man in the street with his ear hanging off, she'd finally found the thug within a warehouse at the Olimpia laundry depot. Seeing him threatening the bound and gagged bullfighter, she'd used her new cell phone to film him. She'd caught him shoving the hostage to the ground and kicking him, before dragging him into a storeroom. But then he'd caught sight of her, and he'd slammed the storeroom shut and come after her while she was still filming. She screamed and ran, hoping she'd lost him after dodging between the machines and back to where the laundry carts were.

Slowly, quietly, she then made her way back to the far end of the warehouse, to see if she could open the storeroom and free the bullfighter. Not just to film him for her news report, but so that he might help her over-come and restrain the savage.

She was just about to open the storeroom door when she turned and saw Benjamin – *Brandon*

Bartholomew – and what the fuck was he wearing? She immediately screamed, thinking he'd also come to attack her, until the thug suddenly reappeared behind him and swung his hammer …

After kicking the shit out of Benjamin, the savage now charged into Elena so hard, her legs shot out in front of her, and her back slammed flat to the ground. Her scalp felt like it was being wrenched apart as he yanked her hair, pulling her away from the door of the storeroom where the bullfighter was trapped, and along the passageway to a loading bay area, full of laundry carts. Being dragged along the ground, she tried to reach for something to hit him with, but her flailing arms simply knocked over some containers of bleach along the way.

Before long, he was sitting on top of her, straddling her, crushing her, with the fingers of one hand tightening around her neck. She could barely breathe.

He was mumbling and muttering to himself, out of his head on drugs – but more so than before, she thought. His eyes were bloodshot, and he looked delirious. He was also clearly sweltering in his leather jacket and with the rucksack on his back, because drops of his slimy sweat were dripping onto her face. The repulsive yob looked terrifyingly unstable, even more so as a pair of secateurs appeared in his other hand.

'I told you …' he was mumbling. 'I told you … to leave the bullfighter to me … in suffering, animals are our equals … in suffering, animals are our equals.'

She tried to wriggle herself free and scratch at his fingers, but his grip was relentless, and the pain in her shoulder had returned, worse than ever. She could only watch, petrified, as he twisted the secateurs in his hand, placing them against her upper left auricle, the fleshy part of her ear. She tried to shake her head, but then the cutters snicked her skin and blood started to trickle from the top of her ear.

'We could have been friends,' he said, salivating. 'We could have had sex. In fact, we still could …'

He moved the secateurs from her ear to the neckline of her loose top, and then started to slowly snip away at the fabric.

She screamed and didn't stop.

Benjamin was lying with his jawbone split, he was sure of it, but the only images swirling through his brain were *bloody* – his bloody nose, bloody mouth, bloody bulls, bloody bullfighters – and why did the image of a bullfighter's bloody breeches suddenly materialise? What was that noise? The psycho had attacked him with another hammer. But now he needed to focus … *what was that noise?*

Screaming …

He slowly managed to stand up. He was dizzy and he could feel the liquid dripping from his mouth and nose. It's blood, but if you don't touch it, you won't see it on your fingers. You can't faint now, Benjamin. Pull yourself together. Nodding to himself, he started to stagger back down the corridor, back in the direction from where he'd originally come. But he could still hear that noise …

Screaming …

It was Elena screaming …

He looked around. He saw the broken wooden pallets scattered on the floor. He picked up the longest piece of splintered wood that he could find, and then ran back towards her screams …

Séverin was panting, boiling, dripping with sweat, and he already felt detached and distant from the gypsy bitch he was straddling, almost as if he was floating above her. He wanted her to admire him. If she only stopped screaming, she'd understand that he was doing a good deed; that he would be erasing the bullfighter because it was the honourable, ethical and legitimate thing to do. Besides, he'd been paid to do it.

'Listen,' he was trying to explain, while snipping away at her top. 'I'm the good guy. I'm just putting the world right. Bullfighters behave badly, very badly, and they need to be eradicated. Do you agree? Do you understand? Stop screaming …'

The extra dose of angel dust he'd taken earlier had been far too strong, and the laundry machine noise was now making him even more paranoid. He was hallucinating, and the image of her beneath him was becoming distorted, as if he was having another out-of-body experience. The secateurs had slipped twice, and it felt like he was watching someone else trying to carry out his instructions. What the fuck was happening to him? What was he seeing? Dragons, demons ... he was roasting ... he was in flames ... monsters were staring at him, plotting to kill him. But he wouldn't let them.

Could she even hear him?

Did she understand what he was saying?

'You're not *listening* to me,' he said, still drooling. 'A righteous man regards the life of his beast; but the tender mercies of the wicked are cruel. That's from the Bible. Proverbs, twelve, ten. You must pay attention ...'

She was still screaming, digging her nails into his hand, and she'd spat in his face, too, which wasn't very kind. Each time he tried to silence her screams, he had to remove one hand from her throat, or let go of the cutters. He was burning, his flesh was pulsating, and so he also started to tug at his own clothes, trying to remove his leather jacket and the rucksack, making it even harder to keep a grip on her.

Then suddenly, he caught sight of a stick, or a short pole, something that was now flapping from the side of his own neck. It didn't hurt, not really, but it was weird. It was kind of just hanging there, floating there ... and ...

'*Get off her,*' someone was yelling.

'*I said get the fuck off her,*' Benjamin shouted again, followed by a searing pain in his jaw.

The freak spun round, distracted by the sight of the

stick jutting out of his neck. This gave Elena space to wriggle away from his cutters, and even more so once he'd lifted himself up to confront Benjamin instead of her.

'What is it with you?' Séverin said, foaming at the mouth. 'Just let me do my job. A job that is morally right … that is righteous. I'm just carrying out my duties, but you keep getting in the way …'

Benjamin, now enraged, stared at him. The sharp lump of wood that he'd jabbed into his neck had missed the external jugular vein, so there was hardly any blood – which was probably just as well, as far as Benjamin was concerned. It still looked very painful, but the psycho didn't seem fazed by it. He'd also reached into his labourer's belt and swapped his cutters for what looked like a butcher's knife. He was swaying, sweating heavily, and his eyes were red and glazed.

Benjamin had seen that look before, many times, mostly with junkies, but there was something different about the crazed figure in front of him. Was it LSD, heroin, or something else? He looked like he was on another planet. Whatever he'd taken, it was clearly helping him to feel little or no pain. He was toxic, he was deadly, and he was muttering away incoherently, partly in French, partly in English. It looked like he was having a problem with his body temperature, too, as he let the rucksack drop off his back before struggling to take off his jacket, moving the knife from one hand to the other as he did so. He finally tossed the jacket on the ground, and the wooden stick also fell from his neck.

Benjamin could see that Elena had got up and backed away. She was pushing some buttons on a wall, and the steel shutter of the loading bay started to open, rising slowly to reveal the near darkness outside. He hoped she was going to run to safety but instead she just stood there. She'd also taken out her phone. Was she calling for help? No, she was *filming*, for fucksake …

'Don't you understand?' Séverin was saying, while staring insanely at Benjamin. 'In suffering, animals are our equals. I have an assignment to carry out. It's a judgement, a deliverance … an act of God … but you're in my fucking way.'

Benjamin had now had more than enough. He felt incensed how this gospel-ranting delirious slob had tried to kill him, before stealing his hire car and the painting, provoking him to be sought by the Spanish police and shattering his professional reputation. More than anything, he now felt sick that he'd been trying to rape Elena. The freak was still waving a butcher's knife, but that wasn't going to hold Benjamin back.

'Yes, I understand perfectly,' he started. 'But look –'

He suddenly sprang forward and headbutted the maniac on the nose. The effect of the impact was instantaneous. Blood and mucus came crashing from the thug's nostrils, but he still just stood there, brandishing the knife and staring dementedly. Meanwhile, Benjamin's head and jaw hurt worse than ever.

'That wasn't very polite,' the psycho was now

saying, either to Benjamin or perhaps to some imaginary figures in his brain, as he rocked his head from side to side. 'Now *you* deserve what's coming to you. It's my duty … my obligation …'

Benjamin took a step backwards. Blood was still dripping from the psycho's nostrils, but he knew what he had to do. It was part of his cognitive behavioural therapy course, exposing himself to the things that he feared. His blood phobia was just a spot of bad neural wiring that needed troubleshooting. He just needed to stare at the blood, to stand up to it, to subject himself to the bleeding.

'*I'll carve you up,*' the freak suddenly yelled. He was still sweating profusely and tugging at his shirt, clearly roasting.

'*Show me the blood then,*' Benjamin yelled back.

Silence.

'*Show me the blood,*' he yelled again.

Then he was on top of him – it didn't take long – because Séverin had backed away, just ever so slightly, unsure what was going on – but it was enough for Benjamin to seize his moment, a split second, which was all he needed to leap forward and kick the psycho's leather jacket up off the floor, flipping it up towards his face, just enough to momentarily confuse and blind him – and then while the freak was waving his arms, trying to free his hand with the knife away from the leather garment, Benjamin kicked him sharply in the testicles, as hard as he possibly could, just to see if *that* was something he could feel.

It was.

Séverin immediately doubled up and the knife dropped from his hand. Benjamin then rammed his elbow into the side of his head – but not hard enough, as Séverin still didn't fall over – not at first – it took another couple of sharp kicks from Benjamin to the side of his knee to force his legs to buckle, and for him to finally crash to the floor. Benjamin was about to leap on top of him, if it hadn't been for Elena grabbing a plastic container of liquid from the ground nearby.

It happened fast.

Benjamin wasn't sure what her plan was to finally subdue the thug, and nor perhaps did Elena, but he watched as she tried to splash him in the face with the liquid. Then only when Séverin, panting erratically, reached out himself for the plastic container, desperate to swig some water, or anything to cool his raging, drug-scorched state of mind … was the battle well and truly won.

Inhaling the vapour of undiluted, industrial-strength bleach can result in stinging eyes and a burning throat. Guzzling it is another matter. As it is corrosive, it quickly oxidizes or burns tissues in the mouth, esophagus and stomach, causing a rapid deterioration of vital signs and mental status, spontaneous vomiting, convulsions, and sometimes cardiac arrest. Ingestion can be benign, though … *if* the patient or victim receives immediate treatment.

But Séverin wasn't going to receive any immediate treatment. Clutching his throat while coughing and spluttering, he stumbled out to the loading bay area and immediately collapsed on the ramp outside. In a flash, Elena had pulled down the steel shutter to keep him trapped out there.

They then stood facing one another. Benjamin's face was blotchy with blood, his mouth and jawbone crooked. Elena's top was ripped open, and blood seeped from the top of her left ear. He narrowed his eyes, trying to curtail his dizziness. He heard her say something, faintly, softly, but it was difficult to hear above the noise of the machines. He thought she said '*gracias*', but maybe he imagined it.

He watched her grab a laundered white towel from one of the carts, then dab her face and ear with it, before draping it over a shoulder to half-cover her exposed front. She grabbed another towel and tossed it towards him. He caught it and held it to the side of his face. Moments later, she was fiddling with her phone again.

'Elena –' he started.

But she ignored him, and instead ran back down the passageway towards the storerooms …

85

Benjamin, Elena and Rafa

Monday 4 June, 9.45pm – El Poblenou neighbourhood, Barcelona.

'Elena, *wait* –' Benjamin called, staggering after her.

Why had she driven off earlier? How come she was here? Did that psycho work here at the laundry? Why had he been yelling about the bullfighter? Was it the *kidnapped* bullfighter? Was he still alive? Where was he being held? Benjamin had come here to clear his name and finally catch the fucker who'd tried to kill him … but Elena wasn't answering any of his questions.

Despite their ordeal, she seemed obsessed with continuing whatever she was doing before he'd arrived. As they reached the area near the storerooms, he caught her eyes sparkling with anticipation as she shot him a quick glance. She then used her phone as a camera again, taking a video selfie, holding it up and speaking to it in Spanish, before pointing it at the store-room door that she'd become fixated on.

Then when she opened the door, the double images returned …

Benjamin wondered if he was in the middle of a psychedelic trip at first. All he could do was stand and stare as a bound, gagged, bloodstained bullfighter slowly emerged from the shadows. He squinted at the apparition in front of him to check he wasn't halluci-nating – but, no, he wasn't. This was no *hallucinogenic toreador* … this was the real thing.

Everything appeared in slow-motion as he watched Elena hold up her phone and start videoing the bull-fighter close-up, while she struggled to loosen his gag with her other hand. She then turned to Benjamin and told *him* to hold the phone, to continue filming her as she untied the bullfighter's hands. Eventually he was free, shaking with emotion, thanking her and embracing her. She then snatched her phone back to record herself speaking rapidly to the bullfighter.

Benjamin didn't understand a word of their snappy conversation, but their body language was agitated, as if they were arguing.

Elena was asking the matador if he was okay. He was, more or less, but he wanted to know where his captors were, saying that there'd been three of them. Elena flicked her eyes towards Benjamin, asking if he was one of them, but the bullfighter shook his head. She said that one of the gang had been overpowered and was out in the loading bay. But the bullfighter started to panic, insisting that it wasn't safe, that they had to leave, they had to leave *right now* –

'Wait, I need to ask you some questions,' said Elena, still recording their conversation.

'No, it's not safe,' came the reply. 'We have to go.'

'It's safe enough for now.'

'*They'll kill me … they'll kill us.*'

'Don't worry, they won't,' said Elena. 'And I'll call the police in a couple of minutes. I'll call your family. I'll make sure you're okay –'

'*No,*' cried the bullfighter, starting to move away. '*We have to run –*'

'*Jesus Christ,*' whined Elena. 'What are you afraid of? Have you lost your balls? Just do me a favour and answer a few questions, will you?'

'Thank you for saving me, but we need to run –' came the reply, as he set off.

'No, wait,' she called out. 'You're supposed to be brave. What are you afraid of? You kill innocent bulls, you cruel little bastard –'

She realised she wouldn't be getting more material than she already had, but maybe it was enough.

'*Okay,* I'll call the police now,' she said, chasing after him. 'You'll be safe …' Her voice trailed off.

All along, Benjamin had been staring at the bullfighter more closely. He looked distressed, tortured, like the tear trickling down from the right eye in the *Toreador* painting – a matador knowing he was about to die, or could have died.

But what else do you see?

He focused on the bullfighter's tie that had been half cut … that green fabric he'd seen flapping on the ground at the service station.

But there was something else …

It was the bullfighter's *ripped white shirt with a missing collar button* … which was when Benjamin finally slumped to the ground.

What else do you see, Benjamin?

What – else – do – you – see?

He reckoned he'd been on the concrete floor in the corridor for only a few minutes, maybe longer, but he wasn't sure. He tried to move, to position himself on all fours to get up, but his body was aching – he needed to wait and build strength. His head was thumping, and it hadn't helped matters having his jawbone pressed against the concrete.

Was he dreaming? There was no sign of Elena, nor the bullfighter, and even the noise of the laundry machines had died down. He patted his pockets, relieved he still had Conso's phone … and then he dug into one of the pockets and found the small button again … the bullfighter's collar button … the button that he'd found at the service station.

Things would be easier now. *Everything* would be

easier. But he had to make contact with Conso and her nephew, to tell them what to search for …

He staggered back down the passageway, clutching the towel to the side of his jaw, and then pushed open a fire-exit. Elena was there, alone, waiting for him. Police sirens could be heard again, and they were getting louder.

'What kept you?' she said.

Benjamin didn't reply.

'The bullfighter ran off, the coward …' she said. 'Wherever he's gone, he'll be fine … but we have to go. I've called the police and told them where he was being held and that I've managed to free him. I don't want to be here when they arrive. I'm in pain. I need to send another report and somehow get back to Girona …'

Benjamin didn't want to hang around for the police either. His name would be cleared and hopefully the police would detain the psycho. He had to finish what he'd come here to do. And he now realised the button was the key to it, the same button he'd picked up at the crime scene at the service station last night. He desperately had to get back to Figueres to collect the painting.

'I'll take you to Girona,' he said.

'You'll take me?'

'I'm going that way …' said Benjamin, nodding.

86

Hendrik Oomen and Officer Soler

Monday 4 June, 9.30pm – Sant Gervasi-Galvany neighbourhood, Barcelona.

At first, neither doctors nor staff had any explanation for the sudden death of Hendrik Oomen, a patient at the Hospital Laforja, who'd been rushed in earlier that day for ophthalmologic emergency care.

None of the medication he'd been given should have provoked any side effects or allergic reaction, let alone cause the patient to die from asphyxiation after choking on his own vomit. But the signs of a struggle around the bedside, and the fact that the bandage over his eyes was smeared with streaks of blood and particles of sick, raised serious concern.

The bedside table drawer had also been left open, his wallet was missing, other personal possessions were scattered on the floor, yet none of the security cameras had identified anything.

Any unexplained death, even in a hospital, had to follow strict protocol and procedures in reporting to the police, a judge and next of kin. In addition, all hospitals in Barcelona were under orders to report any suspicious activity to Vizcaya's incident room.

With Vizcaya leading the search of laundrettes, it was left to Officer Soler to check the report from the Hospital Laforja. She would have dismissed the news of the deceased patient as irrelevant to the investigation if it hadn't been for his job as a laundry driver.

She learnt that Hendrik Oomen, a Dutch resident in Barcelona, had been a driver for 'Olimpia', a group specialising in laundry management for the hospitality sector, which also owned hotels, aparthotels and timeshare properties. Hendrik had apparently suffered a work accident at the group's depot in the *barrio* of Poblenou, not far from the Port Olímpic, where many of the G20 delegates were based. His injuries were sustained after a plastic container of sodium hypochlorite had 'exploded' and spurted into his eyes. With the help of a security guard, he'd been rushed by ambulance to hospital, where he had later died.

As far as Soler was concerned, Hendrik had been an employee at a group that also had a *laundry* business. That ticked a box. As for the container of sodium hypochlorite 'exploding' in his eyes … what was it? Bleach? Other chemicals? *Bomb-making* chemicals?

She called Vizcaya immediately.

87

Benjamin and Elena - Inspector Vizcaya and Séverin

Monday 4 June, 10pm – El Poblenou neighbourhood, Barcelona.

'You'll be fine,' Benjamin said, holding her arm and guiding her along. 'One step at a time … I've got hold of you … you'll be fine.'

She gripped on to him tightly.

He was also still wincing with pain and clutching the towel to his jaw with his other hand. But as they shuffled along, they didn't really raise any suspicions at all. They looked like any other couple on a night out or who'd been drinking all day, staggering along and propping up one another.

She didn't understand how he was going to get her back to Girona until he relocated the old car, parked near the beach restaurant. It was dark now, and there were lasers and flashing lights coming from some music bars and terraces along the seafront.

He helped her into the front seat, asking if she should take her to a hospital, but she shook her head, saying it would be too complicated and she needed to send messages. He wasn't sure if the car would start, but it did, and before long he was following the signs back to the AP-7, towards Girona and France.

Almost immediately, Elena took out her phone again. She then started tapping non-stop on the screen, clicking and writing, occasionally grinning, sometimes even laughing or talking to herself in Spanish. Benjamin asked her what she was doing. Working, she said. There was a silence for a while, and then Benjamin tried to ask her about the taxi business … and how long she'd been doing it.

'Excuse me?' she said, briefly looking up.

'Your taxi … you know …'

'I'm not a taxi driver.'

'There's nothing wrong with being a taxi driver −'

'I know there's nothing wrong with being a taxi driver, but I'm not a taxi driver.'

'Okay,' said Benjamin.

'The taxi is my father's … I told you,' she said, tapping away on her phone. There was a pause. 'I've been training to become a journalist,' she said. 'I tried to tell you that as well …'

'Yes, I remember,' said Benjamin. 'That's great.'

'*Si* …'

'You'll be great as a journalist,' he said.

She looked up, waiting for him to make some crass comment about her having the looks to be a TV presenter.

'You think so?' she said, testing him, trying to provoke it. 'Why?'

'Because you're clearly very insistent,' he said. 'You followed that psycho. You chased your story. You wouldn't let it go, and you saved the bullfighter. It's impressive …'

She stared at him for some time.

'*Gracias,*' she said, finally.

She held up her phone, pointed it at him and took a picture.

'No, not again. Don't, please –' he said.

'One way or another, you realise you're going to have to explain everything to the police, don't you?' she said. 'And very soon … I mean, now …'

'I know,' he nodded. 'But I'm also investigating a work of art and I need to finish it first … discreetly, if possible.'

'*Discreetly?*' she laughed.

'Discreetly.'

'I can help with explaining your story,' she said. 'In fact, you have no choice. It's going to be part of my report. What's your name … really?'

'Benjamin.'

'All of it.'

'Benjamin Blake.'

'*All* of it.'

'Benjamin Brandon Bartholomew Blake.'

She started tapping the details into her phone.

'And your police credentials?' she said.

'Elena –'

'How come you suddenly turned up at the Olimpia laundry?'

'I'd seen a *bugaderia* laundry van leaving the service station last night. Then we'd seen the thug hanging around outside those hotels, remember? I found out that they used the same laundry group …'

Elena was recording him, while tapping away on her phone.

'What else did you see at the service station?'

There was a silence, before Benjamin started mumbling to himself.

'*The ripped green tie … the shirt button … the crime scene's connection to the painting …*'

'*What?*' insisted Elena. 'What else did you see there? You said the psycho had stolen your car … but what else did you see there? You saw the chauffeur's body, didn't you? *Tell me the truth.*'

'I saw a body, yes,' said Benjamin, finally.

'Why didn't you tell the police?'

'I had no phone. It was five in the morning. I told someone who was working at the service station, in the shop, but they got aggressive … I don't think they understood me …'

Elena continued to tap away on her phone.

'Then I found myself as a suspect … but I couldn't and *can't* go to the police … not just yet … I need to finish something in Figueres …'

'*Oh, my God,*' Elena suddenly cried. She started to laugh again. Whatever she'd been sending by email, message or posting on social media, it was clearly having a major impact. '*Oh, my God.*'

The road was clear, with just the occasional lorry or car, and any blue flashing lights now seemed to be concentrated on the other side of the road, coming towards Barcelona. Benjamin was determined to avoid any traffic cops, but he also needed petrol. Elena insisted that they'd be okay, and at the first place he could stop, she took his money, got out and handed fifty euros through a 'night till' window, which enabled him to practically fill the car up. The cashier took the money and clicked the fuel pump into action, without even glancing across at Benjamin.

Once he was driving again, it wasn't long before Elena felt she'd achieved everything she could with her phone. Exhausted, she rested her head momentarily against his arm before leaning back and closing her eyes.

As she dozed, Benjamin carefully extracted Conso's phone from his pocket and saw that he now had a signal again. He considered calling her and Josep but decided to leave it. He hoped to be in Figueres in an hour or so.

Tapping his hands on the steering wheel, he knew he'd been right about something he'd seen at the service station that had conjured up images of the aristocrat's painting. There'd been something he'd *missed* in the canvas. It was something he'd been trying to detect while in the Dalí Museum earlier, comparing *The Face* to the image he'd taken of Jaume's version and had kept on Conso's phone.

At the time, he hadn't been able to pinpoint what it was. He'd been squinting at the facial features of the bullfighter ... but there was something about the chin, or just *under* the chin, that didn't look right.

He now knew what it was.

It was *the button* ...

Elena woke up instinctively on the outskirts of Girona, telling him to pull off the motorway. She told him that her brother was meeting her at a roundabout.

'You'll be okay?' he asked.

'I'll be okay.'

'Look ...' started Benjamin.

'You'll see me again,' she said, smiling.

He watched as she checked her phone once more, but this time it was to then scribble her new number down for him.

'Whatever you need to do, do it quickly,' she said. 'You need to call me in the morning – I mean *soon*, in a few hours' time. I will ask you questions, I will record you again, and there will be someone else who will also follow up. You can speak to your police friends but don't speak to any other media.'

He nodded.

She took another picture of him, leant over and kissed him on the cheek, then ruffled his bushy hair.

'And Benjamin …' she said, lifting herself out of the car. 'Check out the news in the morning.' She looked at her watch. 'Or right now if you like …'

News of the bullfighter's release started to break on social media at 10.30pm, precisely the same time that Inspector Vizcaya arrived at the Olimpia laundry, soon after Officer Soler had called him about the unexplained death of one of the group's drivers in hospital … about thirty minutes after Benjamin and Elena had left.

Initially unaware of the breaking news, Vizcaya was accompanied by two Mossos agents, and they'd cut through the chain on the front gate to enter the laundry depot.

Making their way into the main industrial unit, it didn't take long to detect signs of a violent struggle. There were spots of blood and a butcher's knife on the ground, a discarded leather jacket and baseball cap, plus wads of cash stuffed into a rucksack … but no sign of a kidnapped bullfighter. The blood spots led out to a loading bay area, but there was no one out there.

It was only after Vizcaya pulled out his phone to call Soler and order reinforcements, that he was told about the reports of the bullfighter being released.

According to Soler, the French news agency, AFP,

had posted an exclusive video report from one of their freelance journalists in Barcelona, showing the moment of the matador's release, and it had already gone viral. They said that further reports would be forthcoming, and that they were also making contact with the police in France and Spain.

'*For Christ's sake,*' said Vizcaya, standing in the middle of the laundry workshop, while stroking his walrus moustache. But he felt relief that the kidnap victim had been freed, and a sense of vindication that his theory of searching laundrettes had finally led the investigation team to the Olimpia.

Where, however, was Brandon Bartholomew?

He was told by Soler that the whizz-kid from CITCO, Beltrán Gómez, had since tracked his 'ter-rorist suspect' to Figueres, and he was making arrange-ments to head up there.

Séverin staggered into a late-night pharmacy in the Poblenou neighbourhood, having failed to reclaim the rucksack of cash after the police arrived at the laundry. His face was purple, his nose buckled, his mouth seeping blood. His throat was burning and he couldn't speak, but he grabbed the pharmacist by the neck with one hand instead. With his other hand, he snatched a pen and paper from the counter, then started to scrawl that he needed something – *anything* – to quell the fire in his chest and guts …

88

Benjamin

Monday 4 June, 11.45pm – Figueres.

Shortly after Benjamin had taken the first exit for Figueres off the AP-7 motorway, Conso's old vehicle had had enough. It shuddered and stuttered along the side streets that he'd taken to avoid any police patrols, and he made it as far as he could towards the centre before something exploded loudly under the bonnet, followed by a cloud of smoke. Then the engine had simply conked out.

After slamming the car into neutral, he coasted it up onto a kerb, where it finally came to its pitiful demise near the the entrance to a park. He then ejected himself as fast as possible, tugging at the door handle to get away from the smoking yellow wreckage, anxious that it might blow up.

Soon after, the storm broke.

Towering thunder clouds had been threatening to break the humidity all evening, and when lightning finally flashed across the sky it was a welcome respite. The downpour that swiftly followed was steady, warm and vertical, a heavy pelting of water that splashed fiercely against the rooftops and pavements, drowning out the sound of all else, and rapidly turning the streets into shallow rivers.

Benjamin quickly took shelter in the front porch of a shop, its graffiti-covered metal shutter pulled down and padlocked for the night. With the on-going rain glistening under the yellow glow from street lamps, he briefly considered finding a quiet restaurant or bar to hang out before visiting Conso again, but he knew it was still too risky. Since the cloudburst, there was an eerie feel to the town. The streets were deserted, like a ghost town, and Benjamin felt as if he was the only one around, until he squinted up the road ...

In the distance, he could see the blue lights on top of stationary police vans, and orange lights of municipal or council trucks. Night workmen in waterproofs were positioning crowd barriers along the sidewalks, slowly moving nearer to where he was sheltering. Whatever was going on, he didn't want to stick around. He reached in his pocket for Conso's phone and jabbed the screen to illuminate it as he headed off down a side street, away from the vehicles and flashing lights, sidestepping the pavement puddles yet avoiding the flooded roadway itself, while still trying to keep out of the rain.

He saw a signpost indicating that the Dalí Museum was nearby, and so the street where Conso lived had to be near, too. As he switched on the phone's location services again, he tried to retrace his tracks using the map.

The road up towards the museum had now been blocked off with barriers. Some police officers, despite the rainfall, were already standing behind them. He tried another route, doubling back through a couple of streets to join the road further up – but again it was blocked. Lightning flashed intermittently again, and he was already getting soaked. He had no intention of going anywhere near any police checkpoint, so he started to pace quickly in the opposite direction, and then finally took out the phone to make a call.

He scrolled for the number that he'd received while he'd been in the museum, and soon found it.

'Josep?' said Benjamin.

'Joder … quién es?'

'It's Benjamin.'

'Fuck,' grunted Josep. 'It's gone midnight. What do you want?'

'Where does Conso live again? What street and house number?'

'Are you crazy?'

'No.'

'It's nearly one in the morning.'

'I know, but I'm back in Figueres.'

'She's not there.'

'Oh,' said Benjamin. 'Where is she?'

'She's here, asleep,' said Josep.

'Where's *here?* Where are you?'

'Cadaqués.'

Shit, *of course* … Benjamin could recall Conso saying that her nephew had recently installed new equipment in a studio in Cadaqués. That's where they'd been heading to examine the painting.

'Josep?' he said.

'Yes, I'm still here …'

'Forget doing a radiographic test.'

'Okay.'

'But have you got a gun?'

'A gun?'

'An XRF gun. Do you have one?'

'You mean an X-ray fluorescence gun?'

'Yes … do you have one?'

There was a pause.

'*Josep, do you have one?*' insisted Benjamin.

'Yes, I recently acquired one –'

'*That's great, Josep.*'

'Yeah, thanks … why do you ask?'

'I'll explain … but how do I get to Cadaqués?'

'You have Conso's car, no?'

'No, not really,' said Benjamin.

'Well, there's a bus, but I'm not sure what time it goes …'

89

Beltrán Gómez

Tuesday 5 June, 6am – Mossos Comissaria, Les Corts district, Barcelona.

Despite the single, social media video report of the bullfighter's release going viral and global overnight, the police manhunt for Brandon Bartholomew continued. Or rather, Beltrán Gómez de Longoria's manhunt for Bartholomew continued.

The Olimpia laundry depot had since been turned upside down by Mossos officers and forensics, and the AFP news agency was also being pressed for further details, as was the bullfighter's manager. No further 'exclusives' had yet been posted, but the location of the existing video report had already been matched to the Olimpia depot, with many worldwide media outlets now also trying to contact the freelance journalist responsible for the breaking news, Elena Carmona.

Where, however, was Brandon Bartholomew?

One thing was Inspector Vizcaya and the Mossos confirming where the kidnap gang had held their hostage, in addition to the power-hungry Catalan minister, Isabel Bosch, itching to give a good-news press conference – but Beltrán knew it was his own duty to report back to the Minister of Interior in Madrid, and track down the suspect terrorist and ringleader, still on the run.

The CITCO agent had only allowed himself a couple of hours sleep, slumped at his desk in the incident room, and then he was busy scanning through all the reports again.

At 6am, with dawn breaking, he was informed that all CCTV cameras in and around the Salvador Dalí Museum in Figueres had been double-checked, and it had been reconfirmed that the suspect, dressed in a lumberjack shirt and baseball cap, had entered the museum late yesterday afternoon. As he'd also been identified arriving earlier at Figueres station, carrying a flat case, he'd either dumped the case directly outside the museum before entering it, or nearby.

The suspect had also been the last member of the public allowed in, before the museum had closed for security. More worryingly, there were no images of him leaving the museum, although records showed that a fire alarm had been activated by a member of the public departing through a fire-exit.

Beltrán didn't need further convincing that Bartholomew was now targeting the Dalí Museum.

The G20 wives were scheduled to arrive in Figueres at around 11.30am, with the motorcade delivering them directly to the front entrance of the museum, via Doctor Fleming street and past the Parc del Bosc.

Precisely where a car had been left abandoned ...

It was halfway up on a kerb, on the corner of the square in which the motorcade would pass by, less than a kilometre from the museum.

After bomb disposal officers with sniffer dogs gave the vehicle the all-clear to be examined, a white, blood-stained towel was found on the back seat, with a label stating that it was the property of '*Olimpia*', where the bullfighter had been held.

Beltrán also received details of the vehicle's owner: it had recently been re-registered in the name of Josep Fèlix Puig, a resident of Cadaqués.

Once he'd joined the dots to the SIM card purchase and earlier missed calls made to the Marquès, Beltrán also checked that the local police were keeping surveillance on Josep Puig's studio in Cadaqués, and that reinforcements were available for them if required. Then he finalised his plans to hitch a lift to Figueres himself on a Guardia Civil helicopter ...

90

Benjamin

Tuesday 5 June, 8.15am – Figueres to Cadaqués.

Soon after his late-night call with Josep, Benjamin discovered that the first bus from Figueres to Cadaqués didn't leave until after eight in the morning.

Although the thunder and lightning gradually eased during the night, the rainfall took its time. As a blanket of darkness fell upon Figueres, he tried to steer clear of getting totally drenched, squelching his way undetected around the deserted side streets and alleyways, until he finally located the bus terminal opposite the train station, just off the square where he'd borrowed – okay, *stolen* – a bicycle earlier.

Checking the timetable boards and pinpointing an orange and red *'sarfa'* bus as the one that would eventually take him to Cadaqués, he alternated between trying to doze under a nearby covered walkway, out of sight, and keeping one eye on the empty bus, waiting to seize an opportunity to sneak on board. The chance had finally come at around 5am, once the rain had eased off, and after a cleaner boarded the vehicle and then briefly left the door open while taking away some rubbish.

Despite the bright, post-storm sunlight filling the bus from 6.30am, Benjamin remained flat out on the floor at the very back, tucked as far as possible under the seats. It was just as well. The Figueres local police kept a look out for anyone suspicious arriving by bus or boarding one, but they never checked if anyone had been hiding on one during the night.

In the end, Benjamin was joined by just a few other passengers, and no one noticed, not even the driver, when he quietly lifted himself up and sat with his head down on the back seat, leaning against the window – just five minutes after the vehicle had set off, at 8.15am.

His jaw hurt badly, as did the back of his skull, and the slow-motion feeling had returned, which wasn't great. He knew that he shouldn't and couldn't last much longer without medical attention, but to stop himself panicking he put his brain into action … as good as convinced about the location, time and now *image* of Jaume's Dalí …

He dug his fingers into a breast pocket on his lumberjack shirt and pulled out the bullfighter's shirt collar button. He tugged out the phone from another pocket, pulling out scraps of paper and leaflets at the same time. One leaflet caught his attention. It was the one he'd picked up at the castle-style hotel near Jaume's home in La Bisbal – the *Castell d'Empordà* – where he'd stopped very briefly to see if he could grab something to eat before the journey back to Barcelona.

He read a short description about the history of the hotel. Then he smiled, nodded to himself, and gazed out the window again at the cloudless blue sky.

The breathtaking approach to Cadaqués, the easternmost point of Catalonia, slowly came into view as Benjamin's bus took the single, winding route over the hills from Roses, with the rolling, fertile landscape soon changing to a harsh, arid promontory. The road twisted and turned with hairpin bends, passing abandoned farmhouses, olive groves and scattered grapevines on levelled plots that had been cleared from the splintered rock, like steps.

As the road coiled, curved and dipped, he could already make out a mosaic of boats bobbing and reflecting in the azure waters below, under the piercing morning sunlight. The same light that had drawn other painters to the remote bay, not just Dalí, who'd been lucky to have grown up there. He would conjure up grotesque, monster-like double images for a lot of his work from the rocky crags and cliff-edge formations of the adjacent Cap de Creus, and even called sections of the stunning coastline his 'paranoiac cliffs' – which brought Benjamin, swaying and rocking on the back seat of the bus, full circle to *The Hallucinogenic Toreador* again …

The coach pulled up in Cadaqués at precisely 9.15am. Out of the window, he could see Conso's nephew, Josep, sitting astride his motorbike, an impressive Harley Davidson. An extra crash helmet was hooked through his arm.

Benjamin waited for the other passengers to disembark, then also got off. It was a stunning, clear day, the humidity gone, blown away by last night's storm, and he suddenly felt that he also had a clearer head, albeit battered and bruised.

The first sound that hit him was the raucous squawking of seagulls. It was beautiful. It sounded like laughter.

91

Benjamin, Conso and Josep

Tuesday 5 June, 9.30am – Carrer Curós, Cadaqués.

Josep Puig's studio for his *'Conservacio de l'art'* business was tucked away within the back streets at the very heart of Cadaqués, in the picturesque Carrer Curós. Vibrant colours of bougainvillea and weaving ivy climbed and drooped from balconies on both sides of the narrow street, intertwining in the middle to form a trellis of shade.

The street itself was cobbled with dark slate tiles, wedged vertically into the ground, while the quaint, whitewashed homes, small shops and galleries dazzled with their sky-blue painted doors and shutters. Some even had rich, colourful landscape scenes painted on the outdoor boxes for electricity meters.

Benjamin noticed that there were cats everywhere: sitting in doorways, on balconies, on windowsills, and there was even a 'blue cat' bistro, *'El gato azul'*, right next door to Josep's studio.

He would have dived inside to grab a takeaway or something if it had been open. While on the bus, he'd been longing for coffee and croissants at some water-front café. Somewhere to listen to the murmur of the waves, the masts of yachts clicking in the offshore breeze, and to simply observe the salt-weathered artists and bohemian characters who formed part of this curious world of Cadaqués. But there was no time, it was still too risky, and he had a job to finish …

Josep had first parked his motorbike in an adjacent street to his studio, and once Benjamin had delicately removed the full-face crash helmet away from his twisted jaw and bruised head, they'd strolled through a passageway full of more cats, then went inside.

Josep was keen to practise his English on Benjamin, and he was certainly friendlier than his sullen demeanour of yesterday. He'd forgiven him for the late-night phone call, too, and appeared happy that his visitor had shown interest in the fact that he'd invested in an XRF gun – something that Conso was already setting up, while also clutching a mug of coffee.

'*Oh, God,* what happened to your face?' was her first reaction, after greeting Benjamin.

'Yeah –' he started.

'Are you okay? Are you *okay,* Benjamin?'

No, he wasn't, not really. He didn't feel great. But

he'd already had the same conversation with Josep, who'd reacted in a similar way once he'd met him off the bus. He told him that he'd had a bit of an accident, another 'spot of bother', and that he needed some strong painkillers – and then he'd try to see a doctor or someone later on, perhaps in Cadaqués itself, if that was possible.

With Conso still screwing up her face as she scrutinised Benjamin, Josep returned from the kitchenette, handing his guest a glass of water and a couple of tablets, and then also a mug of steaming black coffee. Benjamin nodded in gratitude. He swallowed the pills while gulping the water, then took some sips of the caffeine.

'And the car?' asked Conso.

'The car?' said Benjamin.

'Yes, how was the car?'

'Fine. Yes. The car was fine. Thanks.'

'Why didn't you drive here?'

Benjamin took some more sips of coffee and gazed around the studio.

'Well, you know, I thought it would be easier by bus,' he said.

Josep seemed keen to start work. He'd already propped Jaume's painting on an easel and was adjusting some equipment alongside it.

'Where *is* the car?' Conso insisted.

'Figueres,' nodded Benjamin, also keen to start work. He dug into a pocket and pulled out the leaflet of the Castell d'Empordà, the old hotel near Jaume's home in La Bisbal. 'Conso, I really want to ask you about the Púbol castle again, you know –'

'Where did you park it?'

'– because I think this might be very important. Sorry?'

'Where did you park it in Figueres? It was a nightmare there yesterday. Roadblocks and security everywhere for the G20 museum visit. Which is why I decided to stay here in Cadaqués … but, anyway …'

Benjamin hoped that was the end of the car inquisition. He didn't have the heart to tell her that the little yellow contraption had finally exploded. He suddenly remembered that he'd promised to help Elena repair the damage on her taxi, too … and he realised he still had to call her. He wanted to speak to her, and she'd offered to help him relate everything to the Spanish police. He checked his watch.

'Púbol?' Conso was now saying.

'Yes, yes, look,' said Benjamin, handing her the leaflet. 'Let me explain …'

Without mentioning the Marqueses de Guíxols or the location of their country home, Benjamin asked Conso to repeat what she'd told him in Figueres about the story behind Púbol. Why and how did Dalí and Gala decide upon that area to search for a fortress to renovate? Who found it for them? Who helped them? Where else had they been searching? What other properties had they viewed before deciding on the Púbol castle?

Conso explained that there were other castles or

'ruins' they'd considered – one in Quermançó, in Vila-juïga, and one in Miravet, on the river Ebro, and there was also –

'This one?' said Benjamin, asking her to read the leaflet properly.

Conso simply glanced at it.

'The Castell d'Empordà?' she mumbled. 'Where is it?'

'Just outside La Bisbal,' said Benjamin. 'Near Peratallada, to be exact … not far from Púbol.'

'And? The leaflet is in English …' she said.

'No, no, Conso, *look* –' said Benjamin, flipping the leaflet over. 'It's in English, Spanish and Catalan. Here, *look* … please read it. They claim in the description that Dalí was once in the running to buy the ruined Castell d'Empordà –'

'Oh, Benjamin, many others have probably claimed that, too.'

'– and I quote, *but when his offer to pay for it with his art was declined, he secured the Castle of Púbol instead* –'

'Oh, Benjamin, *Benjamin* …' said Conso again, but this time she took a firm hold of the leaflet and sat down to read it. After a few minutes, she asked her nephew to connect her to the 'Internet thing' on his desktop computer again …

92

Beltrán Gómez

Tuesday 5 June, 9.30am – Carrer de Carles Rahola, Cadaqués.

The Guardia Civil helicopter ferrying Beltrán from Barcelona to Figueres had been diverted to Cadaqués on CITCO's instructions. The museum in Figueres had been secured for the imminent G20 visit, and Beltrán's presence would no longer be required there.

The local police keeping surveillance on Josep Puig's studio in Cadaqués, however, had reported that a motorbike had arrived with a pillion passenger, and that the two men had entered the premises. One appeared to be the suspect, Brandon Bartholomew. The local police had secured the street and were awaiting Beltrán's arrival and further instructions.

The helicopter landed on the artificial grass of a sports field close to the Cadaqués police station. Since it was a chopper belonging to the Guardia Civil, the

476

Spanish state's police agency with military-like status, it immediately provoked the wrath of some laid-back *Cadaquesencs* sitting outside a café nearby.

Ignoring the Catalan profanity that could be heard from the café as he greeted the bemused local police chief in the street, Beltrán felt euphoric that he was finally closing in on his terrorist, the so-called 'doctor', in order to avert a wider and more catastrophic threat.

Bartholomew had used the Marquès and his Dalí art as a *front*. Even though his kidnap victim had been released, a chauffeur had been murdered and ears had been severed. He was still a ringleader, the *facilitator* for Marcos Constantinos, someone who specialised in forged passports and documents, a fanatic in possession of bomb-making chemicals, possibly acquired from a laboratory under the disguise of examining a work of art, and probably the mastermind behind all 'art attacks' at museums across Europe in the past month.

Today was the official start of the G20. The US President would be arriving mid-afternoon, amid the tightest security ever seen for a visiting dignitary to Barcelona. Beltrán knew what the President's security detail involved, as he'd witnessed it himself while stationed with START near Washington DC.

And nothing, *nothing* could or *would* go wrong in Barcelona … all thanks to young Beltrán dismantling the eco-terrorist cell.

93

Benjamin, Conso and Josep

Tuesday 5 June, 9.45am – Carrer Curós, Cadaqués.

Josep's X-ray fluorescence gun was one of the best, as far as Benjamin was concerned. A portable, flexible spectrometer, ideal for fast, high-resolution, multi-element analysis. He couldn't think how much Josep might have paid for it, but he was certainly impressed.

While Benjamin had been on the bus to Cadaqués, Josep had already been calibrating the apparatus. During their phone call, Benjamin had said he wanted to use the gun on the collar area of the painting, where he thought there might be a button beneath the surface. Nothing had been visible from the infrared reflectography test carried out at MNAC, but that had only ruled out that nothing in charcoal was under the paint. It didn't rule out further paint itself … or at least pigment samples undetectable through IRR.

Conso, now Googling away on Josep's desktop computer, was also listening in on Benjamin's theories about the canvas, while it was being carefully positioned in front of the XRF gun.

'A clear difference between *The Face* in the Figueres museum and *The Hallucinogenic Toreador* masterwork, at least in respect to the collar area,' Benjamin was saying, 'is the button. In the *Toreador* masterwork, there's a button on the collar of the bullfighter, but in *The Face*, it isn't there.'

'Go on …' said Conso, without looking up.

'Dalí himself said it was the *focal point* of the masterwork … where the gaze of Gala, looking down from the upper left corner of the painting, meets the young Dalí's gaze, looking up from the bottom right. Their vision meets exactly midpoint in the canvas, fixed upon the obsessively painted *button* of the toreador's shirt collar.'

Josep was connecting his laptop to the XRF's transmitter.

'Conso,' said Benjamin, looking towards her. 'I think it was Luis Romero who wrote that Dalí told him the button was inspired by one in the *trouser fly* of Matisse, or the fly of the French bourgeoisie, since they always forget to fasten them … did you know that?'

'No, I didn't,' said Conso, laughing, and still searching for whatever it was she was searching for. 'But you are extraordinary, Benjamin …'

'Okay, wait, *wait* …' said Josep, finally satisfied that everything was in position, with the XRF gun now steadily poised, very close to the painting, yet without touching the canvas. 'What are we looking for?'

Benjamin took out the small shirt button from his pocket and held it up.

'This,' he said.

'What's that?' said Josep.

'This,' said Benjamin, 'is the button of the bull-fighter who went missing, who became invisible … who was *kidnapped*. We're going to find out if the double-image of the invisible bullfighter in this painting also had a button …'

'Are you serious?'

'Yes. Totally serious. I want you to point the gun at the collar, just below the chin of the bullfighter in the painting. I believe we'll find a button, in paint, just below the surface …'

Conso was now also looking up.

'… and thanks to your sophisticated gun, Josep, we should even be able to identify whether it was first painted in titanium white or zinc white …'

Josep looked chuffed, yet still somewhat perplexed.

'Why the obsession with a button?' he said.

'Why?' said Benjamin.

Both Josep and Conso waited.

'Reynolds and Eleanor Morse acquired *The Hallu-cinogenic Toreador* when it was still unfinished, and when they saw it exhibited in New York in March 1970,' said Benjamin. 'Dalí, however, said he first needed to trans-port it back to his studio in Port Lligat to finish it … to specifically perfect the *collar button*. Why Port Lligat?

Why *here?* Because this is where he'd practised painting the collar button beforehand …'

He watched Josep switch on the gun.

'I believe this canvas was used to paint *tests* for the collar button during 1969 and was then left here in Catalonia. If it was, then it was painted *before* he brought *The Hallucinogenic Toreador* back from New York to finish it … I imagine in mid-1969, even before the negotiations to purchase Púbol had started. A year later, he was trying to perfect the button on the master-work itself. So, if there's a collar button on this canvas, below the surface and which he then painted over, then it can only be genuine …'

'*Benjamin –*' started Conso.

'Now, confidentially,' continued Benjamin, knowing full well that he could trust them both, 'my client is Jaume Guíxols, the Marquès de Guíxols –'

'*Yes,* Benjamin –'

'The *location* and *dates* are also critical but can easily be established. If we focus on Púbol and the Guíxols' country home – why would the canvas have ended up in the cellar at the home of the Marquès?'

He didn't wait for a reply.

'Simple. Dalí had been searching to buy a castle for Gala in the Baix Empordà region from 1969, bearing in mind the *Toreador* masterwork was painted between 1969 and 1970. We then have the thwarted interest from Jaume's father to acquire the masterwork itself – the possible visits of Dalí to the Guíxols home while trying to acquire, or at least showing interest – *yes,*

Conso – in the neighbouring Castell d'Empordà – now a hotel – and *very* possibly taking the occasional canvas to show the Castell's owner while negotiating to purchase it – before settling on Púbol – and then meanwhile, perhaps accidentally, leaving this canvas study at the home of the Guíxols, or perhaps even gifting it to Jaume's father, for his help in the property search in the first place …'

Conso was clapping her hands and beaming.

'Look at the images,' Josep was saying. 'What else do you see?'

But then there was a sudden, loud bang.

'What's that noise?' said Conso. 'Who is it?'

94

Benjamin, Conso, Josep and Beltrán Gómez

Tuesday 5 June, 10am – Carrer Curós, Cadaqués.

Beltrán Gómez could see stray cats suddenly darting away from all corners of the narrow street, as three agents from the local police started to break down the front door of the studio in the heart of Cadaqués.

Two other agents had sealed off an alleyway at the back, so that whoever was inside would not be able to escape. The local police force was not exactly equipped with anti-riot gear or bullet-proof shields, but its officers were certainly armed, ferocious and capable.

Beltrán had been given strict instructions to remain in the squad car at the end of the lane until the premises were secured, until anyone inside had been disarmed, and any immediate threat neutralised.

As he sat there, stroking his plastered hair, his cell

phone rang. He looked at the screen. It was the old dog, Detective Inspector Vizcaya.

'*Young man ... señorito*,' chuckled Vizcaya, in what sounded to Beltrán as a rather sarcastic and over-gleeful tone. He was clearly gloating about the bull-fighter's safe release.

'This is not a good time, Inspector.'

'When is, *when is*, young Beltrán?' said Vizcaya. 'Unfortunately, you're going to have to make time for this.'

'Am I?'

'Yes, you are ... and why do you always answer me with another question?' said Vizcaya, laughing.

'Do I?' said Beltrán, to the sound of guffaws from the other end of the line.

'Wait,' said Vizcaya. 'We've got someone from London who called us, but she should really be speaking to you. They're trying to show me how to connect the call to you ... hang on, young man ...'

There was a pause. Gazing up the street, Beltrán could see that the agents had now succeeded in entering the art studio, having broken down the front door.

'Señor Longoria?' came a female voice from the other end of the line. 'Señor Beltrán Gómez de Longoria?'

'Who's this?' said Beltrán.

'This is highly confidential, señor Longoria. I'm calling from Scotland Yard's Art and Antiques Unit –'

'Who are *you*?' insisted Beltrán.

'My apologies. The name's Miller. Daniela Miller. Art and Antiques.'

'And?'

'We believe you've been investigating the ALC …'

Beltrán squeezed the corners of his eyes, trying to think.

'The ALC?' he said. 'The Animal Liberation …'

'The Art Loss Consultancy,' said Miller, matter-of-factly.

'What?'

'The Art Loss Consultancy.'

Beltrán was lost for words.

'We believe you've been trailing Benjamin Blake. We've also been trying to locate him. He can be a complex, stubborn individual, but he's really one of our very best investigators …'

Beltrán was now numb. He couldn't quite fathom what he was hearing.

'If and when you make contact with him, can you please ask him to touch base with me. If he's still in Spain, there's an incident in Madrid that he could take a look at for us. I can't divulge anything else. It's highly confidential, I'm sure you understand …'

Beltrán held a palm up in front of him in an effort to pause reality. But no luck.

He was in a bit of a daze from then on. He got out of the squad car, stumbled up the street, then stepped into the art studio through the smashed front door. He could hear shouting from inside, in Spanish, Catalan and English, but then it partly died down. There were two men being restrained by the local police agents, while an old lady was yelling at them.

Beltrán stared, open-mouthed. There was a painting propped up on an easel, with a camera and sophisticated-looking computer equipment nearby. One of the two men being held was clearly Bartholomew – dishevelled, with wild, crazy hair, his face cut and bruised. The other man was younger. He looked like a Hells Angels biker, and he was telling the police not to damage the studio's gear.

Satisfied that no one was in any immediate danger, Beltrán beckoned for the agents to go easy with the two men. He turned towards the old lady.

'My apologies, ma'am,' he said, 'but we'd been searching for the bullfighter, and since this man had –'

'The bullfighter's *here*,' cried Conso, pointing at the painting. '*It's genuine …*'

95

Benjamin, Jaume Guíxols, Conso and Josep

Two weeks after G20 – Fundació Gala-Salvador Dalí, Figueres.

'Thank you,' said Benjamin, acknowledging the applause after being introduced to the audience in a lecture room at the Dalí Foundation in Figueres. 'I'm glad to be back here … and without the police chasing me,' he added, to the chuckles of the gathered throng.

He sat between Conso Puig and the Marquès de Guíxols on the stage. Jaume's little wife was nowhere to be seen, but then nor was call-me-Dixie.

The presentation had gone very well. In front of a select gathering of art historians, connoisseurs, curators and media, Benjamin and Conso had taken it in turns to present their findings, projected on a screen behind them. Benjamin at first detailed his research about where the painting was discovered, referring to Púbol and the Castell d'Empordà, its date of creation, and the timing of *The Hallucinogenic Toreador* being returned from New York to finish the focal point of the entire work: the *collar button*.

'What we now know is that Dalí also painted this remarkable study. It clearly shows his fascination with the button, which he practised painting somewhat obsessively. We can now show you with these final slides. Conso, would you like to take over from here?'

Instead, Conso introduced her nephew, who she said was continuing her work in the conservation and restoration of paintings, and before long he joined her on stage to explain the final examination of the canvas.

'So, under the surface you'll see the *collar button* …' Josep soon declared, enjoying the moment immensely. 'The bottom two layers are original paint. Now, bearing in mind that Dalí used mainly Grumbacher oils while in New York and Lefranc oils in Europe …'

It wasn't long before the audience started applauding. If it hadn't been for his cell phone ringing, Benjamin would have stayed longer on the stage, where Jaume was now answering questions of whether the painting might be put on loan to the Salvador Dalí Museum in Florida …

'Benjamin?'
    'Elena.'
    'How did it go?'
    'Almost finished.'
    'You didn't tell me you had a daughter.'

'Elena, you'd love Sophie.'

'But you didn't tell me. I only found out from reading all the other reports –'

'I didn't get a chance –'

'She's twenty-two –'

'Yes, she's a singer, you'd love her –'

'You're forty-one –'

'Yes –'

'Is there anything else you didn't tell me, Benjamin? Anything else I should know?'

'I don't think so. I have the tickets. Are you still coming?'

Silence.

'Elena?'

'Why Madrid?' she said.

'Something has come up. I'd love you to come with me.'

Silence.

'Elena?'

'We're not a *couple*, Benjamin.'

'I know we're not a couple.'

'We're just, you know … friends … and only *just* friends.'

'I know.'

Silence again.

'Elena?'

Epilogue

Cécile Jousset was incensed. Sitting in her Paris office, it had just been confirmed that an undercover art dealer who'd helped to bust her family's money laundering operation a decade ago was not only still alive, but living under another name – his *real* name.

A wavy-haired brunette with a brilliant criminal mind, Cécile was also ruthless and cold-hearted. She'd taken over the family business from her brother – a heroin trafficker, cash courier and vicious figure in the Parisian world of organised crime. He'd served seven years and was now out on parole. He craved revenge and Cécile had vowed to help him.

She picked up her phone and keyed in his number.

'They've found him,' she said, once connected. 'His real name is Benjamin Blake.'

490

Acknowledgments

This novel has been a long time coming, with a few years first spent writing and developing it as a film, then a TV series (although, who knows, it might still be a film). In the famous words of one of my idols, the late, great William Goldman, referring to what used to be called Hollywood: 'No one knows anything.' Meanwhile, I'm busy writing the sequel.

There are several close friends, family, offspring and adopted offspring, who have encouraged, supported and put up with me while writing this over the years. You know who you are, and I love you and thank you all.

I have researched the work of Salvador Dalí extensively in the writing of this book, with numerous visits to Figueres, Cadaqués, Port Lligat and Púbol. I've read many books and articles on Dalí, too many to list here, but one work in particular proved more than insightful regarding the creation of *The Hallucinogenic Toreador*. Written by Luis Romero and first published as *Dalí* in 1975, the revised edition is *Salvador Dalí*, published by Ediciones Polígrafa in 2003. For additional research into the world of stolen art, *Art Theft and the Case of the Stolen Turners* by Sandy Nairne, also proved fascinating.

I further acknowledge *Death and the Sun* by Edward Levine, for research on how bullfighters travel, and also *The Kidnap Business* by Mark Bles and Robert Low, for an insight into the crime of kidnapping.

This is obviously a work of fiction. However, the events and dates of Dalí and Gala searching for a castle to acquire and settling on Púbol, as well as having *The Hallucinogenic Toreador* painting returned to Spain from the United States for Dalí to finish specific details of it are factual. I learnt about Dalí's obsession with the focal point of the painting through my conversations and correspondence with Joan Kropf, former Chief Curator at the Salvador Dalí Museum in St. Petersburg, Florida, where the painting hangs. I thank her, and also Mercedes Aznar at the Fundació Gala-Salvador Dalí in Figueres, for their kind help with my research and permission to use an image of *The Hallucinogenic Toreador*. The painting referred to as *The Face* in the novel is normally exhibited at the Salvador Dalí Theatre-Museum in Figueres.

Also from the art world, I thank Pedro de Llobet and Benoît Vincens de Tapol at the Museu Nacional d'Art de Catalunya (MNAC) in Barcelona for their generous support, time and expertise.

From the literary world, I thank Anna Soler-Pont, Sarah Nundy, Gillian Stern, Charlotte Seymour, Louise Cook, Lisa Girling, Silvia Querini, Melissa Rossi and above all, Roxanne Rowles. Others kindly read very early drafts, screenplays or sections of the story, and I specifically thank Rick Broadbent, William

Hope, Stephen Maule, Paul Owen, Jane Widdup and Ana Gómez Silvestre.

From the film & TV world, in London I thank Keith Evans, James Cabourne, Anne Morrison, Tim Buxton and Neil Zeiger at Nevision, and also Brian Robertson and Jim Howell. In Barcelona, I thank Roger Gual, Carlota Guerrero, Joaquín Padró, Albert Sagalés, Edmon Roch, Josep Amorós and Pere Roca. With many thanks, too, to Llorenç Perello for his brilliant cover design.

One final note: the novel takes place over a few days in June in a pre-pandemic year, and before the authorities removed some of the tollgates.

Most importantly, thank *you* for reading it.

Look out for *The Madrid Connection* …

Tim Parfitt - March 2023

About the Author

Tim Parfitt has worked in the media in London, Madrid and Barcelona, predominantly for Condé Nast, where he ran the Spanish company, helping to launch *Vogue España* and eventually launching *GQ* in Spain, among other titles. He has also worked for the Press Association, *La Vanguardia* and Grupo Planeta, editing, publishing, launching and re-launching titles as diverse as *Lonely Planet* and *Playboy*.

His first book, a non-fiction travel memoir, *A Load of Bull – An Englishman's Adventures in Madrid*, was published by Pan Macmillan in the UK. It was published in Spain by Almuzara under the title, *Mucho toro – las tribulaciones de un inglés en la movida*.

Tim lives near Barcelona. He can be found at www.timothyparfitt.com and now also on Substack at timparfitt.substack.com

facebook.com/tjparfitt

twitter.com/tjparfitt

instagram.com/tjparfitt

goodreads.com/timparfitt

Printed by Amazon Italia Logistica S.r.l.
Torrazza Piemonte (TO), Italy